Former marine **Elizabeth Moon** is the author of many science fiction and fantasy novels, including Nebula Award winner *The Speed of Dark*, and *Remnant Population*, a Hugo Award finalist. Elizabeth has earned degrees in both history and biology, run for public office and has been a columnist on her local newspaper. She now lives with her husband near Austin, Texas and you can visit her website at www.elizabethmoon.com

To find out more about Elizabeth and our other Orbit authors, register for the free monthly newsletter at www.orbitbooks.net

ENGAGING THE ENEMY

ELIZABETH MOON

www.orbitbooks.net

ORBIT

First published in the United States in 2006 by Del Rey.
Random House, Inc.
First published in Great Britain in March 2006 by Orbit
Reprinted 2006 (three times), 2008, 2009, 2011

A CIP catalogue record for this book
is available from the British Library.

ISBN 978-1-84149-378-7

Typeset in Berkeley Medium by Palimpsest Book Production,

Printe   ne

Dedication

In memory of Ed Tatom, 1958–2005, who defended the weak, helped those in need as quietly as possible, and believed wholeheartedly in the adage about "old age and treachery . . ."

And with grateful thanks to the faculty and staff of Florence High School, who have given our son a wonderful high school experience.

Acknowledgements

As always, the usual suspects from the fencing group were involved . . . they know about more than pointy steel. The helpful veterinarians at Town & Country Veterinary Hospital graciously answered my questions about canine fertility. Test readers for the early drafts included Karen Shull, David Watson, Richard Moon, and those patient enough to listen to me read chunks on Thursday nights. For the later refinements, I thank Shelly Shapiro for catching lots of fossils (remnants of earlier drafts) and reminding me that not everyone wants to hear that much about fly fishing. Mistakes are all my own; don't blame any of these fine people.

ONE

In the afternoon sky, the sound of the approaching aircraft rose above the sea breeze, a steady drone. Nothing to see . . . no, there it was, small to make that much noise . . . and then the sudden flood of data from the implant: not an aircraft, no one aboard, a weapon homing on the airfield's navigational beacon. Visual data blanked, overloaded by heat and light, auditory data an inchoate mass of noise, swiftly parsed into channels again, stored, analyzed: primary explosion, structural damage, secondary explosion, quick flicker of building plans, primary visual restored . . .

Ky Vatta jerked awake, heart pounding, breath coming in great gasps. She wasn't there, she was here, in the dark captain's cabin of *Fair Kaleen*, darkness pricked with the steady green telltales of major ship functions. All she could hear beyond her own pulse beating in her ears were the normal sounds of a ship in FTL flight. No explosions. No fires. No crashing bricks or shattering glass. No reverberative boom echoing off the hills minutes later.

"Bedlight," she said to the room, and a soft glow rose behind her, illuminating tangled sheets and her shaking hands. She glared at her hands, willing them to stop. A deep breath. Another.

The chronometer informed her that it was mid-third-shift.

She had been asleep two hours and fourteen minutes this time. She went into the bathroom and looked into the mirror: she looked every bit as bad as she felt. A shower might help. She had showered already; she had taken shower after shower, just as she had worked out hour after hour in the ship's gym, hoping to exhaust or relax herself into a full night's sleep.

She was the captain. She had to get over this.

This time she dialed the shower cold, and then, chilled, dressed quickly and headed out into the ship. She could always call it a midshift inspection. Her eyes burned. Her stomach cramped, and she headed first for the galley. Maybe hot soup . . .

In the galley, Rafe was ripping open one of the ration packs. "Our dutiful captain," he said, without looking up. "Midshift rounds again? Don't you trust us?" His light ironic tone carried an acidic bite.

She did not need this. "It's not that I don't trust the crew. I'm still not sure of this ship."

"Ah. As I'm sure you recall, I'm on third-shift duty right now, and this is my midshift meal. Do you want something?".

She wanted sleep. Real sleep, uninterrupted by dreams or visions or whatever . . . "The first snack you pick up," she said.

He reached into the cabinet without looking and pulled something out. "Traditional Waskie Custard," he said, reading the label. "The picture is an odd shade of yellow— sure that's what you want?"

"I'll try it," Ky said. He had put his own meal in the oven; now he handed her a small sealed container and a spoon. She glanced at the garish label; it did look . . . unappetizing. Inside the seal was what looked like a plain egg custard. Ky dug the spoon into it. It should be soothing.

"Excuse my mentioning it to the captain," Rafe said, sitting across from her at the table. "But you look like someone slugged you in both eyes about ten minutes ago. I promise to perform all my duties impeccably if you'll go back to bed and look human in the morning."

Ky started to say something about duty, but she couldn't get the words out. "I can't sleep," she said instead.

"Ah. Reliving the fight? It must've been bad—"

That attempt at pop psych therapy almost made her laugh. Almost. "No," she said. "I had my post-manslaughter nightmare the second night. This is something else."

"You could tell me," he said, his voice softening to a purr. When she didn't respond, he sat up and said, "With the matter of the internal ansibles, you have enough on me that I wouldn't dare reveal any secrets of yours."

Maybe it was safe to talk to him; he had been ready to commit suicide rather than let outsiders know he had unknown technology, a personal instantaneous communicator, implanted in his head. "It's not . . . it's . . . I'm not sure what it is." Ky tented her hands above the custard, which was not as soothing as she'd hoped. Something in the texture almost sickened her. "I think . . . somehow . . . I'm seeing what happened back home."

"What . . . the attack?"

"Yes. I know it's impossible; I don't even know if Dad's implant recorded any of it, and I haven't tried to access those dates anyway. But I keep dreaming it, or . . . or something."

"A high-level implant could record it all," Rafe said. "If your father wanted a record, something for a court. Are you sure it's not bleeding over? I mean, if he put an Urgent-to-transmit command on it—"

"It couldn't override my priorities, could it? Everything's user-defined . . ."

"True, but this implant's had two users. It may not know you aren't your father."

"That's . . ." *Ridiculous,* she had been going to say, but maybe it wasn't. She'd had the implant inserted in an emergency, with no time then for adjustment of implant and brain. She'd gone directly into combat, and then the direct connection to Rafe's implant had made changes in hers, changes that essentially reconfigured it into some kind of cranial ansible. That might have damaged or changed control functions. And she'd never had someone else's implant before. Why, she wondered now, hadn't Aunt Grace downloaded the data into a new one? Unless it couldn't be done. "I hadn't thought of that," she said instead. "What do you know about transferred implants?"

"Not much," Rafe said. "I know it's possible to use one; I don't know how much residual control might be involved. That one was your father's command implant, right? I'd expect it to have special features."

"It probably does," Ky said. "It certainly does now, after linking with yours." She looked at the cup of custard and pushed it away. "I suppose I'd better look into that."

"If you don't want to go insane from lack of sleep and nightmares, that would be a yes," Rafe said, pulling his own mealpak from the microwave. "Real food wouldn't hurt, either. How about some noodles and chicken? I can make myself another."

It smelled good. Ky nodded; Rafe pushed the tray across to her, picked up her container of uneaten custard and sniffed at it, then wrinkled his nose and dropped it in the recycler. He pulled out another mealpak and put that in the microwave before sitting down again. Ky took a bite of noodle and sauce; it went down easily.

"See if the implant has a sleep cycle enabler," Rafe said. "They don't put those in kids' implants, but the high-end adult ones often do, along with a timer. It should be in the personal adjustment menu somewhere."

Ky queried her implant and found it: sleep enhancement mode, maximum duration eight hours, monitored and "regulated" brain-wave activity and damped sensory input. Users were instructed not to use this function more than five sleep cycles in a row without medical advice . . .

An Urgent tag came up: "Authorized user request: review sealed files." Ky scrolled mentally to check the priorities of sleep enhancement versus Urgent Message, dropped the priority of the message to allow sleep enhancement to override it, and set a condition for waking. Then she finished her noodles and chicken.

"I'm going back to bed," she said. "Tell first shift I may be late."

Initiating sleep enhancement mode was like walking off a cliff into oblivion. She woke feeling rested for the first time since before she'd put the implant in . . . languid, comfortable. After a shower and change, she went up to the bridge.

"Good rest, Captain?" Lee asked.

"Very good," Ky said. "But I'm going to need to spend a lot of time today exploring data stored in this implant. I suspect it's going to be very intense. So if there's anything you know you need for this shift, tell me now."

"We're doing fine," Lee said. "All systems green—this is a lovely ship, despite the way she's been used. Whatever else Osman was up to, he maintained the ship systems perfectly."

"Call if you need me," Ky said. "I'll be in my cabin."

She puttered around briefly, stripping the bed and

sending the linens through the 'fresher cycle, reluctant to face what was coming. When she realized that, she sat down at her desk and activated the secured files.

In the afternoon sky, the sound of the approaching aircraft rose above the sea breeze, a steady drone . . . but this time she was awake, and viewed the audiovisual data as an outsider, not a participant. Her father's emotions did not flood her awareness; she recognized the silhouettes of the two craft before the implant matched them.

Still, the violence of the explosions was shocking. Her breath came fast. Deliberately, Ky slowed the replay, returning again and again to the same image: were they aircraft with missiles or bombs, or were they the weapons? That hardware could be either. They had come in low and fast; the implant did not record—her father had not thought to look for—the telltale evidence that might tell her which they were.

Ky put a tagger on the best of the early images and told the implant to find any similar images after the explosions, but apparently her father had not looked for the aircraft again, nor had he tapped into the airfield's scan data after that first moment.

Back to the beginning. The implant didn't tell her what her father was thinking that afternoon, but it held his planned itinerary—a flight from Corleigh back to the mainland—and his planned schedule—a meeting with senior management at Vatta headquarters, the agenda including the quarterly financial reports, dinner with his brother and his brother's wife, the next two days a series of meetings with the Slotter Key Tik Growers' Association, the Slotter Key Agricultural Commission, the Slotter Key Shipping Advisory Commission. An address to the graduating class of Nandinia School of Business—Ky ignored the link to the text. All routine: he normally spent at least six days

out of ten on the mainland; her mother preferred
Corleigh's gentler climate except during the main social
season.

His flight plan had been properly filed well in advance;
anyone could have known when he would be at the little
private airfield, and yet no explosion occurred there.

She noted that oddity and went back to the visual record
itself.

The local offices exploded; debris rained from the sky.
Another explosion; the visual output darkened. Along the
margins, a row of red numbers appeared, giving her father's
vital signs. She tried to steady her breathing—was this
when he died?

But no. The visual record returned, as someone pulled
debris off him. She recognized the faces: old George, their
pilot Gaspard, someone she had seen around the office
. . . Marin Sanlin, the implant told her. Her father looked
toward the house, now a tower of flame and smoke . . .

Even seeing it, she could not quite believe it. Surely
the comfortable sprawling house with its tall windows to
catch the sea breeze, its cool tile floors, had not really
gone so fast, so completely. Some walls still stood, as fire
raged inside, consuming everything from her past . . . the
long, polished dining room table, the library with its
shelves of data cubes and old books, the paintings, the
family rooms . . .

The pool, its surface crusted with debris, shards of wood
and ash, and then the horror of her mother's face . . .

Ky terminated the playback, squeezed her eyes shut,
and opened them again to the bland blank screen of the
desk display. Her mother. Beautiful, intelligent, graceful,
infuriating to a daughter who had never felt as beautiful,
as intelligent, as graceful . . . she had been annoyed so
often, rebellious so often, resistant so often to her mother's

advice, and now . . . now she could never tell her mother how much she admired and loved the woman who had given her birth.

Ky pushed away from the desk. It was real; it had really happened; her mother was really dead . . . no mistaking that . . . and she would have to find a way to cope, but not right this moment.

Instead, she headed for the ship's gym. Osman had not run a slack ship, and *Fair Kaleen* had a superb facility for keeping a crew of pirates battle-ready, from the usual run of exercise machines to an onboard firing range. She would work some of this off and counter the effect of all those premium-grade rations at the same time.

Gordon Martin was there before her. She paused a moment, watching him do a gymnastics sequence, rolls and flips. He came upright facing the hatch and nodded to her. " 'Morning, Captain."

"Do you feel like sparring with me?" Ky asked.

His brows raised. "Of course, Captain, but—you seem upset."

She didn't want to explain; she just wanted to hit something. Somebody. "Exercise will help," she said.

"You need to stretch first," he said. Ky nodded, and went through preliminary stretches as fast as she thought she could get away with. Then they squared off on the gymnastics mats. Ky forced herself to start slowly, with the basics; Gordon matched her. They had trained in the same system and they had sparred enough before to have a feel for each other's styles. She was sweaty and sore when they quit, but she felt somewhat better for it.

Going back to the implant's replay was hard. She wanted to skip ahead, but she knew she must not. Her mother's face—distorted by bruises, smeared with wet ash, all too obviously dead—was relieved only by the life signs read-outs along the edge of the visual field. Her father had looked at her mother a long time before someone took her body away, as his own condition worsened. Blood pressure dropping, core temperature, arterial oxygen . . . the implant cut functions not in use, finally managing only the recording she now watched and heard. She saw her aunt Grace through her father's eyes, saw the fierce old woman not as the dotty, fussy prima donna she'd always seemed. Aunt Grace, in that hour, could have been any battlefield commander in a crisis. Any good one.

The implant shut down while her father was being evacuated, apparently because his condition had deteriorated to the point that the implant could no longer get enough energy to record. There was another Urgent file, of a family meeting—Ky could not tell where or when—and then the implant shut down again.

Stella'd said that her father had told Aunt Grace to take his implant. Had Grace accessed these files, marked them for urgent retrieval? Or had her father done that? She found it easier to ponder that than to think about the images she'd seen.

She spent the next hour exploring the implant's capacity, though a short period wasn't enough to access all the organization in detail. A command-level implant held far more, had many more functions, than the one she'd used before she entered the Academy.

The new ansible function she'd acquired in external link contact with Rafe was enclosed in its own kernel and now carried the ISC logo. She would have to ask Rafe about that, but not at the moment. Ship-related functions were actually much broader than she'd realized; she could even override any of her crew at the controls, if she wanted. Though *Fair Kaleen* had not been updated for decades, longer than she'd been alive, the old Vatta command datasets deep in the ship's AI had served Osman well and he had never bothered to delete them. Her implant had already interacted with the AI to bring it up to current Vatta standards. In the financial hierarchy, she had access to all her father's knowledge as of the time of the attack, everything from who held which insurance policies on what to the interstellar potential of the tik trade. Much of that was beyond her; she'd never cared much about the investment end. She'd study it later, or find someone who already understood it. Stella, maybe.

"Captain . . . do you want something to eat?" That was Toby, tapping gently on her door.

"Yes, thank you." She stood up stiffly, feeling the exercise she'd done that morning. She should eat. She should sleep. The implant informed her that she'd been working six hours—six hours? What with the earlier session, exercise, and the second session, she'd skipped one meal already.

Fair Kaleen's mess had seating for twenty. Ky's crew clustered at one end of the long table. The last meal of first shift was the first meal for third shift, so all but Mitt, on bridge watch, were there. Ky sat between Alene and Lee.

"I've got the inventory for all the aired-up compartments done," Gordon said. "I know what the ship's AI says are in the unaired compartments, but I don't know if it's right."

"Do we have anything clearly identifiable as legally owned?" Ky asked.

"Most of it's unmarked or in ordinary shipping containers, but without bills of lading. Osman didn't keep a record of the ships he stole from—at least not one I've found yet."

Her father's implant had a section on laws relating to privateering. The privateer took possession of an enemy ship and its contents, and profited by selling off cargo. Open containers were presumed to belong to the ship that carried them, and went to the privateer without question, but sealed containers with bills of lading were supposed to be sequestered and put in the control of a court-appointed assessor at the next port. If they proved to be genuine shipments, then they were shipped on to the original consignee, but with a reward judgment payable to the privateer for "stolen goods recovery." Sealed containers without proper bills of lading could be tricky. Technically they should go through adjudication, but privateers opened sealed but unlabeled containers to convert them to private use.

She accessed the ship's AI and downloaded the current inventory. Even richer than she'd thought at first. But what could she do with it? Wealth could not bring the dead to life. Even if she rebuilt the house on Corleigh, her father and mother would not live in it . . . her uncle would never sit at the head of the table in the Vatta Enterprises board-room.

She wanted to go back, back before all this, back home, back to the room she knew so well—had known so well—back to a place where every step she took, every voice she heard, was familiar.

And that would never happen.

She forced herself back to the present. "Was Osman's version of the inventory accurate, when you checked it as far as you could?"

"Yes. I was surprised, but I suppose he never expected anyone would have access to this ship's data."

"Then I'm going to assume whatever's in the unaired compartments is the same as the list. It's not as if we needed all that." Which was silly, she knew as she said it. They needed much more if she was going to restore just the physical side of Vatta, let alone strike back at their attackers.

After the meal, she settled into her cabin to consider what next. A year ago—was it really that long?—she had been a happy, ambitious fourth-year cadet in the Slotter Key Spaceforce Academy, looking forward to a career as a Spaceforce officer and a relationship with her fellow cadet Hal. Since then she had been kicked out of the Academy and dumped by the man she loved. Her subsequent career as a trader in the family business—which she had expected to be boring—had been marked by war, mutiny, attempted assassinations, and finally the capture—from a rogue Vatta—of this very ship. Her family and its thriving interstellar business had been almost destroyed. Her own government had sent her a clandestine letter of marque, authorizing her to act as a privateer on its behalf, shortly before refusing to defend or support her family when some enemy attacked. Now she was supposed to save what was left of the family and business, with no allies and too few assets.

Too many changes too fast. She focused her attention on the ship again, checking system by system via her cranial implant. All systems nominal, and her senses told her everything felt, smelled, sounded normal as well. She had no excuse to avoid the larger issues. What was she going to do next? Where would the next attack come from?

Not while they were in FTL flight, at least. She activated the sleep cycle enabler for the second time, and woke eight hours later, this time clearheaded enough to realize that the first sleep hadn't been enough. Now she felt solid out to the edges again. Ready to work. She considered another workout in the gym, but decided instead to work on what she least wanted to do, methodically go through Osman's cargo list and assign her best guess at the value, item by item. Some of it was easier than she expected, thanks to her father's implant. Some was nearly impossible—who could say what someone would pay for prohibited technology most people didn't know existed?

Her stomach rumbled, reminding her that she had been up for two hours without eating. In the galley, she ignored the enticing Premium Gold Breakfast Pak—she felt bloated with all the good food they'd been enjoying—and settled for a protein bar and mug of juice. Someone had left a sticky mug and bowl in the sink; she rinsed it automatically as she considered an array of options. She had two ships now: *Gary Tobai*, old and slow, and this one, larger, faster, and—most usefully—very well armed. The nucleus of a fleet, albeit a very small fleet. If she was going to command a fleet, she needed a staff. Before that, she needed a full crew of capable personnel on each ship . . . and before that, she needed to know how much money she had to hire the capable personnel and supply the ships . . .

" 'Morning, Captain." Gordon Martin reached past her for a bowl and poured a modest serving of dry flakes into it. He looked, as always, like the veteran soldier he had been before he joined her crew. "I've finished the security survey; Osman's bad boys didn't have time to put in many traps. All disarmed."

"That's good," Ky said.

"Do you object to my doing some practice on the firing range today?" he asked. "I've checked the reinforcement of the target frames; it's plenty safe for what I'm using."

"That's fine," she said. She should get in some practice time, too. "Martin, I wanted to talk to you about command structure, now that I have two ships—"

"Think you can keep this one?" he asked, pouring milk onto his flakes.

"I'm going to keep this one," Ky said. "It's a Vatta ship. I'm restoring it to its proper ownership."

"Well, then. You're talking tables of organization?"

One did not say *I guess so* to older veterans, which was Martin's identity no matter what the papers said. "Yes," Ky said instead. "Simple, but something that can scale up."

"Based on Vatta tradition, or . . ." His voice trailed off; he eyed her as he munched on the flakes.

Ky shook her head. "Until we take care of whoever's been attacking Vattas, the old protocols aren't any good. Sure, we need our tradeships back at work hauling cargo and making money, but we can't count on that until we aren't being blown up, shot at, and all the rest. I'm thinking small fleet. I have two ships now. I'm reasonably sure that not all Vatta ships have been destroyed; as we find them, we can bring them into the plan."

"We. Meaning you?"

"We meaning me, my cousin Stella, and you, Martin. And the rest of the crews."

"But with you in command." No doubt in his voice at all.

"Yes," Ky said. "I am the only Vatta I know of with the right training."

"Yeah. I see that . . ." He ate two more spoonfuls, then put the spoon down. "See here, Captain, you have to understand: my background is supply and security. The security duties grew out of supply and inventory control. I've been in a ship in combat, in the Slotter Key System, but I don't know as much as you need about weapons and tactical things."

"What about that organization stuff?" Ky asked.

Another spoonful of flakes as he looked thoughtful. Then he nodded again. "I do understand a lot of that. If you're asking me."

"Martin, the thing that's bothered me since I first took command of *Gary Tobai,* back when she was the *Glennys Jones,* is the lack of a clear chain of command on civilian traders. Sure, the captain's the boss, but who's next? On the smaller ships, it's a muddle. Muddles in war get people killed."

"So what is it you want me to do?"

"Take over training new crew into capable combat-ready crews. Find me some weapons specialists—if you don't know the weaponry, I'll bet you know personnel and can spot the good ones. Help me get this ship organized and ready."

He was nodding along with her words. "Yes, ma'am, I can certainly do that. And I can spend this transit with my head in a cube reader learning the manuals on this ship's weapons, too. I just never had the chance before."

"I know I need a second in command, an exec. I wondered if you—"

He was shaking his head now. "No, ma'am. I'm not the right person for that. I might've made a good senior NCO if I'd kept my nose clean, might even have made a good sergeant major, but I'm a hands-on, feet-in-the-dirt person. The air gets too thin for me in officer country."

"For now, anyway," Ky said. "You might surprise yourself later. So—what do you think of the other personnel aboard?"

"Your pilot's good," he said. "He should shape up with a bit more training—I don't suppose you'd tell them all to get in the gym every day for some physical training?"

"Of course," Ky said. "Good idea."

"That kid Toby's awfully young, but he's smart and hardworking. Can't always tell at that age."

"I hope to get Toby back in school as soon as we can find a safe place," Ky said. Right now she couldn't think of a safe place, but surely she could find something better than the very obvious target they were in.

"Jim's coming along—"

"Thanks to you," Ky said.

Martin shrugged. "Typical young lout," he said. "All he needs is discipline and training; he's got the right instincts most times, though that stupid dog made me wonder. Not officer material, though. Alene's better suited to civilian work than military, but she might fool me in another six months. Sheryl . . . nice woman, but definitely not military." He stopped there.

"And Rafe?" Ky prompted. Rafe had to be part of her plans. She still wasn't sure what she felt about him, but for his connections alone he was a valuable resource.

Martin's expression hardened. "Rafe. Begging the captain's pardon but I was not aware he was actually on crew." He fairly bristled with disapproval. Ky didn't know whether to be amused or annoyed.

"I'm doing the work," Rafe said, appearing with his usual instinct for the critical moment. As if to prove this, he picked up Martin's empty cereal bowl and spoon and Ky's empty juice mug, and went to the galley sink. "But I believe, Martin, you have other reasons for leaving me out of your fascinating analysis."

"You were eavesdropping again," Ky said.

"I was not interrupting an obviously important conversation," Rafe said. "In order to not interrupt but be aware when it might be polite to come in, I had to be within hearing. If you call that—"

"Eavesdropping," Ky said. "And I do."

"I understand your loyalty is to ISC," Martin said. "Not to Vatta, or the captain."

Rafe grimaced. "My core loyalties, at the moment, are highly tangled. I should be most loyal to ISC, yes. But it was our captain here who saved me from a situation in which honor would have required suicide." He swirled a little cleanser into the bowl and mug, and rinsed them. "Thus I have a certain point to my loyalty to the captain, which frankly is giving me a bit of a headache."

"I can imagine," Martin said.

"I doubt it," Rafe said. Ky grinned to herself. Part of that headache had been literal: Rafe found out the hard way that she wasn't much like her cousin Stella when it came to advances. If the rest of the crew knew that she had dumped Rafe on his back for making a move on her, they were all pretending the incident hadn't happened. "There are . . . other considerations." The look he gave Ky had the force of a blow.

"For the present," Ky said to Martin, "Rafe is part of the equation. We have determined that our interests run together, since both Vatta and the ISC have been attacked, presumably by the same organization." Then to Rafe, "Have you had any success digging into Osman's files?"

Rafe grimaced. "The man has the best security I've ever seen outside of ISC research labs, and maybe better than that. I'm working on it. So far I've managed not to let the database destroy itself as I sneak in, but that's about it. I have found some interesting references—already forwarded to your desk, Captain. I'm not sure what they mean, but I thought you'd want to look at them."

"Definitely," Ky said. "But I've been shuffling numbers for two hours. I need some exercise before I work my brain any more. I was planning to spend an hour or so in the gym."

"Want to spar with me?" Rafe asked, with just the slightest edge to it. Martin stirred but said nothing.

"Fine," Ky said. "You probably have tricks I don't know . . ." She kept her voice light, but his eyelids flickered. He knew and she knew. She had surprised him that time; she wouldn't surprise him again.

Ky ran through some simple warm-ups and stretches, noticing that Rafe had his own set, not quite the same as hers. Then they spread one of the mat sets and took opposite sides.

"Half speed," Rafe suggested.

Ky nodded. Her heart thudded; she had always liked hand-to-hand practice and found it hard to go less than full-out, but she had not done this in . . . too long. Rafe's loose-limbed crouch seemed too casual, but she knew it was not. She settled a little more. He had height and reach on her—

He was moving, a smooth glide, deceptively slow. Ky shifted in time with his movement, meeting his strike with a hand placed to deflect then strike on rebound. His foot slid out to hook her ankle . . . she had moved, forcing herself to the same slow rate . . . and for several minutes they ran through a series of attacks and counters, all in slow motion. Ky realized quickly that he was a cunning fighter; his attacks were always multiple, coordinated. She could not react instinctively with the obvious, simple counter without putting herself in the path of the next attack. Her own attacks were complex, too, but she had not gone past combinations of three, and Rafe handled these easily.

"You're quite good," Rafe said, slipping one of her kicks past his hip. "I think I have the edge technically, but you may be faster and that would negate it—" The next kick caught him as he was moving back. "I suppose I don't need to be too ashamed that you got me last time."

"Only ashamed that you tried it," Ky suggested, ducking and weaving to avoid his next series.

"I still think you were lying to the mercs," Rafe said. "You don't really think I'm that repulsive."

"Repulsive, no," Ky said. "You're good looking, in a—" She tried a flurry of strikes, unsuccessfully. "—a certain style of looks."

"Faint praise," Rafe said. His next kick was slow, obvious; Ky shifted sideways and did not take the invitation. "And, damn it, you're too smart. That usually works. Break, please." He backed away to one side of the mat; Ky moved to the other. "I need to talk to you, seriously," he said. "This takes too much concentration. Can we do something else?"

"Sparring was your idea," Ky said. "I'd just as soon try out one of these machines."

"Good. It's about the internal—"

"Ansible," Ky interrupted. "Of course. Let me make it clear. I didn't want it, and now I've got it I don't intend to use it, or tell anyone about it. Is there any way to remove it?"

"Not that I know of. For your own safety, it's important that no one know you have it."

"They won't, unless you tell them," Ky said.

He shook his head. "But if someone finds out, they may try to get at it, or make it work. I was told it would be fatal."

TWO

They were back in her office, and she was about to open the cargo inventory list again when Rafe asked, "Are you going to try a salvage claim? Or just go for a share of value?" For once, his voice had no edge.

"It's a Vatta ship," Ky said. "I'm claiming it as stolen property; shouldn't need to go through the court at all . . ."

Rafe pursed his lips. "You're not law enforcement; you don't have a right to just grab your own back."

Space law, Ky recalled, had been more arcane and confusing than n-space theory. "I suppose it depends on which jurisdiction we land in . . . wonder if Osman has a law library in his database anywhere." Her implant queried the ship database, then dug deeper into the relevant sections. Salvage wasn't an option: not with witnesses to the fact that *Fair Kaleen* hadn't been derelict or abandoned. Reclaiming stolen property . . . no, Rafe was right. Very few jurisdictions allowed that. In fact, the only legal standing she had was as privateer.

And she still hadn't told Rafe she had that letter of marque. If she stayed on that course, she'd have to tell him eventually, but in the meantime she had another person aboard she trusted more. "Excuse me," she said to Rafe. "I really must get this done." He raised his brows at her, but left quietly.

If she had been legitimate military, and Gordon Martin had been her senior NCO, she'd have known how lucky she was. Now she wondered if he'd be willing to stay with her once he found out.

Martin looked at her with a faint but definite smile. "Privateer, eh? Well, they picked a good one this time."

"I beg your pardon?"

He shifted in his seat. "Ma'am, I did serve on a front-line vessel; we . . . knew unofficially, I guess you'd say, about the privateer program. Damned foolishness, I thought most of the time, though I'd like to have been assigned to one."

"So you'll stay?"

"Until you throw me off, ma'am. It doesn't bother me. Privateers are official, just about; they do something that needs doing."

"You do know that the government seems not to be happy with the Vatta family at the moment."

He shrugged. "That's politics, Captain. It'll shift back; it always does. Your family's got a good reputation. And I know you."

That took care of one problem, but she had a raft of others, legal and practical. Staying busy might keep her mind off those scenes the implant had made all too memorable. She wanted to go home; she wanted to go home now. Find the surviving members of her family, find out why Slotter Key had turned its back on them. She could not believe the government had caved in for Osman, of all people.

Slotter Key

In the dark hours between midnight and dawn, the presidential palace was dark except for the duty rooms: communications, security. The President, in his comfortable bed, had finally fallen asleep; his wife, in the adjoining bedroom, snored loudly, but thick walls and doors muffled those annoying rasps and gurgles.

He woke to the sound of a comunit chime, his heart pounding. Who would call at this hour? No calls should have been passed through; his valet should have woken him . . . his hand was scrabbling on the bedside console when he realized that it was his internal unit, his skullphone.

"Look under your pillow," a voice whispered. The line went dead.

Every hair on his body stood up; he was drenched in cold sweat. There could be nothing under his pillow—he always turned his pillows before he went to sleep—but he could not ignore that voice. He turned on the light and lifted his pillow.

The data chip, hardly larger than his thumbnail, gave him no clue. It was there, in that place where it could not be, a tiny, shiny, terrifying presence. He had a chip reader in his room, of course, but he felt a great reluctance to use it. What if this wasn't really a data chip, but something else, something explosive? What if it was toxic and had already poisoned him? The sweat trickling down his sides stank . . . surely he didn't smell that bad all the time.

When he looked around the room, nothing else was out of place. He heard no sound he should not hear, but his heart was pounding so loudly that he could not be sure.

He had to get hold of himself. He had to calm down and think. If he called in the security forces, they would wake up everyone, create a huge mess, and probably not find out anything useful. He knew who was behind this, whether it could be proven or not: Grace Vatta. The old hag was crazy; she'd been in a mental hospital at one time, and they should never have let her out. He just had to find a way to neutralize her.

Gracie Lane Vatta smiled to herself as she watched sweat trickle down the President's face, his ribs, his back. His security should have detected the tap into their own surveillance system years ago, but they hadn't. Now, would he put that chip in the reader, or not? Would he call his security squad? She had plans for each possibility, plans he would find as unsettling as the chip under his pillow. No doubt he would have plans, too, when he calmed down. She knew he was smart enough to suspect her, but she was confident that her plans were better than his plans. She'd had longer to work on them.

A telltale lit on her work board. With one eye on the screen showing the President, Gracie switched that channel to full recording and answered the call. "Found something," a male voice said. Gracie ran the scan through her voice files and her mouth quirked. Master Sergeant MacRobert, Slotter Key Spaceforce Academy. Should she use his name and startle him?

"Identify, please," she said.

"Spaceforce Academy," he said. "I think you know who I am and I'd rather not have my name used. I hear you're looking into the late unpleasantness. In detail."

"Yes."

"That Miznarii kid who got your youngster in trouble—"

She repressed a gasp. "Yes?"

"He had contact from someone who claimed to be a Vatta. Ever hear of someone named Osman?"

"Osman Vatta, yes." She remembered Osman all too well. She'd tried to convince the Vatta higher-ups at the time to have him killed, but she was fresh out of the asylum and that had led to threats of having her recommitted. If Osman was involved, that explained a lot. Osman had known about the bunkers under corporate headquarters, for instance.

"He is a Vatta?" The voice—MacRobert, no doubt about it—sounded uncertain.

"Unfortunately, yes. A most unpleasant piece of work, and long since kicked out, but a Vatta. So Osman paid the student to get Ky in trouble?"

"What he said was that Osman was sympathetic to the Miznarii feelings about biomodification, and suggested that Ky, as a Vatta, would be more likely to help him get contact with a cleric so that he could tell his story."

"What is he, stupid? The boy, I mean."

"He's not the brightest cadet we've ever had, but not actually stupid. Inexperienced. Quite genuinely religious, the fervent kind. Osman also told him that Ky wouldn't get in trouble because she was a Vatta."

"So it wasn't malicious on the boy's part?"

"Not against Ky, at least. He was shocked when she disappeared. He claimed she was the only person at the Academy who befriended him and was nice to him."

"How'd you find this out?"

"He . . . er . . . didn't graduate." MacRobert's voice was grim now. "No matter what was said, Ky was a popular cadet, and no one else was willing to put the time into this fellow she'd been tutoring. He was pretty much shunned. He . . . er . . . committed suicide."

"After telling you all this?"

"No, after writing it all down, as a religious duty. Luckily I got hold of it before a Miznarii chaplain did. I . . . er . . . edited it a bit, but I made a copy. Thought you might want it."

"What I want is some idea of why you're doing this," Grace said. "I suspect you're committing several breaches of regulations—"

"Spaceforce didn't do its job," MacRobert said. "Somebody got to somebody, and I want to know who and how. I think you're likelier to find out."

"We should meet," Grace said.

"No."

She had expected that and had her answer ready. "We need to talk longer and more openly than we can over any com line, no matter how secure. Either you trust me or you don't."

A long pause; then: "Why should I trust you?"

"For the same reason I should trust you," Grace said. "We need each other; it would serve neither of us to harm the other. You care about Spaceforce—"

"And Slotter Key," he said quickly.

"Fine. And so do I. Vatta and Slotter Key both."

"You're on a no-contact list," MacRobert said.

"So are you: Vatta was told not to contact anyone at Spaceforce Academy." Grace said. "Your point is? We need to meet. Do you ever get leave?"

"In seventeen days," he said. "Graduation's over, there's the cleanup period, then I get ten days before the new class arrives."

"What sport?" Grace said.

"Sport?"

She let her irritation hiss out on her breath. "Pick a sport," she said. "Something you do anyway."

"Oh. Er . . . fishing. Up in the Samplin hills; I usually rent a cottage on one of the streams near Tera Lake."

"Fine," Grace said. "Just do that. I prefer dry flies."

"I'm a wet-fly man myself," he said.

"Well, then. Until." She closed the connection.

On her visual, the President got up, went to the bathroom, came back with a glass of water, fumbled in a drawer, and unpeeled an orange pill. "Now that's a mistake," Grace murmured to herself. "You're going to be drowsy in the morning . . ." He had left the chip under his pillow. Another mistake. If the drug made him forget it, and his house staff found it . . . she grinned, imagining the furor when Security got hold of it. She watched until he was clearly asleep, snoring, then played with the room's surveillance equipment, inserting a shadowy figure that moved to and from the President's bed from a closet. They'd find that on the daily review, and whoever was supposed to be monitoring the night shift would be in deep trouble.

Then she reviewed the rental records of holiday cottages on likely fishing streams near Tera Lake, and found that MacRobert had booked through Murrian Holiday Rentals for the past twelve years. In their records, his first preference was Greyfalls, second was Overbrook, and the third was Greentop. All were on Middle Run. He had a current reservation for Greyfalls; the other two were also reserved already. The nearest available property was Brookings Manor, "a working farm with sizable residence suitable for bed-and-breakfast accommodations. Includes fishing rights on Middle Run within walking distance. Available for seasonal or long-term lease, or purchase." It wasn't a bad location at all, and it might serve displaced Vatta family members as an interim residence-headquarters.

After some haggling with the Larger Properties section

of Murrian Real Estate, Grace arranged a year's lease in the name of Stavros' widow, who had—understandably—gone back to using her maiden name. A widow and her relatives retiring to a remote country estate would raise no eyebrows. Helen was presently living in one of the Stamarkos homes; that couldn't go on for too long anyway.

It was so satisfying when one action solved more than one problem. Grace stretched and let herself drop into sleep for a short nap. The one good thing about being old was that she didn't mind not sleeping through the night.

Garth-Lindheimer

Ky Vatta looked around the bridge of *Fair Kaleen* shortly before they were due to drop back into normal space in the Garth-Lindheimer System. Her crew had removed all the evidence of the pirates' occupation except what had been locked away in case evidence was needed. The weeks in FTL flight had given them plenty of time to inventory cargo, purge and reinitialize the computers, and make her a healthy ship for decent crew to ship on. With a new paint job, *Fair Kaleen* could be the flagship of a new Vatta fleet, proof that Vatta Transport, Ltd., was still a going concern.

Or she could be a privateer, proof that Vatta Transport, Ltd., was a going concern with teeth.

When they emerged into the Garth-Lindheimer System, her ship's excellent scan showed nothing suspicious in the system except that the system ansibles were not functioning. Without ansible function, they had no real-time communication with Garth-Lindheimer Traffic Control, so Ky entered their ship's information in response to the automated beacon's request. The convoy, as expected, had emerged ahead of her ship, with the Mackensee escorts positioned to guard either flank. She saw less traffic than expected, and all but two local. Those two carried normal beacon IDs; one had already jumped out by the time they received its signal.

She hailed their escort. "When we dock, the other ships will owe me their percentage for safe transit. Under the circumstances, I could sign that over to you, if you'd like. Or have you made separate arrangements with them?"

Lieutenant Commander Johannson shook his head. "No, Captain Vatta. They still have a contract with you, not with us. It's a legal mess at the moment. Let's keep it simple. They pay you, as they agreed. You pay us, as we agreed. Then we part company." *Forever,* his tone implied.

"I would be glad to supply a statement for your command, if it would help," Ky said.

"I'm afraid it wouldn't," Johannson said. "Any statement by you would be considered contaminated. We'll just take our scolding when we do finally get home."

"I'm sorry we've been such a problem to you," Ky said. She'd had leisure, during the long transit, to realize just how foolish she'd been, and how far the mercenaries had bent their rules to save her and her ship. Should she admit that? "You were right," she said. "About the trap, about . . . everything. I can't regret taking out Osman, but there must've been a less risky way to do it—"

"I hope you keep that in mind the next time you're in a tight spot," Johannson said. His voice had warmed a trifle.

"I will," Ky said. "And I appreciate your standing by us and saving our skins."

"Some skins are worth saving," Johannson said, and then cut the contact.

Ky stared at the blank screen a moment. What was that

about? Her skin? Vatta Transport's? Then she shook her head and called Stella on *Gary Tobai*. "How do you like being a ship captain?"

"I haven't done anything fatal so far," Stella said. "I think Quincy could run this ship herself, though I have been studying hard. But how are we going to dock without a pilot? I can't bring her in, and Quincy says she can't. She's not a licensed pilot, and anyway she doesn't know how."

That was a problem Ky hadn't thought of. Legally, they should not approach within two kilometers of any facility without a licensed pilot aboard. Legally, every ship was supposed to have a licensed pilot aboard, too, but most orbital stations had a pilot service for those whose pilots were incapacitated for some reason. Still, that could be expensive, and it was also a route by which strangers could intrude. She would prefer not to trust a pilot she didn't know.

Ky glanced over at her own pilot. "Lee, how do you feel about a suited transfer back to the *Gary* to bring her into dock?"

He grimaced. "I can . . . if that's the only way. Maybe we'll be lucky and this station will have a tug or pilot service."

"They list one," Ky said. "But after that bonded security service guard tried to kill me, I'm not inclined to trust a commercial service."

"There's a scooter down in number three hold," Rafe said.

"That's better than swimming," Lee said. "But you'd have to wait for me to come back out and bring you in—assuming you're sending the *Gary* in first."

"I was planning to," Ky said. "With us out here armed to the teeth, she's less likely to run into trouble. I hope."

Next, Ky talked to the other captains in the convoy, explaining that her contract with Mackensee would end when they docked. "I will open a new account as soon as we're close enough; you can pay into that."

"But we want to go on," Captain Sindarin of *Beauty of Bel* said.

"Then you'll have to contract with Mackensee yourself," Ky said. "They may be willing."

"Why did we stop out there and hang around for days?" asked Captain Tendel of *Lacewing*. "Mackensee wouldn't tell us anything but that it was safer."

"Pirate in a system we came through," Ky said. "With allies. They jumped you out of the system, went back and dealt with them."

"Oh. But you weren't on scan . . . where were you?" That was Captain Harper, of *My Bess*.

"Bait," Ky said. "My choice. That's where this ship came from."

"Oh. We thought maybe you'd picked up another convoy member. The beacon reads Vatta." Captain Tendel, as always, looked as if she suspected Ky of something.

"The pirate had stolen a Vatta ship," Ky said. "They were operating under our name, illegally."

"So you're taking the ship in for adjudication?"

"I'm reclaiming stolen property," Ky said. "And we can discuss this, if you wish, once we're docked."

Harper nodded; Tendel just glared at Ky until the screen blanked.

"That was interesting," Rafe said from over her shoulder. "I wonder what Tendel has against you. You've got a bigger ship, maybe?"

"Maybe. Doesn't matter, really, as long as she pays her share." Though the cargo on *Fair Kaleen* was valuable enough to cover the fee, if any of the convoy reneged on their payment. If anyone would buy suspect cargo off a former pirate ship . . . but of course they would. Osman had been making a living that way, and a good one, too.

About a light-minute from the main station, a warning message met them. "*All ships on approach. All ships on approach.* Identify yourselves on Channel Eighteen. Report shipname, registry, ownership, organization, captain's name, number of crew. Do not depart from present course without authorization: you are targeted."

"Friendly bunch," Lee said.

"Better than what we were told about Leonora," Ky said. She entered the data for *Fair Kaleen* as if that ship had never been anything but a Vatta Transport ship. Her name matched her beacon chip, at least. Registry, Slotter Key. Ownership, Vatta Enterprises. Organization, Vatta Transport, Ltd. Captain, K. Vatta, crew of six.

Shortly a message came back, voice only. Ky was not sure if it was a live person or computer-generated: "Ownership and captain do not match previous contact. This ship and captain of record are interdicted in this system. Explain."

She had not wanted to explain this over open airways. "Request secure link."

"Secure link available . . ." Status lights blinked, then steadied: lightlag plus a minute or two.

"Go ahead, Captain Vatta," a different voice said. "This is Port Security, and I'm Division Chief Edvarrin." The blurred image on screen steadied to show a severe-faced woman in a green uniform with blue facings. Two rows of silver buttons ran down the front.

"The person operating this ship was not a Vatta employee," Ky said. "I understand you had issues with him?" She waited, watching the communications chronometer readout. Fifty-nine seconds for the message to go . . . fifty-nine for it to return . . . plus whatever time someone needed to frame a message.

Question answered question. "Was he a Vatta family member or using a false name?"

"By birth he was a Vatta, yes," Ky said. "He had been expelled from the family years ago. He stole this ship and represented himself as being part of Vatta Transport when he wasn't. Whatever he was doing, he did it for himself, not with any authorization from us." Again the wait. She tried to anticipate the next question, be ready to answer quickly.

"And your relationship to Vatta Transport's corporate structure?"

That was another sticky bit. How far had news of trouble with Vatta spread? "My father was chief financial officer," Ky said. "Until his death."

"We can't verify that with the ansibles down . . ."

"You should have some records on Vatta Transport," Ky said. "Are any of our ships there now?"

"No. A Vatta ship departed some ten days before the ansibles went down. If you're really Vatta, you should know what ships worked this route."

"A moment," Ky said. She queried her implant, and her father's data came up. Garth-Lindheimer lay on a lucrative trading circuit; Vatta had two ships constantly on the route. "*Connie R.*, captained by Casamir Vatta, and *Tregallat*, captained by Benton Gallat." She paused again. "Unless something messed up their schedule, the ship that departed before the ansibles went down should have been *Connie R.* Sometimes they do overtake each other."

"That is correct. There is another Vatta ship in this group, *Gary Tobai*? It is on our list, with a K. Vatta as captain."

"Yes. That was my ship. My cousin Stella's the captain

now. She took over for me when I . . . obtained this one."

"That is an issue, Captain Vatta. Precisely how did you obtain the ship you are commanding now?"

"Osman Vatta tried to trap me," Ky said. She had been thinking how best to tell it. "He hated my father, because my father and uncle were the ones who banished him from the family. Because the ship had a Vatta Transport beacon, I trusted him initially—"

"But surely you had been warned about him. Do you not use implants, you Vattas?"

"He was banished long ago," Ky said. "I suppose my father thought he was dead, or far away, and that I'd be unlikely to meet him. At any rate, I had no suspicion at first. We were traveling in convoy with a military escort— the Mackensee Military Assistance ships—and they advised me it might be a trap. I didn't agree, and stayed behind when they went on with the convoy. It was a trap, and Osman attempted to board and kill us; he had allies, two pirate ships. We improvised a defense . . . I was able to send a call for help, and after some hours—after Osman was dead—Mackensee was able to come back and take out the other ships before they closed with us."

"So they did not witness what happened? You have no corroboration for your story?"

"They can corroborate that they found his being there suspicious, yes. That I left the convoy to check on him, yes. That I called for help, yes. That there were two ships that when challenged tried to fight, yes. Exactly what happened when he tried to board, no." The usual delay, during which Ky wondered if any of the security recordings aboard *Gary Tobai* would help. With Gordon Martin, Rafe, and herself on this ship, would Stella be able to locate and duplicate them?

"It seems likelier that you yourself were the bait in a

trap set by your convoy," Edvarrin said. "A small, apparently unarmed ship like Gary Tobai, but with military backup, captures a ship like the one you have now? Mackensee isn't known for that kind of thing, but mercs have gone rogue before. Traders just don't have the skills or equipment to deal with a pirate, let alone a group of them." A brief pause, then, "Mackensee informs us that you have a letter of marque from Slotter Key. And that you also have aboard an expert in ISC technology, who has been repairing inoperable beacons. Frankly, Captain, we have no reason to believe that you are in fact a legitimate trader or commercial carrier."

Ky could not think what to say. She had anticipated having to make some argument to gain title of the ship, but she hadn't guessed that anyone might think she herself was a pirate.

"I do have a letter of marque," she said. "But the fact is that Osman Vatta—whom you yourself interdicted—attacked my ship and intended to kill me."

"That will be for a court to decide," Edvarrin replied after a longer pause than usual. "Your military escort confirms your story, but also confirms that you insisted on taking Osman's ship as a prize. Under these circumstances, and in the absence of communication with Vatta corporate headquarters or the Slotter Key government—and with no Slotter Key diplomatic representative authorized to confirm or deny the validity of your letter of marque—we are unwilling to have you bring your ship in under your command. You will take up a station at least twenty-five thousand kilometers from our orbital station, under guard of our insystem security service, and transfer to the station by shuttle. You yourself may appear before a court as specified in the Uniform Commercial Code, Section 82, paragraph 32.b, this court to be convened upon your arrival. This court will then determine the legality of your actions and the ownership of *Fair Kaleen*. Should you choose not to submit to this procedure, you are forbidden to approach nearer than fifty thousand kilometers. On your present course, this intersection will occur in approximately sixteen hours."

Ky looked around the bridge and met expressions as blank as she felt. "That's . . . not what I expected," she said. "It could take days to straighten this out."

"If you go in there, you'll end up in jail," Rafe said. "Remember that *determine the legality of your actions*? If the civil court decides you were wrong to kill Osman and his crew, you'd be facing criminal charges in a system where you don't even have diplomatic representation."

"It's the only way to prove who I really am—" Ky said. "I need to get this ship in my name legally."

"It's the way to be stuck in a lockup with no chance at all to prove who you really are."

Martin gave Rafe a sidelong look, then nodded. "He's right, Captain. They want you to go alone; you don't know anyone here; you don't have any allies. You can't call on the Slotter Key embassy, even if there is one."

"There's not," Ky said. "I checked. Representation is through Fiella Consortium."

"There you are. No allies, no backup—it's insane."

"But if I don't go, they'll say I'm a pirate. And what will happen to Stella and the *Gary*?"

"Stella can take care of herself," Rafe said. "And she'll have Mackensee to speak up for her, as well as the other captains—she didn't make the decisions you made. As your designated representative, she can receive the funds due you from the rest of the convoy and pay off Mackensee."

"I've got to talk to Johannson again," Ky said. "And Stella. But I have to answer them first."

"No, you don't. You've got hours. And by the way, *partner,* I really appreciate your not telling me about that letter of marque. Were you ever going to?"

"Yes," Ky said. "When the time came."

The look he gave her was not reassuring. "Well, the time came at someone else's convenience. I hope you don't have too many more surprises for me. I do my best plotting when I have all the facts."

"No more that I know of," Ky said. "For what it's worth, I hadn't made up my mind to use the letter of marque, since by the time it arrived in my hands, I knew the Slotter Key government had turned against our family. If the ansibles were up, I'm sure they'd have recalled it or repudiated it or whatever they do."

Rafe blinked. "You weren't going to use it? What kind of idiocy is that? It's a marvelous opportunity to rebuild Vatta's fleet, if nothing else. Not every system government is as hidebound as this one; as long as you don't prey on their people and spend enough in port, they won't care."

"But if Slotter Key—"

"Why do you care what they think? They turned on your family, right? Let 'em howl. You have a good fast ship and a letter of marque. You'd be crazy not to use it to the hilt." The others, Ky noted when she glanced around, were staring at Rafe as if he'd sprouted extra limbs. He looked around, too, then back at her, a look as challenging as the flourish of a sword. "What—you haven't gotten squeamish, have you, or stricken with remorse or anything? After the way you killed Osman?"

She shook her head. "No . . . I'm not stricken with remorse. Osman needed killing. It's just—"

He interrupted. "It's just that you've always been a good girl, Stella says. Law abiding, rule following, all that. Well, look where it got your family. Dead, most of them. I'm not saying turn into a vindictive pirate like Osman, but if you want to do the survivors any good, you can't be too worried about what other people think."

Ky was aware of a tense stillness; the bridge crew's attention was palpable. Her mouth was dry; she felt as if she were about to jump out of the ship into vacuum and free fall. A trickle of humor worked its way through—she had done that already. With a bungee cord. And she wasn't the nice rule-bound girl she had been—if she ever had been. She had killed more than once, and she had enjoyed it . . . something she hoped no one else would suspect.

"I suppose," she said, drawing the words out, "if communications come back and Slotter Key tries to withdraw the letter of marque . . . I'll deal with it."

A faint sense of relaxation. She took a deep breath and let it out. "All right. I'm not putting my head in anyone's noose just to see if they'll yank it tight. But I do need to talk to Stella and the Mackensee escort, and as many captains as I have time for."

No one said anything, but there was a collective gust of breath let out.

"We're well stocked for any ordinary voyage," Ky said, as if to herself. "We can't air up the whole ship yet, but there's plenty for us and we have the power to warm up Environmental and let the tanks start producing. Plenty of water, right, Mitt?"

"Yes, plenty. We can go to electrolysis if you want, but it's safer to go slow."

"Well, then. We need to find a destination, within two jumps, and in the books as being relaxed on regulatory operations."

THREE

Stella, when Ky contacted her aboard *Gary Tobai*, stared out of the screen, eyes wide. "You're going to leave me behind? What if they lock me up?" she asked. "Why wouldn't they?"

"You weren't in command when Osman attacked us; you didn't make the decisions or even participate."

"I had a bag over my head and was tied up—" Stella said. "If that's not participating . . ."

"I know that and you know that, but they don't. And they don't need to. You're my cousin; you're a Vatta—or a Constantin, I don't care which name you use here—and you did what you were told. I can name you my agent for financial matters—collecting payment from the others in the convoy and paying off Mackensee. Mackensee will speak up for you, after all. You should still have enough to get where we're going . . ."

"If they don't put me in jail," Stella said gloomily. "It wouldn't be the first time a government punished the innocent because they couldn't catch the guilty." Then, in a different tone, "Sorry. I didn't mean you were guilty, of course. Just what they think, or may think."

"That's all right," Ky said. "But I need someone here

to handle the financial end, and you are, at present, our family finance person."

"Quincy says we need a pilot," Stella said. "Or we'll have to have one of theirs."

"Take one of theirs. It'll lower their suspicions. Of you, anyway. I'll talk to Mackensee and the others."

"I hope you don't mind that we told them about your letter of marque," Johannson said when she called the Mackensee ship. "The locals thought you were Osman trying another trick, or maybe one of his crew or a relative or something. I tried to convince them that you were legitimate, but then they started suspecting us." His expression was that of someone holding a very dead rat by the tail. "I thought the letter of marque would give you some legitimacy, but apparently not."

"I understand," Ky said. She did, but that didn't make her happy about it. "He *was* a relative—distant and unwelcome. At least he didn't have any children." That they knew about, Ky thought suddenly. What if he had? What kind of monsters would someone like Osman have fathered? Was she going to be pursued by his children? She shoved that worry down to deal with the immediate problem. "My concern now is how they will regard Stella. Will it be safe to send her in, or will they throw her in jail?"

"I doubt they'll detain her," Johannson said. "I was able to pry out of them that they had no bias against Vatta as a whole, and *Gary Tobai* doesn't scare them. It's in their database as a legitimate Vatta ship. They may do a closer inspection than otherwise. I hope you moved those mines—"

She had forgotten the mines. Anyone coming aboard—certainly anyone inspecting the cargo holds—would see both the mines and the evidence that one had gone off inside the ship. "No," Ky said. "I didn't have the chance."

He pulled at his lower lip. "Hmmm. That may be a problem. And that ship needed some repairs, didn't it? If you—your cousin, I mean—can make it to another port, perhaps that would be wiser."

"We have to collect the fees from the convoy to pay you," Ky reminded him. "The contract's with Vatta, so Stella can do that—she can set up a transfer account, for instance. And they'll need supplies."

"Ah. But do repairs have to be made before another transfer?"

"I'll ask our engineer, but probably not. Stella will need more crew, though. She's shorthanded now; she doesn't even have a pilot aboard."

Johannson sighed, a sound between resignation and exasperation. "We can supply one for her to dock, but you're right, she'll need one." No port authority would let a ship leave without a licensed pilot aboard.

"That would be a big help," Ky said. "Just getting her to the dockside legally." And a Mackensee pilot wouldn't wander around the ship and discover the mines she'd had no chance to remove.

"I suppose we could claim to have loaned you the mines," Johannson said. "Though that doesn't explain the damage . . ."

"Maybe they won't be noticed," Ky said. "If she can get in, do the financial stuff . . . the ship's a mess but the repairs aren't critical, exactly."

"She can't sell anything remotely suspicious," Johannson said. "That'll trigger a request to inspect the cargo holds. Loading . . . well, she can have her own crew do that, but if that involves new people, people she's not sure of—" He sighed again. "I'd like to offer to help her screen applicants, but I can't. I've exceeded our regs already. You've really put her in a very difficult spot."

Ky wondered if he'd have been half as sympathetic if it had been the lovely Stella who had put her in a spot. "I'm sorry," she said, though she felt she had done nothing but apologize for days.

Stella Vatta went looking for Quincy; the elderly engineer was doing something at the control boards . . . Stella had no idea what, and at the moment didn't care.

"I think Ky's gone crazy," she said.

Quincy looked up. "I doubt it, but what's bothering you?"

"She's not going to dock here. They're insisting on adjudicating possession of Osman's ship, and Ky insists it's Vatta property, stolen and then recovered as a prize. Claims that makes it hers two ways. They're not agreeing; she's going to pull out, she says. That's insane. Leaving me here with a ship I don't know anything about—"

Quincy gave her a hard look, not the sympathetic one she'd been hoping for. "You've been aboard how long? And she appointed you captain tens of days ago . . ."

Stella tossed her head. "I've been trying, but I never had the ship background. And anyway, even if I did know all about this ship, it's not right for her to just hare off somewhere and leave me—"

"We could go with her," Quincy said.

"She says not. She says we're supposed to stay behind and handle all the financial stuff with the convoy and Mackensee."

Quincy's brows rose. Stella nodded at her.

"Now do you see what I mean? I can just imagine what the other captains will say. And Mackensee. And she's left me to straighten out whatever messes she's caused—"

"You are trained in finance, though, isn't that right?"
Quincy asked.

"Well, yes, but—"

"Do you really think this is something you can't do?"

"Well, no, but—"

"So she knows you're capable of it, and she's left you
a job you can do. It's unfortunate that she has to pull out,
and I admit I'd be more comfortable if she were going to
be around—" That in a tone suggesting Quincy wasn't at
all convinced Stella was competent. "—but I don't see that
it's as bad as you're making out."

Stella stared at the old woman. "You—you agree with
her?"

"Whether I agree with her or not on any given decision isn't the point. The point is she's saved us—and this
ship—twice now, and for me that's a record worth
respecting. She's asked you to do something you're capable
of doing—"

"I got that already," Stella said.

"Good. Because that's what's important. If she'd asked
you to fight a space battle, I might think that was crazy.
If she asked you to pilot the ship into dock yourself, I'd
know that was crazy. But asking you to sweet-talk some
ship captains and handle finances? It should be eating
cake with cream for someone like you." The look Quincy
gave her made clear what assets the old woman thought
Stella would use on the ship captains. Stella felt her blood
beginning to sizzle.

"We don't even have a pilot," Stella said, struggling to
keep her voice level. "It's not legal. We have to have a
pilot to dock."

"And undock," Quincy reminded her. "But pilots are
always for hire at major ports like this. We can call for
one, to get in, and I'd be very surprised indeed if you

couldn't hire any crew you wanted once we're docked."

"You don't think they'll ask questions?" Stella said. Quincy looked blank. "About the damage," Stella went on. "Where Ky the genius nearly blew a hole in our ship and knocked us all out."

"It didn't go anywhere near the hull," Quincy said. "And there's no reason a hired pilot would need to be down there in cargo anyway."

"We'd better hope they don't have a good nose," Stella said. To her, the emergency access passage still had a meaty aroma though the others claimed they'd swabbed it repeatedly and there weren't any visible stains from Osman's gory demise. She was sure minute traces of blood remained that could be found by any good forensics team. Not to mention a certain gory package in the back of the freezer; Ky had wanted a tissue sample to prove identity if she needed to.

Quincy leaned against the bulkhead and folded her arms. "Stella, I can tell you're upset, but for the good of Vatta you need to get over whatever it is. You and Ky must work together—it's our only hope."

"I was willing to work with her," Stella said. "But she isn't working with me: she's just doing what she wants and she expects me to follow along like . . . like that idiot puppy." Quincy opened her mouth but Stella ignored her and rode the rush of anger that had finally gotten loose. "I'm not her puppy or even her kid sister. I'm older than she is, I've been out in the universe longer, and she treats me like some low-ranking employee, not a colleague or family member!"

"That's not fair—"

"You're right it's not fair." Stella knew what Quincy meant, but shook her head and went on. "Everything she does gets us in worse trouble. It's as if she wanted trouble, wanted danger. I suppose she gets a kick out of it; that's probably why she went to the Academy in the first place. But it's not the way to rebuild a business!"

"She saved your life," Quincy said, as loudly as Stella. "She saved all our lives. You might at least show a little gratitude!"

"Gratitude for being tied up helpless with a sack over my head and then having my implant fried by that EMP burst? I don't think so. If she'd had the sense to listen to that Mackensee commander and leave Osman well alone—"

"He'd still be out there hunting us," Quincy said, biting off each word. "Do you really think he wouldn't have reported us passing through that system to his allies? Do you really think we'd be better off with Osman in that ship than Ky? Use your head, Stella! You're smarter than that."

The anger withdrew, but not all the way. "And then there's Rafe," Stella said. "She's got some kind of relationship going with Rafe, I can feel it. And he's dangerous; she doesn't have a clue how dangerous."

"And you do," Quincy said, with a sly smile. "Don't try to fool me, young woman: I've seen too much jealousy in my life not to recognize it when it's standing red-faced in front of me. You wish Rafe were here not for Ky's sake but for yours. Your heart rate speeds up at least fifteen percent when he looks at you."

"I do not," Stella said, but she knew her voice lacked conviction. "I set Rafe aside years ago—"

"And then you ran into him again. I agree, he's a dangerous man, but you underestimate Ky if you think she'll do anything foolish because he has a glamour about him. She's not the one who—"

"Oh, for pity's sake, don't bring *that* up again," Stella

said. "It was over ten years ago and I've never done it again."

"Sorry," Quincy said, her face flushing.

"And it's because she has less experience that I worry about her," Stella said, trying to recover some high ground.

"Well, don't. At least, don't worry about her on that account. Worry about how she'll get along if you turn on her, if you and she can't work together."

"I don't see how we can work together if she's not even here." Stella knew that sounded sulky, but she still felt sulky. More than that, she still had the cold, vast hollow inside her, the vast fear she had endured, lying bound and hooded in Ky's cabin while Osman attacked. Yes, she had volunteered for that so that Ky would be free to act, but she had not expected to feel quite so helpless, so vulnerable. The others had known what was going on; the others had been able to *do* something, but she had been left without any clue at all, not knowing who would come into the cabin next until she was actually freed.

In her mind, that fear flowed into the next, when Ky had suddenly ordered them all into suits and had gone by herself to deal with Osman. None of them had known what was going on, then, until Ky did something—told someone—to trigger one of the EMP mines and the surge knocked them all out. Once more, she'd been helpless, this time in a helpless ship, while Ky—the only one awake and capable—killed Osman.

She could not forget—she would never forget—the blood, the stench, when Ky came in that time. Ky, her little cousin, the good girl of the family, the dreamer . . . she had looked, in the aftermath of her battle with Osman, like a hideous monster. Even after she showered and changed, something lingered, some essence of the killer. It was as if Ky had absorbed something of Osman,

his brutality, his delight in dominating, causing pain . . .
but she could not quite believe that. Not Ky. Yet . . .

"She's changed, Quincy," Stella said. "Before she got
that ship, she was all Vatta; she cared about the family
and the company above all. She didn't care about the letter
of marque; I believe she had no interest in using it. Now
that she's got a ship like that, with weapons and all, she's
changed."

"You think she doesn't care about the family? After the
way she protected you and Toby?"

"After she put us in danger," Stella said, but this time
without heat. "I'm afraid she'll go after the pirates by herself, in some crazy attempt to get revenge. And Toby's with
her. She'll get them both killed."

"I don't think so," Quincy said. "I've been with her
longer than you have. She's not going to take on something she knows she can't handle, and she's not going to
think a single ship can fight off a lot of 'em."

"I hope you're right," Stella said. With the outburst,
she felt exhausted and on the edge of tears. She was not
going to cry in front of the old woman. Quincy would,
she was sure, take it as an attempt to manipulate her. "I'd
better go tell the others—"

"The ones that didn't overhear you yelling," Quincy
said, with some tartness.

"Yes. Well, I need to talk to Mackensee and the convoy
captains, and of course the station, as well as the crew."

Stella looked at her tiny crew gathered in the rec area and
shrugged as she told them what Ky had said. "We don't
have much choice," she said. "Ky can't come to the station without being tied up in legalities for a long time;
they think she's a pirate."

"That's ridiculous," Alene said.

"It may be ridiculous, but to them it's prudence. For our sakes, we have to be as bland and uninteresting as we can possibly be. Businesslike, of course. Professional, but cool. We don't know, for instance, if anyone is still stalking Vatta ships and family members, so we have to be careful. But we're not looking for trouble." Before anyone could ask awkward questions, she went on. "We need a pilot to get to dock; I'll see about taking one on. We'll be hiring additional crew at this station, including a permanent pilot. If any of you want to leave the ship here, please let me know at least a standard day before we dock, so I can get the paperwork ready. Alene, start scanning the local listings to see what we have that might be marketable."

"What about those things in cargo?" Alene asked.

"What things?" They weren't carrying any contraband that Stella could think of.

"Those mines," Alene said. "The ones that came in with the cleaning supplies. We can't let some Customs clerk see those, or we'll be locked up tighter than tight."

Stella had almost forgotten the remaining mines. Just the thought of them made her feel sick to her stomach. Ugly things, menacing even when just sitting there on the deck.

"Lock them back into their carrying containers and put them in the number two hold, along with anything else consigned to a specific destination. We can then trade out of the others."

"The captain—Captain Ky—did something to them, remember, after she unpacked them. Do you think it's safe to move them?"

Another loose end Ky had left for her to take care of. Stella wondered how she was going to ask Ky about the mines without revealing to any listening ears that there *were* mines. "I'll check with Ky," she said. "Unless, Quincy, you know——?" But Quincy shook her head. "Well, then," Stella went on, "is there anything else we need to ask Ky about? Because she's changed course and this will be difficult in a few more hours."

It was impossible, Stella found, to ask whether mines needed to be deactivated and, if so, how, without making it clear that something was being concealed, if not what.

"I needed to ask you about those cargo items that were involved in the . . . er . . . attack. As you recall, some crates were opened when we were . . . trying to make some barriers and things . . . and some of those items may have been rendered unsafe . . ."

"You mean the . . . oh," Ky said. Her face expressed some emotion that might have been consternation or just concentration. "Er . . . nobody's moved them, have they?"

"No. My question is . . ."

"Well, yes, you'd want to inspect and remove anything . . . er . . . damaged in Osman's attack and clear a space for repairs. I understand that."

"With the reminder that no one in my present crew is experienced in this particular kind of——"

"Yes, yes," Ky said, cutting her off. "Quincy is probably your best choice for this, as some of it is technical. Is she available?"

"She's down in cargo. I'll transfer your call," Stella said. Typical of Ky not to let her finish her sentences. She called Quincy to the relay screen and listened in.

"Quincy," Ky said, "Are you concerned about the items we took onboard at Lastway, from that supply company—— the cleaning supplies, deodorants, and things?"

Quincy's brows rose; then she smoothed her expression. "Yes, Captain. If you recall, Environmental thought some of the canisters might be useful in defending the

ship. But I'm wondering about corrosives that might cause
leaks or impair air quality."

"Yes. And you don't have Mitt over there anymore; I
think he was in charge of that. I'll just ask him." She cut
the sound, but Stella could see Ky turning away, talking
into another device, presumably connected to *Fair Kaleen*'s
Environmental section. Would anyone really believe that
they'd tried to use canisters of deodorant for weapons?

Ky's voice came back on. "Mitt says it's just a matter
of making sure the lids are fastened tightly. There's a snap-
on part—the actual locking device is on the side."

"I saw that," Quincy said. "There's some kind of status
marker or something?"

"Yes—the instructions are in there somewhere. You'd
want it to be dark or green, not orange."

"Do you think Mitt took the instructions with him by
accident? Or what would I look for?"

"If you can find the original crate, there's a readable
version . . ."

Stella listened without comment. Surely anyone listening in would immediately recognize what was being
talked about.

Quincy and Ky went on, until Quincy gave a little grunt
of satisfaction. "Ah. Now I see it. Thanks, Captain—I've
got it and it's clear that none of the . . . uh . . . canisters
has leaked. The contents appear stable."

"Then if the container is still in one piece, just repack
them." Ky looked as calm as if they'd been discussing
tubes of sealant. "Stella, I'd suggest you put that crate and
the other items that were on consignment into one of the
holds and move items you might want to trade to
another—"

"I already thought of that," Stella said.

"Good," Ky said. "Now is there anything else?"

There was, but not something Stella wanted to get into over an open channel. "I would like to know where you're headed next," Stella said. "So I can rejoin you later."

"Oh. Of course." But Ky said nothing more for a moment, instead staring at nothing, with the slightly blank expression of someone accessing complicated implant information. Then she focused on Stella again. "Stella, do you have Vatta route information in your implant?"

"Only the main routes," Stella said. "Maybe Quincy has it in hers."

"I do," Quincy said.

"Good, then. Section six, standard route, alternate three's second stop alternate. Don't say it."

"I have it," Quincy said. "Not recommended, right?"

"Right. The Vatta code should begin with VXR—"

"That's it," Quincy said.

"Let Stella know, but no one should reveal it here," Ky said.

Stella wanted to say *ridiculous,* but maybe it wasn't. "I am authorized to hire crew here, am I not?" she asked instead.

"Of course," Ky said. "You're the CFO; you know what we can afford and can't."

"See you in a few weeks," Stella said, hoping that would be true.

"You'll be fine," Ky said, and signed off.

Stella glared at the blank screen for a few seconds before putting in a call to the Mackensee ship. She would have sent a string of curses after Ky if she'd had a way to do it. Here she was, stuck without a real captain or a pilot, short-crewed otherwise, and Ky was off somewhere doing something—probably getting herself in trouble, as she usually did. How was she supposed to hire reliable crew in this situation?

She fell back on older experiences and tried her best smile on Lieutenant Colonel Johannson. Men in authority usually liked being asked for advice. "How can I find reliable crew?" she asked. "My cousin's left me in a difficult situation . . ."

His answering smile was a bit grim. "You Vattas have a talent for getting in difficult situations. I'd be tempted to do a subsidiary contract with you, except for my experience with your cousin. However, for a fee I can lend the services of our intelligence unit to check out candidates for employment, if you wish."

"That would be most helpful," Stella said. "I'm sorry Ky was such a problem to you."

"She didn't intend to be," Johannson admitted. "But I suspect she's one of those drawn to trouble—or trouble's drawn to her. You may be one of the peaceful Vattas—if there are any."

"We thought we were," Stella said. "Most of my family are—were—ordinary business people. Wore suits, went to the office, came home and in their off hours followed individual hobbies. Or, for those on ship duty, did whatever duty they were assigned."

"Hmmm. Sounds peaceful enough."

"Except for competition between companies," Stella said. "My father could be pretty cutthroat in doing deals, but personally I never saw him as anything but a respectable businessman. Even boring, I thought when I was a youngster, but I had grown out of that." Her only comfort, after her father's death, was that she had, after all the turmoil earlier, gained her father's trust and respect as an adult.

"It's odd that such a massive attack was aimed at your corporation," Johannson said. "I know—at least your cousin said—that she had no idea who had done it, or why; she was convinced it was connected to the attacks on ansibles, but I couldn't think of a plausible connection."

"I can't, either, really. I'm hoping that Osman was behind it somehow—certainly he intended harm to us, and his connections at MilMart suggest a wider-ranging capability—"

"Wait—I hadn't heard about that. What connections at MilMart?"

"He taunted us—said our defensive suite wouldn't work against actual missiles—"

"But we checked it out—our techs said it was fine—"

"Well, it wasn't," Stella said. "I don't understand how it was done, but somehow it showed up fine on scans, but there were bad components. Osman bragged that he had an agent in MilMart, that he'd told them to sell us a compromised system. Ky didn't tell you this?"

"No, she didn't. I suppose it could have slipped her mind—"

"We fixed it," Stella said. "Or rather, Quincy and the Engineering crew did. Replaced the defective parts."

"We buy from MilMart," Johannson said; his tone was now grim. "They have a good reputation, but if they've got someone in their organization who's cheating customers, that's something our headquarters has to know. Fair trade—that pays for our help in screening potential crew for you."

"Thanks," Stella said, astonished.

He didn't explain further, but went on. "Send us a list of the crew you want to find, and we'll check with hiring agencies."

Stella had considered at length what appearance would best suit her needs, studying local broadcasts and newsfeeds. Few visible humods and a human population skewed to the short and dark. Their broadcast entertainment, however, featured one tall blonde after another. For once her beauty might work for her; if she couldn't be one of them, she could be what they admired.

"Aren't you worried about security?" Quincy asked as Stella prepared to go onto the station and arrange financing options.

"Not a great deal," Stella said. "I really think the impetus for attacking Vatta came from Osman. I don't think he was the whole show—he could hardly have managed to damage all those ansibles himself—but I don't think I'm in that much danger."

"I hope you're right," Quincy said.

"I also," Stella said. She put on a smoke-blue dress suit, arranged her hair carefully, and went to meet the Customs and Immigration team at dockside. All male, all fairly short and dark. Their eyes widened as she stepped out onto the dock.

"Er . . . Captain Vatta?"

"I'm Stella Vatta, yes," Stella said. She could see in their expressions that she was having the desired effect. "I don't have a uniform," she said, putting on her most wistful smile. "My cousin was the captain, but when she left, she appointed me."

"And your experience—" That was a stocky older man with a little gray in his dark hair. His name tag read NIMON KNAE.

Stella looked down and allowed her cheeks to flush. "Actually—I'm more of an accountant than a ship officer. But she left me a very capable crew."

"She turned a spaceship over to someone who isn't even a ship officer?" His eyebrows had shot up, almost comically.

Stella nodded. "But I'm a family member, you see. She said a Vatta ship had to have a Vatta captain."

"That's hardly fair to you. How are you supposed to know what to do? What if something goes wrong?" He had taken on the protective tone she knew so well from her father; her eyes filled without her intent even as she recognized that she had found a point of contact.

"I do worry about that," Stella said, blinking back the tears. "But I've been reading the manuals, and I do have a very capable senior engineer. Of course, I plan to hire more crew here—and maybe one of the Vatta ships on this circuit will come in while I'm here."

"She shouldn't have done it," Knae said. "She put you in a very dangerous position."

"I know," Stella said. "I was scared stiff most of the time. But what else could we do? That horrible man was trying to kill us—" It was almost too easy to play the help-less, immature beauty for this man; she was annoyed with herself for the ease with which she fell into the role.

As Knae continued to question her about their voyage, about Ky, about Osman, about the mercenaries, Stella struggled with her own feelings. She and Ky had talked about the family disaster only in brief snatches, information-only. This was the first time she had told the story straight through, from the attack on her family back on Slotter Key through the attacks by Osman. She felt like two Stellas: one in control, carefully manipulating tone of voice and expression to have the best effect on the officials questioning her, and one adrift in waves of emotion she had not taken the time to recognize. From the first, she had been reacting or doing what she was told—by Aunt Grace, by Rafe, by Ky.

Those minutes—was it only minutes?—she had lain on the bunk with a sack over her head came back to her with terrifying intensity. It was hard to breathe, even now, when she thought of it; the fear dominated everything . . . when was he coming? Would Ky be able to stop him?

Knae kept on asking detailed questions, some she couldn't answer, questions she now understood were important in many ways. But in the brief time between waking from the stun to her implant and Ky's leaving for the other ship, she hadn't asked enough questions, or the right questions. Ky should have told her, somehow, exactly what had happened and how; Ky should have understood that she was too dazed by events to take in everything right away.

Her control slipped; she felt more tears on her face, and knew she was shaking.

Knae's face softened and his voice was gentler as he asked, "Can anyone confirm any of this? Even your crew?"

"Quincy could. Quincy Robin. She's as old as the ship, near enough, she's been with Vatta all her life." Stella took a deep breath and managed to steady her voice. "Our escorts certainly know about attacks on Vatta ships and personnel—they witnessed attacks on us at Lastway. Lieutenant Commander Johannson will confirm what happened from Lastway to here."

Finally they seemed to have run out of questions. Knae looked at the others, who looked back and shrugged.

"I need to get to the bank," Stella said. "If you don't mind?"

"Go ahead . . . but don't leave the station without permission."

"I wouldn't know how," Stella said, smiling at them. She wondered how Ky would have fared, when even her beauty had barely softened their attitude.

FOUR

"I'm sure you don't want someone you've never seen before trying to get access to corporate accounts," Stella said, putting full force charm into her voice. The Crown & Spears account manager nodded, eyes wary. "Even though I know the account numbers and passwords—of course even with the best security such things have been compromised. But I want to open a new corporate account. We have funds coming in, owed us by the convoy that just arrived, and I want the same terms as in the other Vatta account."

"Er . . . that seems reasonable," the man said. "And if you really needed . . . perhaps something could be arranged . . ."

"No need," Stella said, smiling at him, watching him react as nearly all men did to that smile. He was certainly more susceptible than Customs and Immigration's Inspector Knae. "But I don't want to be paying higher bank charges than the regular account; it will annoy our people and give me a black mark."

"Surely not," the man said. "In such an emergency—"

"You don't know my aunt Grace," Stella said ruefully. "She doesn't believe in excuses."

"A close family firm," the man said, smiling now.

"There's a dragon in every family, isn't there? With me it was my mother's mother. Until she died, we were all hauled up at least once a tenday." He shook his head. "Let's see, then. In the present state of things, with financial ansibles down, we aren't taking credit transfers from outsystem institutions, but we are accepting hard currency or trade goods from incoming spacers."

"Of course," Stella said.

"Existing Vatta corporate accounts fall into our Preferred category; I believe you'll find the amenities acceptable." He passed across a hardcopy sheet; Stella glanced over it quickly.

"Yes, that's quite acceptable. Now if you can refer me to a licensed appraiser . . ."

"Certainly. Ballard Valuations is bonded, quite reputable. So is Actuarial Appraisals."

Stella flipped a mental coin and chose Ballard. Two of Aunt Grace's diamonds produced a respectable first deposit to the new Vatta account. Stella sent the necessary information to the other convoy captains and instructed them to make their deposits promptly, then told Mackensee that she had done so.

She had just returned to the ship from Crown & Spears when the station security chief called.

"We've checked your story with the Mackensee commander and your crew personnel; we are now satisfied that you are not a pirate and that you are in legitimate command of your ship, though you are not actually qualified . . . but that's not your fault. We accept that in an emergency you did what was necessary. Nonetheless, we require that you hire an experienced captain and necessary crew before proceeding."

"Thank you," Stella said. "I fully intend to hire someone who knows more than I do."

"We are not yet convinced that your cousin is as blameless as you think, however. She failed to submit to our judicial investigation."

"Ky is . . . impulsive sometimes," Stella murmured. "She was always very upright, however."

"That may be, but she is now running an armed vessel to which she has no adjudicated title and she claims to have a letter of marque and thus a prize claim—"

"She has the letter of marque," Stella said. "I've seen it."

"And there's the matter of the person with her whom you think is working on behalf of the ISC. But he didn't fix *our* ansibles the way you say he fixed others."

"Did you ask him to?" Stella said.

"Well . . . no." A longish pause, then a grudging nod. "All right. I see your point. We didn't ask for that help, and we weren't being overly welcoming to your cousin. I suppose if she felt she had to exit the system, he could hardly have jumped ship into vacuum."

"Precisely," Stella said, smiling. "And now, I'd like permission to unload my cargo and go about my business— trading business."

"Quite so. Go ahead, then. We've greenlighted your cargo access."

Three shifts later, the first of the convoy ships had made its deposit into her new account, and she had made the required transfer to Mackensee for their escort service. Their own cargo, small as it was, sold for a good price; she now had enough in the account to hire new crew.

Balthazar Orem had lost his ship to dock charges; with no transfer credit and a cargo that didn't compete well in the current market, he'd been unable to keep up, and the station had seized his ship. "I'll be glad to work for a company like Vatta," he said in his recorded interview. "I know Vatta's had problems, but it'll recover. It's always been a respectable line. Maybe I can save enough to start over m'self someday, but realistically—" He rubbed his left hand through thinning gray hair. "I'm gettin' on for that. Just to be in space, just to have a ship, that's what I want. All my papers are in order; I've never had a judgment against me."

"He's the best we've found," Johannson said. "He worked up to his own ship from cargo handler; he knows his job and he has a good reputation, other than being 'too small to compete.' "

"I'll take him," Stella said. "At least, I think I will, but I still want to meet him myself."

"Pilots are a bit chancier," Johannson said. "We found you what we think is the best available onstation, but she's got a reputation as a handful. Here's her interview." He flicked on the vidscreen. The hard-faced redhead sat bolt upright, looking as if she might explode any moment.

"I'm a pilot," she said. "Not a navigator, not an engineer, and for sure not a cargo worker. Pilot. Best one around, and that's why I insist that I'm just a pilot, nothing else."

Stella tried to imagine that personality in her crew and almost refused.

"I don't get in rows, I don't cause trouble—I'll do my share of general shipwork, in the galley and so forth. But I'm a specialist, see? This is a small ship you're talking about, and sometimes these small ships think everyone can do everything. They can't. I need to run my sims every day to keep my skills up and stay sharp."

That didn't sound as bad.

"She's abrasive," Johannson said, "but she passed our skills test with a very high score."

"I'll take her," Stella said. She needed skills more than a sweet personality.

Orem came for his interview within minutes of her call; he must have been waiting just outside the dock space. Stella recognized the same quiet competence that characterized many Vatta captains. It was hard to make herself ask more questions, and she finally shook her head and said, "This is ridiculous—you're clearly qualified, Captain Orem, and I hope you'll accept this position."

"Thank you, ma'am; I'll be glad to."

"Just give me time to move my things out of the captain's cabin—"

"You don't need to do that, ma'am. I can bunk anywhere."

"Of course you'll have that cabin," Stella said. "It's set up for communications to the bridge." She didn't really want to bunk in crew quarters, but she knew better than to shortchange her new captain.

By the end of that business day, she had hired an excellent environmental technician as well, and Orem had already worked up a watch schedule for the old and new crew.

"I like him," Quincy said to Stella in the rec area. "He feels solid to me. And she's prickly, but qualified." No question who *she* was . . . the new pilot.

Over the next few days, as Orem settled into command of *Gary Tobai*, Stella completed the financial transfers from the convoy to the new Vatta account. It was tedious, as not all the convoy captains had accounts with Crown & Spears, and two of them had to wait for their cargoes to sell in order to clear the amount needed. Stella suspected that Ky would not have had the patience to keep after the various ship captains without annoying them too much.

She had told Quincy to organize a priority list for

repairs; now she told Orem how much they now had available to spend. Repair crews moved into the damaged cargo hold and began rebuilding the wiring. Stella looked at their balance—much healthier than she'd expected, even counting the cost of repairs—and went in search of trade goods. With traffic down, what would the market on Rosvirein be looking for? Or, assuming a reasonable course, something she couldn't predict with Ky, the next logical port, Sallyon?

If Vatta was to rebuild, it would need contacts on as many stations as possible. Garth-Lindheimer had been a prosperous and respectable trading station for some time; the system had several habitable planets, and insystem trade sustained the economy even with the ansibles down. No interstellar traders headquartered here, but she visited the branch offices of those who had regular routes through Garth-Lindheimer. Everyone's business was down, pirate activity was up, and no one wanted to subcontract with Vatta, even for short runs. She paid a visitor fee to make use of the Captains' Guild, where she expected the dining room gossip to more than repay that expense. At first she heard nothing new, just complaints about the time it was taking ISC to repair the ansibles, the apparent increase in pirate attacks, lost revenues, rapacious insurance companies.

"So what is Slotter Key like?" asked Captain Parks of *Amber's Dream* on her third visit; he offered to buy her lunch, and she accepted.

Stella shrugged, letting the soft knit dress she was wearing almost slip off one shoulder. He appeared to be only a few years older than she, sandy-haired with pale blue eyes. She'd seen him watching her before; perhaps he would be less cautious than the other captains. "It's my home world; I think it's beautiful. Pretty much standard type for unmodified human colonization. More ocean than most, I'd say."

"And why are you all the way over here?" he asked, his eyes straying to her cleavage.

Stella took a calculated breath. This kind was the easiest to pump for information. She explained, briefly but emotionally, about the attacks on her home and family. "And then my cousin went off in the other ship, and left me to take care of things here."

"That doesn't seem fair," he said. He was leaning forward now. Stella sat back.

"It's not, but what could I do? I had to find someone to help me with the ship. I'm not a licensed captain, as you know."

"You could have asked me," he said.

This was too ridiculous. "You have a ship already," Stella said, with just a hint of tartness. "And I am asking your advice now. What sort of cargo do you think will be profitable if I were headed for, say, Bissonet? And is Rosvirein the best way to go, or should I head for the Topaz Cluster?" Stella had picked Bissonet as most obvious populous system beyond Rosvirein and Sallyon.

"Bissonet? They're a major manufacturing center, and your ship's too small to carry any raw materials they might want." Parks moved his wineglass a centimeter. "I'd try culinary additives, art glass, things like that. Tricky, if you haven't been there before."

"I've got to do something," Stella said, shrugging. "If I'm going to rebuild Vatta, it has to start somewhere."

"A hard task," Park said. He leaned forward, elbows on the table, inadequate chin resting on his hands. "You are young for it, but then the young and beautiful find many things easy that others would find impossible."

He was impossible. If he leaned any closer, he would upset the whole table in her lap.

"You flatter me," Stella said. Usually she enjoyed a game of flirt and fly, but now it seemed as juvenile as a child's circle game. What she wanted was information, useful information, not admiring glances and barely veiled lust. It was her own fault, she admitted to herself; she had dressed to arouse, but it was still a bore.

"What an excellent fish," she said, applying herself to the pink-fleshed fillet in front of her. It was good; Ky had said that the food at the Captains' Guild dining rooms was nearly always good.

"It is," the man said, starting in on his own pair of chops. "If you like fish," he added.

Stella smiled sweetly at him but went on eating. When she had finished, she thanked him and excused herself. "I'm sorry, but my ship tells me there's a call waiting— it was a lovely meal, and you were most generous."

His smile brightened. "Perhaps I'll see you this evening, if you stop by the bar—"

"It will depend on business," Stella said. If you couldn't leave them laughing, you could at least leave them hopeful. Not that she wanted to fan his hopes, but no need to leave him feeling used.

In the days that followed, while the repair crew finished their work, Stella picked up small amounts of a varied cargo. This was much more her sort of thing than running a ship. She had always had a knack for recognizing what would become a style trend well before it did; she could read quality in merchandise types she didn't know as if it were printed in bold on the surface. Now this led her to pick up bales of handwoven cloth, several crates of art glass, some spare parts for larger ships' environmental systems, two crates of porcelain dishes, and

250 Kospar Infini toilets, top of the line across the galaxy. Captain Orem told her about those when they came up on the auction board.

"I thought toilets were toilets," Stella said. "Mature technology, been around thousands of years—I mean, I know the name, and they're nice, but to haul around on spaceships?"

"All Kospar products are first-rate," Orem said. "But the Infini model is what the rich and famous put into their homes and private offices. Kospar limits the manufacture every year, well below demand. Designers beg for them. What was in your father's house?"

"Kospar," Stella admitted. "Benites upstairs, and there was an Infini in the master bath and the main guest bath, but I never used those. What's the difference?"

He shrugged. "What's the difference between synthsilk and real silk? Grape juice and wine? For one thing, each is unique in some way: color, texture of the exterior, inclusions—"

"Inclusions?"

"Decorative elements incorporated into the structural material. I saw one once that had ferns . . . it was a work of art, not just a basic human necessity. For another thing, they don't break. They never require cleaning. They never need repair or adjustment. Anything that damages one of them will destroy the house around it. They all monitor for a wide range of health concerns. And they have the most comfortable seats. They also cost, of course, and the profit on them, even for the shipper, is quite generous."

"So you think we should take them."

"We should take twice that many if they were available. I don't suppose you'll sell many on Rosvirein—though the criminal element has never been noted for austerity—but if we do go on to Sallyon and Bissonet, I'd expect a very nice profit indeed."

The toilets came aboard, along with hand-knit scarves of wool from a local game animal, bright-painted religious icons, packets of freeze-dried "wild" meat and fish, and anything else that caught Stella's eye and passed Captain Orem's experienced trade sense.

Ky brought *Fair Kaleen* into Rosvirein's system cautiously. Rosvirein had the reputation—according to her father's implant and Rafe's memory—of a rough place in which few questions were or should be asked. The automatic beacon when they arrived requested confirmation that the beacon ID was correct, nothing more. Ky checked the scan. Twenty-eight ships insystem, twenty of them carrying trade beacons, and eight of them showing as armed, weapons hot, under the Rosvirein Peace Force logo. Twelve of the twenty traders were in space; the others were listed as docked.

A list of system rules came up on screen. Armed ships were welcome, but if their weapons went live they would be fired upon by Rosvirein Peace Force. Military personnel must declare their organization and current contracts, if any. Privateers must declare any letters of marque currently in force and provide a facsimile of such documents. Pirates were advised that any attempts at piracy insystem would be severely dealt with. Patrons were welcome to carry whatever personal arms they wished onstation, but were held responsible for any damage caused to persons or property. Registered bounty hunters could locate and identify fugitives, but not capture or kill them.

The last line read: "Be advised, the death penalty is frequently imposed and we do not have an appellate court system."

"It may not keep us alive, but anyone who attacks us will be taken down," Rafe said, reading that. "Cold comfort, though. And did you notice, their ansible's live. The bad guys have been here, if they aren't here now."

"So we can expect attacks." She would have to have security if she left the ship; that meant Martin and Rafe.

"Maybe not. If Osman was the real push behind the attacks on Vatta, the other bad guys may not care. And if you act like you think he was the real cause, and they don't have other reasons, they'll be glad to let things lie."

"That's so reassuring," Ky said, for want of anything better. A trickle of sweat ran down her backbone.

"It could be," Rafe said. He eyed her. "Nervous, Captain?"

"A little, yes," Ky said. "Can you find out through these which ansibles are functional?"

"I can if they have a list up," Rafe said. He sat down at the console and queried the local ansible. "Ah. Repairs have been made to thirty-seven percent of the ansibles originally down, but some of those aren't considered stable. Slotter Key's still not up. Garth-Lindheimer is; it just came back online eight days ago. I'm not sure I find that good."

"Why not? I can contact Stella if she's still there."

"It strikes me as suspicious that an ansible starts working just after we leave a system . . . at least, when I had nothing to do with it. Either a legitimate ISC repair crew showed up there, or . . . or something."

Ky felt a cold chill. She hadn't wanted to leave Stella back at Garth-Lindheimer; if something happened to her cousin or that ship, it would be Ky's fault.

"Stella's smart," Rafe said, answering her unspoken fear. "She's been in tight places before. And she's less confrontational than you are."

"Confrontational . . ."

"It's the military training, I suspect. Meet trouble head-on."

Ky thought of explaining that sound military theory was against direct confrontation if sneakier maneuvers were available, but thought better of it. She did have a history that suggested confrontation, even though she hadn't meant to take that route. And experience was teaching her that getting into arguments with Rafe rarely accomplished anything but raising her heart rate.

Rosvirein's Customs and Immigration looked over the facsimile of Ky's letter of marque with what looked like practiced boredom. "Slotter Key, right. Here's the rules for privateers. You can't take ships in this system unless you assign half the prize to us prior to the attempt. If you fail to take the ship you indicate, you still owe us half the prize value as assessed prior to. However, you are welcome to gather information and guess where your target ships are going next and attack them there. Onstation, we don't want trouble. Or, we don't want trouble that interferes with trade. We're a free-trade system. No limitations on merchandise categories."

"I'm here to trade," Ky said. "No targets in sight, and I don't want trouble, either."

"That's what they all say," the officer said, grinning. "Trade's reasonably active now, but we've had reports of unidentified ships bouncing in and out of the system, and with that and all those ansibles down, some of the traders are talking about traveling in convoys. Not that I'm brokering or anything, but if you're in the escort business as well as trade, you'll probably find someone interested."

"I'll think about it," Ky said. Thinking about it was all she could do, until she had the whole ship aired up and weapons crews to operate the weapons. First she had to sell some of her cargo so she could hire people, and even before that she had to avoid being killed. Tempting as it was to think that Osman's death ended the threat to Vatta, it could be fatal to make that assumption. Especially on a station with Rosvirein's reputation.

With Martin and Rafe along, and her own personal weapon loaded and handy in its holster, she set out for the Captains' Guild.

The concourse bustled, as busy as Lastway's and subtly more varied. Dress ranged from plain shipsuits to elaborate costumes Ky would have expected at a formal diplomatic affair. Visible personal arms included swords, firearms, shocksticks. Local security, just as obvious, wore full battledress, faceplates up, carried combat-quality firearms, and walked in pairs.

Ky watched a group of women, all in lush blue velvet pantsuits, lace ruffles at wrists and throat, lace headdresses, stroll along looking at shop windows. They turned in, finally, at a display of custom electronics. Out of a grocer's came a woman in a blue uniform dress and white headdress, shepherding a line of small children, each clutching a fruit of some kind. A humod with four forearms, two hands carrying books, one a briefcase, and one rummaging in the briefcase . . . another with a floret of tentacles on one shoulder, all rolled into a compact mass; the other arm appeared normal.

The Captains' Guild onstation looked like any upper-level spacer bar, with its protective doorman. Ky checked in, listing *Fair Kaleen* as having cargo to sell, crew vacancies, and no firm destination.

"The status boards are in there, the bar's over there, and we have three private meeting rooms, if you need them," the clerk said, pointing in various directions after she'd finished signing in. "We don't see Vatta captains in here that often."

"The ansible problem has a lot of people off route," Ky said.

"We've heard. Luckily we've got our own techs. Annoys ISC that we don't call them every time a blip happens, but we're not stuck like the rest of the tame sheep who depend on ISC for everything. Slotter Key's your headquarters, right? And its ansible's still out. Guess you people are on your own now, no one to tell you what to do."

"Something like that," Ky said. She didn't look at Rafe; she could imagine what he was thinking. She looked at the status board. Ten ships in dock, counting hers. Those docked when she arrived insystem had left, except for two. She'd already noticed that *Bal's Tiger* and *Ratany* had been there a long time. Captains R. Taylor and G. Pinwin. Awaiting cargo, according to the Captains' Guild board. Others had come and gone, finding cargo. Something to be wary of, no doubt. Still, she could use more crew, and ships that stayed too long in one place often had crew who wanted to move on.

"The local market's hot for custom and specialized electronics right now," the clerk went on. "Woven fabrics is cold—the local system produces and exports excellent natural-fiber fabric. Foodstuffs, unless you've got something really exotic, are also cold. Munitions always have a hot market here. Fine arts—it depends. High-end furnishings are the same."

"Thank you," Ky said.

"And since you're looking for crew, or you have something specific in mind, I might know a connection . . . ."

"I'll need to consider our cargo in light of what you've told me," Ky said. She wasn't about to give this one information he could sell on.

Her first priority was resupply anyway, and that meant she needed quick cash. The ship's limited hydroponics space hadn't begun to replace the air lost to space when the air lock blew out, and she wanted those now airless cargo spaces aired up so they could be inspected and the reserves replaced. Rosvirein's air charges were high, but not impossibly so. She would contact Crown & Spears first, see about accessing the corporate accounts, and if that proved impossible then she'd sell something—anything—to pay for air.

FIVE

Slotter Key

The man assigned to watch a particular scattered remnant of the Vatta family wished the assassins would hurry up. A pleasant hill-country job, practically a vacation, he'd been told. Sweet summer breezes, beautiful flowers everywhere, a paradise. People paid good money to spend part of the summer up here in the hills, he'd been told.

People were crazy. He had never been so bored and so miserable. The house and gardens had an efficient alarm system—sensible enough, with all the attacks on Vattas—so he had to stay at a distance, hiding hour after hour in the lee of a rocky outcrop. The camping outfit he'd rented back in the city turned out to be useless, a bright-colored tent he dared not use, a portable chemical toilet that clogged up the second day, and foodpaks that tasted like hay and sawdust. He had been rained on, sunburned, bitten and stung by more nasty small creatures than he'd known existed, and all to watch a grieving widow, her orphaned grandchildren, and a dotty old lady.

Grace Lane Vatta may have been a war hero once—he had found reference to her guerrilla activity—but now she was a dotty old lady who didn't appear outside until after supper, when she tottered around the orchard and garden in typical old-lady clothes: big hat, saggy skirts down to her ankles, long sleeves, a fuzzy shawl around her shoulders, and sensible shoes. The middle-aged widow looked almost as frumpy as she followed two young children around. Her grandchildren, they were supposed to be. The children were children, vacation-grubby.

Their routine didn't vary. The children played outside in the morning, sometimes riding two sluggish ponies around and around a paddock just beyond the garden. Their grandmother was always nearby. Afternoons, everyone was indoors, and other than the after-dinner stroll, they were inside in the evening, lights out shortly after dark. They'd had no visitors other than the grocer's van, no excursions in the ten too-long days he'd been watching. Why be rich, if it meant living such boring lives? At least they would be easy targets for the assassins, if the assassins ever showed up.

He had dismissed the assistant who covered the night watch, because these people went to bed shortly after dark and slept all night. He could use the extra money, to make up for his own miserable working conditions and the cost of the hard bunk at the hostel where he slept, since he couldn't stay in the tent.

His head hurt and the light stabbed his eyes painfully. He ached. He was sure he was coming down with something. His right leg had a big swollen pink patch on it, and he had another on his right side, just above belt level. He'd pulled horrid little bugs off him in both places; they'd been attached firmly. Probably sucking his blood. His back itched, no matter how much he scratched at it with a stick. He needed a doctor.

He tried to contact his backup, but got no answer. He couldn't reach his employer, either. Easy to imagine the man relaxing in a seaside café back in the capital, cool and comfortable, safely away from biting bugs and the wonders of nature, probably taking a long lunch hour with some beautiful girl.

In late morning, he gave up in disgust after finding three more of the flat, blue-black bloodsuckers crawling on his clothes. The old lady wasn't going anywhere, and he had to get something to keep them off, as well as medicine for his aching head. He struggled up, stiffer and more miserable than ever, and made his way up to the mail road, carefully keeping out of sight of the house windows in the distance. He paid no attention to the ponies whose ears were pricked as they watched, the vultures whose monotonous soaring above the rock outcrop ended as they rose on thermals and went looking for something else dead or dying. He caught the local van to town and asked directions to the clinic.

He planned to be back in a few hours, but once the emergency clinic medic saw the red circles and heard about the bloodsucking bugs, he found himself whisked into bed with IVs attached. The medic had plucked two more of the things from his back. "You're not going anywhere," a doctor said firmly. "You've got bluetick fever, no doubt about it. I can't believe you didn't come in as soon as you found the first one attached. Didn't you pay any attention to the warnings about blueticks? You were lying on the ground, weren't you? It's the same every summer; you city people come up here and ignore precautions, and then when you get sick you want an instant cure."

Her voice made his head hurt worse. "I have to get back . . . ," he said.

"Well, there's no instant cure for bluetick fever, young man," she said. "You're going to have a very unpleasant eight to ten days, but at least you won't die of it. If you hadn't come in today . . ." The doctor shook her head and walked out. He wanted to get up, insist on leaving, but the pain in his head redoubled and he couldn't move.

An early-afternoon thunderstorm grumbled its way along the slope beyond the river, cooling the muggy air as it blocked the sun. Grace Lane Vatta, dressed in worn but impeccably tailored fishing clothes, rod and creel in hand, waders slung over her shoulder, paused in the gateway between the gardens and the near paddock to watch the storm and the pleasant sweep of land between the house and the water meadows below. The mail road, higher up the slope, carried the right amount of traffic for the time of day. Behind her, the house dozed, quiet at this hour since Helen insisted on the grandchildren—Jo's orphans— taking naps so that she could rest.

Nothing moved in the grass that should not move; nothing interfered with the grass's response to wind. She had checked that from an upper window, but she made no rash assumptions. The children's ponies loafed in the shade of a tree, switching their tails idly, proof that no one lurked near the paddock. Those greedyguts would be trying to beg a treat if anyone were near. The vultures that had circled and swooped low over a stony outcrop every day were high up this afternoon, riding the storm's thermals. They had moved away in late morning. Whatever had piqued their interest the past week was gone. Grace hadn't bothered to check; animals were always getting sick or dying, and vultures always found them. Blueticks were abundant near that outcrop, even more so after she'd collected a jarful from a farm dog down the way and put them in the handiest place for a spy to lie watching.

The storm continued to move toward the lake and the hills beyond. Grace took a last quick look around and moved out across the paddock. Both ponies lifted their heads—*food?*—and one turned around and took a few steps, but she continued steadily, and the ponies both stayed in the shade. She climbed the stile at the far side, and eased down the steeper slope of head-high brambles and gorse, following one of the many sheep paths. From above, an aerial observer would have seen the logic in her twisting progress; no one would want to struggle through the dense thorny growth. Grace, armed as always with a variety of useful tools, would have done so if necessary, but in this instance the sunken sheep path served her well. No one was likely to spot her even if they knew where to look.

When she came to the river, she spent a moment in the fringe of willows, looking upstream and down. MacRobert, she knew from several days of observation, preferred to fish the lower reach of his cottage's permit range in the morning, and the upper reach in the afternoon. She had watched, from across the river in a hide she had made herself, arriving before dawn each day and staying hidden until dusk. Long experience in the country had provided her with effective repellent, a small but efficient waste-disposal unit, a compact solar-powered foodbox. She had taken wicked delight in imagining the watcher assigned the house lying among the rocks, miserable and with any luck being bitten by blueticks, while she had a comfortable seat. She didn't know if MacRobert knew she was there—if he was as good as she hoped, he would—but she had wanted to ensure that no one else was watching him. So far it looked good.

She sat on a flat rock to put on her waders, custom-made for her years before and repaired regularly, and looked at the river. No change in level from the day before. Upstream, a narrower, rougher section, water tumbling over rocks, but here by the flat rock the river ran deceptively smooth, its glassy surface concealing its speed. Downstream, it curved left around a point, a cluster of older, taller trees, and just before that curve, on the far side, an old snag had created the perfect hiding place for a fish.

Grace stood up, stomping her feet in the waders, making sure she was secure, then picked up her creel and slung it from its shoulder strap. A last pat of pockets, ensuring that each held what it should. She looked again at the water, the angle of light, the cloud of insects hovering, rising, hovering above the water . . . time to choose the first fly. In the difficult years after the war, when she had struggled with memories and emotions she must hide—when she had faced the threat of permanent confinement in an asylum—she had learned to tie her own flies, a task that demanded concentration on the immediate, a task that looked harmless.

She chose her favorite, old and frayed as it was, tied it on, and moved out into the water, feeling her way into its flow. Gravel under her feet, the push of current on her legs, the pressure of water flattening the waders against her feet. The water's surface, smooth or rough, bulging here and hollowed there, revealed its bed. She cast, the line flying from the tip of the rod in easy arcs, and her fly, light as air, rested on the water, moved with the water into position.

A swirl, a glimpse of something, and her fly disappeared. She felt that first faint resistance, resisted the urge to jerk back—then delicately, delicately, drew the line in . . . and set the hook in one quick move. The fish shot forward, raising a welt in the water; Grace grinned. It was headed downstream, just as she'd hoped, and she let out line before resisting. It jumped then, an arc of silver striped with red, and shot upstream. Grace argued, through the line. *Not that way . . . this way.* The fish turned downstream again; Grace again gave it more room, following along the bank.

She knew the man was there, where she had expected him, as he had expected her. Still, she played the fish, and he played the courteous fisherman who yields to someone with one on the line. She was sure there were no watchers, but if there were, they would see only what anyone would expect to see. At last she had it in the shallows, almost in reach of her net, a huge trout for this water, fifty centimeters at least.

"Want some help?" the man asked.

"Please," Grace said.

He stepped past her with his own net and skillfully slid it under the fish without damaging it. "Release or dinner?"

She thought about it a moment. She enjoyed Beckmann trout, but the fish, big as it was, would not feed the whole family. "Release," she said.

"Do you want to, or shall I?"

"I'll do it." She laid down her rod. He held the fish properly, firmly but without damage, the fins folded down; she removed her barbless hook from the bony jaw and stuck it in her vest. "My release."

"Of course."

He held the fish until she had lifted the net, then stepped back. Grace carried the fish—a good heavy one, but she wasn't going to weigh it—to deeper water. She loved this part, the feel of the fish in her hands, its quivering impatience to be free. The fish gaped, gills working, then it flexed and she opened her hands. It fled upstream, back to its home under that log.

"Very nice work," the man said now. "Beautifully played, and on a barbless hook, too."

"Thanks for your help," she said. And with a nod to his tackle some yards away, "A wet-fly man, I see."

"And you're a dry-fly . . . takes a light touch, that." After a pause, he went on. "You are aware this is private water?"

"We're leasing Brookings Manor up the hill there; our privileges run from the lake to Bender's Bridge."

"I'm sorry, I didn't realize . . . I'm leasing Greyfalls Cottage; guest rights go from that point"—he nodded to it—"downstream a kilometer. My name's Anders MacRobert, by the way."

"I'm Grace Lane Vatta," Grace said. "Would you like a sandwich? I brought some in my creel."

"Thank you," he said.

They sat on another of the granite boulders near the river, where the rush of water would frustrate any hidden listening devices in the trees twenty meters away; Grace handed him a wrapped sandwich and unwrapped another for herself. He handed her a bottle from his creel.

"We have a problem in Spaceforce," he said, looking out across the river. His lips barely moved.

Grace resisted the temptation to glance around, and took a bite of her own sandwich. "I'd agree. Do you know what?"

"It's related to the privateer program," he said. "Do you know about that?"

"That Slotter Key uses privateers instead of a real space navy, yes. That certain officers function both in the official Spaceforce and as advisers on privateers, yes."

"Your niece Ky has a letter of marque," MacRobert said.

Grace felt the blood draining from her face. "She *what*?"

"She has a letter of marque. It's all official, though it's not quite . . . usual."

"I . . . should think not." Grace had not expected to

be surprised at whatever MacRobert wanted to tell her; this, she admitted to herself, was definitely a surprise. "The government's turned on us—"

"This is from before," MacRobert said. "It was issued before the attacks on Vatta—which, by the way, I certainly didn't anticipate."

"Did her father know? Her uncle?" Vatta officially, she was thinking. "It's been against our policy to accept letters of marque."

"I know that," MacRobert said. He ate the rest of the sandwich without speaking; Grace waited him out. "The thing is," he said finally, "I knew something was wrong about what happened to Ky in the Academy. The cadet who caused the trouble wasn't really the type. Someone had to put him up to it. I had this feeling—something was more wrong than anyone knew—and I knew she was out in space somewhere with no idea what had happened or why, and she was on an unarmed little tradeship. She might need help. So I . . . arranged it."

"You didn't tell anyone at Vatta," Grace said.

"No. Nor a few other places."

"But the government had to know . . . someone signs those things. They'll rescind it . . ."

"I don't think so." He took a long swallow from his bottle. "She's not exactly on their records . . . well, not on *all* the records. She has a valid letter of marque, yes. Duly signed by all the right people." He paused again. Grace wanted to strangle the rest out of him, but suspected that wouldn't work. She took a sip from her own bottle. "There are different kinds of letters of marque," MacRobert went on. "Some are more specific than others, limiting that captain's actions. Some are more general. Some are . . . special. Hers is special."

"How did you get it to her?"

"Courier to Lastway. Knew she was going there. I sent a letter, too, and if she followed my instructions she has some useful weaponry, as well."

Unexpectedly, Grace felt a surge of raw anger. "You just made her more of a target," she said. "There's no way she can fight effectively with that old crate she's in, and now you've given our enemies even more reason to go after her."

He did not react to her anger; he might have been the granite boulder they sat on. "She'll make a better privateer than regular officer, actually," he said. "I think she's better off."

"As if you had the right to make that decision," Grace said. "She's not your family."

"No. But I watched her for the years she was at the Academy. Intelligent, quick, capable, and if I'm not mistaken the true killer instinct."

Grace felt her stomach clench. "I hope not," she said.

He turned to her. "Why?" Then, seeing something in her face, his expression changed. "Oh. You've—of course, I know something of your history."

"She's alone," Grace said, hating the hoarseness of emotion in her voice. "It's going to be a shock to her if . . . when she finds *that* in herself. Stella doesn't have it: she can kill, but she hates it so much that she's never tempted. If Ky—"

"She had four years of military discipline," MacRobert said. "That will help her more than you know."

"I suppose." Grace folded the sandwich wrapping into a tight cube and put it back in her creel. "So—what did you expect of her as a privateer?"

MacRobert frowned at the river. "I thought, since she had more military training than most captains, that she could pick up information for us in places where known privateers hear nothing. I was sure something was coming, something big, and hoped she could find out what it was."

"You could have just asked her to spy for you without tempting her to try privateering."

"I could, yes. But that would have required setting up lines of communication specific to spying. Privateers can report directly to local consuls; I . . . have access to those reports."

"Why do I feel you are more than a master sergeant of cadets?" Grace asked the sky.

"We should get back to fishing," MacRobert said. "Just in case."

"You're right," Grace said. "Meet you on the river tomorrow?"

"Certainly. You know my habits, I'm sure. At least, I hope it was you camped over there across the river. Very discreet. I'm sure you were there days before I happened to notice it."

"I hope so, too," Grace said. "Good fishing to you."

"And to you," he said.

Grace worked her way back upstream against the current, forbore to bother the big trout under the log, and went after the much smaller ones well upstream, frolicking in clouds of midges.

When she got back to the house, the grocery truck was there; the delivery driver had another story to tell about idiot tourists. Someone had overturned a boat in the lake in a particularly stupid way, and there was another case of bluetick fever who had walked into the clinic thinking he just had a headache.

"What about the children?" Helen asked. "They're outside all morning, at least—"

"You use repellent on 'em, right?" the driver asked. "The good stuff, in the blue bottles?" Helen nodded.

"They'll be fine. Check 'em over every evening—"

"We do that," Grace said. "Bathtime."

"Well, then. Shouldn't be a problem. But if one of 'em complains of a bad headache, get 'em to the clinic. This tourist must not have used the right repellent and lay down someplace where sheep had been; the medic—he's my brother-in-law—said there were tick bites all over him and a couple of ticks on his back."

"Will he be all right?" Helen asked.

"Probably," the delivery man said. "But he won't be out of the clinic for at least ten days, Sam said."

"That's too bad," Grace said. Helen looked at her sharply; Grace said nothing more.

Grace was in bed reading one of the old books that had been in the house when they came when Helen knocked on her door. The book was a mystery, which she didn't ordinarily like, since she could nearly always figure out who the criminal was by page fifteen, but this one was old enough to be interesting for its historical data. "Come in," she said.

"You put those ticks out there," Helen said.

"Out where?" Grace asked.

"Wherever—how did you know where he'd be?"

"There are four good places to hide from the house while watching it, and be unseen from the road," Grace said, without looking up from her book. "I put a good-sized jar of blueticks in each, yes."

"So—you made him sick."

"I hoped to, yes."

"That doesn't bother you?"

Grace laid the book facedown on her chest and looked at Helen. "Bother me to give tick fever to someone working with those who killed your husband, Jo, Gerry and Myris, and all the hundreds of others? Not a bit."

"You knew someone would be watching us—you figured out where—are there more?"

"Not that I know of, no. That fellow had someone on night shift for a few days, but for the last while it's been just the one, in daytime."

"You knew this and didn't tell me? The children—"

"He wasn't after the children, Helen, or I'd have taken him out. He was watching us, reporting to someone else, and that someone might have done something—sent assassins or whatever. But I'd have known that in time to protect you."

Helen's mouth was still open slightly. "You . . . Stavros always said not to underestimate you. How do you know things?"

Grace smiled. "People talk to old ladies. I listen very well. And although your daughter and Gerry's both thought of me as a stuffy, priggish old harridan, Stella soon discovered my secret."

"Which is?" Helen said.

"I have no morals," Grace said. Helen's face changed. Grace made a bet with herself what Helen would say next.

"You don't mean—you do mean that," Helen said, her tone changing midstream.

"Yes. I had them once, or at least a semblance of them. I was quite conventional as a girl, which is what passes for morals with most people."

"Why are you telling me this now?" Helen asked, tension in every line of her body.

"Several reasons." Grace pushed herself up in the bed and laid the book down beside her. "Our family is under attack. We're living together, and thus mutually dependent. You need to know what I'm capable of."

"You can kill, I know that," Helen said. "That doesn't bother me, and I don't see that it means you have no morals."

"It doesn't," Grace agreed. "But you were shocked that I planted ticks to make a spy sick, that I didn't care whether he lived or died. Right?"

"Yes . . ." Helen drew the word out, clearly thinking. "Now that I've heard your reasons, I'd agree it was the right thing to do—"

"Which is something else you have to understand about me, Helen. I don't really care whether you agree or not. I'm going to do what I think is best, regardless. And I won't always give reasons. I may not always have reasons; I may be working on instinct."

Helen's mouth opened and shut again. "I . . . suppose I should be glad you're on our side."

"Yes, you should," Grace said. "If we're to get through this, my skills will be necessary. In fact, I have some things to teach you."

Helen stiffened; her chin came out. "For instance?" she said.

"How to make fruitcake," Grace said, picking up her book. "And why," she added, focusing on the page again. "Good night, Helen."

She didn't look up to see Helen's expression; she waited until she heard the gentle thump of the door closing, then put the book aside and turned out the light. When the glow of Helen's light on the ivy outside the window ceased, Grace waited another half hour, then padded barefoot over to the window and extended a whisker microphone to Helen's window. Only the sound of someone sleeping; Helen didn't exactly snore, but she did make a soft sound that would probably have been a snore if she'd been heavier.

Without turning on a light, Grace retrieved her clothes from under her pillows and changed into a black body-suit meant for climbing. Thin, flexible climbing shoes on

her feet; the headlamp on her head. She had insisted on
the room with the trellis . . . now she slid over the win-
dowsill and eased down the trellis to the top of the first-
floor windows, where she had left open a transom in the
library. For ventilation, she'd told Helen, and shown Helen
the alarm sensor that would pick up anything the size of
a cat that managed to find a way in.

Now she tapped the control panel Helen had not seen,
a hand span from the window frame, hidden in ivy. The
alarm system went dormant. The transom let her in; the
bookcases that framed the window made it easy to find a
way to the floor. She had scouted this route when looking
at properties to lease. Once on the floor, she reset the
alarm system to ignore her but remain alert to everything
else. That much was easy; this was not the first night she
had crept downstairs to continue what she considered her
mission, finding the guilty and making their lives miserable.

The real difficulty came with establishing an untrace-
able connection to her taps into the presidential palace.
She'd had neither the time nor the means to prepare this
house for that kind of work, and the prior owners had
been boringly straightforward. She had her field kit—
tucked behind a row of old legal texts—and now she pulled
that out, still working by feel.

The library had three rooms, two with windows and
one interior. The windowless room had apparently been
used both for the rarer books—old hardcopy works—and
accounting. It contained a desk, several primitive safes,
and a communications console as well as sealed, dust-
proof bookcases. Grace moved into this room, closed the
doors on either side, and switched on her headlamp. Now
she could hook into the console and begin the task of
foxing her signals.

She had two main objectives tonight. She wanted to pay the President another little visit, and she wanted to find out just what kind of "special" letter of marque Ky had been sent. She began, however, with a secondary objective, contacting her agents around the planet. So far they had not been able to identify which district she was calling from, but she checked that first every time.

SIX

Rosvirein Station

According to the Commercial Code, the contents of a privateer's holds belonged to the privateer. However, special tariffs were usually imposed on privateer imports, and easily identifiable articles might trigger legal action by the original consignors or their insurance companies. Ky looked over their inventory—as best they knew it, with some holds still unaired—and tried to decide what would bring the most profit and the least suspicion.

"Two bales of Engen currency . . . is that any good?" she asked Rafe.

His brows went up as he looked at the inventory and then the sample Lee had brought forward. "I wonder where he got that. It's real, it's not counterfeit, it's not dependent on the financial ansibles being up, and nobody can prove who it belongs to, other than you."

"But we're not in Engen, or near it . . ."

"No, but it's a recognized currency. My guess would be that most of the currency dealers will give you seventy percent of the face value."

Ky was going to argue the unfairness of this, but realized

that it was found money anyway. "Have you calculated the value?"

"The bales are labeled as ten million each. Whether they really contain that—" He shrugged.

Fourteen million. Maybe. It would surely be a start, more than enough to air up the ship at least. "I'll call Crown & Spears," Ky said. Within a few minutes she had confirmed that the bank would indeed take a sizable deposit of Engen currency at 72.1 percent of face value. "We'll deliver it ourselves," Ky said. "And then go on to the ISC local office."

"Too conspicuous," Rafe said. "Use one of the bonded delivery services; the bank should hold it for inspection until we get there."

Martin nodded. "He's right, Captain. It's not just robbery that's a concern, but assault. Best decide on some other merchandise, and have the delivery company handle it all; that'll be safer."

It took another couple of hours to find consignees for some of Osman's other more respectable merchandise, a bale of Hurriganese furs, second quality, and three five-hundred-liter cases of dried milk replacement for orphaned calves, and then arrange for pickup by one of the bonded delivery companies.

By then Martin had already detected that the first attempt to penetrate their security system had come less than five hours after they docked.

"You expect that sort of thing," Martin said, showing Ky the log. "Place like this, particularly. There'll be people who want hooks into our system just to learn something, as well as access to the ship or personnel."

"The ones who attacked Vatta?"

"Not necessarily. I'm sure those are around as well, but I'd expect others who just routinely try to infiltrate all ships' systems."

Ky chewed her lip a moment. "We need to know if it's just thieves and rascals or a serious threat—"

"I'm working on that," Martin said. "But we're going to need more crew."

"I'll list positions open—what do you think we need?"

"Osman was overcrewed, but then he needed muscle. So will we, if you're going active as a privateer. We need backups for every department: Pilot, Navigation, Engineering, Environmental. Enough cargo hands for any actual trading you want to do. And people to operate the weapons systems. Think a Spaceforce ship."

"People who know weapons systems are the most likely to be bad guys," Ky said.

Martin rubbed his nose. "Not necessarily. Take me— there are reasons besides incompetence or treachery for someone not to get along in a regular military. But yeah, you want to be careful." His voice lowered. "What about Toby? Are you going to keep him as crew? The kid's talented, but—"

"But he's too young for a fighting ship. You're right, Martin, but I don't know where to send him—or how— that he'd be safer than with us. But thanks for reminding me. I'm sure we can get him more educational modules here. And maybe a tutor."

"He doesn't need a tutor to learn," Martin said. "Just the modules; he's a self-starter. Someone his own age would be a help, though I'm not suggesting taking on another kid." His forehead creased. "And . . . um . . . what about Rafe?"

"Rafe's not exactly regular crew," Ky said. "I think of him as an ally, though."

"Maybe," Martin said. "And maybe not. You still have him under partnership bond?"

"Something like that," Ky said. The leverage that her

knowledge of his cranial ansible gave her was more than a partnership bond, she hoped, but she wasn't going to tell Martin about it.

"Well . . . I wouldn't necessarily trust him when it came to hiring people."

"No," Ky said. "I'm not planning to. But if he thinks someone's not trustworthy, that's worth consideration."

When Ky left the ship to go to the bank and the ISC branch office, she was surprised to find a small crowd just outside *Fair Kaleen*'s private dockspace offering themselves as potential crew, as trading partners, as local guides.

"I've never been this popular," Ky murmured aside to Rafe as they headed from dockside to the local ISC office. Behind her, Martin and Lee formed her rear guard; she was glad to have the extra muscle. Her skin felt tight all over; she made herself breathe slowly. Either an attack would come or it wouldn't.

"Get used to it," Rafe said. "It's that command presence you have sticking out all over."

"I do not."

"You do. And it's not even in full bloom yet, which frankly scares me silly. Of course, it may also be that they suspect what your cargo's worth."

"Do you think any of them know about the . . . um . . . *things*?"

"The—" Rafe gave her a horrified look. "You mean the . . . er . . . ship things?" Clearly he wasn't going to name them out on the concourse. "Ky—Captain—you mustn't sell those! It could destabilize—"

"I haven't decided to sell them," Ky said. "The databases, though . . ." Osman's illicit cargo would bring more profit than milk replacement powder.

"You might want to let me check around," Rafe said.

"I'm likelier to find useful contacts than you are."

"You've been here before?"

"No. But some of what I imported to Allray came via Rosvirein. I knew someone here at one time, but I don't know if she's still here."

"Find out," Ky said. "I have no experience at all selling that kind of thing."

Counting the Engen currency at Crown & Spears took only moments as the counting machines whirred; Ky signed the papers and put the adjusted total in the ship's account. From there, she prepaid the air fees; in twelve hours or so they would have all the compartments back to full pressure. From Crown & Spears to the ISC offices was only a short stroll.

The ISC entrance was tiled in the gold-gray-and-blue color scheme of ISC. Gray-uniformed ISC guards stood either side of the doorway. One of them moved forward as Ky and her group approached.

"Do you have an appointment?" he asked.

"No," Ky said. "I wanted to speak to your local system manager—does that require an appointment?"

"In present conditions, yes," the guard said. "Most business may be conducted by wire, and the site contains current status of ansible function as we know it."

"I have information pertinent to your operations," Ky said, carefully not looking at Rafe.

"May I have your name, please?" the guard said. "I will inquire . . ."

Ky handed over her identification.

"Are you the same Vatta who was at Sabine?" he asked, his voice a trifle warmer.

"Yes," Ky said.

"Just a moment." He went back to the doorway and turned his back while the other guard stared past them with a bored expression that Ky knew masked complete alertness.

They were ushered in very shortly, to meet a grave older woman shorter than Ky, her black hair streaked with silver.

"Captain Vatta, what a pleasure. We heard about your exploits in the Sabine System." The woman extended a hand. "I'm Station Manager Selkirk."

"Thank you," Ky said, shaking hands. "I believe I have information useful to ISC, this time concerning ansible malfunctions."

"Ah. We should go to my office . . . perhaps your . . . people . . . might wait here; I will send someone with refreshments."

"I'd like Rafe to come along," Ky said. "He's got more technical expertise than I have."

"Does he?" murmured Selkirk. "Then by all means . . ." She glanced around. "We need two chairs, and light refreshments in the lobby." Ky saw no device, but almost immediately a door opened at the end of the counter and a man pushed out a dolly holding two chairs. From a door at the other end of the counter came a man with a tray. The chairs were placed, the flowers on one of the small tables moved to the next, and the tray set on the table. Martin and Lee sat down at Ky's gesture, though Martin didn't look happy about it.

"This way," Selkirk said. A door opened in the right-hand wall, and Selkirk led Ky and Rafe into a carpeted hallway; a guard stood by the door they had just passed through. Ky's skin tingled. Selkirk's office, when they reached it, was a corner office with a window overlooking a garden that wrapped around the corner. "It's part of the security," Selkirk said, gesturing at the window. "We need the airspace between us and our neighbors. My security chief wanted to make it all smooth cerroplast, but this way we get an oxygen credit and it costs us less, even counting in the gardener's salary."

"And it's beautiful," Ky said. The garden had real trees screening the neighboring walls, as well as a water feature complete with waterfall and decorative bridge.

"Yes," Selkirk said. "But enough of that. What brings you to us and what information do you think you have?"

"I was on Belinta when the ansibles failed," Ky said. "In fact, I was in contact with my home office on Slotter Key at the exact moment; at first I didn't know if it was a problem in local equipment at either end or an ansible problem." She paused, but Selkirk merely nodded. "It soon became obvious that Belinta's ansible was out; by the time I reached Lastway, I knew that several others were. We found uncrewed ansibles with their mailboxes stuffed, nothing moving in any directions."

"Ah . . ." Selkirk's expression brightened. "That entire sector's still out of touch. We've had only one emergency ship in there, and it reported that it'll be months before we get all the units back up."

"At Lastway," Ky said, "we found something else. The Lastway ansible appeared to be working—"

"It never went out," Selkirk said. "We don't get direct messages from there much, but we do get relays."

"The station manager was bent," Ky said. "He was passing some messages and sequestering others—"

"Are you sure?"

"Yes." Rafe spoke for the first time. "Captain, may I speak frankly to Manager Selkirk?"

"Of course," Ky said.

He stood; Ky saw the woman tense as he approached her desk. "Don't worry, ma'am; I merely want to show you a code that Captain Vatta does not know." He wrote on the notepad on her desk, then stepped back and sat down, avoiding Ky's gaze.

Selkirk stared at what he had written; Ky wished for

the ability to look down from the ceiling. Then Selkirk's head came up; her face had paled. "You are—"

"You will want to check that," Rafe said. "Against your books."

Her fingers raced over the plate on her desk; she focused on some display Ky could not see as her brow furrowed. When she looked up again, she looked more worried than pleased. "It matches. This is . . . a surprise. Does your— the captain know anything?"

"She is aware that I'm a covert agent for ISC, yes," Rafe said. "What more she knows, or has surmised, you would have to ask her. I owe her my life; I was over at Allray when this mess started; it is thanks to her that I am this close to headquarters."

Selkirk transferred her gaze to Ky. "Captain, you astonish me."

"More to the point," Rafe said, "I have technical data you need, including a report on the situation at Lastway when we left there. It may bear on the relationship between the attacks on our ansible system and Captain Vatta's family and home world." He glanced at Ky. "Some of this should be transmitted back to Nexus Two as quickly as possible. Is your link there still reliable?"

"Yes," Selkirk said. "We lost ansible service here for only six standard days. We had contact with ISC headquarters before that, and that link functioned as soon as we were back up."

"The locals claim they fixed the ansibles here, instead of an ISC repair crew," Ky said. "Is that true?"

Selkirk flushed. "You have to understand Rosvirein culture, Captain Vatta. They're a very proud, impatient people and they do have considerable technical expertise. I was told, when I was assigned to this post, that it was advisable to allow their crews to assist ours in case of technical difficulties before calling for a repair crew."

"That would be a yes," Rafe said. "And was the problem found to be in the interface circuitry in the spatial . . . er . . . area?" He glanced at Ky and away.

"Yes," Selkirk said, folding her hands.

"I suggest that the decision to allow Rosvirein crews unsupervised access to the ansibles should be reconsidered. I'm not prepared, at this time, to recommend action against them, but some emotional conflict is better than compromised communications."

"I see," Selkirk said. She glanced at Ky again. "Captain, I mean no insult, but would it be possible to discuss proprietary matters with your crewman alone?"

"He's not my crew," Ky said. "He's your agent. Would you prefer that I leave now—in fact, I have nothing more to contribute on my own—or that Rafe come back later?"

"The matter may be urgent."

"Then I'll take my leave," Ky said. She could not help feeling a little annoyed, but she didn't have to show it. And after all she had plenty of other work to do. "Meet me later, Rafe," she said. "Shall I leave you an escort?"

He grimaced. "I think I can take care of myself, Captain, thanks all the same."

Ky wondered if he would tell Selkirk about the shipboard ansibles. She hoped not. She didn't want to turn them over to the ISC.

She picked up Martin and Lee on her way out.

"Rafe's staying?" Martin sounded wary.

"He is ISC, after all," Ky said. She still felt twitchy out in the open, even though she saw nothing more menacing than a uniformed woman shepherding a line of children whose voices would have pierced armorplate.

"He's trouble," Martin said. "You know what I feel about trusting him, Captain."

"Only half as far as I can throw him," Ky said. "But that's a tidy distance."

Martin snorted and shook his head. "Captain, sometimes you're funny. So is he coming back?"

"I hope so," Ky said. "He says he has that contact here for trading some of Osman's less legal cargo. But in the meantime, let's look at getting some good crew aboard. We're all overworked at the moment. With all due respect to Lee, we need another pilot, at least, maybe two. Engineering—we need to replace Toby, let him go to school—" If they ever found a safe place for him, that was.

"Weapons crews," Martin said, as they turned into the docking bay entrance.

"I've never hired weapons crews," Ky said. "I don't even know what to look for. We could get along just with regular ship crews—maybe they could learn—"

"We could, except that we're an armed vessel," Martin said. "If you're not armed, you might or might not be attacked, but if you're armed, and can't use your weapons, you're an exceptional prize for those who can take you. We've been lucky so far, but we can't count on being lucky."

"Luck follows preparation," Ky said, quoting from a lecture at the Academy. "I know, but—"

"You can't just bluff everyone," Martin said. His brow furrowed. "Captain, if you want to disarm the ship, that's one thing, but—"

"I get your point," Ky said. "We have weapons; we need weapons crews. I just . . . this is where I would be looking to plant agents aboard other ships, if I were the pirates."

"Sure they would, so we have to be careful. I'm not expert in weapons, Captain, but you said before you think I can spot rotten apples. Trust me for that."

Ky nodded. "I do trust you, Martin, and you have experience. What about working with Rafe on this?"

As usual when Rafe was mentioned, Martin's expression soured. "Well, he has experience with rotten apples, I'll say that for him. But I just said—"

"I know. But on this I think he's trustworthy. If he's with us he won't want to be killed by having approved the wrong crew. Now—do you have any idea how many we'll need just to fight the ship?" How much would it cost, how much cubage would be needed to supply that many people?

"We have eight missile batteries—we'll need a crew for each. Spaceforce had what they called a team for every two batteries, eight to a team. So we'd need four teams of eight, that's thirty-two. Two beam weapons, those can be controlled by one board on the bridge. You do need someone expert on that, and then one or two senior weapons masters to coordinate. Say thirty-six, all told."

"Plus what we need for regular crew." Ky shook her head. "We'd better sell off a lot of our cargo; I'm guessing that weapons-qualified crew won't come cheap, and I want good ones."

Rafe reappeared a few hours later, with the news that he had found his former contact. "You'll have to come with me," he said. "She won't deal through me; she wants to meet you. But I'll be armed. You can bring someone else, too, if you want. I'd suggest not Martin—he's too obviously military."

"Lee?" Ky said to her pilot. "Want to come along?"

He grinned happily. "Sure, Captain; I've nothing else to do in port." As before, he had outfitted himself from Osman's store of personal weapons until he fairly bristled. Rafe cocked an eye, clearly amused; his own weapons were, like Ky's, concealed.

Rafe's contact met them in a dingy storefront a quarter

of the way around the station. She was a hard-faced woman with streaks of burgundy and green in her gray hair. She had a yellow ribbon tied around the left sleeve of her gray jacket, and two green ones tied around the right. Signals of some kind, Ky was sure.

"I dealt with Osman," she said, when Rafe introduced them. "You have the same kind of merchandise?"

"I have the same merchandise," Ky said. "Osman's dead. I took his ship."

"So he said." She jerked her head at Rafe, then looked Ky up and down. "You hardly look tough enough to take on Osman."

"Both of us Vattas," Ky said. That got a wry grin in response. They dickered briefly, but the woman wanted Osman's merchandise and eventually agreed to pay what she would have paid Osman.

Ky told herself that the goods Amy was buying—the contents of cranial implants transferred to other media—had already been taken from their owners, and the owners were dead. She told herself that repeatedly, but her stomach churned all the way back to the ship.

In the next days, Ky was glad that Martin had taken over the hiring of the fighting crew. She had enough to do with rest of the cargo—deciding which to sell and where—and interviewing regular ship crew. As the list filled, she realized that Osman's crew had been none too large for this ship in its fighting configuration. She felt uncomfortable with so many strangers coming aboard, but there was no alternative.

In civilian tradeships, the senior engineer often functioned as the captain's second, but this would not work in a privateer. On Spaceforce vessels, the distinction between officer and enlisted was clear, as was the chain of command, but she had no idea how other privateers handled the interesting problem of blending the two functions.

She was still puzzling over this when Martin brought back the first of his finds for her approval: an entire weapons team.

"They were part of a small mercenary company—Calvert's Company—and then the commander died. They didn't like his successor, so they left. They're all one family and they want to be hired as a unit. I looked up Calvert's and it was legit. Small, but good. When Ben Calvert died, his junior commanders—a nephew and a longtime friend—squabbled over who'd take over, and one of 'em died in a training accident, so called. This team walked, along with about a third of the rest."

"What are they like?"

"Solid, I'd say. They claim combat experience with Calvert's, and familiarity with the kind of weapons we have. You want to see them?"

"Of course." Ky wondered what she could discern that Martin couldn't. She looked over their files while Martin went to fetch them. Jon, the oldest, was over fifty; the youngest were twenty. Five of the eight were sibs; the other three were first cousins. It reminded her of Vatta.

They filed in, wearing obvious uniforms with darker rectangles where unit or rank patches had been, and lined up stiffly across from her, five men and three women. She could tell nothing from their faces except that they looked biologically related.

"At ease," she said, hoping it was the right command. They shifted smartly to parade rest.

"This is Jon Gannett," Martin said, nodding to the man in the center. "He's their leader."

"M'rating was master gunner," the man said. He could have been carved from a block of tik wood; his skin had not paled with years in space.

"Master Gunner Gannett," Ky said. "Chief Martin has explained what we're looking for, I gather?" She noticed, from the corner of her eye, that Martin had startled slightly at the title she'd given him.

"Yes, Captain. You need weapons teams for missile batteries, and you plan to fight pirates."

"That's right. You have the right qualifications, on paper, but you're used to a strictly military setting. Privateers are technically civilian ships. I need to be sure that you understand the distinction."

"Would we be expected to do civilian chores?" There was an undertone of contempt.

Ky raised her brows. "You'd be expected to do whatever I order," she said. "It's unlikely that any work on this ship could be considered strictly civilian, aside from the actual selling and buying of cargo . . . for which you're not qualified. Ship maintenance, though, of course."

His mouth quirked. "Understood, Captain. Your—Chief Martin says you are qualified to command a warship—"

Ky glanced at Martin, trying not to show her surprise.

"We mean no insult, Captain Vatta, but we need to know that we're not going to be commanded by—" She could see his struggle to find a euphemism for *idiot,* and waited it out. "—someone who has no experience," he finally said.

"I'm sure the chief's given you the book version," Ky said. "I am young, but not unacquainted with danger and violence." She grinned, letting some of that dark force into her smile.

Gannett nodded abruptly. "If I may introduce my team, Captain?"

"Please," Ky said.

As he spoke their names, the other team members took a step forward: "Arnold, Podtal, Rory, Hera, Gus, Ted. Arnie

and Pod are my crewleaders. You'll make your own decisions, I understand, but they're good. We all grew up in
the business; Gus and Ted are the youngest, but they
enlisted when they were just fifteen; they're twenty standard now."

Ky thought of Toby, now nearing fifteen. Had the hard-
faced men before her ever been as young as Toby?

"You left Calvert's because you didn't like the new commander, is that right?"

"Yes." That in a flat voice that invited no questions.

"You broke a ten-year contract to do that," Ky said.
"Does this mean you'd prefer a short-term contract with
me?"

That question surprised Jon; she saw the shift of expression. "We're not lookin' to leave anyone, ma'am," he said
slowly. "We'd like a permanent place, if you have one, but
we need a job, worse'n anythin' right now."

Ky thought of a dozen things to say, and ask, but her
instinct was that this family group was straight. She
glanced at Martin and gave a slight nod.

"All right, then. Your files look good, and I'm offering
you a place as my number one weapons team. In our tradition, that's the forward portside batteries."

"Thank you, Captain," their leader said. He didn't mention if their tradition was the same, a sign that he understood things were as they were here.

"Chief Martin will show you where to bunk and stow
your gear," Ky said. "And we'll get you some patches for
those uniforms." As soon as she could have them made
up; it was yet another detail she hadn't thought of.

Ten days after first docking at Rosvirein, *Fair Kaleen* looked
and felt much more like a fighting ship. A new starboard
air lock, all compartments fully aired up, environmental

supplies complete, new crewmembers busy about their tasks. The Gannetts had settled into the berthing area for the portside first and second batteries; they'd inspected all the batteries and related supply compartments, and reported to Martin that all were in satisfactory operating condition, but the missile racks were not full.

Ky wondered where Osman had expended those missiles, but ignored that stab of curiosity and authorized the purchase of replacements. Meanwhile, a second weapons team, this one made up of two different crews, moved into starboard batteries one and two, and Martin continued to comb the applicants for more he could approve. Environmental filled all positions, then Lee found a good pilot prospect while onstation shopping.

When she made her way through the ship on her daily rounds, her implant cued her to the names that went with the faces she saw: Barton, environmental tech class 3, a humod from Cantab with chem-sensing tentacles for direct assays of pollutants; Leman, engineering tech class 2, from Allray. Her original crew, at first a bit wary of the strangers, soon warmed up, and she came across little gatherings in the crew spaces. Even Rascal, at first inclined to growl and nip, relaxed enough to roll over and let some of the newbies scratch his belly.

Best of all, she had found two competent officers with good records, cast loose when their captain couldn't make the daily docking charges and pay the crew. The captain himself approached Ky on their behalf.

"Hugh's the best first officer you could want," the man said. "He's honest, hardworking, and gets along with crew. You're a privateer, the board says—well, he spent five years with a merc company until he lost his arm, and then he chose to civ rather than stay, which makes sense to me. As for Laurie, she's a genius with anything technical.

Engines, environmental, communications . . . she eats that up . . ."

Ky interviewed them that afternoon.

"You do understand I'm a privateer," Ky said to Hugh Pritang. "It's not like a tradeship, and we will probably be in combat." She was trying not to look at Pritang's left arm, in case he thought that was rude, but the cluster of appendages at the end did not look like fingers.

"That's fine, Captain," he said. "I thought I wanted safety when I left the Rangers, but I've been eight years with Janocek's ship and frankly I was bored. If the ansibles come back up, you can access my combat record—"

"As long as you understand," Ky said. "That's what I wanted to know."

"This is a functional arm," Pritang said, holding it up. "It looks odd, I know, but actually I can do things with it that I couldn't with the original. I'm not disabled in any way. My wife couldn't stand it, though."

That was clearly a challenge. Ky made herself look: those heavy ridges in the forearm area had to be reinforcing for extra muscles; the appendages included three fleshy near-fingers and two tentacles, one with what looked like a sucker tip and one with an obvious dataport probe. "I've never seen one like it," Ky said.

"But it doesn't bother you." That was more statement than question.

"No," Ky said. "It doesn't bother me. Do you want this job?"

"Yes," he said.

"Then welcome aboard; there's plenty of work." She introduced him around; she could tell that he and Martin took to each other right away.

Laurie Sutton had the look and attitude of good engineers everywhere, practical and focused. She asked the right questions about the ship systems, and took a quick tour. Though she was much younger than Quincy, Ky felt the same confidence about her. By the end of the shift both had signed on and moved their gear aboard. Now if she could just find a qualified weapons officer; she really needed someone at that station on the bridge.

And when would Stella get there? She made an ansible call back to Garth-Lindheimer, but *Gary Tobai* had left the system days before. Ky tried to smother her own impatience and plan for the future. She still didn't see how she was going to combine rebuilding Vatta with taking down their attackers—at least not in the same time period—but she began to lay out a sequence for each.

Her own trips offship were infrequent. Hugh quickly took over many routine duties, but other things shipboard demanded her attention. She did try to get to the Captains' Guild every few days, just to check on the eyes-only information there. But finally, when she felt confident that the ship would get along without her for a few hours, she decided she could afford to take a break.

Though no one on her crew had been attacked, she wasn't about to go out carelessly; she had full clips of ammunition, and the Rossi-Smith in its holster was loaded. She chose Rafe and Jim to accompany her, leaving Hugh to continue the provisioning of the ship. Her ostensible errand was to the chandler's, to see what was available in crockery, as Osman's stores were not sufficient for the full crew. A proper Vatta ship used proper crockery and eating utensils, not the recyclable ephemerals Osman had apparently given most of his crew. She was determined to feed her crew off decent ware befitting a respectable ship.

SEVEN

Bendick's Ship Supplies, the first chandler's they came to down the concourse, carried only ephemerals. "Fully recyclable," the clerk said. "No washing necessary."

Ky turned away. Recyclables required energy, and most produced by-products that no one wanted.

The next three chandlers on this section of the station also carried only ephemerals. By then it was nearly mid-shift, and Ky decided that was reason enough to look for a place to eat lunch.

"Any problems?" she asked Rafe.

"None I see," he said. "It passes belief that the bad guys don't have an agent on Rosvirein, but so far I've seen nothing suspicious. That by itself raises my suspicions, but we should be all right for lunch, as long as you don't choose the most dangerous dive in the place."

"You've been onstation more than I have," Ky said. "What do you recommend?"

"There are three reasonable cafés within easy walking distance," he said. "Mama Jo's serves mostly Alganese food—diced meat and vegetables in pocket bread, fairly spicy. They're really crowded at lunch; people like to eat in, and they have only ten tables. Section Three Bakeshop specializes in pies—two crusts and a filling. Mostly bland, to my taste, but if you like creamed chicken in pastry, it's good. Good apple tarts, too. They do a lot of take-out, so they're not as crowded. Tony's does grilled stuff on skewers and a good mixed fry; their bread is superb. Plenty of table room if we get there in the next few minutes."

"Preference?" Ky asked.

"Bakeshop," said Jim promptly, while Rafe said "Tony's" firmly.

"Tony's," Ky said. Bland creamed chicken in pastry didn't interest her. Her mouth had watered at the mention of "grilled stuff on skewers."

"Too bad," Rafe said to Jim. Jim managed not to scowl.

On the way to Tony's they passed Empire Embroidery, where the ship patches had been made. Ky was startled to see one of hers displayed in the window, along with a dozen others, as "examples of our work." Rafe, noticing her glance, shook his head.

"We need to get out of here soon," he said. "Not that everyone hasn't known about your ship, but that patch tells anyone interested that something's up. I don't suppose you have any idea how long Stella will be?"

"None. Wish I did."

"I don't see why the new patches make a problem," Jim said. He was slouching along, hands in pockets, until Ky turned to look at him; then he pulled out his hands and tried to stand straighter.

"The sword," Rafe said. "That's new for Vatta. It's a challenge."

"I didn't think of that," Ky said. "But we needed something—"

"I'm not saying it was a bad thing. But it's eye-catching. Not just that Empire Embroidery put one in their window, but every time one of your crew goes onstation wearing it."

Tony's, when they got to it, looked as if someone with not quite enough money had tried to convert a standard station business cubage into a half-ruined castle on a planet. The fake stone facing of the entrance was obviously fake, and the fake amber-glass light globes all had blackened areas where the plastic had oxidized. But the smells coming out were delicious—Ky watched a platter of skewers go by and wanted to grab them away. The proprietor, a cheerful balding man in a white apron, ushered them to one of the decorative alcoves.

"Menu's on the table," he said. "Just punch it in; you're ahead of the rush, so it'll be quick."

It was quick and delicious. Ky hadn't had fresh, unprocessed food in a long time; she was more than halfway through a skewer of lamb, mushrooms, and vegetables before she looked up again. Jim was shoveling down the stew he had chosen, but Rafe was looking toward the entrance and crumbling a cheese roll as if it annoyed him.

"What?" Ky asked quietly. She hoped nothing was going to interrupt her meal. Two well-dressed men were near the entrance; when Tony bustled up to them, they spoke briefly, and he led them to a table on the other side.

"Nothing," Rafe said, with a small shake of his head. He bit off a piece of roll. Ky went back to her skewer, and stripped the rest of the items off it, all but one mushroom that would give her an excuse to pick it up again. She glanced again at the entrance. The men were sitting quietly at their table. She didn't see either one look at her table.

The second skewer was more than she could eat. She hoped Tony's had take-out bags, and nibbled on one of the raw carrot sticks. "Nothing with you is ever nothing," she said to Rafe.

"Nothing yet," Rafe said. "One of those men who came in is Borrie Difano. Usually eats lunch halfway around the station, at Luca Seafood Bar. I suppose he *could* have a sudden yearning for lamb instead."

"Change in pattern?"

"You could say so, yes. I don't know his companion. Borrie's not muscle, but he runs muscle." Rafe glanced up to be sure she understood. Ky nodded. "His territory's over there; he's on Damien's pasture over here."

"Damien."

"About equivalent in rank, in the local infrastructure of irregular transactions."

"Criminals."

"I suppose you could call them that. But Rosvirein's definitions are somewhat looser than whatever you grew up with."

"Spare me," Ky said. "If we have a situation approaching, I'd prefer not to be distracted by your need to show how sophisticated you are." Her left hand slid down to check the flap of the holster.

"Ouch." Rafe took a sip of his drink. "You are sensitive today, aren't you? All right. No need to fumble around for it; your weapon's right where you left it. And Borrie's not the muscle; he doesn't like to get involved, he claims."

Jim's head came up; he stared at Rafe, then at Ky. "Is he—?"

"No," Rafe and Ky said together. Rafe shrugged and Ky went on. "Just finish your meal, Jim. We have work to do."

Jim nodded, spooned up the last few bites of his stew, then grabbed a roll out of the basket and stuffed it in his mouth. Ky reminded herself to tell Martin to work on Jim's table manners.

A group came in, and another behind it; the place was

filling up. The table flashed READY FOR BILL?

"We should leave," Rafe said. "They'll need our table."

Ky punched in her station credit code; the display changed to reflect payment, and NEED CARRYOUT? Ky punched YES, and in a moment a girl darted up with an insulated container. Ky tipped the remains of her skewer into it, and the girl began to clear the dishes onto a tray.

As they stood, she noticed that one of the men across the room had left—at least he wasn't at the table anymore. They worked their way through the crowd now waiting to be seated; Ky's back felt itchy again, but nothing happened. Outside, as they headed farther down the passage, Ky glanced around but noticed no one following them.

"It's not their way," Rafe said, after the third time she'd checked behind them. "Besides, I'm watching, too. We're beginning to look like we think we're being followed, and that's going to interest a freelancer if you don't stop it. Jim and I are your escorts; you're supposed to trust us."

"Sorry," Ky said. "I think I'll stop and make some calls. Surely someone carries real crockery and not that recyclable stuff."

"Good idea," Rafe said.

Ky found a public booth, and the two men placed themselves to watch her back. When she found a chandler with the merchandise she wanted, it was almost to the far side of the station. She gave Rafe the address. He nodded. "I know where that is, or close to. We should take a tram; we'll walk our legs off otherwise and be well into nightshift as well. Don't want to be there after the dayshift change."

"Should we do it another day?"

"No . . . I don't think so. But let's catch a ride."

The intrastation tram took them around to the far side

in less than an hour, and their station was only a few minutes' walk from Carson Brothers.

"Of course, Captain, we carry all classes of crockery and flatware both." The lean, stooped older man who identified himself as Lemuel Carson had dual cranial bulges and one artificial eye whose focusing mechanism buzzed as it changed. Ky wondered how he tolerated it. "Everything from Delian fine porcelain and full formal services of gold on platinum to your basic plain white glazed pottery and stainless-steel flatware. All imports, though some of it's secondhand and we have a few antique sets, if you fancy a delicate floral pattern with silver-gilt edging—"

"No, I'm looking for good-quality shipware," Ky said. "I don't know if you're familiar with the Vatta Transport logo—"

His face brightened. "As a matter of fact, we have several sets; let me just check the inventory—" After a moment, during which Ky assumed he was querying his implant, he nodded. "A ship called *Nocturne* carried service for one hundred with the Vatta logo only, no shipname. The paperwork said it was taken on trade for new with a shipname."

One hundred . . . more than ample for one of the larger tradeships with full crew . . . they wouldn't have to clean up but once a day. Not standard, that.

"I'd like to see it," Ky said.

"Certainly," Carson said. "This way . . ."

The crates were transparent, showing each dish and the cushioning between them. Carson's stocking 'bot lowered the crates to the floor so that Ky could see the logo on the centers of the plates and bowls. The blue T with the red V overlaid on it showed clear; it looked authentic.

"Eight of the plates are chipped," Carson said. "So are

eleven of the cereal bowls. I said a hundred, but actually there are only eighty-seven mugs. Naturally I would only charge for the items actually here, and with adjustment for poor condition."

"Naturally," Ky murmured. What ship had these come from? What captain had wanted to replace company-supplied tableware with something he or she had to pay for? And so much of it? Successful captains often did order tableware with their ship name on it, but usually only in small amounts, for serving customers dinner aboard, for instance. Was it plunder from the attacks on Vatta ships? Could she eat off it, if it had been taken from the dead? Yet she wanted to touch it, return it to the family, almost as if it had been a captured ship. It was part of the way things had been—

"Is this the only set?" she asked as he opened the crate of plates and she took one. It felt solid, reassuring in its sturdy simplicity. The red-and-blue logo was crisp, its colors unfaded.

"No, there are two more, but they're smaller. We have ten place settings of the old logo, the VTL form, but no provenance for that. It's been here for years. Then we have five places of the new logo with the name *Briar Rose,* but the design is blurred, and the paperwork indicates this is why they were sold off. Do you want to see either of those?"

"I'll take a look at the old logo," Ky said. She remembered her mother's silk twill scarf with that design printed in gold and gray on blue, no doubt gone up in smoke with the house. One of the old sets of porcelain at home had the same design, the letters all blue, with gold highlights and gray shadows and a red line. It hadn't been used on ships for thirty years at least.

The stocking 'bot scurried off to find it. Carson tipped

his head to one side. "If you'll take it off my hands," he said, "I'll give it to you at less than the space cost. Nobody wants it; it's been here for years. I keep telling myself to send it to recycling, but . . . it's merchandise."

The 'bot came back trailed by a single-wheeled crate. Carson touched the top with his thumb, then ran a finger along the seal; it popped open. He lifted out one of the old plates and handed it to Ky. It felt different, lighter; the blue letters were edged with gold on the left and upper margins, and dark gray on the right and lower. A narrow red band bordered the logo. She felt as if she'd had ice poured down her back; her eyes burned. It was the same; it had to be the same. She tapped the plate with her fingernail and Carson nodded as it rang slightly.

"It's good stuff, and old," he said. "If it didn't carry such a well-known logo, I could get a good price for it. Unusual to see that quality shipboard."

It had not come off a ship, she was sure. The logo, yes, but such porcelain had never been bought for ship duty. It had come from a Vatta home. It had been *stolen* from a Vatta home.

"What's your price for this and the big set?" she asked. "Minus any that are chipped, of course."

The price he named seemed reasonable, but she would have paid more. She went through the motions of inspecting every item, discarding the chipped and crazed, noting the missing, and at the end authorized a draft on her account, and asked about delivery.

"I'll get this right out to you," Carson said. "It's near shift end; it'll be delivery-free if you can wait until tomorrow, but I'll have to charge for delivery off-main shift. Have to hire someone."

Surely Stella wouldn't turn up in the next twelve hours, and even if she did, she'd need to resupply. Still, Ky wanted to have that china—the old pieces in particular—safely in her possession. "How much would the delivery charge be?" she asked.

"Fifty credits."

"Send it on over, please," Ky said. "I'd rather get the galley organized quickly." With that chore out of the way, Ky called back to the ship. Martin answered, and she told him to expect a delivery of crockery within two hours.

"When will you be back?" he asked. "Rosvirein Traffic Control reports three heavily armed ships just down-jumped into the system, and put out an all-ship advisory that these might be pirates. Rosvirein's insystem defense is on full alert. These ships are days out, but—"

"Coming straight back," Ky said. "I should be there in an hour or so, assuming we catch the next passenger tram. I'll call if we don't. It's shift change." Her heart was racing; images of the last time she'd been docked when raiders entered a system came vividly to mind. "I'm going to call the stationmaster, have us put in the queue for departure. If Stella brings *Gary Tobai* in here, I want to be out there where I can protect her."

The stationmaster, sounding harried, gave Ky a departure slot six hours away without argument. "If you can't make it, let me know right away. I'm sure someone else will want your slot."

By the time they made it back to dockside, shift change had crowded the passages; Ky threaded her way through the traffic, hand near her weapon, and Rafe and Jim on either side. The gate to their dockside was open; she could see someone's back and a cargo cart stacked with crates. Several of the Gannett family and Martin were near, along with a man in delivery company uniform.

* * *

Pietro Duran received his orders in silence. It was the kind of job he hated, high risk and low return. Eventually, something would go wrong, and he'd die, and that would make the boss happy because he had it in for Pietro. And for no reason, really; it wasn't his fault that Gustaf the baker had decided to spend the last of his savings on a blowout when the diagnosis of incurable degenerative brain disease came through, instead of paying his usual protection money to the Organization.

But the boss refused to understand that, and thought Pietro should have been more persuasive. By then Gustaf was dead, an obvious suicide, and moreover he had left the record of his protection payments in an unencrypted file that the local snakes had discovered. The local snakes had demanded three times their usual payoff to ignore or lose the evidence: that, Pietro knew, was what really made the boss mad. Now Pietro had survived a string of high-risk assignments but the boss still didn't give up.

Intercepting the package had been no problem. The Organization had a finger in every delivery company on the station. They didn't steal directly, but it was a handy way to transport prohibited goods from place to place, concealing them in legitimate packages. All Pietro had to do was mention to Giff that he had an interest in packages to a certain destination, and would prefer to make a hand delivery, and Giff alerted him when the next shipment came through.

"It's kind of rush," Giff said. "They want immediate delivery, same-day service. Can you manage that? We're short-staffed today; I've got two out with personal problems."

The right code words. Pietro said "Sure, Giff. I'm off-shift now; I'll come right down. Which pickup?"

They talked a bit more, the usual thing—recognition codes, and so forth, and Pietro turned up at the cargo delivery station in the correct uniform, with an actual delivery service ID. It wasn't one package, but two: large cartons marked FRAGILE and THIS WAY UP. Pietro checked out a pallet mover, attached the suction pads to the cartons, and transferred them to the pallet mover, entering the correct destination code into the control panel. On some stations, he'd heard, package delivery was completely automated; he wondered what the equivalent of the Organization did there when it needed to intercept packages. They would think of something, he was sure.

Here, packages too heavy to hand-carry had to be accompanied by a delivery person even if a robotic pallet mover could have found its way to the right dockside. Very handy. So was the requirement to have human inspection of each piece of cargo at the end of any automated segment. He had an excuse to unseal the packages if necessary for inspection, using the delivery service's licensed tool, which left the correct code on the seals when he replaced them.

The manifest, coded into the seal itself, told him that this was "dinnerware, used, sales tax and export tax paid in full" and gave the number of plates, mugs, cups, and so on in each carton. Dinnerware. That made it easy. Inspection required opening both cartons. He ran the tool's tongue-probe down into the carton: no breakage in the first carton. He resealed that one and opened the second. No breakage here, either. Now—where to put the contact code? It must be accessible to the agent aboard the ship, but he didn't know that agent's position in the crew, just a name and flatpic of the face. He could put it on a plate, but some crew didn't handle plates except to eat off them. He could put it on the carton itself, if the agent handled cargo. At some time or other, almost everyone on a ship did, but would the agent find it before the cartons were unpacked and then recycled?

Both, he decided. He applied one of the several code dots he had to the back of the topmost plate in the second carton and another to the inside of the carton lid, then resealed it with the official tool. Then he walked beside the pallet mover as it moved slowly out into the concourse following the control line laid into the decking and swung left to head for the docking area.

In the bustling cargo center, Pietro had recognized other Organization operatives here and there; they all knew each other and he assumed the others were on assignments, as he was. Other personnel he ignored; the cargo center was always full of spacers and locals both who had come to send or receive packages small enough to use the intrastation cargo lines. He could not possibly keep up with all the ship patches, though he knew most of the stationers' uniforms.

He did not notice the two spacers who noticed him, and whose quietly skillful movement through the crowds on the concourse kept him unaware that he was being followed.

"That was interesting," Jon Gannett said. "He just put a telltag on that carton."

"Two," Hera Gannett said.

Jon didn't doubt it. Hera had several unobtrusive humodifications, including a telescopic lens implant in what looked like a normal eye. She couldn't quite read a telltag at a kilometer, but she could certainly see better than he could at a distance.

"Where's it going?" he asked.

"Our ship," Hera said. "That's a legitimate badge he has, and a legitimate cargo handler's inspection tool."

"Something bent," Jon said.

"Number one-eight-two," a clerk announced.

"I'll get it," Hera said, and moved forward. Jon had ordered a surprise treat for number one battery three days ago, and they were carrying it themselves rather than having it delivered. Old traditions on a new ship, something to connect them to their past and toast the future. Jon kept a casual glance on the fellow now moving slowly away with the pallet mover.

Hera came back with their package.

"He's headed back," Jon said, as they moved toward the cargo center exit. "We follow?"

"Should we warn the dock watch?"

"Wasn't enough for explosives . . . I think we just follow and keep him contained." That would be no problem, even if the man was armed—and Jon assumed he was.

The nondescript man in the delivery service uniform took a direct route with no stops or detours: the pallet mover followed its embedded line, and he paced beside it. Jon and Hera moved with the shift-change crowds, steadily and without appearing to watch the pallet or its escort.

"Heads up," came a voice in his implant. "All crew onstation, return to ship. All crew onstation, return to ship immediately. Acknowledge."

Jon tapped his station com, a code that meant "on the way." The captain must have almost everything she wanted aboard already; this pallet they were following might be the last load. Ahead now he could see the fat glowing numbers that designated dockspaces, and the number for their ship. The pallet mover turned into their dockspace and paused.

Jon and Hera moved up to the dock entrance. Ahead of them, Pod was working dockside security, checking the delivery. He glanced up from running a diagnostic wand down the side of the cartons when Jon moved closer.

"All crew report to First Officer Pritang," Pod said. *All crew* was family code for "anything wrong?"

"Go on, Hera," Jon said. "Tell him we're back; I'll hang out with Pod, here." More family code. Hera's name plus *here* in the same utterance meant "the problem's here."

Pod continued to wand the pallet mover and its cargo as if unconcerned. Jon flicked him a hand signal, from behind the deliveryman's back, and a moment later Pod's wand emitted a high-pitched squeal.

"This stupid thing!" Pod said, shaking the wand. "It does that all the time and there's never anything—"

Jon had noticed the man stiffening when the wand squealed. His left hand had twitched toward his side . . . a left-handed shooter? Now, as Pod continued to shake the wand and complain about its frequent malfunctions, the man relaxed slightly.

"I'll bet it won't react this time," Pod said, running the wand down the carton again. Of course it would, Jon knew. But the man was relaxed, not worried now. Probably thinking how to explain the telltags if they were found, probably thinking they wouldn't be noticed. The wand squealed again.

"I hate those things," Jon said, moving a little to one side; the man glanced at him, but didn't seem concerned. He would recognize Jon's position, but if he was what Jon suspected, he would be sure he could handle it. "Let me try, Pod; maybe I can make it behave."

Pod handed it over. "I hope so. Martin says open anything that squeals but these are just dishes. They called over a couple of hours ago about 'em. The captain saw 'em packed; there can't be anything wrong."

Jon fiddled with the wand controls. "That should do it. I don't know why we have to use this stuff anyway. We have area scans—" He stepped close to the man to wand the cartons on this side. The man moved away, out of politeness or the desire to keep Jon from coming too close. He seemed to be looking around the docking area.

"You have a crewman named Julio Calixo?" he asked suddenly.

"Julie?" That was Pod. "Sure. Cargo handler."

"Listen, I know his sister Bea. Think I could speak to him?"

Jon could feel the change in Pod's alertness from two meters away. He hoped the deliveryman couldn't.

"Sure, I'll call," Pod said. He used the exterior com rather than his implant phone, and without using any family code at all—the person answering must not be one of them—said Julie had a visitor dockside, someone who said they knew his sister.

"His sister Bea," the man repeated, and Pod added that.

Interesting. Jon recognized a code phrase when he heard it.

"He's coming out," Pod said.

While the man's attention was split between Pod and the gangway, Jon pressed a control and the wand squealed again. "Damn it! I thought I had it fixed." The man barely glanced his way as Jon shook the wand. So his priority was to meet this person, pass a message? Tell this person where the telltag was? Jon glanced toward the gangway and saw Gordon Martin coming out with Hera.

"Here comes trouble," he said. "Hera and the big guy." The deliveryman looked at him. "Sorry—I'm going to have to open the cartons now; he'll have heard the wand and he has his rules."

"That the captain?" the deliveryman asked.

"No. That's the security chief. Captain's a lady."

"Got a squealer, eh?" Martin, Jon could tell, scared the

deliveryman. "Let's open 'em up and take a look. You—delivery—let me see your badge."

"I'm legit," the man said. "Nothing's wrong with this cargo; it's that wand. I checked contents myself at the cargo terminal: nothing broken, nothing prohibited."

"Looks all right," Martin said, after a cursory inspection. Jon wasn't fooled, not when Hera'd had time to tell Martin what they'd seen. He, too, was playing for time.

"It's the wand," Pod said. "I told you before it's broken."

"Are those my new dishes?" Jon turned to see the captain, the mystery man Rafe, and Jim-the-bonehead in the entrance. Martin didn't like Rafe, that had been clear from the first day, and Jon already respected Martin enough to take his opinion of Rafe. But at the moment, Rafe and Jim were properly positioned for escorts. Would they recognize that something was wrong here?

"Yes, ma'am," Jon said.

"Then let's get them aboard; we're about to leave," she said.

"This hasn't cleared security yet, ma'am," Martin said. "We're working on it."

"We're in the queue for departure," she said. That was new; she must have contacted the station authorities on her way back from this shopping trip. Why the hurry, Jon wondered.

"Yes, ma'am. We'll make it," Martin said. "Just don't want any unpleasant surprises. It won't take long to do a visual on these things."

"Right," she said. She moved toward the ship, keeping herself out of all conceivable lines of fire. Jon nodded to himself. She wasn't going to second-guess her security chief and she didn't try to micromanage . . . but she recognized a threat. Rafe had moved to cover her, but Jim still lagged, staring at the carton as if it had snakes in it.

Jon didn't know Julio Calixo—he didn't know most of the new hires yet—but he was fairly sure the youngish man who came out of the gangway now and headed toward them was the contact the deliveryman wanted to make.

"Where *is* Bea?" Calixo said loudly. "She missed Grandma's birthday party and no one's heard from her since."

"She's fine," the deliveryman said. "She was through here last month; she's working on an old lady's yacht and asked me to let you know if you came through. With the ansibles down, she couldn't let you know. Can you imagine Bea washing dishes for a rich lady? And packing and unpacking boxes of stuff?"

As code, it was ridiculously transparent. Dishes, boxes, unpacking. Jon didn't think much of the deliveryman's smarts, but if he hadn't known there was a telltag on a dish and on the carton, it could've sounded innocent enough.

"Since you're here, Calixo," Martin said, "you can help inspect these—the captain's in a hurry. We need to get these signed off and put aboard."

"Oh, sure—sure," Calixo said. The deliveryman stirred, as if to help, and Martin shook his head.

"Not you. You know the rules. We can't sign off until we're sure it's as ordered, but we do the inspection here. It won't be long. You can call your office if you need to." The deliveryman shook his head. "Calixo, you do that carton; I'll do this one." And he didn't have to say, *You Gannetts stay alert.*

Jon moved again, this time taking the angle on Calixo; Pod stepped back, as if returning to his primary duty of dock security, and Hera had a standard cargo databoard, or what looked like one.

Martin opened the carton with the telltags and spoke

to Calixo, who had opened the other. "I didn't know you knew anyone on this station," he said. "It's not in your interview transcript."

Calixo stiffened for a moment, then went on burrowing into the packing materials. "Well, it's not like . . ." He paused. "I mean, we're not close friends or anything, he just knows my sister Bea and that's how I know him."

"Um." Martin lifted out the top plate, turning it in his hands. "So . . . what's his name?"

"Uh . . ." Calixo cast a swift glance at the deliveryman, blinked, and then said "Pete . . . well, Pietro, actually, but like me he doesn't use his formal name."

"I see," Martin said. He was looking at the bottom of the plate. Jon saw the glisten of sweat on the deliveryman's neck. "So . . . this little telltag thing here wouldn't be a coded datadot he wanted to get to you, and calling you out here wouldn't be a way to let you know where it was, then?"

"No!" That was too quick, too sharp, almost panicky. The deliveryman twitched, controlled it.

"Because," Martin said, "if this telltag, or the other one on the inside of the carton lid, is a secret coded message from him to you, I'm going to be very displeased, and I'm going to have to know what it's all about."

"I don't know anything about anything," Calixo said. Jon didn't look at him; he watched the deliveryman instead, watched another tensing and relaxing, the change of color on his neck.

"Well, that's fine," Martin said. "I'm glad for your sake that you don't, but . . ." Out of the corner of his eye, Jon saw Martin turn toward the deliveryman. "That leaves you. You're the only person to open this shipment since it left the store."

Jon knew that Calixo moved suddenly because Pod's

weapon emitted a soft but distinct noise followed by the sound of Calixo hitting the deck. "Look at that," Pod said. "Accidental discharge . . . it's like the wand, everything's acting up today." He hit the controls, sealing the dock off from the concourse.

"Well?" Martin said to the deliveryman. "What's your story?"

Jon had his own weapon out, as did Hera now; the deliveryman was pinned, and knew it.

"I—I'll tell you everything," he said. "I will, really— just don't kill me."

"That depends," Martin said. "You're armed, I'm sure. Put your hands straight out to the side. Jon, search him."

The deliveryman had more weapons than any one person needed, plus both mechanical and electronic lock-picks, and a coil of R-387 moldable explosive wound around his left leg.

"Aren't you the busy one?" Martin said, eyeing the array laid out on the deck. "So, start talking."

"I can't here," the deliveryman said. "He'll know. He'll get me. But I can tell you things you need to know. Take me along, please. Take me away from here; it's my only chance."

Martin frowned. He glanced at Jon; Jon understood that glance. "He's really frightened, sir," he said. "He might have something."

"If you don't, we'll space you," Martin said. "All right. Cuff him, get him aboard, you and Pod. I'll tell the captain and get someone out to clean up this mess."

"Is he—is he dead?" the man asked, with a look at Calixo's limp body on the deck.

"That's not your concern," Martin said. Jon sealed the cuffs he'd put on wrists used to cuffs—the man had known how to position his wrists for them, and Jon had made the necessary correction—and nudged the man forward, toward the gangway.

Hugh Pritang met them in the ship's entrance. "Captain's going to want a complete report," he said to Martin. "I'll take care of dockside." Jon wondered what that meant. What would station law enforcement say? Technically, dockside belonged to the ship, and ship captains had the power to administer justice there, but most stations took an interest in dockside deaths, and the man certainly looked dead.

But his job was the prisoner, for now, so he kept going without a backward glance.

EIGHT

"This is a situation we didn't need," Ky said. "A dead man and a prisoner . . . I can just imagine the local reaction to that." And possible pirates in the system, and Stella somewhere between Garth-Lindheimer and here, maybe jumping into trouble. Rosvirein Station's advisory to ships in the system had made it clear Rosvirein Peace Force thought these ships were dangerous.

"Hasn't been any yet," Rafe said.

"Somebody's bound to have heard the shot," she said.

"Begging your pardon, Captain, but I doubt it," Hugh said. He looked, as always, completely professional and relaxed at the same time. "The shot was inside our dockspace, and you'll remember we have a standard acoustic barrier, even when the gate's open. Drops the volume thirty or more decibels. And Pod—the shooter—used a quieted weapon. The victim's your crewman, who was clearly conspiring against you, and he tried to draw on your security forces."

"Um." Ky thought about it. She hadn't given the order to kill, but she'd made it clear she wanted the ship secure. Which made it her responsibility.

"Would've been worse if he'd shot Pod," Rafe said.

"I can see that," Ky said crossly. "I'm not trying to

second-guess my own security. I'm just thinking what to do now. We hired the dead man here, after all. He's bound to have other contacts—"

"Who aren't going to be asking questions, if he was undercover for someone," Hugh said. "This is Rosvirein, which helps. I've been here five standard months, while Captain Janocek tried to make ends meet; I don't think there'll be any problems."

"So did we get all the blood off the deck?" Ky asked.

"Complete biochem cleanup," Hugh said. "I did the entire dockside and then reminded the station environmental squad that we were due a refund of the deposit you paid when you arrived for cleaning their grungy dock thoroughly so they didn't have to do a complete decontamination. They argued about it, but sent over an inspector, and you'll find the deposit refund in your accounts."

Rafe grinned at him. "Hugh, I think you're almost as devious as I am."

"Not at all," Hugh said with a straight face, though his eyes twinkled. "I'm merely doing my job to see that our departure is trouble-free, as any good first officer would."

"Which leaves us the matter of our prisoner," Ky said. "I understand he said he was willing to tell us why he placed the telltags?"

"Yes. I think you should let Martin and me question him," Rafe said.

"I think I should be there," Ky said.

"I agree," Hugh said, as Rafe opened his mouth. "Someone from command must be there, and the captain bears ultimate responsibility. I can keep us moving on our departure schedule; the captain needs to be on the bridge only for the last part of that."

"Word's gone out. No more killin' Vattas." The man's head lolled back; his eyes focused on nothing. He had not resisted their questions; he had even suggested himself that they might want to use interrogation drugs if they had any.

Ky had hesitated. Surely taking someone prisoner and questioning them privately was against the law—she knew it was against the law on Slotter Key—but Rosvirein's laws were notoriously lax as long as nothing bothered its own citizens. And chem-based interrogation wasn't physically painful. She really did need to know what this man probably knew. Yet she had the uneasy feeling that she was about to cross some line she had never crossed before, a line that Osman would have crossed without thinking about it. Maybe she'd already crossed it, when she hadn't reported the altercation dockside . . .

"Reliable?" Ky now asked softly.

Martin shrugged. "Maybe, maybe not. Chemicals are always tricky, and we don't have an enzyme scan on him."

"Said it's stupid," the man mumbled. "Vatta right here, lemme do it, money's good. No money, th'said. No more killin' Vattas. Done enough. Blame Osman that slime. Just put the telltag on the carton and let Calixo know."

Ky felt her brows going up. "So even his allies didn't like him?"

"Nobody like Osman," the man said, even as Martin shook his head at Ky. "Osman's bad link. Ga—t'boss glad he dead." His head rolled around, came up slightly, and his blurry eyes almost focused on Ky. "Y'pretty, honey. Wanna play?"

Martin's knuckles whitened, Ky noticed, but his voice stayed even and soft. "Not playtime, sonny. What about t'boss?"

"He don' like Osman. He don' like anybody do more'n

he told 'em. He—" A sudden flush ran up the man's neck.

"Damn it," Martin said very softly. He grabbed one of the other syringes laid out on the box and stabbed the man's arm. But the flush deepened, pink to red to rose-purple. "He's got a suicide link. To the boss, whoever that is. We're going to lose him, if this isn't the right anti-dote—" Then to the man, louder. "Boss name—who?"

"Boss?" The man's breathing had quickened to gasps. "Boss he don' like . . . he . . . Ga—Gammissss." And on that hiss, his body convulsed against the straps as his skin went from purple to blue-gray.

Martin had the oxygen mask on his face; Rafe helped unstrap the man and they laid him flat. But nothing worked. He was dead.

"What was that?" Ky asked.

"Suicide circuit, probably in his implant. Some of them trigger on any interrogation drug, some are keyword-specific. There are different drugs they use: cardiotoxins, neural solvents. This was clearly an oxygen decoupler." Martin shook his head. "Propagates really fast in the bloodstream, and just about impossible to reverse. If you have a hemoglobin replacement and a lot of other equipment, you can sometimes save 'em, but otherwise not. And their implants are always wiped."

"Keyword was his boss, or the boss's name," Rafe said. He and Martin were stripping the body now. Ky wondered what they would do with it.

"Gammis something," Martin said.

"Gammis . . ." Rafe paused. "There was a pirate gang operating over near Woosten maybe five years ago, and someone said the head of it was named Gammis some-thing. Turek, I think. Supposedly he had some kind of protection racket going on with the system government and local ships. But he was leaving ISC alone, so I didn't pay much attention."

"Captain, how long till we leave?" Martin asked.

"Just a couple of hours," Ky said. "What are you going to do with him?"

"If it's that quick, we can just stick him in cold storage and dump him in space later. His friends aren't going to be asking the authorities about him anytime soon anyway." Rafe had brought a packing wrap and laid it out. He and Martin rolled the body onto it.

"We can't just—" Ky began, then stopped. They could. It was wrong, certainly against the law, but so was killing someone in an interrogation. For a moment, the weight of the deaths she had caused lay on her shoulders.

"If we try to dump him on the station," Martin said, "we could be observed. Probably would be. Even if we got away clean, our record here would be tainted. If he just disappears, they might suspect something but they wouldn't know. Another scum with a record vanishes, who cares?"

It made sense, but it made sense that felt uncomfortably close to the dead man's values.

"Wait a minute," Ky said as the other two started to fold the shipping blanket over the man's face. She knelt beside the corpse, ignoring Rafe and Martin except to ask, "What's the name on his ID?"

"Pietro Duran," Martin said. "A fake, I'm sure of it."

"But it's the name we have," Ky said. She had said no words over the first men she killed; they had been trying to kill her, and she had felt no impulse to speak for them. But this Pietro, evil as he might have been, had done her no direct harm, though by his own words he would have if his boss paid for it. Saying words over his body felt right, something more real than real. She looked at his face, blue-gray and sharp with death. "Go in peace, Pietro Duran," she said. "If you had those who loved you, may they find peace without you, and if there is life beyond life, may you have a better one than you had here."

When she stood again, she felt better, more solid to herself.

Martin and Rafe looked confused, and no wonder. "I didn't know you were religious," Rafe said.

"I haven't been practicing for a while," Ky said. "But I needed to do this."

"Does it bother you he's dead?" Martin asked.

"Not particularly," Ky said. "Though the thought of having a suicide circuit in an implant disgusts me." She shook her head. "Get him into the freezer and this cleaned up. I'll be on the bridge, making our farewells." That would make *two* corpses in the freezer. Even Rosvirein's relatively lax law enforcement would probably detain them for having killed two people, if they suspected.

Ky made the usual round of calls, trying to leave Stella with the best possible arrangements at the bank, with the Captains' Guild, with merchants, and finally with station authorities. She noticed, on the system status board, that other captains were also reacting to the arrival of the armed threesome.

"Cleared," the stationmaster's office said at last. "All accounts green, no outstanding warrants, no complaints. We understand about your cousin. Fair travel, Captain Vatta. Did you want to list a destination?"

"No," Ky said. "Outsystem only."

"Very well. You're cleared for a least-boost course to jump point gamma. At this alert level, you must have clearance from Rosvirein Peace Force to deviate from that course."

Ky scowled. "I was going to take the slow route and see if my cousin showed up."

"No. We want all ships insystem either docked or

boosting out, not hanging around where they could interfere with system defense. Remember that if you attack a
ship in this system, we will retaliate."

"Even if they fire at my ship?" Ky asked.

"Yes. Keep your weapons cold; our forces will fire on
any ship that goes hot. Is that quite clear?"

"Very clear," Ky said. She hoped Rosvirein's defensive
forces were as good as they thought.

Undock went smoothly; behind them, ships peeled off
Rosvirein Station like beads off a string, with *Fair Kaleen*
leading the parade. Ky watched the system scan, high-
lighting the incoming ships with threat icons. Nothing
happened as the hours passed. Were they pirates after all?
Had she skipped the station for no reason? How upset
would Stella be, to find her gone? She stared at the plots,
trying to make *Gary Tobai* appear by the force of wishing,
but it didn't.

After the first uneventful day on insystem drive, Ky
called Rafe and Martin aside. "We've got to figure out
who's behind all this," she said. "This Gammis Turek or
whatever—what is he after? What does he want?"

"This is more than one pirate gang could do," Martin
said. "It'd take a space fleet, near enough."

"He worked with Osman," Ky said. "What if he worked
with other pirate gangs? Got them to cooperate?"

Martin snorted. "Cooperate? Pirates? They're too independent for that."

"Maybe," Rafe said. "And maybe not. It would make
sense—organized crime's a lot more profitable and safer
than the same criminals doing things on their own."

Martin gave him a look that clearly conveyed *You should
know;* Rafe sketched a salute.

"Of course I have reasons to know," he said. "I'm still
right. Enough pirates working together, linked by ansible,

could overpower any one system's defenses, especially if
it was cut off from others, if its ansible failed. There's no
organized interstellar force. Just a few privateers running
around with no coordination, even if they are authorized
by the same government." He stopped and looked
thoughtful a moment. "Just how many privateers does
Slotter Key have out, anyway?"

"I have no idea," Ky said. She felt the glimmer of an
idea, but couldn't quite bring it to consciousness.
"Martin?"

"I never heard," Martin said. "I suppose . . . twenty?
Thirty? And Slotter Key's not the only government that
uses them. Let's see—there's Mannhai. Cirvalos.
Bissonet."

"The original signatories to the Commercial Code all
had privateers at one time," Rafe said. "But only a handful
do now. Not worth the bad publicity."

"Which Slotter Key just ignored," Martin said. "Cost
us diplomatically, some said."

"Making Slotter Key the logical target for a group of
pirates that wanted to expand its influence," Ky said. She
could almost see it now, the pirates' whole plan. "If you
could show that privateers weren't effective protection—
for that you'd have to attack tradeships—then you could
convince governments and shippers they needed better
protection—"

"It worked over in Woosten," Rafe said. "The protection end, anyway. I don't think they ever had privateers
there. Not a bad system to test it in . . . Woosten's too
poor to interest many of the big firms."

"So they cut off communications and hit one particular shipper really hard. Probably chose Vatta because of
Osman—"

"Or because Vatta is big, well known, and had never

been part of Slotter Key's privateer fleet," Martin said.
"Lots of publicity, less risky—no Vatta ship was armed."
He paused, frowning. "But for the attack on Slotter Key
itself, they must've pressured the government somehow.
From what Stella said, someone knew about the bunkers
under your headquarters and placed charges belowground.
You can't do that from outer space."

"But if this is what's going on, and we can find more
clues, we can tell people—" Ky said.

"Tell them what?" Rafe asked. "That there's danger?
They know that. Just giving them a man's name won't
help."

"I'm thinking of the other privateers. We need to find
them, get them working with us."

"Working with us? You mean to find out more?"

"As a . . . a fleet," Ky said, as the concept she'd been
groping toward came clear. "If Slotter Key has as many as
thirty, and the others have that many, too, we'd have a
fleet bigger than the pirates."

"First, we don't know how big their fleet really is," Rafe
said. "For all we know, they have hundreds, thousands,
of ships. Second, you'll never get fifty or a hundred independent privateers to agree to fight together as a fleet."

"Even if they were trained to fleet maneuvers," Martin
said, nodding. "Which they aren't."

"Nobody could support a fleet of thousands," Ky said.
"Not without more resources than could be put together
in the past few years. Hundreds, maybe. Slotter Key's a
wealthy world, and we have fewer than two hundred real
warships, plus the support craft." She ran the figures in
her implant again: that was right. The economy would not
stand more without adjustments that had not been made.
"As for training," she went on, "Slotter Key puts Spaceforce
officers aboard its privateers, and they're trained in fleet

maneuvers. Maybe others do the same, or maybe we can borrow fleet officers."

Martin looked at Rafe. Rafe opened his mouth. She held up her hand. "No. Don't tell me why it won't work. Help me find the right way to do it."

"But—"

"Captain, you don't understand the difficulties—"

In her mind a cascade of possibilities rained down, glittering like polished coins. "I do understand," she said, putting an edge to her voice. "I understand that we are one ship—that Vatta has, to my knowledge, only two ships, one of which is an old, slow, toothless tub. I understand that the enemy has many ships, efficient communications, and the advantage of initiative. But I also understand—and you had better understand—that this family, *my* family, is not finished. I am not finished. My aunt Grace is not finished. I don't intend survival—I intend victory."

The moment she heard the words, she thought how brash they sounded, how unlikely to be true, but Rafe and Martin both looked at her as if they'd heard trumpets.

What had she done? Did she really have command presence? She pushed that question away and went on quickly.

"The pirates have a combined fleet right now. Even if it falls apart, it will cripple trade and communication. The resources to deal with that are already out here, if we just put them together."

Rafe had recovered his breath. "And you think you can do that."

"I had better do that," Ky said. "No one else seems to be doing it."

Martin nodded slowly. "Combining privateers might work. But what about the space fleets in systems that have them? Wouldn't they be more use?"

"They'd be a big help," Ky said. "If their governments

released them. But most operate in their own system only. Some don't even have FTL capability; they're like block police. What we need is a true interstellar force."

"What about communications?"

Ky grinned. "Those shipboard ansibles," she said. "We have enough to equip at least a strike force—it puts us equal to the pirates. And we can have more built."

"No," Rafe said, paling. "You can't do that. You mustn't do that."

"Yes," Ky said. "Rafe, the tech's already loose in the universe. You can't suppress it now. Chances are some of your renegade development people are already manufacturing them. You've looked at Osman's inventory lists. How many do you think are out there?"

"At least sixty," Rafe said. His shoulders slumped. "But I don't see why we can't try to destroy them with the ships—"

Sixty ships with constant real-time communication independent of system ansibles . . . Ky shivered. She had hoped for fewer; she'd need a lot of allies to take on that many—or more.

"We can't defeat them without communications parity," Ky said. "Tactically, instantaneous communications between ships at scan-lag distances gives them incredible advantages in command and control."

"If the system ansibles come back up, we could use those."

"And if they don't? And considering how vulnerable they are to skilled attack? No, Rafe. The only way to fight them is to use those ansibles ourselves."

He shook his head but said nothing. The ship's intercom bleeped.

"Captain!" That was Hugh Pritang on the bridge. "More ships downjumping."

"On my way," Ky said. She hoped one of them would be *Gary Tobai,* perhaps in a convoy. On the bridge, she found tension almost as thick as Aunt Grace's fruitcake.

"Four more armed ships," Hugh said, pointing them out on scan. "No sign of your cousin. Rosvirein Station hasn't—ah, there they go."

The station's automated message center displayed a crawler on the lower edge of the navigation screen: ATTENTION ALL SHIPS. ALERT STATUS XENO. HOLD COURSE OR BE FIRED ON. MAINTAIN WEAPONS LOCKDOWN OR BE FIRED ON. SHIPS MAY ACTIVATE DEFENSIVE SHIELDS ONLY. ALERT STATUS XENO. SYSTEM ANSIBLE NOT AVAILABLE FOR PRIVATE USE.

"Shields up," Ky said. "Lee, give us a calculation on time to jump if we don't wait for the jump point."

"Twenty-two minutes at present acceleration," he said. "I've got it running, along with an estimated downjump variance."

"Good," Ky said. "Engineering: get the FTL drive on standby for an emergency jump." She was not going to be caught, as at Belinta, no matter what happened here.

On scan, Rosvirein's embedded systems defenses showed up as red dots, as did the system's ships. Ky looked at the ship plots. The three original problem ships, inbound for Rosvirein Station . . . the outbound traders, some of them undoubtedly privateers just like *Fair Kaleen* . . . Rosvirein's own Peace Force ships . . . and the four newcomers, which had come through the jump at high delta vee relative to the system and showed no signs of deceleration.

Ky's stomach clenched. Eight Rosvirein ships, shadowing the first three, were now bracketed between them and the newcomers.

"That's not good," Hugh murmured even as she thought it. "C'mon, get yourselves out of there."

"Scan lag's almost an hour," Lee said. "What's done is done."

All Ky could think of was Stella, Stella in a small, slow, defenseless ship . . . minutes passing like hours as she watched the outdated scan, as the newly emerged ships spread out, as the shooting began, from ship and embedded platforms both.

It was hard to remember that what she saw was almost an hour old, when shields flared.

"They're not after ships," Ky said. "They're after system defense, the embedded installations." The attackers' shields flared under Rosvirein Peace Force fire, but none had failed yet.

"Look at that!" Lee pointed; Ky had already noticed one of the ships in line behind them veering from its assigned course. "Armed tradeship *Iron Gate,* and she's loading on the delta vee." She was much closer to them than the seven attackers; they were able to watch her in near real time.

"Course estimate," Ky said.

"Nowhere near us; looks like she could be on a least-time course for . . ." He paused. The navigation screen showed the first blunt arrowhead of *Iron Gate*'s course change narrowing as the acceleration closed her options. "The system financial ansible platform."

"A decoy attack," Ky said. "These others are just covering the attack on the ansible. They have to know that ship weapons won't—" But a flare on the screen belied her words; one of the embedded defense batteries was gone. "Prepare for transition," Ky said. Even as she said it, another crawler came on the screen.

ALL SHIPS ALL SHIPS READY FOR UP TRANSITION. ALL SHIPS JUMP IN ORDER OF DEPARTURE, 30 SECOND INTERVAL, FAIR KALEEN FIRST. SHIPS NOT UPJUMPING WILL BE TAGGED AS HOSTILE.

"They want us out of here," Hugh said. "If they have more of whatever that was, Rosvirein's system defenses are in trouble."

"So are we," Ky said. "Lee?"

"Fifty seconds."

It felt more like fifty minutes, but *Fair Kaleen* slipped into transition with the smoothness of perfect alignment.

"That was . . . interesting," Rafe said. "I hope it's over with before Stella gets there."

It was the first time he'd expressed concern about Stella; Ky looked at his impassive expression, wondering.

"I hope the right side wins," Ky said.

"They should," Hugh said. "Unless a fleet follows that probe, Rosvirein's Peace Force has plenty of firepower to run those raiders out. I read it as a test of the system's defenses—"

"They blew an embedded installation," Ky said.

"I'd bet it's a peripheral automated one," Hugh said. "Let's look at the scan data when the ship's secured for FTL flight—"

"After we set up a training schedule," Ky said. "Clearly, we can expect trouble anywhere but in FTL. I'll take bridge watch; you and Martin rough up a schedule for me."

"It's almost shift change," Rafe murmured.

"It was my watch next anyway," Ky said. "If you're tired, you're off duty." Through her implant, she checked ship functions, one after another. No problems: *Fair Kaleen* hung suspended in indeterminacy.

"I meant, the captain's a long way from her last meal," Rafe said. "Aren't there rules about that?"

Ky started to say she wasn't hungry, but now that immediate danger seemed past, she was. And with the ship fully crewed, she now had galley staff; she called down and requested a meal. "Satisfied now?" she asked Rafe.

He put his hands together and bowed slightly. "I have only the captain's welfare in mind."

"I'm sure," Ky said, trying to keep the same light tone.

Three hours into the new shift, Martin and Hugh reappeared with a training schedule and more questions about her plans.

"How are the tradeships going to know we aren't pirates, too? How are the system governments going to react? And the mercenary companies?"

"We'll figure it out," Ky said. "The traders . . . well, Vatta still has a reputation for honesty, Osman aside. I can talk to them. Unless the mercs have thrown in with the pirates, they have no reason to attack us. They make their money out of insystem conflicts, anyway. Governments—"

"Governments that don't like or trust Slotter Key, remember—" Rafe said.

"I know, I know. First things first. We find the other privateers. One at a time if we have to, but I'll bet they're already joining forces if they've run into the pirate gangs."

Two days out from Rosvirein, Ky called Rafe into her office. "Did you tell that ISC manager about the shipboard ansibles?"

He looked shocked. "Good gracious, no! She's not cleared at that level. Why?"

"Is there any way to use these shipboard ansibles to hook into local communications networks?"

"Not really," Rafe said. He steepled his fingers. "The difficulty in integrating shipborne ansibles with local facilities is one of the big problems with using them. It's easier to call ship-to-ship across systems than to access the local communications network. The system's just not set up for that."

"That doesn't make sense," Ky said. "It's closer—"

"Closer physically, yes, but that's not the point." Rafe frowned. "This is getting into proprietary secrets again, but you need to understand at least part of it. System ansibles access local-system communications through hardware and software that ensures cross-identification. The ansibles themselves are protected by requiring all incoming messages to carry valid initiation and destination codes, which—except for ship coms, which are in another database—are preloaded at manufacture. Each system ansible is custom-made to respond to its destination's signals. Got that?"

"Yes, I suppose. It's an expensive approach—"

"True. But it's kept ansibles safe from the kind of takeover that used to happen with planetary and system-wide nets. Meanwhile, ISC sets the parameters for the system's lightspeed net to match those of the ansible to form a unique connection. Part of our monopoly agreement is that systemwide nets will not link with other ansibles. Ansible-to-ansible links are possible, of course, but access to the system lightspeed net is limited to one ansible."

"But some systems have more than one—many have both a financial and a commercial—"

"We—ISC—will manufacture more than one ansible with the same internal code, of course. But there's only one connection code for each customer system, and our service agreement ensures that the customer can't connect with any other ansible. If ISC opened customer systems to shipborne ansibles, that would mean a massive security hole."

"There's got to be a way around that," Ky said. "I can't believe that Osman and his allies weren't contacting locals with theirs. It would keep their communications secure from any surveillance that ISC was doing through the system ansibles."

"If they did, they had tech we don't know about," Rafe said. "Not that it's impossible. Some of ISC's research division have been unhappy with the no-proliferation policy for decades. Management has suspected that they're using ISC funds for research we never see."

"Let's assume they had that tech," Ky said. "It's safer that way. And then let's assume you can figure it out and build us an equivalent."

Rafe stared at her. "Me? I'm not a designer or engineer. I can't possibly—"

"Rafe, you're the one person we have who's expert in ISC hardware. Until we find a designer or engineer who wants to work with us, you're it. I'm sure Osman had information on this somewhere. Find it."

"But you need me to help you with the contacts—"

"Yes. You can do both. It may slow you down."

"To a dead stop," Rafe said.

"Not really. If you can even define what we need to know, we can start trolling for more expertise."

"I'm getting close to the edge of what I can do," Rafe warned. "My primary loyalty is still to ISC. You're asking me to help subvert it."

"It's my contention that in order to help ISC, we have to have communications that work," Ky said. "ISC's enemies already have the tech I'm asking you to find—we're not making things worse. We're using the new tech to help."

He scowled at the table. "Maybe. And maybe not. I'll have to think about it."

"Don't think too long. By now the enemy knows who we are."

"What about Stella? How will she know where you've gone?"

"I've left her a message, at the Captains' Guild."

"She's not going to be happy about that."

"I know," Ky said. "But we didn't have a choice. On the way we can stop off and . . . er . . . practice some things."

"Drills," said Rafe with distaste.

"It's not as if you didn't have your own drills," Ky said.

At the next jump point, Ky ordered the ship to lay over a few days. She took them close enough to one of the larger masses that debris from their successful shots at components of its ring system would stay in that area, not complicate the jump-point transit for other ships. The two corpses vanished in the first salvo.

Watching things blow up was less fun than it had been when she and her cousins set off illicit fireworks on the beach, but in three days she knew that the Gannetts were definitely a superb gunnery team and the others were as good as what she'd been shown in the Slotter Key Spaceforce. Osman had kept his weaponry and supporting electronics in superb condition, so only slight adjustments were required. On the fourth and fifth days, she and Hugh set up simulations for the crew to play through.

"I wouldn't like to be the odd pirate that tried to take us on," Hugh said, after the first round of simulations. "When do we go hunting?"

"We need to do more than pick them off one by one," Ky said. "That could take a lifetime. There may be sixty or more with the portable ansibles. That's how many Rafe thinks were dispersed just through Osman's services."

"Ouch. You're right; we need a fleet. But assembling one—"

"Is not going to be easy, certainly not if I try to talk to governmental entities. I'm hoping to find some privateers at Sallyon, though. Surely they'll be more willing to listen."

He nodded without much enthusiasm, and she went on. "We also need more than gunnery drills, Hugh. That last fire-emergency drill was pitiful, response far too slow. Keep us awake nights if you have to, but I want to reach Sallyon with a crew that's thoroughly familiar with every compartment and every procedure."

"Beats scraping paint," Hugh said. Ky laughed.

In the next FTL passage, she had reason to wish she had not said *keep us awake nights,* because the drills he devised interrupted everyone's sleep repeatedly. Power loss, environmental leaks, hull breaches, fire in the galley, armed stowaways holed up in cargo, artificial gravity failure . . . and the captain had a role in every emergency, usually involving getting to the bridge in nothing flat. She wondered where he'd found the variety of drill-enhancing objects and substances that smoked, stank, flared, and made scary noises like escaping air, crackling flames, gunshots, and gurgling liquids. Or the makeup that turned some of the crew into gory "wounded" or "dead" heaps here and there about the ship, and others into strangers—stowaways, assassins, the enemy.

"At least it's not boring," Rafe said one day, when they were hunched over the table eating a hasty meal after two hours of struggle to control an imaginary flood. "The man shows real creativity in his approach to drills, I'll say that for him."

"Thank you," Hugh said, coming in behind them. "And I'm pleased to report, Captain, that performance has been steadily improving, reaching commendable on the past three drills. With the captain's permission, I'd like to let up now. I think they need a reward for good work."

"You have the captain's permission," Ky said. "The captain would like a full night's sleep—or any shift's sleep—

so I don't get to Sallyon looking like this—" She gestured at herself.

"The captain is always impeccable," Hugh said. She gave him a look. "And diligent as well," he added. "Some captains would've told me to lay off days ago; I appreciate your willingness to let me push this crew to a higher standard."

"You're welcome," Ky said. "And I appreciate the work you put into this."

"Mutual admiration," Rafe murmured and rolled his eyes. Hugh looked at him with a mild expression that seemed to convey something far less than mild; Rafe suddenly turned red and got up hastily.

"Interesting young man, that," Hugh said to Ky.

"Very," Ky said. "My cousin Stella knew him awhile back; he showed up with her at Lastway."

"He is . . . er . . . attached to her?"

"No. At least, I don't think so. They had a legal partnership; I had one with him myself after Lastway, because Stella said he would honor a partnership."

"Is it operative now?"

"No, it's long run out. I forgot to renew it."

"And yet he chose to be on this ship with you. Interesting."

"He had the expertise with communications systems," Ky said. "I needed him."

"Ah." Now the mild look was turned on her. "He's quite good looking."

"Not you, too," Ky said. When he said nothing, she went on. "Martin worries all the time that I'll fall for him or something. I won't. He's not my kind." If she had a kind, which with Hal's defection she wasn't sure of. "I'm going to bed," Ky said. "And I would appreciate it if there were no surprise drills for the next eight hours."

"Certainly not, Captain," Hugh said. She hoped that was not a twinkle in his eye.

Three days later, they dropped into the Sallyon system and eased in toward the Sallyon Main Station.

NINE

Sallyon had placed a remote surveillance station only fifteen light-seconds from its mapped jump point; *Fair Kaleen* no sooner cleared downjump turbulence that Ky found herself facing a Sallyon Immigration Control official onscreen.

"Sallyon inbound clearance station to arriving vessel. Confirm beacon ID, owner of vessel ID, commanding officer ID, last port of call, ansible status at last port of call. All vessels must have clearance from this station before proceeding to Sallyon Main Station." Along with that came a datastring for the ship pilot, directing the rate of deceleration and course.

"Shipname is *Fair Kaleen*," Ky said. "Owner, Vatta Enterprises. Captain, Kylara Vatta—"

"Our records show this vessel's captain should be Osman Vatta. Explain this discrepancy."

"Osman Vatta was a pirate," Ky said. "He stole this ship from Vatta Transport. You should have a warning on file from Vatta repudiating ownership and responsibility for Osman Vatta—"

"We do."

"Osman Vatta is dead," Ky said. "I should be on your list as captain of either *Glennys Jones* or *Gary Tobai,* depending on your latest update information before the ansible troubles—"

"Er . . . yes."

"This ship, *Fair Kaleen,* is now returned to the Vatta Transport list; in order to prevent confusion, I intend to re-register it under a new name."

The face on the screen looked both confused and cross. "But who are you? What authority do you have?"

"I'm Kylara Vatta," Ky said. "My father was Gerard Vatta, chief financial officer of Vatta Enterprises, which included Vatta Transport, Ltd. That list from Vatta should have included a brief bio and visual—"

"Well . . . yes . . . but what are you doing with that ship? How did you get it?"

"My cousin Stella and I have been authorized by Vatta headquarters—" If any such thing still existed. "—to reestablish Vatta trading routes and recover any Vatta ships we can locate. I also hold a letter of marque from Slotter Key, which authorizes me to take prizes. Osman is dead; this was a Vatta ship until he stole it; I have returned it to Vatta service."

"It's an armed vessel," the officer said.

"Yes, of course," Ky said. "Osman was a pirate."

"You haven't disarmed it."

"No. As I said, I hold a letter of marque—"

"Your weapons must be locked down and sealed; we must inspect the seals. An inspection team will board before you dock at the station."

"Of course," Ky said.

"Now—what was the ansible status at Rosvirein when you left?"

"The ansibles at Rosvirein were working while we were

docked there, but we left because we were informed by Rosvirein authorities that a threat existed, and we observed a ship apparently heading for their financial ansible just before transition to jump."

"Do you have any recorded evidence of this?"

"I can make a copy of our scan log," Ky said. "There was some exchange of fire—"

"How many invaders?"

"Three ships came through in formation; that's when Rosvirein advised all outsystem ships at the station they must either leave or stay for the duration of whatever happened. I chose to leave; I'd been caught in trouble before, at Sabine. Rosvirein had their own ships shadowing the first three, and everyone else had been told to lock down their weapons and stay out of the way. We were a little more than a day out of Rosvirein Main Station when four more ships jumped in and fired on one of the Rosvirein defense batteries. Then one of the ships in the departing line veered off and appeared to be headed for the financial ansible. That's all I know."

The man grimaced. "I doubt that. Someone like you, in a ship like that . . . all right, I'll give your ship provisional clearance to our main station; you'll have to halt ten thousand kilometers out for boarding by a weapons inspection team. Resistance to boarding will be interpreted as hostile intent, and you will be subject to severe measures . . . is that clear?"

"I'm not going to object to your weapons team inspection," Ky said. "I already told you that."

"Then you will be cleared for docking, but I warn you, you had better stay out of trouble. We don't tolerate subversives."

"Subversives?"

"Half the rabble we get from Rosvirein are troublemakers," the man said. "Organized crime is rife over there; pirates come and go without hindrance. You say you are legitimate but you're in a very dubious position, Captain Vatta."

"I'm not your enemy," Ky said. "The pirates are my enemies; they killed my parents; they tried to destroy my family's business."

He didn't respond to that, but continued. "Your ship's navigational computer has received the assigned course data. Proceed."

As ordered, *Fair Kaleen* slowed to a crawl and finally parked at zero relative velocity to the weapons inspection team's shuttle. Ky extended the new docking tube that had been replaced along with the air lock, and aired it up; a team of eight came aboard. Sealing the weapons took almost two hours, but the inspection team, unlike the Customs officer, showed no excessive suspicion. "Welcome to Sallyon, then," their officer said as he prepared to take his team back to their shuttle. "Local Traffic Control will guide you in."

Onstation formalities, once they were docked, went smoothly. Clearly trade was down; the station wasn't crowded with ships, and they had been assigned a berth in a section normally reserved for passenger liners "to balance mass," as the stationmaster explained. Ky looked over the list of ships onstation, and was startled to notice one with Slotter Key registry: *Sharra's Gift,* commanded by an N. W. Argelos. Maybe it would have news from home.

The officer at the head of the ship's gangway had a very military set to his shoulders; the crew were brisk and businesslike.

Ky walked up to the dockside barrier, gave her name, and asked to speak to the captain.

The young woman with the compad looked her up and down and called to the man at the gangway. "Visitor to see the captain."

He came nearer. "Your business, please?"

Ky felt herself straightening even more. "My name is Ky Vatta; we just arrived from Rosvirein. I'm from Slotter Key and saw that this ship also carried Slotter Key registry. I'd like to meet with your captain to exchange information important to our system."

"Vatta, eh? How long have you been away from Slotter Key?"

"I lifted from home on seventeen Berith, last year," she said. "I know about the attacks on Vatta headquarters and personnel; my father—Gerard Vatta, the CFO—was killed along with my mother when our home was destroyed."

"I see. Wait here, please; I'll contact our captain." He touched his temple, indicating an implant call. Ky eyed the dockside. *Sharra's Gift* was onloading sealed pallets that looked remarkably like arms. "You can come aboard," the officer said. "Captain Argelos will see you, but he can give you only a half hour."

"Thank you," Ky said. She nodded to the Slotter Key flag painted beside the hatch; inside, a young woman waited to lead her to the bridge.

Captain Argelos was a thickset man near her father's age, black hair streaked heavily with white. "So you're Gerry's daughter," he said, shaking his head. "That was a bad business, the attack on your family. My condolences, Captain."

Tears stung her eyes; she blinked them back. It was the first time anyone had said the conventional words, offered the conventional sympathy. "Thank you," she said.

He sat in silence a moment, looking to one side. Then he nodded, as if coming to some conclusion. "It has made us all nervous," he went on. "To think that our Spaceforce could not protect our citizens on our home planet—"

"I can imagine," Ky said.

"I don't know—Vatta has never been part of—but are you aware of Slotter Key's privateer program?"

"Yes," Ky said and offered an explanation she hoped would make sense to him. "I was at the Spaceforce Academy before I joined the family business."

"Ah," he said. "Then you know that Slotter Key privateers operate most of the time as ordinary traders or freight carriers. Pirates never knew where we were, how many we were, or which we were. We have broad discretionary powers, and we carry sufficient weaponry to make us a match for most pirates. But now . . . it's clear that something has changed, that pirates are operating in larger groups."

"You're telling me that you yourself are a privateer?" Ky said.

"Yes, I am," he said. "I am trusting you with this information, to explain why, although we share the same flag, I cannot afford to be associated with you at this difficult time." He sighed, and rubbed one hand over his hair. "When the trouble started, I wanted to offer assistance to any Vatta ship we met—serve as an escort, lend some of our personnel for security duties and the like—but my Spaceforce adviser argued against it. Strongly. We were here to protect Slotter Key shipping, I said to him, but he said that was the wrong way."

"And what did he say was the right way?" Ky asked, keeping her voice light. Was this man's Spaceforce adviser in league with the enemy?

"Hunting for the pirates," he said. "Which we did. We found some, too, but they were in numbers we couldn't match. Nor can you, Captain Vatta. It's suicide to try. If all of us—all the Slotter Key privateers, that is—were a single fleet, it would still be risky."

"Space warfare is always *risky*," Ky said from a dry mouth. "But sometimes it's necessary." She drew a deep breath. "So—you have information about the way the pirates are operating now?"

"Yes. Unfortunately, I have no way to get it to Slotter Key, with the ansibles down, other than going there. Without guidance from the government my options are limited—"

"What about other privateers? Do you know where they are? What they know?" Despite herself, she could hear in her voice a rising excitement.

"No . . . we use commercial ansibles to communicate, the same as everyone else. Two ports back I ran into another of us, but he didn't know any more than I did."

"You didn't think of working together, combining your forces?"

"Two of us against pirate fleets that might be as big as fifteen or twenty? What good would that do? If we can get in touch with Slotter Key again . . . when the ansibles come back up . . . if ISC can even do that much . . ." He scrubbed at his hair again, a man clearly nearing the end of his rope.

"Who's your adviser?" Ky asked. "Maybe it's someone I knew—"

"I don't know if I should tell you. I'll have to talk to him. I think I'll just go home, see what the government says. If they want us to combine—"

"If they're not compromised," Ky said.

"Compromised?" His brows rose.

"You said yourself it bothered you that they weren't able to protect citizens onplanet. What that says to me is that someone got to the government at some level.

Someone wasn't doing their job. Perhaps someone didn't want to do their job."

He scowled at her. "That's—you're asking me to believe that the government *wanted* Vatta attacked?"

"Not officially, no. But pressure could have been applied. What if someone knew about the change in pirate tactics, knew that Slotter Key's insystem defense couldn't stand against a pirate fleet, and was offered the choice— sacrifice one family, or lose everything—"

"That couldn't . . ." His voice trailed away; he looked down. When he looked at her again, his eyes were troubled. "Is our local defense really that weak?"

"Ask your adviser," Ky said. "But it's not just Slotter Key's problem. Ansibles are down all over; other governments may be under pressure." She stopped, switching internal gears. "Did you ever hear of a pirate named Gammis?"

His expression changed. "Gammis? Gammis Turek? Nasty fellow, that one. Ten, twelve years ago we almost got him ourselves, but he got away. Left us a message at the next station we came to, threatening all sorts of things. I didn't pay much attention—we'd won, after all—but I started hearing things from other captains. Two years later, one of my crew turned up missing, and four days later station police found the body. Flayed. With a recording of what had been done stuffed in the mouth. Others have had similar experiences after a run-in with him."

"I think he's behind this," Ky said. "We had a rene- gade Vatta—a distant cousin of mine, ousted from the family. He stole one of our ships—"

"Osman Vatta," Argelos said, nodding. "We knew about him; your family put out a bulletin years ago."

"He came after me," Ky said. "Vengeance on my father and uncle; I think he's the source of the attacks on Vatta—

the reason for choosing Vatta, I mean. But he wasn't working alone. He was under someone else, and I think that someone else was named Gammis."

"I suppose that could be," he said. "What made you suspect Gammis?"

"After Osman died," Ky said, "I started looking for the person behind him . . ."

"Osman's dead? How did that happen?"

"I killed him," Ky said. "Surely you recognized the ship I came in on."

A slow flush rose to Argelos' cheeks. "Yes, but—"

"And you must have wondered if another Vatta had gone renegade, if I was perhaps his daughter or something—"

"Not after learning you were Gerry's daughter," he said. "But . . . yes. That's certainly what my adviser thought."

"I can't imagine any reason for attacking only Vattas— and attacking them so thoroughly, in so many places— other than personal grudge. At any rate, when Osman and I met up, I was able to kill him and capture his ship."

He nodded. "Where did you have it adjudicated? Any problems with the courts?"

"I claimed it as a prize," Ky said. His eyes widened; she grinned, enjoying his shock. "I have a letter of marque, too, Captain Argelos. I don't know why, or how, but it was waiting for me on Lastway."

"But Vattas have never been privateers—"

"I know. But there it is, so I took over *Fair Kaleen* as my prize."

"And no one gave you trouble about it?"

She wasn't going to talk about Garth-Lindheimer. "They weren't too happy at Rosvirein, but they agreed it was legal. And business is business."

"This is a dangerous time, Captain Vatta," Argelos said.

"I don't think business as usual is a good model. I will consult with my adviser and be in contact, but do not expect much, would be my advice. I believe he would have doubts about the validity of your letter of marque, as, quite frankly, do I." His expression made it clear that was the end of his patience.

"You can come aboard and look at it," Ky said. "Thank you for your time, Captain Argelos. I hope to hear from you soon."

A few hours later, Argelos contacted her and asked permission to come to her ship. Ky agreed willingly, hoping this meant a positive response. When he came aboard, his face showed no warmth.

"My Spaceforce adviser thinks you're crazy," Argelos said. "Just out for revenge for your parents' deaths. I told him what you said, and he swears your letter of marque must be forged. Vattas were never privateers, he says, just as I said."

Ky nodded to the frame on the wall. "There it is. See for yourself."

"If you'll pardon me . . ."

"Of course."

"Let's see, now . . ." Argelos was up, peering closely at the letter of marque. He had a small tube in his hand that Ky guessed was some instrument for determining the validity of the document. "Did you study much about the privateer system? How it works in practice?"

"No. Borderline pirates, is what we were told. We certainly were not told that they were an integral part of Slotter Key's defense system. That came as a complete surprise."

"Um. This reads just like mine. Superficially at least it seems to be the same. Impressions the right depth; ink and paper the right kind. A good forgery, if it's not genuine. I have to wonder, though, if the government was removing protection from your family as you suggest, why it would give you a letter of marque."

"I wondered that, too, frankly," Ky said. "I wondered if it might be a fake, intended to get Vattas into even more trouble, but it came from a source I can hardly doubt."

"Can you tell me what?"

"Spaceforce," Ky said. "Someone I know personally."

His brows went up. "Spaceforce? Are you sure?"

"Yes. The source was . . . unimpeachable."

"I don't think I understand at all," he said. "Unless someone's feeling guilty. Are you fully aware of all the law governing privateers?"

"No, no more than I knew about how privateers work. I hoped to find someone from home who could help me out with that. You're the first I've found."

"Hmmm. I suppose it wouldn't hurt to send you a copy of the pertinent regulations and things. But about working together—"

"Perhaps if I talked to your adviser, I could explain—"

"He wants nothing to do with you. He was quite adamant on that point; apparently he thinks some past contact would . . . er . . . contaminate, is the way he put it, any cooperative action."

"He knew me?" Ky asked. "He was at the Academy?"

"Or on one of the training ships. I'm not sure which; he declined to say. He considers you a loose cannon, that much is certain. Overenthusiastic and not overhonest, he said. He's only been assigned to me within the past year; my former adviser developed health problems and had to take medical leave."

Ky immediately thought of her nemesis at the Academy, the cadet whose lies to her had caused her expulsion, but he should not have graduated yet. Who could this be?

"I don't see that, myself," Argelos went on. "And young-sters can mature, grow some sense. I was wild enough, in my young days. Still . . . I'm not ready to go against his advice."

Ky tried again. "Sir, I still say we should work together— all the privateers—to take care of these pirates. I think it's essential—"

"That can't possibly work."

"Why not?"

"Well . . . as I said, there aren't enough of us. Not from Slotter Key alone, anyway. And we don't have any way to communicate. And privateers from other systems aren't likely to cooperate—"

Ky wondered if this was the right time to play her best card. Surely it couldn't hurt. "We can solve the commu-nications problem."

His brows went up. "Really? How?"

"Captain Argelos, have you ever heard of shipborne ansibles?"

He scowled at her. "Ansibles on ships? That's not ISC technology. Do you have any idea what kind of trouble we'd be in—?"

"The pirates have them," Ky said. "How else do you think they coordinated their attacks? Besides, we found a number of them on Osman's ship."

"But the ISC will interdict our home world if we use non-ISC communications—"

"No, they won't," Ky said. "They haven't been able to protect the system ansibles. That was the source of their monopoly—they could supply, and protect and main-tain—that vital system. Now they've failed—not just in one system, and not just for a short period. It's been over half a standard year, and dozens of systems are still cut off. Systems will have to protect themselves. They won't

care what ISC says, if they have another way to communicate."

"Do . . . do these work just like system ansibles?" Clearly
he was interested, leaning forward, eyes alert.

"Not exactly," Ky said. "ISC has set things up so that
lightspeed communications can interface with only those
system ansibles installed by ISC—ansibles manufactured
with preset origination codes specific to each customer."

"Then they're useless—"

"No. What it means is that we can't connect directly
to system communications webs with these ansibles, but
ship-to-ship communication is quite possible, as is ship-
to-system-ansible if the system ansible is functioning. It's
a parallel system."

"How hard is it to install? To operate?"

"Osman's ship had one installed," Ky said. "We haven't
had to do an installation, but I do have a manual for both
installation and operation."

"I would worry about detection," he said. "How do you
know that this device isn't transmitting your whereabouts
to the pirates? System ansibles have a locator code."

"We're still alive," Ky said. "I imagine that if the pirates
knew where my ship was, they'd have attacked me by now."

"Except that you killed Osman, you say. That might
give them pause."

"Not if they're as strong as you say," Ky said. "You said
they could gather ten or fifteen ships at a time; no one
ship would stand a chance against those odds."

"What's the difference between their protection racket
and what you propose?"

"A true interstellar space navy subordinate to civilian
governments? Quite a lot. The pirates are saying *Pay us or
we'll attack you.* I'm saying *Fund a space navy and they'll
attack the pirates or anyone else.*"

"But both cost the citizens directly."

"Sure they do. But in one case the citizens get to choose who protects them, and how. They agree on price beforehand."

"You make sense, Captain Vatta, but I still . . ." His voice trailed away. "I'm still bound to listen to my adviser. I can try to talk to him, but . . . I don't know."

Ky sensed that she had pushed him as much as she could; she hoped he would come to agree with her later.

"Thank you for coming, Captain Argelos," she said. "I understand your concerns, and hope we can continue this conversation another time."

His face showed relief; he shook her hand before leaving.

A few days later, Ky had just finished her daily inspection of the Environmental section when an alarm called her forward.

"What's happened?" Ky asked, coming onto the bridge.

"Empire Line's *Princess Philomena* just arrived insystem, squalling like a banshee," Rafe said. "Apparently the pirates hit Bissonet and have taken over the government—blew through the planetary space militia as if they weren't there. Threatened to scorch the cities if the government didn't give in. They're imposing tariffs and blowing up ships that don't cooperate. Just like they did to Vatta, they're saying."

"As we expected," Ky said. "Did they have a name for themselves?"

"The Deepspace Benevolent Association. Commanded by—again no surprise—one Gammis Turek." He nodded at the screen. "This is what he looks like, they think."

He was tall, dark, and missed handsome by only a small margin.

"He's probably charming," Ky said. "Rogues often are."

"Ouch," Rafe said, glancing at her and away. "Actually, they're saying he's terrifying. Can go from calm to hysterical in a nanosecond, and kills on whim."

"Ummm." Ky studied the picture. He looked older than she was, younger than Osman or her father. He wore an outfit that looked like leather or a good synthetic, the deep burgundy jacket decorated with strips of metal. Probably bonded to personal armor. The pants, an even darker shade not quite black, had a burgundy stripe up the outer leg. Black boots, of course. One hand gloved, with metallic strips that were probably useful in a bar fight. The other bare, showing a tattoo, the design half hidden in this view. "He's certainly dressing the part, isn't he? Big bad pirate chief."

"I suppose. Yes. Only wants a hat with a feather."

"He'll have it on his helmet," Ky said. "Flamboyance is useful, of course."

"Yes. There's only one vid clip of any of his people . . ." Rafe called up the next image. Turek was standing, arms crossed, while two men in burgundy shipsuits seemed to be searching someone, and a third read from a list.

"Same color, different fabric," Ky said.

"I never knew you were so interested in clothes," Rafe said.

"Clothes are data," Ky said. "He's chosen those clothes for a reason; if we understand that, we know something about him. We can see, for instance, that he prefers a showier material for his outfit than they wear. No problems with privilege, I'd say. The color—that's trickier. If we knew where he was from, what his background was, that would help. Colors mean things to people, but not the same thing to all people."

"Red without having to flaunt it?" Hugh suggested.

"He's not worried about flaunting," Ky said. "He's a

peacock for vanity, I'd say. No, the burgundy has a reason. Red plus. Fire and smoke? No, he'd go more orange. Red and black, maybe . . . danger and death. Interesting."

"I don't see what difference it makes what he wears," Martin said. "What he does tells us who he is, what he's really like."

"What he wears tells us who he thinks he is," Ky said. "Military psych class—understand your enemy's viewpoint."

"Give me enough weapons and I don't need to understand my enemy," Martin said. "Just blow 'em away."

"Understand them, and they'll put themselves in your sights," Ky said. "Much more efficient."

"I suppose," Martin said, grinning.

"I would not have suspected you of subtlety, Captain," Rafe said. The others gave him a sharp glance, but Ky laughed.

"Hardly that, Rafe. Simple good straightforward military analysis."

"Be that as it may, what are you going to do about this fellow?"

"Kill him," Ky said cheerfully. "When we can, at least."

The Captains' Guild buzzed like a kicked beehive. Insystem captains, long-haul captains, all talking at once by the noise level. Ky signed in with the reception clerk. "Any chance of a table for one in the dining hall?"

"Another hour, then yes, Captain Vatta."

"Very good. Put me on the list, please." She glanced around; the bar was jammed—clearly no seats there.

"Captain Vatta!" There, across the reception area, she caught sight of Captain Argelos. "A word, if you please."

She noticed as she moved toward him that a convenient lane opened up for her. No one else spoke to her, but they were obviously aware of her presence. No wonder: he had called aloud.

"You've heard about the *Philomena,* of course . . . ," he began.

"Yes. The whole Bissonet system attacked, the government falling . . ."

"What you said before . . . you were serious?"

"About privateers combining to make common cause? Yes, completely." Around them, conversations had muted; she was aware of that, as if she could see ears elongating and waving in the breeze.

"Captain Bisdin says the pirates had a whole fleet. Fourteen ships at least. There's no way one of us could meet that alone and survive."

"Ummm." Ky made the noise just to encourage him to keep talking.

"It'd take more of us . . . more than just you and me."

"Yes, it would," Ky said.

"I don't see how . . . we don't even know where the others are. And I don't know how to fight a fleet action."

"I do," Ky said.

His eyes widened. "You—? You expect to command?"

Now a circle of silence surrounded them; she could hear faint shushing noises toward the edges of the room. This was not the best moment to publicize her plan.

"Perhaps we should discuss this somewhere else," Ky said.

Argelos flushed and his mouth tightened. Then he said, "All right. Where?"

"I'm dining here, when a table opens up. After that, you'd be welcome to visit my ship."

"We could share a table," he suggested.

Was that too eager? Was he perhaps more than another privateer captain? She smiled at him anyway. "I make it a rule not to discuss business during meals," she said. "But aside from that, we could indeed share a table."

"Excuse me," said a woman who'd been a few feet away. "You're one of the Vatta family?"

"Yes," Ky said, glad of the interruption.

"Was your ship attacked like other Vatta ships?"

"Yes," Ky said. "More than once—but unsuccessfully."

"She claimed Osman Vatta's ship as a prize," Argelos put in.

"Osman was the family black sheep," Ky said, answering the question not yet asked. "Apparently he joined the same group that attacked Bissonet, and we suspect he's the one who made the Vatta family their first target, in revenge for being kicked out." Heads nodded. Family conflict and vengeance were familiar experiences. "So he attacked me, and I managed to defeat him and take his ship."

"What about the ship you had before?" someone asked from the back of the circle.

"My cousin took it over," Ky said. "She had a contract to complete elsewhere."

"Do you think Vatta's no longer the target?" the woman asked.

"I think everyone's the target," Ky said. "All of us. These pirates want to run things for themselves, have everyone paying tribute to them. Our system governments wouldn't cooperate and fund a real space navy, so there's no interstellar force to deal with them."

"So it's hopeless." That was a stout older man. "We can't fight 'em; we might just as well pay what they demand."

"I didn't say it was hopeless," Ky said. This was not how she'd planned to launch her proposal, but it was a moment to seize.

"I say it is," the man said. Heads turned to watch him.

He shrugged. "They have more ships, more weapons. Bad enough when we met them only out in deep space, a long way from our ports. But if they can replace governments, destroy the little protection we had insystem, then there's no way we can move cargo without being seized and plundered."

"One government isn't the whole sector," Ky said. "The same thing that's kept us from having a real interstellar space navy makes it hard for them—they have to overthrow each system separately—"

"That won't be a problem," the man said. "My government was already worried just by the attacks on Vatta. Now, hearing that a whole system was overthrown, they'll be looking for ways to 'reach an accommodation' as soon as possible."

"Not my government," said the woman who had spoken first. "Kessel-Tinian doesn't cut deals with anybody." She glared at the man, who glared back.

"Are you saying my government—"

"Enough," Ky said. Somewhat to her surprise, they all fell silent and looked at her. "We won't solve this by bragging or by giving up—or by waiting for our governments to do it for us. They can't even communicate with one another while the ansibles are down."

"Well, you surely don't think *we* can do anything, do you?" asked a tall man. "We're just civilians; our ships don't have any weapons—"

"There are merchanters with armed ships," Ky said. "Think about it."

"Privateers!" the man said. "As bad as the pirates, the way I see it. Probably in league with them."

"Not all of them," Ky said. "I'm a privateer, and I'm not on their side."

Silence again. Then, "You?"

"Me."

"So . . . Slotter Key is standing up to the pirates? Then how come you Vattas were attacked?"

"Slotter Key sends out privateers—you all know that. That may be why a Slotter Key family was attacked. Bissonet doesn't license privateers, so we don't know whether the pirates would have insisted on taking them over."

"But how do you think we can fight back? Without weapons, without our governments supporting us?"

"Yes—is there really any hope?"

Ky looked around. It was absurd, the way they were watching her, as if some miraculous answer would appear on her forehead. "Of course there's hope," she said. "But it won't be easy . . ."

"You have a plan?"

"I have ideas," Ky said. "I'm not going to tell you everything about them here. One or more of you may be working with the pirates, after all."

A hiss of indrawn breath, and the crowd around her shifted, faces turning to eye their neighbors.

"You think one of us would help them?" That was the angry bald man.

Ky shrugged. "Someone who's been threatened, then offered immunity for spying on other captains . . . where better than the Captains' Guild, after all, for picking up all the gossip? We're not all saints, are we?" A chuckle at that. "So I'll tell you I think there's hope—the pirates aren't that strong yet, though if we wait until they've coerced a lot of systems into helping them they will be. I won't tell you more about my plans, not in an open gathering like this. But if you want to know more, talk to me quietly." She smiled at them, then said, "Excuse me, please."

*　　*　　*

The next morning, she was called to the stationmaster's offices.

"Captain Vatta, we have concerns." The stationmaster, two other men in civilian dress, and a woman in the uniform of the station police sat around the table of a small conference room. "Sit down, please." The chair indicated put her in bad light, but Ky sat down anyway.

"Concerns?"

"Yes. We understand that you are talking to ship captains about forming a fighting force."

Ky said nothing, but raised her brows.

"These rumors about pirate fleets—I'm sure they're exaggerated," the stationmaster said.

"You have contrary evidence?" Ky said.

"Well . . . we've never seen a pirate force larger than two ships, maybe three. Our local patrol ships are more than a match for them. We haven't had a successful pirate attack in decades."

"Do you think *Princess Philomena*'s captain is lying? He seems a very honest person to me," Ky said.

"Not lying," the stationmaster said. "But he doesn't have your background of military training. Whatever happened there, I'm sure he magnified it in his fear. Don't you find that happens more often than not?"

"Underestimating a threat causes as much trouble," Ky said. "Have you looked at Captain Bisdin's scan data?"

"No. It's only a civilian tradeship; the scan isn't as detailed and accurate—"

"I have," Ky said. Silence. They looked at each other. "There were indeed fourteen ships involved in the attack. Five others were insystem at the time. Three of those innocent ships were destroyed while Bisdin was in scan range. Captain Bisdin made it here; he doesn't know what happened to the fifth ship." She looked around the table. They were all a shade paler.

"But . . . but maybe that's all they wanted, a secure base—" That was one of the men.

The police officer turned on him. "All they wanted? Of course it's not all they wanted. You can't think they'll stop—"

"We can hope so," the man said. "I mean, it's too bad for Bissonet, but why would they need more than one system?"

Ky and the police officer locked gazes a moment; Ky shook her head. "You could ask that about humans in general. But more specifically, if their goal is control of interstellar shipping—an enormously profitable business—then interdicting one system at a time, while communications are down, would be the way to go about it. With the resources from such trade, they could rule the known universe."

"But surely—" the man began. The stationmaster held up his hand, and the man subsided.

"Captain Vatta, even if you're correct and there is evidence for concerted pirate activity . . . these are criminals. They won't hold together for long. There's no need for civilians to take on unauthorized military functions—"

"There's every need," Ky said. "Interstellar trade depends on secure ports of call, good communications, and minimal piracy in deep space. We are out of communication for days to weeks at a time in FTL flight, so that even when the ansible net is working, we need to know that the space we're coming to is secure from piracy. You don't know—none of us knows—where this pirate fleet will attack next. We don't know how many agents they may have on various worlds, who might cooperate with them. If they pick off the busiest ports, gain control of those governments, interstellar trade will collapse—and if it does, pirates will control your supply lines. When they control your supply lines, they control you."

"That's a scary scenario," the stationmaster said. "I still think it's unlikely. And I have concerns about civilians trying to take on military functions. It's too dangerous, a lot of untrained civilians putting weapons on their ships and going out to hunt pirates. Stirring up trouble, it seems to me, and the perfect way to get a lot of innocent people killed. Speaking as chair of the council, I want it stopped."

Ky bit back the angry words she wanted to say and tried instead to gauge the reactions of the rest.

"We have insystem patrol," the police officer said slowly. "We haven't had problems with pirates, and they'd find us a tough nut to crack. I admit a fleet of fourteen might stretch our resources, but I'm confident that we could handle it."

"If the system ansibles are still down, you'll be limited to lightspeed ship-to-ship communications," Ky said. "The pirates have shipboard ansibles."

"That's another thing," the stationmaster said. "You've told people this, but no one's ever heard of such things. What makes you think they're real?"

"The ship I captured has one," Ky said. "Complete with operating manual. Osman was a pirate, and in his data files I found evidence that he was working with—or for—a group headed by the same man Bisdin reported as the leader of the pirate fleet."

"It's absurd," one of the men said. "Ansibles are huge—massive—there's no way to fit one on a ship. The power supply alone—"

"Nevertheless," Ky said. "There's one on my ship."

"I don't care," the stationmaster said, putting both hands flat on the table. "This disruptive behavior has to stop, Captain Vatta. Even if the pirate threat is real, your course of action is not the right way to meet it. You're panicking people on this station; we're swamped with complaints and demands. We can strengthen our local force; we can hire mercenaries. We do not need—and will not put up with—a bunch of rogue traders trying to pretend they're a military force. If you persist in your attempt to persuade and organize the other captains, I will insist that you leave this system—or you will be arrested."

"I see," Ky said.

"No more meetings, no more clandestine visits to your ship—"

"Clandestine?" Ky let her voice express surprise. "There was no secrecy because there was no rule against such visits—"

"All right . . . but from now on they would be clandestine. Unless you are actively trading merchandise—nonmilitary merchandise—I want you off this station in forty-eight hours. And in that forty-eight hours I want no more of your rabble-rousing, is that clear?"

"Quite clear," Ky said. Anger roiled her stomach. How could they be so stupid? How could they not understand the traders' point of view, when they depended so on trade?

"You will be accompanied by a member of the station police, to ensure that you obey these strictures." The stationmaster glanced at the police officer, who looked less happy than before but nodded.

The meeting ended on that note; Ky managed to keep her temper in check until she was out the door.

TEN

The police spy—as Ky thought of him—assigned to her was a stolid young man who said very little. He followed her closely on her way back to dockside. When she turned into the Captains' Guild entrance, though, he put a hand on her arm.

"You're not supposed to talk to them."

"I have bills to pay in here, since we're leaving," Ky said. "Come with me and see."

"If you talk to the other captains—"

"I'm not forbidden to talk to them," Ky said, with waning patience. "Just to talk about certain things."

She stopped at the desk, checked her balance, and paid it. "Any other charges, I'll authorize payment by my bank," she said.

"That's fine," the clerk said. "You have a stack of messages—" He rummaged in the pigeonholes and pulled out a mix of data cubes and hardcopy messages.

"I'll take those," the policeman said, reaching out.

"No, you won't," Ky said, keeping a firm grip on them. "The stationmaster said nothing about interdicting my mail."

"I'll have to ask—"

"Ask away." Ky put the messages into her case and

locked it. The policeman looked blank: accessing his skullphone, she assumed. She decided to make her own call,
and reached the stationmaster's office assistant. "I need
to speak to the stationmaster."

"Who is this—oh. Captain Vatta. Is there a problem?"

"My escort tried to take my mail. I don't believe that's
appropriate or necessary."

The stationmaster's voice replaced his assistant's.
"You're not supposed to communicate with other captains—"

"About the topic you named, yes. You didn't say I couldn't
pick up my mail, something other people sent me."

"About the conspiracy . . ."

"It's not a conspiracy, and I expect the mail has more
to do with trade. I had deals pending with several onstation merchants."

"I'd like to be sure of that."

"Sir." Ky squeezed her eyes shut for a moment. "I am
trying to comply with your request that I leave this station. That means closing accounts, finalizing pending
deals, and so on. I agreed not to continue organizing a
useful resistance to the pirates, but I did not agree to not
doing business with my customers. Let your man do his
job but let me do mine."

"As long as it is just business . . ."

"It's just business."

A dramatic sigh. Then, "Very well, Captain Vatta. I
will not insist on monitoring all your incoming messages,
but this does not mean you are free to continue as you
were—"

"I understand," Ky said.

"Good. I'll inform the police."

Very shortly, the policeman turned back to Ky. "All right.
They say you can keep your mail."

"Thank you," Ky said. Several captains she knew had come into the reception area in the meantime, but seeing the policeman they stayed at a distance. Ky made no effort to contact them. Instead she spoke to the clerk. "Post *Fair Kaleen* for departure in thirty-six to forty-eight hours, please."

"Destination?"

"Haven't decided yet, but we've made all the profit we can here. I'll let you know when I've decided."

"Any open cargo space?"

"Yes, four cubic meters. Go on and post that. I'd like to travel full, if I can."

Back at the ship, Ky told the policeman to wait on the dockside.

"But they said—"

"They can monitor my communications with other ships," Ky said. "I have no objection to that." She did, but protesting would do no good, she knew. "My decks are foreign territory, however; you have no jurisdiction there."

"I'll have to call."

"Go ahead." Ky went on in, told her security detail to shut the inner hatch, and went straight to the bridge, where she placed calls to Argelos and others who had shown interest. "I've been asked to leave the system," she said. "I cannot discuss it with you. I'm deciding where to go next; that will be posted at the Captains' Guild. I do have four cubic meters of open cargo space, should anyone want to ship that amount to my destination."

Her implant pinged her, warning of an incoming priority call. It would be the stationmaster, she was sure. It was. "I told you—" he began.

"I have told other captains that I'm leaving. I'm sure you monitored the transmissions—"

"You said you were asked to leave."

"Yes, because I was. I told the truth."

"You're trying to drum up sympathy—"

"No, I'm not. They'd figure out that much on their own; they're not stupid, Stationmaster. I was asked to leave; I'm leaving; I have some cargo space open if anyone has cargo going my way."

"Which is?"

"I'll decide that in the next twenty-four hours. Probably less. I'll post it. Whatever you think, Stationmaster, I am not engaged in conspiracies."

"So you say," he said, and closed the connection.

"So . . . do I surmise that they're annoyed with you for telling the truth?" Rafe asked.

"Something like that," Ky said. She was suddenly, ravenously hungry. "Lee, would you ask someone to bring me something from the galley?"

"Sure, Captain."

"Which truth upset them?" Rafe asked.

"They'd rather not believe the pirate fleet is a real threat. They started out wanting to believe that the *Philomena*'s captain just panicked and there weren't that many pirates. I pointed out that his scan data showed pretty clearly how many there were. Then they shifted to the hope that the pirates would be satisfied with gobbling up one system. Or maybe the pirate alliance will fall apart because everybody knows pirates can't cooperate. But it wasn't even the reality of the pirate menace that had them so upset. It was the thought of mere civilian traders daring to work together—form an armed merchant fleet—to fight off the pirates."

"It is an untried theory," Hugh said. Ky looked at him. "I'm not saying it won't work," he said. "Just that I can understand why it makes them nervous."

"Not just nervous. Hostile. I don't see why they can't understand that it's more dangerous to just sit and wait around. Unless they're all in league with the pirates—"

"Probably not," Rafe said. "Or the pirates would be here, and we'd be dead. I'd guess they're just worried and don't know what to do about it."

"So . . . how are we going to convince them?"

Rafe shrugged. "We can't. The pirates will, eventually."

"Too late, though," Ky said.

"Maybe. Maybe not. At any rate we've done what we can here. At least some of the other captains are thinking about the possibility. If enough do, what the local governments think won't matter. Of course, that's probably what the pirates thought, too. It's a copy of their strategy."

"Puts us behind, doesn't that?"

"Not really. Lead time is their one real advantage; they're outnumbered—"

"We think." Unwillingly, Ky found herself repeating Rafe's arguments back to him.

"Almost certainly. I'm willing to bet that at least half their fleet—probably almost all of it—was there in Bissonet. There are hundreds of merchant ships, several dozen privateers we know about, and that's not counting the mercenary forces."

"Which would be very expensive," Rafe said. "Who could afford to hire them?"

"Trying to do war on the cheap is what got us into this mess," Ky said. "Cost is why we don't have the kind of interstellar force that could control, if not wipe out, piracy. But since our governments don't see it that way, we'll have to convert them." She stretched. "But the first thing to do is pick a destination. I want to go back to Slotter Key and find out what is going on there."

"I don't think that's wise," Rafe and Hugh said together;

Martin nodded. They looked at each other, then at her.

"I need to know why I have this letter of marque," Ky said. "And why the government cut off our family. Who was bribed?"

"Jealousy?" Rafe asked.

"I don't think so," Ky said. "We were rich and powerful, yes, but not a threat to the government."

"You are now," Rafe said. "Seriously. They turned their backs on you; your family was nearly destroyed. Now you come back, and they see vengeance in your eyes."

"I don't—" Ky stopped. "I suppose . . . I do want revenge for what they did. If they did anything themselves. Mostly I want answers. I want to know why."

"With all due respect, Captain," Martin began. Ky nodded. "Fight your war first, then ask questions. If you go back and they arrest you—or even if they just rescind the letter of marque, which I think they would—who's going to take the fight to the pirates?"

Rafe nodded. Ky stared at the table a long moment. "You really think I can . . ."

"I don't think anyone else can," Rafe said. "If ISC had the capacity, the ansibles would be back up by now. And we—they—have always ignored everything but ISC property. That was partly to gain political support for maintaining the monopoly, sure, but it kept our costs in bounds. You not only saw what was needed—which a lot of people have done—but you've taken steps to start it."

"Not very effectively, so far," Ky said.

"Effective enough to get thrown out of a system," Rafe said. "That's a start. Stay away from Slotter Key until you can go there in strength."

"Where, then?" Ky said. She put the Traders' Directory in the cube reader and put it up on screen. "Where will the pirates go next and where should we go?" No one said anything, and after a few moments she answered her own questions. "If they can take over the backbone systems, they can interdict seventy percent of the trade . . . so I'd bet they won't leapfrog more than one of those systems . . . maybe just hit the next in line. Let's see . . . the jump-point index . . ." A complex graphic appeared onscreen, the tangle of lines representing mapped routes. "We don't have the resources to guard all the backbone systems— but they don't have the resources to attack them all, either. If we just knew where they were going next . . ." An idea hit her; she looked at Rafe. "Rafe, can we trace the other shipboard ansibles with ours? When they make contact, can we find out where they are?"

He pursed his lips. "We might . . . but not without letting them know where we are, and that we have the equipment."

"Oh. That won't work, then."

"It might, if we can figure out a way to fake the back-connection. Though of course they may have figured that out, too. They must know by now that Osman's dead and you have his ship. They'd know he had a shipboard ansible. They may or may not know about the others."

"Not a good idea, then," Ky said.

"Not unless I can figure out some way to protect our end. But I'll think about that."

"Back to basics," Ky said, staring at the graphic. "What will the enemy do next, and where, and what can we do to frustrate that?"

"If he has the resources to take more than one system at a time, I think he'd go for the big crossroads first. Cascadar. Moscoe Confederation. Blunt. Allray. Parry's World. All first-tier, all with multiple routes converging."

"Let's be extravagant and assume he has a hundred ships," Hugh said. "More than we think, but I'd rather overestimate him than underestimate him. Twenty ships per system . . . that's five. He needs to keep some at Bissonet. He might hit four . . ."

"What about ISC headquarters?" Ky said. "Nexus Two, isn't it?"

"They wouldn't—oh." Rafe looked blank for a moment. "I suppose they might try. Nexus Two is really our trade center, and we—they—do have a very good insystem defense capability."

"So did Bissonet," Ky said. "And the prize is much bigger if they could get control of the ansible system at its source. They've already shown negative control—they can make it unusable—but if they can turn it back on, there'll be those who think it doesn't matter who controls it as long as they keep it working. ISC's lost a lot of respect in these past few months."

Rafe nodded slowly. "Then I suppose I must agree that the interests of ISC now march with yours, Captain, and my duty to ISC is no longer in possible conflict. Though I don't think we should go charging off to Nexus Two, especially not if we're trailing a ragtag assembly of privateers. The ISC defense force is likely to shoot first and ask questions later."

"So where can we go to communicate with them and not be shot to pieces?"

"I'm sure they've repaired the Nexus system ansibles, if those ever went down," Rafe said. "Next over hubward would be Maricana." He pointed it out on the graphic. "Four jumps from here. It's pretty much a dead-end system; its only mapped routes are to Moscoe Confederation, which is how we'll have to go in, and Nexus."

"And Moscoe Confederation, you said, is one of the likely targets for the pirates. If they got that, then . . . it looks like Nexus is somewhat cut off."

"No, the Nexus jump points—there are two, though one is a very long way out—have five or six mapped routes."

Ky eyed the chart again. "We'll go to Moscoe," she said. "I'm not so sure about Maricana. Maybe the Moscoe ansibles will be working. Post the destination, Lee. It's far enough away that it ought to make these idiots happy."

In the next four hours, two captains called to offer cargo bound for Moscoe Confederation. Ky accepted both consignments, insisting that the shipper waive insurance coverage. As she'd expected, the station police insisted on inspecting the shipments.

"I'm already an armed vessel," Ky said. "What are you worried about?" But she told her crew to open the containers; she wanted to be sure what was in them, herself. One was full of implantable prostheses, each extremity or limb in its own sealed pouch of nutrient liquid. The consignee was the West Cascadia Rehabilitation Centre. Another was full of bioelectronic components going to the same customer. "I had no idea you had that level of expertise here," Ky said to the shipping agent.

"We don't," he said. "That's been waiting here for seventy standard days; the ship we were supposed to transfer to never came in. Yours is the first chance."

Ky was about six hours from undocking, well ahead of the deadline, when *Gary Tobai* appeared on longscan. Much as she had worried about Stella and the ship, this was a very inconvenient time to have them appear. She needed to talk to Stella, and she cursed herself for not having installed a shipboard ansible on the little ship. How would Stella deal with the suspicion she herself had raised?

The stationmaster called her. "That is your confederate?"

"That's my *cousin*," Ky said. "The ship is an unarmed trader, as you can tell."

"But she is related to you. She must not pursue the same ends."

"I'm sure she won't," Ky said. "How could she? *Gary Tobai* has no weapons."

She had to undock long before Stella would arrive. This would not, she was sure, make Stella happy. Two days after undock, she was close enough to use short-range secure com to contact her. A strange man's face appeared on the screen, but he nodded and quickly fetched Stella.

"You're leaving again," Stella said before Ky could speak. She looked very composed, which with the younger Stella could mean either calm or anger.

"There's a situation," Ky said. "Stella, do you have the resources for another jump?"

"Afraid not." Stella sounded uncharacteristically curt. Ky winced inwardly. She did not need an angry Stella to cope with. "I've got new crew; it cuts our range somewhat. Why?"

"This system's not entirely friendly. If you can load what you need and leave, that would be a good idea. I'm headed for Moscoe Confederation. I have more information on the people we're interested in. That system may be dangerous, so come in carefully."

"Every system you've been in seems to be dangerous; Rosvirein wasn't exactly a vacation spot."

"I'm sorry—I tried to wait for you but they insisted I leave—"

"Apparently you know how to make yourself unwelcome," Stella said. "Some ships were still docked there when we arrived; *they* said undocking was optional."

Stella had not been with her at Sabine; she could not understand the compulsion to get back into space, to have maneuverability. "I'm sorry," Ky said again.

"We made a good profit anyway," Stella said. "I sold

over half the toilets." Toilets? What was she talking about? "I don't suppose you've had time to do any actual trading . . ."

"I did," Ky said, stung. "Didn't you see the balance in the accounts on Rosvirein? I left them for you."

"And I suppose that appalling woman who showed up to ask if I had any data for sale is where it came from?" Stella's expression was that of someone finding cat vomit in her shoe.

"Appalling woman?" For a moment Ky couldn't imagine what Stella was talking about. Then she remembered Rafe's contact. "Oh . . . Amy? Why did she come to you?"

"Because, she said, it might run in the family. I don't know what you sold her and I don't want to know, but . . . she said there was someone went missing right after you left. She was sure that's why you'd run out before I got there."

"I didn't run out, Stella! I left because I didn't want to be locked on to the station if you arrived in the middle of some row, and you needed me—"

"So—if I needed you, you'd be here in Sallyon, instead of where I was. Just like now, when I might need you in Sallyon, you're leaving for somewhere—where was it again?"

"The Moscoe Confederation." Ky took a breath. "And before you say anything more, you need to know what's happened." Stella opened her mouth; Ky held up a hand. "No, just listen. The pirates took over Bissonet System."

"What!"

"One of the Empire Line's fast passenger ships got away and brought the tale. We think they may hit the busier trade routes next."

"How many pirate ships?"

Maybe Stella was thinking again. Ky went on. "The passenger ship thought fourteen were at Bissonet, but Rafe thinks from the serial numbers that sixty shipboard ansibles are out there somewhere, and I don't know how accurate that ship's scan is."

"Oh, good," Stella said in a tight voice. "I'm glad we're still outnumbered enough to make it sporting."

Ky couldn't think of anything to say for a moment. Then Stella said, "I have a message for you from Quincy."

"What's that?"

"She said to tell you that I'm a lot more restful as a captain than you were, and so is the captain I hired, so she may not retire after all."

"I'm sure," Ky said.

"How's Rafe?" Stella asked with a tone so colorless it almost shrieked tension.

"Rafe's fine," Ky said. "Plotting, of course."

"Are you and he . . . uh . . . ?"

"No," Ky said firmly. "Why don't you tell me what happened with you?"

Stella gave a concise, organized report that Ky could tell had been thought out well in advance. Moneys received from the convoy captains, moneys paid to the Mackensee escort, trade goods sold, cargo purchased, new crew hired.

"Sounds good, Stella. Could you tell how the Mackensee commanders were, at the end?"

"How angry they were with you, you mean? I think it was somewhere between angry and admiring. They were nice to me. Helped me vet the new crew, for instance."

"That's good. Look, Stella, I'd rather you didn't go to one of the obvious high-risk systems. Either follow me to Moscoe, or you could go back to Slotter Key."

"No," Stella said. "I'm not going back until we have more to show. Aunt Grace would have my hide. I'll go with you to the Moscoe Confederation, but I still need to resupply here."

"All right. Be meek and mild; they think anyone associated with me is a dangerous rabble-rouser."

"You? What have you been up to?"

"Nothing but a little common sense. Didn't suit. If I were you I'd get in and get out. Don't talk to other captains much."

"Fine. See you there, then." Stella signed off. Ky couldn't tell if Stella was still as angry as she'd seemed at first, or if the exchange of information at the end had calmed her down.

The intermediate jumps and transits between Sallyon and the Moscoe Confederation passed without incident. None of the system ansibles was functional, and Ky did not pause to let Rafe work his magic on them. There was an ISC ship in one of the unpopulated systems; it seemed to pay no attention as they translated in and out again.

"At least they're trying," Rafe said.

"Yes, but service has been interrupted a long time now. People will be ready for alternatives, who never thought of it before."

"Well, they shouldn't. We—ISC—has a huge network and has delivered reliable service for a very long time. It would cost far too much for anyone else to duplicate that." For a rebel, Rafe could be remarkably conventional, Ky thought, watching his face. He flushed suddenly. "Showing my roots, I suppose."

"A little, yes. The thing is . . . who are your potential competitors? You mentioned the research division inside ISC, the ones who wanted to spread the newer technology. Would they be capable of getting a competing system in place?"

"I don't know. Maybe. Not sectorwide, but for a few systems . . ." He sighed. "I just don't like any of this."

"No one in their right mind would," Ky said, thinking of her family dead and scattered.

Their transition to Moscoe Confederation space went smoothly; the communications boards lit instantly. "Ansible's up," Rafe said. "Local authorities are demanding identification and want to speak to you."

"Interesting," Ky said. "Hook me up, then." When he had made the connection, she entered the ship data, her name, and waited for an answer. It came so quickly she knew there must be a deep-system watchpost as at Sallyon; the face on the screen was a balding, bearded man in a forest-green-and-blue uniform.

"On our records, the ship identified as *Fair Kaleen* is captained by Osman Vatta, not Kylara Vatta. Explain." No *please,* Ky noticed.

"Osman Vatta stole this ship decades ago from Vatta Transport," Ky said. She found it easier to tell the story each time, and ended with, "So I claimed the ship as a prize under UCC regulations, and by right as a representative of the original owners."

"Only privateers can claim prizes," came the reply. "Legitimate Vatta ships have never been privateers."

"I have a letter of marque from Slotter Key," Ky said. She transmitted an image of it. "It will of course be available for inspection by your Immigration people."

"And it will be inspected," he said. "Do you carry any cargo, or are you here just to bounty-hunt?"

"I have cargo consigned to a rehab facility here," Ky said. "Originally shipped from Goskone, with transfer at Sallyon, but there were no ships bound this way until mine."

"Ah . . ." He looked down for a moment, then nodded. "Yes. There's an overdue shipment of prosthetics and bio-electronics." His voice warmed slightly. "You may proceed on your present course; you will obey Traffic Control for an approach lane; you will lock down all weapons systems on their command. Do you agree?"

"Yes," Ky said. "I noticed your system ansible is functional; do you have a list of live nodes?"

"Yes, but it may not be up to date. Slotter Key is still down, if you were thinking of reporting to your headquarters."

"You have heard about Bissonet . . ." Ky said.

"Yes. We are on full alert," he said. "If those scum try anything here, they'll be sorry. How did you hear?"

"An Empire Line passenger ship escaped the carnage and came screaming into my last port, Sallyon."

"Escaped or was sent?" he asked.

"Excuse me?" That was something Ky hadn't thought of.

"Wasn't there an Empire Line ship implicated in that mess at Sabine awhile back?"

"Yes, but—"

"And—wait a moment—weren't you there? A Vatta was, I know that, something starting with *K*—?"

"That was me," Ky said. "Yes. And the captain and a few officers of that Empire Line ship were apparently in league with a pirate. But I can't believe the Empire Line itself—"

"Fast ships, good reputation. Almost as good as Vatta Transport, before this started. I'm not saying management has anything to do with it, but a few captains suborned . . ."

"But why?"

"Figure it out, Captain Vatta. I have work to do." With that he cut off the contact.

Ky looked around the bridge. "Well, anyone else think that's simply paranoia, or does he have a point?"

Martin pursed his lips. "Anytime someone's supposedly

above suspicion, it's time to get suspicious, or that's what I learned working security for Spaceforce. Those are the ones that can really hurt you. The scallawags you're always keeping an eye on and have on a short leash. If there are enough Empire Line officers working with the pirates, that's as good as a secure courier service."

"So . . . maybe Bissonet wasn't actually attacked and taken over?"

"Or it was and the idea was to spread fear as widely as possible. Or maybe there were more ships there . . . the other ones we are pretty sure they have. Or maybe it all happened just as the man said, and it was an honest lucky escape."

Ky shook her head. "I need reliable data. I heard about the fog of war, but this is ridiculous. How long has it been since I started looking for answers, and all I have so far is Osman, who's dead, and the name of someone who might be the pirate leader. It's not enough!"

"Actually," Martin said, "we have a bit more than that, begging the captain's pardon. If you'll excuse me, I'll go do what I should've done already and pull some things together for you."

"Do that," Ky said. "While I try to figure out where to go next and what to do when ten thousand pirates show up on my tail."

Her father's implant gave her all the information Vatta Transport had on the Moscoe Confederation. Three inhabited worlds, one of them the second largest moon of a gas giant. Traffic Control directed her to the approach lane for Cascadia, the most populous, where the rehabilitation center was located. It was a long insystem run, as Cascadia was on the far side of its primary.

By the time they came to final approach, Ky was familiar with all the Traffic Control officers on the Cascadia lane. All had a family resemblance though they didn't look like clones. Tall, big-boned, muscular, fair-skinned, eyes from light brown through hazel to blue, hair from brown to reddish to blond, attractive in an outdoors sort of way, even though some of them clearly spent their careers on a space station. Her father's implant offered no clues to the consistency.

"Small gene pool to start with," Rafe suggested. "Amazing they aren't all idiots."

"Not with half-decent medical facilities," Ky said. "You know it's not that hard to select for specific characteristics. But why'd they pick this, I wonder. With their sun's spectrum, you'd think they'd have gone for higher skin melanin."

"They're not ugly," Rafe said.

"No . . . just wondering," Ky said. "Maybe it's a hereditary position, running Traffic Control. Stranger things have been done."

The screen lit again. "Hi, Captain," said the current duty officer, who had told Ky to call her Terri. "You're right on course, thanks. Six hours to dock. Please confirm weapons lockdown."

"Weapons locked down," Ky said. "Here's the visual." She had recorded a visual of the weapons racks with seals in place.

"Very good," Terri said. "Now eight seconds of reverse on your insystem, please, on my mark . . . three, two, one, mark."

Lee had complied with this, and Terri nodded as the numbers came up.

"That's great," she said. Ky began to feel like a child whose teacher is trying to coax her past some childish fear. "I'll be calling for three more reverses—in about forty-five minutes, then in another several hours, then the final one to match our station for docking. In case you're wondering, these early ones are to clear other traffic."

Ky wondered whether to say she knew that already; her own nearscan showed the other ships. But best let Traffic Control do its thing, she decided.

The six hours seemed to last twelve, but the planet grew steadily larger on scan, its readouts showing the usual human-habitable world with plenty of open water and an oxygen-nitrogen atmosphere. Its continents were bigger than Slotter Key's; its oceans speckled with fewer island chains; its ice caps were substantially larger. At last they were close enough to see the main orbital station on external visuals. Ky blinked. Though many small orbital stations had unusual geometry, usually for some specific commercial purpose, most main stations, where interstellar trade came in, followed a standard design: they looked like giant wheels or disks rolling slowly through space. Large stations simply "stacked" the disks on their central axis.

"Ummm . . . Terri?" Ky said.

The woman laughed. "You saw it, did you? Know what it is?"

"Not really," Ky said.

"It's a tree. An Old Earth conifer: our emblem. Old Mick, our founder, said now that everyone had artificial gravity generators, there was no reason why stations had to look like wheels. He got the design from a holiday ornament, he said."

Ky looked again. Two isosceles triangles intersected at right angles, bisecting each other: the tree itself, she supposed. Their bases were toward the planet; the tip pointed away, toward deep space. A cylindrical section stuck out from the base of the triangles, and now that she looked closely, she could see that the cylinder continued at least partway to the apex of the triangles. Its axis lay across her flight path, the wider base gradually obscuring her view.

As she neared it, she could see that the jagged "branches" were docking slots—this unlikely shape provided docking slots for a hundred ships, and they could access their slots without interference with other traffic.

"Pretty slick, isn't it?" Terri asked. Then, without waiting for an answer, she said, "Your tug's coming up on your starboard side. Split your screen and I'll introduce you."

Ky did so, and the tug captain turned out to be a strikingly handsome brown-skinned man with black hair and green eyes. So much for limited genetic pool. "Hi, Captain Vatta," he said. "I'm Tugmaster Stanish Madera. You're for North-third-four. Let's start getting you oriented to the Tree. The branches go out in four directions: we use north, south, east, west."

"I'm used to that," Ky said.

"Good. So you're on North, the third branch from the base, the fourth dock slot on North third. That's the outer slot. We assign dock slots on the basis of your reported mass, to balance the Tree, so if you have any doubt that your reported mass is correct, please let me know right away."

"It's correct as far as I know," Ky said.

"Good, then. Terri, we're ready for drive-cut."

"Captain, please cut your insystem drive."

"Drive shutdown confirmed," Ky said.

"I'll be grappling in five," Madera said. "Five, four, three, two, one, contact—"

"Confirm contact," Ky said as the ship's skin sensors reported it.

"You shouldn't feel a thing," Madera said. Ky watched the station loom closer and closer, until they appeared to be hanging motionless a meter away.

"Station grapples out," Madera said.

"Contact," said another voice. "Cascadia Station welcomes Captain Vatta and *Fair Kaleen*. Please remain as you are until we confirm docking complete." A longish pause, then, "Docking complete, Captain Vatta. You may extend your life-support and power lines for connection, please. Our next communication will be over your secured lines."

"Understood," Ky said. The screen flickered and went off, only to light again moments later as the dockside crew connected *Fair Kaleen*'s umbilicals to the station.

"Welcome again," the voice said, this time from the face on the screen, a female version of the tug captain's. "We will need you to give our Immigration officers access, please, within an hour, to inspect your weapons and ascertain crew identity."

ELEVEN

Ky wondered if the Customs officers would also show a family resemblance, or be more what she thought of as normally varied. The officers who waited on the dockside were all red-haired, though she didn't notice that for a moment because the biggest had what looked like silver horns curling around his head from his brow to his ears. Ky blinked, then realized what they were. Enhanced implant plug-ins, probably mobile sensors.

"Captain Vatta? I'm Senior Inspector Vaughn."

"Yes, I'm Captain Vatta."

"May we come aboard?"

"Yes. Follow me, please." She led the way toward the weapons bays. From the expressions of her crew, most of them had never seen that kind of implant plug-in, either. As she'd now expected, the tall man's "horns" uncurled to reveal a sensor tip, which he ran over the racks of missiles and then the visible surface of the missile tube backlocks.

"Very good, Captain Vatta," he said. "We will now place our seals, which must remain intact while you are here; they will be inspected again prior to your departure. I understand you have cargo to deliver here?"

"Yes," Ky said. "This way." She led him to the containers bound for the rehabilitation center, and he opened them, extending one of the tendril-like plug-ins down into the container.

"Quite correct," he said, retracting it. "Now I need to see the identification of your crewmembers, if they are going to leave the ship; we do not care about those who stay aboard. Oh, and if you have any livestock—"

"No livestock, but a dog," Ky said. "We certainly won't allow him off the ship."

"You have a dog?" His brows went up almost as high as his horns. "What type of dog?"

"We were told it was a terrier; I don't know much about dogs, myself."

"Dogs are very popular here. If he is for sale—"

"No," Ky said. "He belongs to a young relative of mine."

"That's too bad. He would be worth as much as this—" He put his hand on the container of prostheses. "We have very limited genome material for dogs, and terriers, in particular, are both popular and in short supply. Your relative could make his fortune."

Ky had known from childhood about the vagaries of trade—that something worthless in one place might be highly prized somewhere else. But she had never considered that the miserable pup Rascal was good for anything but keeping Toby busy and happy.

"I'll tell him," she said, "but I'm sure he'll want to keep the dog."

"Perhaps a DNA sample . . . that alone would bring a good price," Vaughn said. "More if the dog is male and could produce a sperm sample."

Ky didn't want to speculate on that. "I'll tell him," she said again. "Now, about the crew. All but three might want to go offship; your station seems to have good facilities."

"We do indeed," Vaughn said. "Excellent shops, local craftwork, fine dining—"

"Then tell me what you need in terms of identification. I can assemble the crew for you."

"Oh, I just need the paperwork. Scans are fine. Then you must agree to ensure that each has read and understood the local regulations. We take regulations very seriously, and enforce them rigorously. It is the only way to deal with outsiders."

"I see." Ky raised her voice slightly. "Jameel, will you bring down the crew ID dossiers, please?"

"Yes, Captain," came the response from the ship's intercom. In a moment, the cargo clerk came in with a hardcopy stack; Vaughn took it, scanning it quickly with one of his plug-ins. Jameel's eyes widened as he watched, Ky noted with amusement. She was beginning to find it natural.

"Hand out the regulations," Vaughn said to his companions, still scanning dossiers. They reached into the shoulder bags they carried and each handed Ky a small bundle of what looked like booklets with bright green-and-silver covers. "There is also a data cube, Captain Vatta, but this saves you printing out copies yourself. Each foreigner who comes onto the station must have a copy of the regulations in his or her possession while on the station, to ensure that there is no excuse for breaking rules."

"I see," Ky said. With her thumb, she opened the cover of the one on top. A table of contents, with headings that looked very organized, if a little odd. Buying. Selling. Eating. Excreting. Sleeping. Conversing (not in the course of buying, selling, eating, excreting). Helping. Fornicating. Obstructing. Damaging. She paged over to Damaging and found a definition of *damage,* and rules for damaging without incurring the death penalty. "It seems very . . . thorough . . . ," she said, running her gaze over the rules for damaging, for receiving damages, for adjudicating damaging.

"It is no more thorough than we found we needed,"

Vaughn said. He retracted his plug-in and squared the pile
of ID dossiers. "Are these copies I might take and file, or
originals?"

"Copies," Ky said. "You are welcome to take them."

"You are most courteous, Captain Vatta. We do appreciate courtesy. You may notice that in our regulations."

She had. One of the rules for damaging was that the
person intending to damage someone or something was
expected to give notice "in a quiet and courteous voice;
it is an offense to speak too loudly or use foul language."

"Do please inform your kinsman of the market value
of his dog," Vaughn said. "And please inform Customs
when you are ready to certify that all your crew have read
and understood the regulations."

"I will do that," Ky said. "Thank you." She wasn't sure
what she was thanking him for, but if he wanted courtesy
she would give it to him.

"My pleasure, Captain," Vaughn said, and led his team
back out to the hatch and onto dockside.

Ky closed the inner hatch and went to the bridge. She
wasn't sure how she was going to explain this one to her
crew.

"For a society that started with a bunch of backwoods
renegades, they certainly do have a thing about politeness," Rafe commented when he was halfway through the
booklet.

"And it's their own peculiar definition of politeness,"
Martin said. "Have you gotten to fornication yet?"

"No," Rafe said. "I've been here before." Ky looked at
him in surprise. "Notice the penalties," he said. "They kill
people for a lot of things. But politely. 'The executioner
will always give the condemned sufficient time to recover
from any embarrassing exhibition of emotion; condemned
need not fear that they will be exposed to public ridicule

as a result of inability to control bodily functions.' "

"That's grotesque," Lee said. "Providing clean pants for someone about to be killed?"

"They consider it minimal courtesy," Rafe said.

"I wonder you survived a visit, then," Martin said.

"I am always polite," Rafe said. "It is one of my few virtues."

Martin and Lee both started to speak; Ky quelled them with a glance.

" 'Fornication is legal among all classes of persons, foreign or citizen, provided that due notice has been given of all relevant diseases and conditions, and that no offer of payment is made by the pursuer, and all payment is made in advance if payment is requested by the pursued,' " Martin quoted. "So what does that mean—do they have prostitutes or not?"

"It means if your chosen partner wants to do it for money, you have to give them money," Rafe said. "They have much the same system on Allray. Not the bit about due notice given, though, or the part about parental responsibility, or the use of objectionable language during the acts themselves."

"Very direct, I'd say," Ky said. She read on, fascinated.

Before Ky had finished exploring the peculiarities of Cascadia's legal system as it applied to transients, representatives of the West Cascadia Rehabilitation Centre called about the prostheses and bioelectronics.

"The expiration date is critical; the shipment is overdue. Can you confirm that the expiration date has not been exceeded? We have damages owing if it is—"

"I'm not the original shipper," Ky said. "The materials were held up because of widespread interruption of trade; surely you knew that."

"Yes, but you're in charge of them now—"

"I was on my way, in transit here, within twelve hours after picking up the shipment," Ky said. "None of the delay is my fault."

"But the expiration date—"

"Hasn't been exceeded yet, not if the date on the container is accurate. However, it will be in another five days."

"We'll send for it right away. We have priority for cargo space in shuttles. How soon can you offload it?"

"When I'm paid," Ky said. "Because this was an unscheduled transit, and the original consignor was not available by ansible, I agreed to take it as pay-on-delivery. Now given the nature of the cargo, and its humanitarian importance, the charges will be only seventy percent of what other cargo of equal mass would be." She named a figure.

"Where did you say you picked it up?"

Ky gave the name again.

"Just a moment." After a pause, the caller reappeared onscreen. "That's quite satisfactory, within the usual parameters. Thank you, Captain Vatta. To what account should we direct the transfer of funds?"

"I just arrived; I'll be setting up a ship account with Crown & Spears under my name, Kylara Vatta." She spelled it.

"Within the hour, then," the caller said. "Or is that too soon?"

"No, that's fine," Ky said. "And your representatives can pick up the cargo as soon as I have confirmation of funds transfer. The containers are standard one-meter shipping cubes."

She called the local branch of Crown & Spears next.

"Aye, we saw a Vatta ship was inbound," the woman on the vidscreen said. "So you want to see the Vatta

Transport balances? Do you have the account numbers and passwords?"

"Yes, but I want to set up a separate account for my current business," Ky said. "Under my own name, Kylara Vatta. There'll be a funds transfer coming in from the West Cascadia Rehabilitation Centre shortly—"

"Oh, you brought the prostheses?" Without waiting for an answer, the woman rattled on. "We really need them, you know. Or I guess you don't. We had a huge industrial accident months ago and there's a lot of people waitin' for 'em. My brother lost his left arm."

"I'm sorry," Ky said.

"Not your fault," the woman said. "But of course, if you need an account to take that transfer you will have to come by the branch for personal identification procedures."

"What's the shortest way?" Ky asked. The listing in the station directory gave an address by direction and branch connection, but no map.

"Get yourself a leader-tag," the woman said. "They're free to visitors; there'll be a booth as you enter the concourse. Type in our name, and it'll program the leader, and then it'll tell you the best route."

"Thanks," Ky said, thinking that a map would have been simpler.

"People get turned around," the woman said. "Leader-tags save a lot of confusion."

The kiosk dispensing leader-tags had both keyboard and voice input; it recognized "Crown & Spears" and spit a green tree-shaped tag into its output bin. Ky picked it up.

"Hold pointing tree tip facing away from you," a tinny voice said.

Ky turned the tag in her hand until it pointed forward.

"Turn fifty-eight degrees right."

She almost laughed, but instead turned until the tag said, "Walk ahead."

By the time she got to the Crown & Spears entrance, she was heartily tired of the tagger's voice. It didn't seem to have a volume control, so everyone nearby got to hear its fussy warnings. "Do not walk into trash bins—turn thirty degrees right—now thirty degrees left . . ." As she came to the entrance, the tagger announced, "You are here. You are here. You are here," and then "Task over. To reactivate, place in input bin of leader-tag kiosk. If not returned to kiosk within one hour, alarm will sound."

Ky entered Crown & Spears, the familiar silver-gray-and-blue décor comforting.

"May we help you?" said an elegant young man in black suit and white shirt.

"Excuse me—where can I put this tagger thing?"

"Oh, we have a kiosk. Most businesses do." He took it from her and put it in a smaller version of the kiosk she'd used tucked between two ornamental pillars. "Now—may we help you with something else?"

"I'm Captain Kylara Vatta; I am opening a new account here."

"A moment." His eyes blanked, then focused again. "Yes, of course. You spoke to our senior account executive before. She will be pleased to meet with you now, if that is quite convenient."

"Certainly," Ky said. "Thank you." She followed him across the dark shining floor, past large desks each with its attendant, and then down a carpeted hallway to a large office on the right.

"Mellie, this is Captain Vatta; Captain Vatta, Melanda Torrin."

"Captain Vatta, what a pleasure." The woman she'd

seen onscreen now looked older, less exuberant. Black suit cut to show her figure, white blouse with a frill of lace at the throat, gold earrings, a thick mop of red-brown hair, shoulder length. And startling blue eyes.

"The pleasure is mine," Ky said.

"Our laws require that we meet new account owners in person, and confirm identity. That is hard to do these days, with multiple ansible failures, but I believe we have Vatta family DNA samples on file. You would not object to a comparison?"

"Er . . . no." She had not anticipated this. "But doesn't that take a long time?"

"For a reasonably close family resemblance, no. Let's see. Two years ago, a Captain Vatta came through: Josephine Iola Grace. Would you know how closely she might be related?"

"If she listed her father as Stavros, she's—she was—my first cousin. Her father and mine were brothers. She—they're—all dead."

"I'm surprised to hear that. She was quite young," the woman said.

"Her ship was blown up," Ky said.

"You said all dead . . . do you mean your father?"

"Yes. Father, mother, brothers . . . and my uncle Stavros and much of his family. You had not heard?"

"I had not, no. I'm sorry, Captain Vatta. I did not mean to offend."

"You didn't offend," Ky said. "You didn't know."

"Do you have no one, then?"

"Some survived," Ky said. "Jo's sister Stella. Her mother, Stavros' wife, Helen. I don't know about her children." She had never met Jo's children; they'd been born while she was in boarding school or the Academy.

"I shall hope they are safe," the woman said.

"I, also," Ky said. "But I don't know . . . the Slotter Key ansible is down."

Grace looked out her window before dawn. She had no need to stand in front of it; she used the excellent optics she'd installed and scanned everything in view on that side of the house, methodically sweeping back and forth, working her way out from the crazy-paved walk below, past the strip of grass, the roses trained against the wall, the wall itself, keying to the angle she'd arranged to see its far side, where a striped cat crouched, tail twitching, about to leap on a rabbit nibbling berries a few yards along. Beyond, a stretch of rougher grass to the perimeter fence. Another rabbit, a pair of them, frisking. Courting. Mating. Well, they were rabbits. She wished the cat luck. Beyond the perimeter fence, the land rose in gentle waves to the hills and the road. A bulge of hill cut off any view down-valley to the east; the road curved around it.

Right about now . . . yes . . . the first traffic of the day, a truck whose engine had made the same squawk and growl when its driver shifted for the downgrade every morning since they'd come. It was too early for birds to show her if anyone lay hidden in the rock outcrop, now a dark blur on slightly lighter dark. Movement caught her eye. She scanned the top of the outcrop . . . small, alert but uninterested in the hollow below, ears cocked to something uphill. It stood and trailed its bushy tail over the rocks as it slid down on the riverside. Fox. What had alerted it?

The gentle *tonk-tonk-tonk* of sheepbells came to her ears, and now she saw, pouring off the road in a slow torrent, a flock of sheep. Two shepherds were with them, and four dogs. Sheep and dogs passed the rock outcrop; one of the dogs leapt up to the top and sniffed, tail wagging wildly, but jumped down and went on when a shepherd called it.

Without moving from her comfortable bed, Grace checked the other sides of the house. Nothing. Ponies up near the house end of the paddock, waiting for the children to run out and feed them. Their girl Caitlyn from the town on her bicycle, leaving a dark trace in the silvery dew as she rode on the footpath instead of the road.

Grace turned off her system and let herself doze as light brightened in the room. She had been up until almost four, interfering with the sleep of the wicked, making them nervous enough to call each other on what they believed were secure lines, and she knew were not. She had recordings; she had made copies; she had transmitted copies to various locations. She needed to think about what they'd said, make sense of it, make plans . . . but she was tired, and hated the years that had stolen her ability to stay up two nights running.

A cry woke her, completely alert in an instant. She was halfway across the room, bare feet slapping on the floor, weapon in hand, when she thought to grab the security system's master control and plug in her implant.

The paddock. One pony down, legs thrashing. Justin, Jo's elder child, sprawled in the grass. Helen running. The other pony standing stiff, head thrown up, ears pricked, with Shar, the younger child, clinging to its mane.

They weren't supposed to ride until after breakfast. It *was* after breakfast; she'd overslept and Helen hadn't woken her. She threw the scans to full power. There. A glint in the briars. No time to get downstairs, outside—

She was across the second-story bridge to the far side of the house, out on the balcony, peering through the exuberant flowering vine and its equally exuberant bees, when the assassin stood up to get a better shot at the other pony or its rider. Or at Helen, who was ignoring the obvious danger and running straight for the fallen child. Ignoring the bees, ignoring Helen's yells and the second pony's sudden bolt, Grace focused her whole attention on drilling a hole through the assassin.

He fell. Grace scanned the area again for any other threat. No. A lone assassin? Stupid of them, and she wasn't sure she believed it. Movement in a neighboring field caught her eye. A rabbit, streaking away from where it had been quietly nibbling grass. Her gaze tracked the streak back, back, to another tangle of briars. There—her vision aided by highly illicit processors in her implant—she detected heat radiation. And there, aided again by other highly illicit bioelectronics, she directed her next shot.

Helen had reached Justin, thrown herself over him as a protective blanket. For all the good that would do, Grace thought. *Stay down, Helen,* she wanted to yell. The second pony had slowed from its wild bolt; the child still hugged its neck, unhurt, mouth a round O, eyes wide. The pony flicked its ears back and forth, then suddenly lowered its head to snatch grass; the child slithered off, unbalanced by that move. Unhurt, apparently; Shar threw a leg over the pony's neck and tugged at its mane, trying the trick they'd taught the pony two weeks before, to raise its head and lift a child rider to its back.

Grace didn't want to leave the window, where she had the best view . . . but she had to. Downstairs, she heard voices, exclamations, the scurry of feet. She was still wearing her night clothes, the close-fitting black garment with pad-protected elbows and knees in which she'd climbed out of her own window at midnight and back into it at four in the morning. When she went downstairs, Caitlyn saw her and gasped, fist to her mouth. Grace thought of what Caitlyn was seeing—a slim black figure holding a very nasty-looking weapon. One of *them.*

"It's all right, Caitlyn. It's just me—"

"But . . . but . . . Miss Grace—"

"Caitlyn, go in the kitchen and stay there."

"The police—"

"Don't call them. I will or Helen will."

"The doctor?"

"One of us will call if a doctor's needed. Stay in the kitchen until you're called, can you do that?" A nod from Caitlyn, still paler than she should have been.

Grace moved to the back of the house. The garden, from above, had an obvious plan, but from the ground presented too many obstructions and distractions. She wanted to hurry; she might be needed now. But hurry brought her too predictably to walks and open spaces easy to range. They—if any such were still out there—would expect the hurry, the predictable direct approach through the main aisle in this garden, wide enough for a small tractor and its implements. Grace chose a slower route, but not much slower for someone who had prepared carefully, for whom the straight lines of apparently solid walls and hedges had gaps ready for use by those who knew them. She knew them all.

Now she came to the paddock, where the injured pony still made those unhorselike sounds but more quietly. One leg was gone, ending in a mangled stump still spurting blood. The other legs kicked less vigorously. She should kill the pony humanely, but she had humans to check on.

"Helen," Grace said, just loud enough above the pony's groans. "How bad is it?"

"Not hurt," Helen said. "Just stunned. Shar?"

Stunned could kill, as they both knew. "Shar's fine," Grace said. Down the paddock, Shar was back astride the second pony, kicking hard, but the pony didn't want to approach.

"Are they coming?" Helen asked.

"Not those two," Grace said. "I'll get Shar."

"I meant the police," Helen said.

"Not for a while," Grace said. "Not until after we call them, so don't."

"Don't call—?"

"No." She walked up to the first pony, whose glazing eyes barely turned to see her, squatted down, and aimed carefully at the crossing of the X made by lines from right ear to left eye and left ear to right eye. "Sorry," she said to the pony, and fired. The pony jerked and then went limp.

"What did you do?" Helen asked.

"Gave it peace," Grace said. "Get Justin inside, if you can. I'll get Shar." She walked down the paddock, itchy with tension, an easy target, to the far corner where the second pony was grazing in quick, nervous snatches. Shar, sitting bolt upright on the pony's back, stared at Grace as if she were a stranger. Perhaps the child didn't recognize her. She herself felt more at home than she had in decades, the carefully constructed veneer of slightly batty and prudish old lady falling away to reveal the same familiar interior Grace, a Grace perfectly at home in black climbing suit with a weapon in hand.

"Easy now, Buttercup," she said to the pony. And to the child, "Shar, your mother wants you. It's time to go in."

"He won't *go*," Shar said. She looked so much like Jo at that age that Grace almost choked.

"He's scared," Grace said. "You sound a little scared, too."

"What happened to Rosy?" Shar asked. "Did you shoot Rosy?"

"Rosy broke a leg. It was a bad break. It couldn't be

fixed. Come down, now." She started to reach for Shar, but the pony sidestepped and she had only one hand, the other being still occupied with her weapon. Shar had tilted toward her, and now slid too far off balance, falling to the ground just as something slammed into Grace's left arm, whirling her around as if in a dance. She fell, furious with herself, knowing instantly what it was and that there had been more than two. The pony bolted again, the quick thuds of its flight scarcely faster than the rhythm of her heart.

She was on the ground. Shar, facedown and head-up, stared at her. "Stay down," she said to Shar. "Stay flat— put your head right down and be quiet and hold still no matter what." Waves of pain washed over her, nausea racked her. She turned her head and saw, without surprise, that her arm was lying folded up all wrong, in a widening pool of blood. "Damn," she muttered.

"Bad word," Shar said. "Gramma says . . ."

"Quiet," Grace said. "You be the baby possum, like in the story." She had to do something about the bleeding or she would be dead, like the daddy possum in the story. But that would mean letting go of her weapon, something she was sure the assassin would like to see.

She heard a crackling in the brambles beyond the paddock fence, footsteps, and willed herself to stay conscious until she could shoot the scumsucker in the gut . . . there was the dark shape, in a suit similar to her own, but with a hood and mask. She struggled to bring her weapon to bear . . . and then the figure staggered, fell facedown, and behind it was someone she recognized too slowly as MacRobert, bloody fish-gutting knife in hand.

"You—" she said.

"You're having an interesting morning," he said. He moved up beside her, grabbed her left arm, and shoved what felt like a spear into the bone. She knew it was his thumb on the artery, but that's not what it felt like.

"I got two of them," she said, and wondered why she was justifying herself to him.

"Good," he said. "Because I don't think I could sneak up on any more that way. May I take your weapon if I need it?"

"Go ahead," she said, relaxing her grip.

"I heard their shots, but no answering fire," he said. "Took me a while to make it from the river—"

"Glad you did," Grace said. Her vision was going; she was peering down a dark tunnel at a small bright image.

"Stay with me now," he said. She felt his hand at her mouth, a tiny hard something on her tongue that tasted bitter. "Bite that."

She bit. She had tasted it before, and military-grade stimtabs hadn't changed that much. The tunnel shortened, then disappeared; she saw very clearly, with little bright halos around everything.

"You may lose this arm."

"I thought so," Grace said.

"Aunt Grace . . ." That in a near-whisper, from Shar.

"This is a friend, Shar," Grace said. Or maybe not, but she could not at the moment cope with the possibility that he was one of them.

"Can I get up?"

"Not yet," MacRobert answered for her. "Just lie quiet, and let me help your aunt Grace."

He had placed a tourniquet now, doing it one-handed with a deftness that indicated he'd done it before. Grace thought of offering to replace his thumb with her right hand for arterial pressure, then—as another wave of nausea hit her—decided to just lie there and let him work.

The stimtab and her own biochemistry finally reached

equilibrium about the time he had the tourniquet tightened and started to straighten her arm out. She rolled her head to see.

"Better not look," he said.

She looked anyway. A mangled mess where her elbow had been, only a shred of skin holding it on. Beyond, her undamaged left hand, now looking like the corpse it was, bloodless.

"Might as well take it off the whole way," she said.

His brows went up. "I'm no surgeon."

"It's not an arm, at this point," Grace said. She felt only mild regret, which she knew to be shock and drug combined. Still, two live children for one lost arm was a good bargain.

"As you wish." He cleaned the gutting knife carefully, something she appreciated fully only later, and cut the arm free. Grace felt nothing physical, but despite her determination to accept the loss, there was something profoundly wrong about her arm—*her* arm—lying there with no connection to her. It was not her arm; it could not be her arm . . . it must be someone else's arm. What a disgusting thing to leave lying in the paddock, where a child might find it . . .

She had a dim memory of MacRobert helping her back to the house, of his voice assuring her the children were safe, Helen was safe, everyone was safe, when she opened her eyes to find herself in bed, floating above the mattress in a pink cloud. That was so unlikely that she closed her eyes again, willing herself to dream properly and wake up completely. On the second try, she recognized the drifting sensation as drug-induced, and the memory of the morning's—that morning's?—events appeared in chunks, accessed by her implant's recording.

"—Transfer to regional trauma center immediately—" she heard a voice say. She wanted to argue, but her mouth was full of very dry cotton. "Should have called immediately—"

"She said—" That was Helen's voice.

"*She* said!" A pompous voice, full of scorn. Grace felt anger stirring. "Why would you listen to a woman missing an arm, a woman in shock? People in shock say all sorts of stupid things."

Her tongue was working its way through the cotton. "Na'stoo-id," she croaked. Even to herself it sounded more like a frog than a human.

A stranger's face appeared on one side, Helen's on the other. "Grace!" Helen said. "You're awake."

Not really awake, she wanted to say. Too full of drugs to be really awake. But the other face annoyed her, as full of self-righteousness and scorn as the voice had been.

"Who you?"

"I'm the local doctor. Please stay calm. You've had a rather serious injury, some kind of hunting accident. These idiot summer visitors never seem to think about how far their shots go . . . missed a rabbit, I daresay."

And he had called *her* stupid. Three hunters, shooting at and missing three rabbits?

"Where Mac—" She couldn't say the rest of his name.

"The man?" Helen misunderstood the word. "The fisherman who helped you? He's gone to help the police find the . . . the hunters."

So there was a reason for the stupidity about hunters. She wished she could think what it was.

TWELVE

The ceiling of the regional trauma center's amputation ward had been designed for the entertainment of those who must lie flat in bed. Grace had a choice of programs to display: games, news, sports. None of them served her purpose. She had been overruled by doctors, psychologists, and worst of all Helen, all of them certain that a woman her age needed the specialized services here, rather than specialists in attendance *there*.

Surreptitiously, she hitched herself up in the bed until she could use the headboard to tilt her head forward and look across the room. Through the glass sliding door, she could see the man in uniform seated just beside it. The careless-hunter story had broken down; provincial authorities knew that the shots had been attempted murders. Her life, they said, might be in danger. They were not happy with her weapon, though she faced no charges for having wounded (unhappily not killed) the assailants. An unlicensed beam weapon was an indictable offense, she'd been told. Hadn't she realized? Her explanations had been received in silence, without comment afterward.

Her stump ached. No, calling it an ache was a euphemism. The attendants used euphemisms. *Are we feeling some discomfort, dear?* It wasn't discomfort and it wasn't an ache.

It hurt, a lot. The med dispenser button lay just under her right index finger. She didn't push it. No one died of pain, and she wanted to think. They had cleaned up the stump of her arm; the bulky wrappings prodded her ribs. She wanted a cloned prosthesis; they were saying she was too old, and she needed a way to convince them she wasn't.

Using heels, hips, and her right arm, she pushed herself headward a few more centimeters. It was never good to lie still too long. She couldn't turn on her side; the arm board and IV line to her right arm made it too awkward, and she wasn't about to try lying on her stump. But by the clock, she had eighteen minutes until the next official attendant check.

The man outside the door alerted; she saw his head come up, his arm drop to his side. Her chest tightened. Then he relaxed, smiled, stood up. Helen already? She wasn't supposed to visit until tomorrow. Grace made herself breathe more slowly. No use panicking the attendants.

MacRobert peered through the door, winked at her, said something to the man in uniform, then came in. He had a sheaf of flowers wrapped in green paper.

"You're looking better," he said.

"Thank you," Grace said, meaning more than the words or the flowers.

"You're welcome," he said. He looked around for somewhere to put the flowers, and chose the pitcher from the bedside table. "Just a moment." He took the pitcher and flowers into the tiny adjoining bathroom—to which Grace had not yet been allowed access—and came back with them. "There. Nothing makes a hospital room really cheerful, but flowers can't hurt."

"They're lovely," Grace said. She did not believe for a moment that he had brought her flowers just to cheer her up. But as long as she was stuck in a ward with full patient monitoring, how could they communicate?

He gave her a sweet smile, something so at odds with what she thought of him that she felt herself scowling back. "Are you in pain?" he asked. "You're frowning." Then, as if reassured, "I was due extra leave, and it was granted, so I thought I'd stay in the area until you're out of the hospital. My time is up in the cottage, but— your niece, is it?—graciously invited me to stay at the manor with her and the children. I offered to do the back-and-forth for her; the children are upset about the pony."

Grace blinked. "That's . . . very nice of her. Of you. Of course, we do have fishing rights to that whole area. I hope you're scaring some fish."

"A few, yes." He pulled one of the chairs around to sit facing her. "Wouldn't you like the bed elevated?"

"I would, yes, but they wouldn't, and the bed reports to the nursing station if I do it. In would come the efficient attendants to put it back down and remind me not to hit that button by accident."

"Control enthusiasts, aren't they?" MacRobert said. "Helen says they're bucking about a cloned prosthesis instead of bioelectronic?"

"They think the clone won't take, or it's not cost-effective or something."

"How long does it take?"

"To grow an arm? Minimum of eight months. Four for the initial stage, then implantation, then another four to eight of boosted growth and a lot of physical therapy."

"Mmm."

"And I resent every day of it. I knew there was more than one; I knew there might be more than two. But I had to go get Shar . . ."

"Of course you did," MacRobert said. "The bioelectronic prosthesis is faster, though, isn't it?"

"Supposedly, yes," Grace said. "Hook up the nerves, attach the prosthesis, and then it's forty to sixty days of training. But it wouldn't be *my* arm."

"They could make it look—"

"I don't care about looks!" That came out more angrily than she meant to sound with MacRobert. "I care about function," she said more quietly. "It's easier to interfere with the signaling in a noncloned prosthesis. It's less reliable. I can't afford to worry about who might be programming my arm."

"Oh." He looked taken aback.

"Bad enough I'm out of action when Helen needs me. A shorter time out would seem better except . . . I don't know when, or who, or how many."

"Perhaps you could recuperate back at the manor while making that decision," MacRobert suggested.

"Get out of here? Everyone seems convinced I need to be here."

"Until you were out of danger, yes. But now? Don't you have some recovery time before they can start either approach to a prosthesis?"

"I . . . think so, yes."

"You would be as safe, from a security standpoint, at the house as here. The level of medical support you need is much less . . . the last time I stopped by, you had tubes and wires everywhere." He grinned.

"I don't remember." She did not remember a visit from him at all. How long had she been unconscious?

"Blood loss and shock," he said. "You've made a remarkable recovery." He did not add *for a woman your age,* which the attendants kept mentioning. She felt absurdly grateful.

"I intend to make a full recovery," she said. "I have

things to do." One of the most frustrating things about being locked up here was having to leave the guilty at peace.

"I'm sure you do," he said. "But if you feel up to roughing it in the country, we can both put pressure on the staff."

"Just a moment," Grace said. She felt around on the keypad under her right hand. There. That was the bed control. A motor whined faintly and the head of the bed came up. "It's hard to argue effectively while flat on your back."

His grin broadened. "Indeed. Shall I barricade the door so the attendants can't get in, or—"

She didn't feel at all dizzy. "No, you're going to help me get out of bed and into the bathroom."

"I am?"

"You are. Here—give me your arm—" He held out his bent arm; she grabbed it and pulled herself upright. Now she was dizzy for a moment, but it passed. Sitting upright on the side of the bed felt much better than lying in it. Her bare feet, hanging over the side of the bed, looked pale and oddly unnatural.

"I'm going to stand," she said. "I'll have to lug this damned IV pole with me—"

"You're sure? Never mind, you're always sure." He positioned himself to make it easy for her to slide off the bed, his other arm ready to steady her if she needed it. She felt lopsided without her left arm, but not unsteady. He put a firm hand on her back as she reached out to the IV pole, and together they started a very slow walk across the room.

They were halfway to the bathroom when an attendant came bustling in. "Now, now, dear, mustn't play with the bed control—*what* do you think you're doing? You—whoever you are—get away from her—"

"No," Grace said. "I need his help. I'm going to the bathroom."

"You can't!"

"I most certainly can, and I most certainly am." She glared at the attendant. "It's a shame that this gentleman is more use to me than you are, but it can't be helped. I certainly wasn't going to use a bedpan in front of him."

"You should have rung!"

"You should quit treating me like an idiot," Grace said, feeling better with every step. "If you want to help, unhook me from this blasted pole. Or help bring it along."

"I'll have to call the doctor," the attendant said.

"And I have to use the toilet," Grace said. "Are you going to help, or not?" The longer she stood up, the more she wondered if this had been a good idea, and she really did need to get to the bathroom. The attendant, muttering, finally reached for the pole. Grace transferred her grip to MacRobert's arm and took another step. Better.

The attendant didn't want to leave her alone in the bathroom, but MacRobert drew him away and shut the door. Grace sat, feeling limper than she liked, but also triumphant. She imagined pacifying pharmaceuticals rushing away, and when she was through, she stood up by herself—with a good grip on the IV pole. That brought her face-to-face with the mirror. The person staring back at her was only partially familiar. It wasn't the missing arm that bothered her but the stooped posture and slack, puffy face with the hazed eyes. She dismissed the ridiculous hospital gown as an irrelevant accident.

She forced herself upright. Better. Glared at the puffy face. Better again. Made faces at herself in the mirror until the attendant knocked on the door.

"Are you all right?"

"I'm fine," Grace said. "I'm coming out."

On her way back to the bed—which seemed much farther away than it had been on the way to the toilet—she said, "I'm going home tomorrow."

"You can't!" the attendant said.

"In law, I certainly can," Grace said. "I am a competent adult, and thus allowed to discharge myself from a medical facility at any time, whether or not it imperils my life." She sat down on the bed, trembling with exhaustion. "And since I am a competent adult, this won't. I will have medical assistance at home."

"But—"

"You really do not want a legal battle with me," Grace said.

"She's right," MacRobert said. The attendant looked at him, then back at Grace, and let out a huge sigh.

"I'll have to talk to the doctor," the attendant said, and left in a hurry.

"Idiot," Grace said. She was perched on the edge of her bed and had no idea how to lie down again without hitting her stump. It hurt enough already; she did not want to bang it on anything.

"Here," MacRobert said. He put one arm behind her and presented the other for her to hold with her good hand. She would have glared at him except that he was doing the obvious best thing without fuss. She let him ease her back to the bed, but managed to get her legs up onto it before he reached for them. He laid the cover over her lightly. "You really are one to take an idea and run with it, aren't you?" he said. "When I suggested recuperating back at the manor, I wasn't thinking of tomorrow."

"I'll rest better," Grace said. "And I'll be there if—"

"If nothing. I'm there. You're not in action right now." He cocked his head. "You're a very determined woman."

*   *   *

Grace arrived back at the manor in a medical transport, clearly marked as such. This obvious signal to the other side that she was helpless infuriated her, but the medical staff had insisted that she could not travel safely without attendance, and Helen backed them up. She was tense all the way, feeling like an obvious target, but the trip went without incident. Perhaps MacRobert had arranged protection; she felt inclined to believe that he had.

She let herself be moved through the house in a hover-chair, vowing silently that she would be on her feet as soon as she got rid of the worriers. She wanted to see the children above all, but Helen was worried that they'd upset her.

"Auntie Grace?" That was the younger, Shar. She turned her head.

"Yes, Shar."

"Gramma said it's a bad word but sometimes it's all right for grown-ups to say bad words."

"Excuse me? What, Shar?"

"That word you said when you fell down and there was all that blood. I told Gramma you said it and then your arm fell off and there was all that blood. I thought it made your arm fall off to say the bad word, but Gramma said no."

The pure absurdity of that brought tears to her eyes and a snort of laughter at the same moment. Shar looked at her with concern. Grace blinked the tears away. "Shar, I'm sorry. I'm fine, but that just hit me funny."

"You cry when something's funny?"

"Sometimes." How to explain to a five-year-old . . . she wouldn't even try. "Shar, you did very well that day."

Her lower lip trembled. "It was scary. Buttercup bucked me off *twice,* and Justin was laying there and Gramma was screaming and you—"

"Yes, it was scary," Grace said. "But you did very well. You didn't scream. You did what I told you."

"I wanted to—"

"But you didn't. Do you still need to scream?"

Shar looked down. "Sometimes. But it's bad—it upsets Gramma."

"Not at the right times. When something's been really scary and you couldn't scream then, sometimes you need to scream or cry later."

"Really?"

"Oh yes," Grace said. "Sometimes I scream." Shar smiled through tears, and then left. Grace wondered when MacRobert would show up. Soon, she hoped.

Her next visitor, however, was Helen, who shut the door behind her and stood by it. "I haven't thanked you yet for saving the children." Her voice was tight, as if she spoke around a block of ice.

"Helen . . . say what you mean."

"It's—I can't—" Helen, always so remote and cool, collapsed on the chair suddenly, shoulders shaking. Grace cursed her own weakness. "Stav and Jo and the children almost—"

"But they didn't get the children," Grace said.

"But they almost did. If you hadn't been there—"

"If I hadn't overslept, I'd have known they were there before the children went out," Grace said. "How's Justin?"

"Oh, he's fine. A bump on the head, that's all. He's upset about Rosy, of course." Helen sniffed. "I've got to stop this . . . all this crying."

"You have a lot to cry about," Grace said. "So do the children."

"You aren't crying," Helen said. "And you're the one who lost an arm."

"But not a husband and children," Grace said. "Can

we stop this comparison of grief? I certainly don't think less of you for grieving."

"Oh. Yes." Helen blew her nose, wiped her face, and took a deep breath. "It just hits me at the oddest moments. And I did want to thank you."

"You're welcome. Now—what happened to the assassins?"

"I don't know. The police kept telling me to take care of the children and not worry when I asked. They took your weapon away, I do know that."

"Just the one I had with me?"

"You have others?" Helen's brows went up. "Here?"

"I certainly hope so," Grace said. "Not that I'm in shape to use them, but I'd hate to lose them. Any more trouble?"

"No, nothing. The police have been here, of course, and that fisherman who knew you—MacRobert."

"You meet the nicest people on the river," Grace said. "Quite the gentleman he is."

"You did know he's in Spaceforce?" Helen asked.

"Is he?" Grace said, closing her eyes.

"Grace. Don't do that. I know you knew; you know everything about everyone five minutes before you meet them."

Grace opened her eyes. "Do I? All right, I knew MacRobert was in Spaceforce. I did check out who was renting cabins on the river when we leased this place. That was an obvious way for someone to gain access. But when we met on the river, he was all right. I watched for a few days to see; he's a wet-fly fisherman, and he was fishing like any other."

It was hours later, while she was napping, that MacRobert came. He knocked on the door; she woke, mumbled something, and he came in.

"You have a nice system here," he said, looking around

the room in a way that indicated the locations of system elements.

"Thank you," Grace said. "Now why were you so anxious to get me out of that hospital?"

"Events. Would you like to check your system and see that it's functioning?"

"Yes." Grace accessed her implant's security subroutines, linked into the house system. All well so far. "If you'll hand me the controller in the drawer of the bedside table . . ." It looked like the remote for a vidscreen; MacRobert handed it to her. She ran through the diagnostics, something the implant could not do without a direct physical access. All correct. The system was on at the highest level, as it should be. "Clear," she said.

"Good." MacRobert sat down in the chair near the bed. "You had obtained information on the actions of officials in high office; you had transmitted that information to certain persons—am I right?"

"Yes," Grace said.

"I would like to see that information. We are concerned that those persons are not the ideal agents in this instance."

"*We?*"

He gave her a steady look. "We have a common cause. We have a common enemy."

"Do we?"

"Yes." No wiggle room in that statement. "Whoever attacked Vatta did so not alone to destroy Vatta, but to terrify the government. And my best guess is, not this government alone. It would not surprise me to find that other ansibles than ours are out of commission, and that atrocities have been committed in other systems, all to cause governments to weaken or fall. Here, in the one system where we can obtain hard data, we know that the highest level of the government is involved."

"Who are *we*?" Grace asked. What she really wanted to ask was *Who are you?* but the answer to the other might make that clear enough.

"Spaceforce is tasked with external security issues," MacRobert said. "That's public knowledge. We were deliberately misled and kept from knowing things that then allowed the transfer of weaponry from a nonallied space fleet to this planet, and activation of that weaponry by at least one such ship. The attack on Corleigh Island's Vatta offices and household was made using high-level weaponry controlled from space. By the time we could ascertain that, the ship involved was beyond our borders, and we were ordered not to pursue it. Then the ansibles went out, and we were ordered to contract our perimeter to two light-minutes." He paused; Grace nodded her understanding and he went on. "This caused us some concern. Us being that part of Spaceforce tasked with security analysis."

"I see."

"Not completely, you don't, and I'm not authorized to share all our sources with you. Though I believe we share some sources of which we are not aware. At any rate, though my nominal position is senior NCO in the cadet barracks at Spaceforce Academy, my actual job is, as you've surmised, in the security sector. It's just that I could learn things fairly easily from homesick cadets that other operatives had to dig for."

"So what is it you want from me?" Grace asked.

"I want you to share what you've learned with me, and let us use that information to take down the President," he said. "You've set the wrong kind of hounds on his trail. Kill him your way, and he'll be a martyr."

"I want him dead," Grace said.

"Quite so." His tone was level; Grace noted that he showed no shock or disapproval. That surprised her; he was developing a habit of surprising her, and she surprised herself by not resenting it. "And *we* want him discredited," MacRobert went on. "If you didn't want that, too, why collect the chain of evidence you've spent so much time on? We can accomplish both, if we work together."

"I would have to trust you," Grace said. To his credit, he didn't use *I saved your life* to persuade her, but just sat there, waiting. She closed her eyes. He said nothing. She wanted to trust him. She wanted nothing more than she wanted the President both dead and dishonored. But could even Spaceforce accomplish that? More important, would they?

She opened her eyes. "Do I have your word, MacRobert-whatever-your-rank-really-is, that you will not let that weasel escape?"

"Yes. And I can have a high-ranking officer come here and speak with you, if that will help."

Grace hoped her expression carried sufficient disgust with that appeal. "Admirals and generals are feather-weights, MacRobert. You, I choose to trust. All right. I'll need to get downstairs to the library, and onto my secure line. What time is it? Damn. Better get me downstairs now."

She was sweating with pain, her hand and feet cold, by the time he had her installed in the chair and helped her hook up the external communications she'd established. With exquisite courtesy, he withdrew to the library proper while she sent out the coded message that meant "stop, cease, await next orders." Confirmation took hours, hours during which she passed from merely tired to utterly exhausted, fighting off the pain and weakness to stay upright in her seat, acknowledging each reply within the appropriate time frame, each having its own unique reply code.

At last it was done. MacRobert got her back upstairs and into bed.

"You had better get it done," Grace said, with the last of her strength. "Or I'll come after you."

"I believe it," he said. "But I promise, we'll get it done."

The President yawned as he sat behind his polished desk. Though he had slept better the past dozen nights, he still could not stop yawning. On his desk was the Order of Rescission that would invalidate all Slotter Key letters of marque and order all its privateers to cease operations. It seemed futile, since they had no functional system ansible, and thus could not recall the privateers now in operation, but he hoped it would placate the pirate horde. At least, with that old woman out of commission, he had only one enemy to fear.

His door opened unexpectedly; he glanced up to see his personal assistant and behind him someone in uniform.

"Mr. President, the Commandant of Spaceforce Academy."

The President looked up, into the steady gaze of a man he had despised for decades. His assistant backed out and shut the door. "Commandant," he said, unable to put any real welcome in his voice. "What brings you here so—"

"Without an appointment? That." The Commandant nodded at the President's desk.

"Excuse me?"

"Mr. President, let's not play games. You're proposing— no, you've decided—to rescind all letters of marque without the advice or approval of Council. You are on the point of signing the Order of Rescission."

"How do you know that? Have you been spying on me?"

"Don't be naïve." The Commandant sat without being invited to sit. "Everyone spies on everyone else; it's why we have security systems." He put a scrambler cylinder on the desk and thumbed its controls. "Someone may be able to penetrate even this, but it will take skill. Mr. President, we at Spaceforce—since we are tasked with the external defense of this system—have been looking into the attacks on the Vatta family compound and headquarters—"

"That's not external," the President said. Sweat sprang out on his back. They could not know . . .

"In origin, yes, they were. And they represented a clear threat to our system integrity, so they are well within our defined mission."

"What has this to do with the Academy?" the President asked. "You're head of the Academy, not all of Spaceforce."

"True. You appointed Cair Tlibi the Spaceforce Commandant, didn't you?"

It was a matter of record; they both knew it. What was this leading up to?

"Yes, I did. What of it?"

"A distinguished officer, with a fine record," the Commandant said. "Would it surprise you to know that he had a history of offering and accepting bribes?"

The President knew his own face was shiny with nervous sweat, but he dared not wipe it away. He scowled. "I would not believe it," he said. "It's a politically motivated attack on an honorable man . . ."

"Hardly that," the Commandant said. "He's confessed, you know. Bribery, extortion, and collusion with an external enemy."

The President felt faint. Not Tlibi, not the gruff, hearty

man who had always been the most accessible, most affable military man he'd ever known.

"And I must mention, Mr. President, that he has—I'm most sorry to have to say this—named you as one of the people with whom he had illicit monetary arrangements. Given his record, we do not accept this on his word alone, of course, but I'm afraid that there must be an investigation—"

Shock and rage swamped prudence. "How did she do this?" the President heard himself saying.

"She?" In that one word was all the warning he needed to pull himself back to his usual control.

"Never mind." He took a deep breath. "Needless to say, I repudiate everything you've said. I don't know by what means you forced an innocent man to confess to crimes he had not committed, but I refuse to believe that Tlibi has done anything that heinous, and obviously I'm denying any such acts on my own part."

"I understand, Mr. President," the Commandant said.

"And now I must ask you to leave," the President said. "I'm quite busy already and I will consult with my legal staff at once about this . . . this disgusting matter."

"No," the Commandant said. "I'm not leaving."

"But you—" The President stabbed at the emergency button on his chair. Nothing happened.

"Mr. President, for the moment you are . . . cut off from communication. The Council are considering what to do, and I am here to ensure that you communicate with no one and take no actions related to your presidency."

"How dare you!"

"On orders from the Council, Mr. President. They have been apprised of the relevant facts, and it was their request—no, command—that you be guarded by a high-ranking officer of Spaceforce who was already in possession of the same facts." His voice changed timbre. "Sir, I would not reach into that drawer if I were you."

The President removed his hand from the drawer in which he kept his personal weapon. "You are wrong," he said. "You are completely wrong and I will be exonerated in court. After which, your career will be in ruins."

"It is the risk one takes in the military," the Commandant said, with a twitch of the shoulders that was not quite a shrug. "Doing the right thing has its risks, and we accept them."

"I could have killed you."

"I doubt it." The Commandant smiled, not the easy, affable smile that the President had enjoyed from Tlibi, but a smile that brought ice to his heart.

He wanted desperately to know how they had found out. Was it Graciela Vatta, that horrible old bag? She was supposed to be dead, or near enough. She'd had her arm shot off; she was in an amputee ward. Surely someone in an amputee ward wasn't able to arrange this, even if she'd had the knowledge . . . and there was no way she could have the knowledge . . . "I want to know—" he began.

"I'm sure you have many questions, Mr. President," the Commandant said. "But I'm not allowed to answer them."

"This is outrageous," he said. It was what one said in these situations, but he realized that by itself, with no one listening who cared, it sounded ridiculous, like the bluster it was.

"Except," the Commandant said slowly, removing from his tunic a small round container, "with this." He opened the container and set it on the President's desk, within his reach. It looked like—it was—a small pillbox. Inside was one small white pill.

The President felt his insides twist into a hard knot of terror. It could not be. It could not be anything else.

"Such behavior would unfortunately deprive us of the information you have that is relevant to your case," the Commandant said. "I would be censured severely for not anticipating such an act on your part and preventing it. On the other hand, from the perspective of the person facing intense interrogation with regard to the alleged acts of malfeasance and treason, it might be preferable, though of course it would be seen as an admission of guilt."

The small white pill seemed to swell, blotting out the future. The President's mouth filled for an instant with sour liquid; he swallowed. "Is it . . . does it . . . is it . . . painless?"

"No," the Commandant said. "But it is quick."

His thoughts raced, tiny pictures flickering through his mind. His election, his inauguration, his many speeches, his many conferences, those conversations with party leaders, with prominent business leaders, those confidential chats, those significant glances and one or two words in the right places. He knew—he had made it his business to know—how effectively information could be extracted from prisoners. Those who had been his allies, his friends, would expect him to protect them. Or would they? Were they even now figuring out how to deny their complicity? Were they even now in custody, even now revealing everything to save themselves?

A wailing voice in his mind insisted that he had not been a bad president. He had not done anything everyone else hadn't done, at least not until the threat that could have doomed his government . . . *We have targeted you and your family, too* . . . himself. And he could have done nothing else then, no one could. The government needed him, needed his familiar face and voice to reassure them through the crisis. If one family had to suffer unfairly for it—if it was unfair for one family to suffer—then for the good of all . . .

The Commandant's gaze ripped through that reverie; the man had a drooping eyelid as if he were going to sleep, but even so the intense scrutiny was like a searchlight. The President knew that this man would not listen, and if he listened would not agree with that whining voice.

Now the President's mouth was dry; his voice rasped in his throat. "You think I should . . ."

"I have no opinion," the Commandant said. "Or rather, I have an opinion but it would not be appropriate to state it."

"I—I need time to think—"

The Commandant glanced at the clock on the wall; the left corner of his mouth twitched. "Do you? That might be unfortunate."

"You could have said it was painless!" That came out in an aggrieved whine that sounded childish even to him.

The Commandant shook his head. "I don't lie," he said, without even a hint of emphasis on the pronoun. Other men had said that, and other men had been lying when they said it. The President had long experience of liars great and small. But this time, with this man, habitual honesty was as obvious as habitual dishonesty was in others. It was not a boast. It was not an attempt to convince. It was a simple fact: he did not lie.

Damn the man. Damn the arrogant, self-righteous, stiff-necked, ramrod-up-the-rear priggishness of him. Why couldn't the Commandant at least have the grace to be crudely triumphant, amused, something—anything—despicable that he himself could fix on, could feel superior to?

The President felt the sting of tears and closed his eyes. He would not cry in front of this man. He would not beg for mercy where no mercy existed. His eyes dried, burned with the effort not to cry. His hands twitched against each other, under the desk, but he was sure the Commandant knew that even if he could not see it.

"My wife—" he said, pleased that his voice was steady. "She is certainly not involved in any of the alleged incidents."

The Commandant nodded. "No one, Mr. President, suspects your wife of anything."

"And I categorically deny that I myself have done anything illegal or . . . or improper."

"I understand, Mr. President."

"Whatever evidence you or the Council think they have seen, it is all faked, a malicious plot against me."

"I understand, Mr. President." A pause. "Time is passing, Mr. President."

Somewhere outside his office, men were searching through files and closets, questioning clerks and secretaries, housekeepers and cooks. The quick imagination that had made him so effective a politician, so able to see others' viewpoints and how to circumvent them, what means would work with which opponent, now provided a stream of images: employees backed into corners of an office, eyes wide, muttering to each other, families disturbed at breakfast, on vacations, children crying, spouses indignant and frightened, the incredible mess left behind any official search.

The pill in its box seemed to pulsate in time with these images, alluring and terrifying all at once. He had always considered himself a brave man: what would a brave man do? Face the coming investigations, the inevitable trial? Drag his wife and his relatives and friends through the muck? End his life with a hood over his head so the official witnesses at the execution didn't even have to see his face, as the glass wall protected them from the unseemly smells of sudden death? Or die now, quickly if not painlessly, and hope that his death would take much of the ardor from the investigations? That they would be content with his death?

He wanted to ask how much it hurt, how bad was the pain, but even in the roil of emotions, he knew that the Commandant could not answer that question. If it was really that—really death, in that small compass—no one had lived to say how bad it was. Or how quick.

He had never considered himself indecisive. He had always been firm in his opinions, in his positions, unswayed by anything but the practicalities of his office. Yet now he was wavering, hating himself for that wavering.

Even through the closed door, he heard a noise in the passage outside.

In a flash, without really thinking, he grabbed the pillbox, shook the pill into his hand, then into his mouth. The pill dissolved, a bitter taste, and a second later pain wrenched his body, outlining his bones in white fire.

"Good for you," the Commandant said, past the pain and the roaring in his ears. For an instant, he was grateful for that small commendation. Then sound and pain met, went beyond bearing, and he lost himself in that chaos.

THIRTEEN

Moscoe Confederation

After setting up the new ship account, Ky asked about access to the other Vatta accounts.

"Of course," the account rep said. "You have been identified as an authorized person, captain of a Vatta ship. What did you want?"

"I want to transfer a small sum to the ship account, to be transferred back when the West Cascadia Rehab Centre funds come in and clear. We need to pay docking fees, air fees, that kind of thing."

"You'll need about a thousand, then," she said. "Here are the balances of the various Vatta accounts. There's the general corporate account, and each ship has its own—"

"I'll transfer from the general," Ky said. "What's your clearing time on transfers from the planet?"

"For an entity like the rehab center, four hours. We have to run a verifying query to their branch, that's all."

Ky mentally added up the charges so far. "You're right, a thousand should do it." That transfer took only seconds. Ky then authorized payment of the outstanding charges, which came to 978 credits, and headed back to the ship with a freshly programmed leader-tag. She was able to anticipate most of its chirpy directions, and dumped it happily in the bin outside the dock entrance.

The status display outside the ship now showed green: all charges paid. No local police were visible, as they had been when she left. A very practical way, she thought, to ensure that no one pulled out leaving unpaid bills behind. The little blue bar at the bottom of the display puzzled her at first, but when she touched it, the text explanation came up. 48 HOUR CREDIT LIMIT APPROVED. So she wouldn't have to transfer again even if the rehab center's funds were delayed . . . good.

Back inside the ship, Toby met her before she got to the bridge. For once, the dog was not at his heels. "You're not going to make me sell Rascal, are you?"

"What? Of course not, what gave you that idea?"

"There've been inquiries coming in. It's all the cargo they're interested in, and they're offering a lot of money . . . and he's caused so much trouble . . ." Toby looked near tears.

Ky put a hand on his shoulder. "Toby, listen. Rascal is not cargo. He's crew. Granted, he's a noisy, dirty, smelly, mischievous little terror, but he's *our* dog, officially, and *your* dog in reality."

"It's a whole lot of money," Toby said, doubt still clear in his voice. "Martin said you might need it."

"So just how much is a whole lot of money?" Ky asked.

"Er . . . um . . . thirty-seven thousand."

"For a dog?" That seemed impossible. What were dogs good for, other than to make messes and cheer up orphans?

"Yes. And Martin thinks they'll go higher . . . we haven't even advertised."

"Well, I wouldn't sell *you* for thirty-seven thousand, or thirty-seven million," Ky said. "And I'm not selling your dog." The numbers danced in her head anyway. "But if you weren't offended at the idea, maybe we could market his sperm."

"You trust them?"

"No. But if we hired a vet, I'm sure there's some way to do it on this ship, something that wouldn't harm him permanently but could get your trading nest egg started." And pay for his education, if it turned out his parents were among the dead.

"He's only a puppy—"

"He's grown a lot since Lastway, Toby, and so have you. Let's see . . . if dogs are so scarce and valuable here, they may not have a canine vet on the station, but there's bound to be one onplanet who has expertise in artificial insemination. Let's see."

The station directory listed only two vets, both certified for "livestock import/export health certification and quarantine procedures." One listed the species for which he was certified, including some Ky had never heard of, but not dogs. The other's ad said, "Practice limited to health certification of large animal (hoofed) livestock."

Cascadia's directory included only five "canine specialists," and one of those listed "reproductive services." Ky checked the time zones against the listed office hours. Seven hours until they opened. She glanced at Toby. "So where did you hide him?"

He flushed. "In . . . a crate behind some stuff in the gym."

"Don't you think you ought to let him out?"

"Yes. I just worried—"

"Well, don't. You're not going to lose your dog. Go on now, let him out before he destroys the crate." She just managed not to add her usual *and keep him out of trouble.* Toby didn't need to hear that at the moment.

"Yes'm." Toby took off at a jog, neatly avoiding Rafe, who was just coming onto the bridge.

"A boy and his dog," Rafe said, coming in as Toby left. "I suppose you told him you weren't going to sell Rascal?"

"Yes," Ky said. "Though we're looking at vet services. If they're that eager for a dog, I'm thinking frozen sperm might be worth something."

"Mercenary lot, you Vattas," Rafe said, but without much sting to it. "I noticed that our dock-watcher disappeared. I suppose that means the transfer came through?"

"It hadn't when I was at the bank, but I moved some funds from another Vatta account to clear our accounts onstation."

Her skullphone bleeped. Ky motioned Rafe back and answered it.

"That transfer you were expecting just came through from the rehab center." A visual display gave her the number and name of the caller, though she had already recognized the voice as the person she'd spoken to at Crown & Spears. "We should get confirmation by the close of business, this shift; do you want us to transfer the thousand back to the Vatta corporate fund when we do?"

Ky queried her implant about the Moscoe Confederation's history with Vatta Transport. Under its heading, her father had noted ". . . requires steady, mature captains with uncommon interpersonal skills; these people are ferociously courteous but occasionally capricious. Under no circumstances should ship crews reveal the presence of small pets, especially dogs. There is a pervasive belief in this society that their dogs were stolen from them by merchant ships, and they will insist that any dog is one of those stolen, or the descendant of same. They have few dogs, owing to the same problems as many terraformed worlds where the native wildlife is highly toxic to dogs."

Ky could almost hear her father's voice in those familiar cadences. Just so he had explained things to her or thought aloud, filling in each corner, finishing off each idea precisely. Grief swept over her. She could not believe she would never see him again; that if she returned to Slotter Key, he would not be there to greet her. She knew—she believed what Stella had said—but it seemed a fantasy, unreal.

She wanted to go home. She had never been really homesick at school or the Academy or even on the first voyage. The memories had all been comforting, not distressing. Now she felt the pull of Slotter Key, the familiar sights and smells, the familiar stars in the familiar night sky, the particular green of the tik plantations, the feel of the rain on her face, the cool tiles of the hall under her bare feet, the colors of the flowers. It did not seem possible that she would never walk that hall again, never throw herself down on that bed, never see again any of the childhood keepsakes in that closet, never see or hear . . . she let herself think of that for a moment . . . her father, her mother, her brothers. The visuals stored in her father's implant showed the moment of destruction, what her father saw, but not what came after . . . was anything left at all?

She blinked back the tears and made herself concentrate on the current situation. So she shouldn't have let the locals know they had a dog . . . how bad was this going to get? Should she warn Toby? Finding a good place to hide the dog seemed prudent, as did making sure they were full up with supplies in case they needed to button the ship and leave in a hurry. And she could check local statutes relating to dogs on their legal database.

Sallyon

Stella Vatta Constantin listened to the litany of complaints about her cousin Ky's behavior and wondered what Ky thought she was doing. Her aims had seemed straightforward enough back on Lastway: survive attacks, find and join up with other Vatta survivors, try to reorganize Vatta as a commercial entity. Hiring the mercenaries to protect them had made sense in those terms; forming a convoy to offset the cost of hiring the mercenaries made sense as well. But ever since the Osman affair, as Stella thought of it, Ky's behavior had changed, and Stella wasn't sure Ky still put Vatta—the family and the business—first.

Stella had fought with her own memories of the stubborn, bossy child Ky had been, trying to understand the person Ky had become in those years they hadn't met. The trim, compact, decisive young captain on the dock at Lastway had clearly changed, matured. Whether that was the influence of Spaceforce Academy or something else, Stella didn't know, but she'd begun to like and trust that Ky and believe that Grace was right in saying that Ky should lead the family through this crisis. She'd appreciated that Ky was quite clearly going through the same struggle to see Stella as she was now, not as that-idiot-Stella.

Now she wasn't so sure. Why had Ky refused to accept her father's implant until a moment of crisis, the most dangerous time to attempt an implant change? Why hadn't she accepted the mercenaries' offer of assistance if she hadn't trusted Rafe? Why hadn't she listened to the mercenaries' advice to get out of the system rather than make contact with the suspiciously convenient "Vatta" ship that turned out to be Osman? Ky had risked so much—risked all of them, as well as herself. The boy Toby, who should have been protected first and last. She'd actually talked to

Toby about suicide, something Stella considered horrible, given Toby's past experience.

And as for the battle itself . . . she had struggled not to let Ky see how shocked and alarmed she'd been by the way Ky conducted it—and herself. That feral grin of triumph, so different from the sick guilt Stella felt the times she'd killed . . . Stella had the feeling, dread mixed with nausea, that Ky had enjoyed killing Osman, that she felt no remorse at all.

She'd been relieved that Ky left her behind on *Gary Tobai*, and at the same time appalled. How could Ky leave a complete novice in command of a ship, even with the experienced senior crew she'd inherited? For that matter, how could Ky think of trying to run a damaged ship—about which she knew nothing—with just a skeleton crew?

Ky's decision to leave her in charge at Garth-Lindheimer rather than submit to adjudication of Ky's claim to Osman's ship had come as a shock as well. Refusing adjudication bordered on lawlessness. That wasn't like Ky; she'd always been the most stubbornly legalistic child.

And now she was faced with more evidence that Ky wasn't what she'd seemed at Lastway, that she might be a young Osman: brilliant but erratic, a charismatic leader with overweening ambition, without a conscience. A killer.

She smiled pleasantly at the dour-faced officials who interviewed her. "I'm really only interested in resupply and trade," she said, for the fourth or fifth time. "I'm sorry my cousin upset you, but as you can see this is an unarmed cargo ship, and a very small, slow one at that. My focus is on restoring Vatta's reputation as a common carrier, not on some plan to rid the universe of pirates." She let a hint of humor creep into her voice, the older relative about a wilder youngling.

"Do you think she's dangerous?" one of them asked.

A hard question; Stella wished she knew the answer.

"Not to anyone not allied with the pirates," she said finally. "I don't know if she told you about the attacks on our family?"

"Yes," the man said. "But we weren't sure we believed her."

"It's true," Stella said. "Her parents were killed; my father was killed. Both of us lost siblings and many other relatives. Vatta ships were attacked in other ports; in Allray, for instance, we lost an entire ship and crew but for one boy who was offship on an errand. I have been attacked myself, and our ship and personnel were attacked at Lastway. I'm sure if she had a chance, she would harm those who did this."

"So she said. But she claimed she had a letter of marque from her government—"

"She did. I saw it myself. I don't know anything about letters of marque—you will understand that my duty in the business, until now, was onplanet, not shipboard."

"And yet she left you in command of your ship—"

"As an emergency measure, and with very experienced crew, yes." Stella was not going to help blacken Ky's name, even if she had her own concerns about that. "I hired a licensed master at the next port, of course, along with additional crew."

They stared at her and she smiled back. Finally one of them shook his head. "Well. I find it hard to believe that you are involved in her conspiracy building, but should you find yourself in her company anytime soon, inform her that neither she nor her ship is welcome in this system until further notice. You may trade, but we prefer that your crew not go onstation, and all trades must be approved by our security staff. Is that clear?"

"Yes," Stella said. It would be a bother, but not impossible.

"You may attend the Captains' Guild, but you will be accompanied, when offship, by one of our personnel."

"I'm delighted," Stella said. "In case someone is still out to get Vatta family members, I would want an escort in any case, and an official one should be much more effective."

From their expressions they had not expected her response. What *had* Ky actually done or said? Stella felt a twinge of resentment again. It wasn't fair that she had to clean up Ky's messes.

When Stella checked in at the Captains' Guild, she felt the intense interest of everyone from the clerk at the desk to the other captains chatting in a corner of the lobby, one of whom immediately broke off and headed for the bar. She was used to being stared at, and she had dressed to accentuate her looks, but she was sure it was more than her beauty drawing attention this time. Her police escort nudged her. "Remember, no talk about alliances or conspiracies."

"I know," Stella said, forcing her voice to serenity. "And if someone else brings it up, I'll cut them off."

"See that you do," the escort said sourly. She was a stocky short woman with a broad, blunt face; Stella knew from the moment they met that the woman recognized and resented Stella's tall, elegant, blond beauty and was not about to admit it, even to herself. She'd been the target of that kind of resentment all her life.

Now a tall gray-haired man came out of the bar and approached her. "Captain Vatta?"

"Yes," Stella said.

"Pleased to meet you; I'm Rogier Sanlin, Porodin Shipping. My ship's the *Curry Town*."

Stella checked her implant. Porodin Shipping was a

four-system firm, running one circuit route with eight ships. A minor competitor when Vatta had been strong.

"Nice to meet you, Captain Sanlin," Stella said. He had eyed her the way most men eyed her, but was being polite about it. "What can I do for you?"

He glanced briefly at her escort. "Don't worry, they've told us all what not to talk to you about, and I wouldn't anyway. Porodin is pure shipping, no interest in anything else. I was wondering if you had cargo to transship to one of our destinations, or if you had cargo we might be interested in."

"I might," Stella said. "Let's talk." It took only minutes to establish that he might buy her custom textiles, but only if she would accept cargo space in trade.

"With the financial ansibles still down so many places, money's tight," Sanlin said.

It was only the first of several such conversations; Stella quickly caught on to the intricacies of trading cargo-space futures, and by lunchtime she was already eight hundred credits up in hard money.

"Aunt Grace always did say I was born to print money," Stella said to her police escort, "but I think she meant marry it." The woman glowered.

Stella ran her sales cube through a reader so her escort could check it for clandestine merchandise; the woman seemed annoyed that she found nothing to complain about.

It was almost time for lunch, and she considered annoying her escort by having lunch in the Captains' Guild dining hall, but that felt too much like something Ky would do. Still, she was tired of the ship galley. Her crew seemed unperturbed by having to stay aboard, but they were all professional spacers. She wasn't. She looked at her escort.

"Can you suggest a good place for lunch?"

"You can eat here," the woman said. "But I come with you."

"Of course," Stella said. "But here it's likely that other captains will approach me; I didn't want to concern you."

"It doesn't bother me. I would just stop you."

Stella just managed not to roll her eyes. She went to the registration desk instead and spoke to the clerk. "I've been stuck on a very small ship for a very long time," she said. "I'd like to find a place for lunch that has good food, where I won't be bothered with business for at least an hour. Can you suggest something?"

"Melandra," he said. "You'll need a reservation. One?" Then a glance at her escort. "Two?"

"Two," Stella said. She smiled; he made the call and then gave her directions.

"It's very expensive," her escort said as they came back out into the concourse.

"I'm sure," Stella said. "Places that protect you from interruption usually are. Do you mind?"

"No," the woman said. "I've never been there. I hear they have all natural foods, no vat-grown."

Melandra, when they reached it, had a simple gray door with the name in gold script. Stella paused. "Stella Vatta," she said. The door opened on a carpeted hall, the walls gray pin-striped with burgundy, then closed behind them when both were through, shutting off the bustle of the concourse. Somewhere, a mellow stringed instrument was playing.

"This way please," a pleasant voice said from near the floor. Stella looked down. A knee-high artibod, its body metallic burgundy, blinked emerald eyes at them. It moved ahead of them down the corridor, turned left, and led the way into what looked like a rustic bower in a fruit orchard on a day somewhere between spring and summer. A single table, draped in white, stood between padded benches under a trellis supporting a grapevine. A white-flowered tree grew against one wall; one thick with shiny red fruit grew beside it. A light breeze moved its leaves; the air smelled of roses and grass and earth. "Be seated please," the artibod said. Stella slid onto one bench, her escort onto the other. She felt beneath her the bench reshape itself to her body; a back extension extruded to support her back in perfect comfort. Her escort looked startled, but said nothing.

"The season is programmable," the artibod said. "Controls are on the table; the menu will appear there shortly. Would the ladies prefer artibod or human service?"

"Artibod," Stella said, just as her escort said "Human." They looked at each other; the escort shrugged. "Artibod," Stella said again.

"Command the table when you are ready to order," the artibod said, and rolled away.

"I had no idea," her escort said. "There's really just one table?"

"In this alcove, anyway," Stella said. "I'm sure they have others." She looked at the table controls. They were, indeed, on a setting between spring and summer; the temperature was cool in the shade, warm in the artificial sunlight. "Are you comfortable?"

"Yes." The woman looked around again. Stella relaxed into her seat, which adjusted to the shift in weight. "You can't bribe me, you know."

"Excuse me?"

"Taking me to a fancy place like this. It won't work, if you're trying to bribe me to let you talk conspiracy to the other captains."

"I don't want to talk conspiracy to other captains," Stella said. "I just want a nice lunch, uninterrupted, so other captains can't say things to me that you will object to." Her escort looked puzzled. "What would you think," Stella went on, "if one of them had come up and started asking questions about what Ky's doing?"

"I—would tell you to stop."

"Even though I hadn't started the conversation. Yes. So I wanted to have a peaceful lunch, where I wouldn't be bothered with that kind of thing. This is a nice place. What are you going to eat?"

The menu, now visible on the tablecloth, included both standard fare and exotics, with explanations available at a touch. Stella chose roast chicken with vegetables, a green salad. Her escort scowled at the menu. "They don't have just plain sandwiches."

"They may, if we ask," Stella said. "Any particular kind?"

"I usually eat at a kiosk on B; fried soy cubes and onions in a flatbread wrap."

"Ah. I'd guess the Pocket Grill is the closest to that. I'm having chicken."

"It's more expensive."

"It's on my account; don't worry about it."

"I—I would like the chicken, too."

Stella nodded and entered the order. Another artibod rolled up with the drinks she had ordered, and in a few minutes came back with their meals, rising to table level to roll them off onto the table. They ate in silence at first. Stella waited to see if the food would have any softening effect. When she suggested dessert, her escort said, "You aren't like your cousin."

"Excuse me? I'm having the torte—what are you having?"

"What's a torte?"

Stella explained, then entered the order and went back to the previous topic. "What do you mean, I'm not like my cousin? I mean, I know I don't look like her."

"It's more than that." The woman leaned forward. "She's trouble, that one."

"Really? What did she do?"

"She's part of a conspiracy to overthrow the government," the woman said. "She was trying to get all these traders to join her."

"Overthrow the government? Surely not . . . is that what she said?"

"That's what my supervisor told me. She argued with the stationmaster, very loudly. They told her to go away and not come back."

"Do you know exactly what she said?" Stella asked. "Because I know she wanted to rebuild Vatta—"

"She didn't talk about Vatta," the woman said. "She talked about war."

Quincy met her at the main hatch. "What happened?" she asked. "You look furious."

"I'm not sure I want to talk about it yet," Stella said. "The good news is that we have a buyer for the textiles we bought. The bad news is that Ky has gone out of her mind."

"Mmm." Quincy glanced around. "Perhaps in your cabin?"

"Right." Stella led the way, trying not to glower at the crewmembers she met. When they were in her cabin, hatch closed, Quincy sat on the bunk while Stella paced the four steps back and forth. "Ky," she said finally, "is an idiot. All right, I know she's brave and I know she's not actually stupid, but . . . she's now alienated two different systems, at least, and for all I know she's busy making us more enemies where she is now. I don't know how she thinks making people angry is going to help our family recover—"

"What are they angry about here?" Quincy asked.

"She has this harebrained idea that all the Slotter Key privateers, and anyone else they can get to join them, should form a united fleet to fight the . . . I don't even know who." Stella sat down in her desk chair and ran her hands through her hair. "Whoever it was that attacked the Bissonet System, I suppose," she said. "Apparently she is convinced that they're all connected, the attacks on Vatta, the nonfunctioning ansibles, the increased pirate activity, and now this system attack . . . and yes, I know, she was talking like that before, but she had her head straight on priorities: Vatta first. Now—I don't think she has the slightest concern for Vatta's reputation. We are not a military organization. We transport and we trade. I don't know what she thinks she can accomplish; it's not like she has any actual experience. That Mackensee officer, Johannson, was right: she's a very loose cannon, and we're the ones who will suffer for it."

She felt better for saying it. Across the small cabin, Quincy nodded. "She does get wound up about what she wants to do. I worried about her myself. But her record's good. It's not everyone who could've gotten us out of that mess with Osman."

"It's not everyone who would've gotten us *into* that mess with Osman," Stella said. "All we had to do was follow the advice of the professionals we hired and go on our way." Maybe this time Quincy would understand the point she'd tried to make more than once.

"And Osman would still be out there plotting against us," Quincy said. "That wouldn't be good."

"No . . . but what we have isn't good, either. Whatever happened to putting Vatta back together again?"

"Do you really think that's possible, Stella?" Quincy leaned forward. "So much has been lost . . . all those ships, all those people."

"I don't know if it's possible or not, but it's what we set out to do. It's not time to quit on that yet. And she's got Toby—"

"She'll take care of Toby," Quincy said.

"I'm not sure of that," Stella said. "She's likely to get him killed, or turn him into another like herself."

"Are you sure this isn't more about you than about her?" Quincy asked. "Maybe because Grace sent her your father's implant and used you like a messenger girl?"

Stella snorted. "Aunt Grace has used me as a messenger—and other things—for years. I'm not jealous of Ky. I didn't want her father's implant—or my father's, for that matter. But Ky isn't any more suited to run Vatta than I am, if she can't keep her mind on trade and profit and the family. All this flashy pseudo-military behavior proves it. She's just like Osman—"

Quincy's mouth dropped open. "No, she's not!" she said firmly. "Not at all. Stella, I served with Ky from the time she left Slotter Key. I spent over a year on the same ship with Osman when I was young. She is *nothing* like that man. She's honest, she's kind, she cares about her people—"

Stella blinked at the vehemence of Quincy's reply. "But Quincy, she's also reckless and impulsive—"

"That's not the same thing as dishonest and cruel. For pity's sake, Stella, the best traders are risk takers to a degree. Risk avoidance is a low-profit strategy. I'll admit Ky can be bolder, quicker to act, than just about any captain I've served under, but in times like these that's the margin of survival. I was scared witless, I don't mind admitting, when we tangled with Osman, but I don't think anyone else could have gotten us through that with so little damage."

"So you think I'm not qualified?" Stella regretted that

the moment it came out of her mouth; even to her it sounded juvenile and whiny.

"No. I think you're differently qualified." Quincy sighed, and ran a hand through her thick white hair. "Stella, I've served the Vatta family for nigh on seventy years now. The one thing I know about Vattas—and that would include you, whatever you think of yourself—is that you're full of surprises. Not one of you is predictable, not really. You're not all the same: some of you obviously qualified for ship duty, some for desk work, and your great-aunt Frances was a research genius who never got her nose out of her lab, according to your father, while her brother Ismail tinkered about for years without amounting to anything practical. But he's famous among musicians for inventing three new instruments. Strong character, all of you. Your talents are not the same as Ky's, but you have them."

"There are good surprises and bad surprises," Stella said; she knew she was losing but she could not let it go. "Ky's being irresponsible, at least where the family's concerned."

"I don't think so. Though starting a feud within the family would be, in my opinion." Quincy's direct look conveyed a warning. "The family needs you, Stella—you and Ky, both of you. Don't give up on her."

Stella tried to tell herself Quincy was too old to understand, perhaps too blinded by having worked with Ky. She couldn't quite make it convincing; Quincy was known for her earthy wisdom, and Ky had, after all, succeeded so far.

"I'm not giving up on her," Stella said. One way or another, that was true, and she knew better now than to express her doubts about Ky openly.

FOURTEEN

Cascadia

Ky wondered where Stella was. If she had resupplied quickly, as Ky suggested, and followed on, she should have appeared in this system about ten days after Ky . . . should be insystem now. It would take that old ship longer to move in from the downjump radius, but the new FTL drive Ky'd installed at Sabine had cut their jump time considerably. Had something happened to her?

"I doubt they'll hold her," Rafe said when she mentioned her concern. "She hasn't done anything—at worst, they'll send her off all the sooner, because she's related to you."

"Then she should be here. I wish I knew more about that captain she hired."

"She'll be fine," Rafe said, and patted her shoulder.

Ky glared at him. "Do not try to soothe me like a child, Rafe. You know as well as I do that there's danger, and she doesn't have any weapons . . ."

"Those mines," Rafe said.

"Which she hasn't a clue how to use," Ky said.

"You know, she's not stupid, even if she is beautiful," Rafe said, hitching a hip onto the table.

"I never said—"

Martin came in with the day's training report and gave Rafe a dark look. Rafe shrugged. "I'm only trying to calm the captain down, Martin; she's worried about sweet Stella."

"With some reason, I'd think," Martin said. "No word yet, Captain?"

"None." Ky moved data cubes from one stack to another. "I know she's upset; that was clear. I can't blame her; she's had to trail me around to three different systems, cope with whatever I left behind."

"It's not like she's never traveled," Rafe said.

"I know that. But it's different when it's your ship, when you're not just a passenger." She sighed. "I just hope they don't give her too much trouble on Sallyon."

"There's nothing you can do about it even if they do," Rafe said.

"That's the problem," Ky said.

Worrying about Stella was only marginally better than worrying about what was going on back on Slotter Key. She dragged her mind away from both, and onto the dog problem. Should she contact that veterinary clinic onplanet, or not? It was too late to hide the existence of the dog, but she'd insisted that no pictures be posted.

She shrugged and placed the call.

"Eglin Veterinary Clinic, small-animal practice only, canids a specialty. How may we serve you?" The voice-only channel gave scant clues to the speaker, but the high breathy voice suggested young and female.

"This is Captain Vatta; we're docked at your space station. I need information on reproductive services."

"Species, please?"

"Canid," Ky said, crossing mental fingers.

"Oh." The voice faded, then came back. "*You're* the one! You have a dog aboard! Is it for sale? Where did you get it?"

"We rescued a dog at Lastway Station," Ky said. "It was going to be killed."

"Killed! They kill *dogs*?"

"Indeed they do. We intervened. I understand that dogs are a valuable commodity here, but we are not interested in selling the dog. However, it is a male, and I presume gametes are also marketable."

"You may be unaware of this, Captain Vatta, but we once had plenty of dogs. They were stolen by unscrupulous spacers. That's why dogs are so valuable here." The speaker's tone had shifted quickly from prim to resentful. "We would have to test your dog to see if it's descended from the dogs that were stolen; in that case, our government would demand its return."

"Do you know how far away Lastway is?" Ky said. "And they have plenty of dogs; they have no need to steal them."

"You traveled the distance," the voice said, "so could someone trafficking in dogs."

"I'm not trafficking in dogs," Ky said, "despite the outrageous prices offered by your people. The dog is not for sale and never has been."

"You could be just holding out for a better price." That was said in tones of deep suspicion.

Ky managed not to say *This is ridiculous* and held her temper. "All I wanted to ascertain was whether it was possible for you to obtain sperm from this dog, without pain or distress to the animal, and whether it would have any market value. I understand now that it would be far too expensive and complicated, so I'm sorry to have taken up so much of your time." She closed the connection.

"That was odd," Rafe said.

"I should've checked my implant before I told them we had a dog aboard," Ky said. "It didn't occur to me."

"Think it will give us trouble?"

"It could. Everything else I've done and not done has," Ky said. "Evidently what seems simple and straightforward to me is all wrong."

"There's a Vatta icon insystem, Captain," Hugh said. "But it's not Stella."

"Not Stella . . . who else could it be?" Ky said. She looked at the plot. "One of our bigger ships . . . damn. It's that idiot."

"Which idiot?" Hugh said, grinning.

"That's *Katrine Lamont*," Ky said. "And if I continue to have a bad day, Furman will still be captain."

"That's the one who—"

"Gave me all that trouble at Sabine, yes. My very first captain when I was on my apprentice voyage. Doesn't like me at all."

"Ah, but does he have the weapons to blow us away?" Rafe asked.

"No, but we can't use ours," Ky said. "I wonder what he's doing over on this side of the sector. He had that really plush route—remember, he was furious at being pulled away to go to Sabine."

"You didn't tell your father to send him to the back of beyond?" Rafe said.

"I wouldn't do that," Ky said. Rafe rolled his eyes at her; she shook her head. "I wouldn't. Besides, being almost next door to Nexus isn't the back of beyond. Cascadia's had human settlement longer than Slotter Key."

"Yes, but it may not be as good a route for him, especially if he had established relationships with customers on the old route."

Ky quickly accessed the information in her father's implant. Furman had been in the minority as a senior captain who was not by birth or marriage in the Vatta family.

He had earned his promotions on his record: he had the second best on-time record in the fleet, and he had made Vatta dominant in his former route, taking business share away from rival shipping firms. All this was good. His personal fitness reports were marred only by the occasional complaint of his rigidity.

Until the Sabine affair. Apparently he'd been unwilling to be pulled off his lucrative route, and then . . . Ky felt her brows rising as she accessed the classified file that contained what he had said to her father and her father had said to him. Downgraded from triple-plus to one, transferred to the Virnidia–Moscoe–Nexus–Bondeen route . . . she wondered that he hadn't quit. Retirement, probably. Or maybe he really was loyal to Vatta. She was amazed at the depth of her father's wrath.

She could've wished for anyone else but Furman.

"He crossed my father," Ky said. "It was the Sabine thing, but I didn't start it. He called me a fool, which was probably fair, and my father didn't like it."

"No," Rafe said, "I suppose he didn't. What do you think will happen now, when you have no father to throw his considerable weight on the scale?"

"I don't know. Furman doesn't like me, but he should know by now he can't control me."

"He doesn't know you have a letter of marque, does he?"

"No. But if he knows about Osman, he may think Osman is here because this is Osman's ship."

"And he'll do what?"

"Tell the authorities it's an outlaw ship, assuming he knows that. Of course, I told them the truth about it. If we could just get the beacon changed I wouldn't have these problems—"

"And we'd never have caught that outlaw back on

Rosvirein," Martin said. "There are advantages to a bad name."

Rafe slanted a glance at him. "Indeed there are. I didn't expect you to make my argument."

"Enough," Ky said. The two of them would bicker all day if she didn't stop it. "What benefit do you think we'll get out of Furman thinking this is Osman's ship?"

"I have no idea," Rafe said. "But anytime you shake the righteous prigs, bits of information fall out of their pockets. We'll just have to see."

Katrine Lamont was on a fast approach; as a familiar unarmed ship on a regular schedule, she was granted priority. Ky wished she knew what Furman was saying to Traffic Control and what they were saying to him.

Meanwhile, she had enough to keep busy. Moscoe Confederation's Ship Registration Commission was sitting on her request to change the ship's name and beacon ID. They had agreed that her letter of marque gave her the legal right to claim it as a prize and file ownership papers. She had done that, and they had processed the change in ownership in just a few days, only insisting that it must be registered to her, and not to Vatta Transport. A corporation could not hold a letter of marque, and a prize was the property of the captain holding such a letter of marque. Later, perhaps, she could transfer ownership to Vatta Transport, but that would have to be by sale, not gift. They had agreed that having a ship formerly owned by someone with a bad reputation was an embarrassment. But they had not yet decided whether ownership gained by capture allowed the new owner the privilege of changing the ship's identity . . . and when, if it was legal, it could be done. How long should it be delayed awaiting legal challenge?

Another complication was the continuing pressure to sell Rascal. They had been offered a number of substitute pets, from Terran cats of all shapes and sizes to exotics like Tamburine alloes—furry, with black masks like Old Earth raccoons and bright green tongues. They were said to be completely odorless, nonallergenic despite the soft fur, affectionate, and docile; they excreted dry pellets, which they were easily taught to put in receptacles for pickup. Ky had refused all these. She still wasn't that fond of the pup, but Rascal and the need to care for him had certainly put Toby on an even keel. The boy had blossomed on the voyage, willingly tackling challenging tasks related to the drives as well as continuing his studies and caring for Toby. He was centimeters taller, muscling up as he worked out in the gym under Martin's guidance. She wasn't about to upset him by taking away his dog. The more they pressured her, the more she resisted.

"Captain Vatta." That was the stationmaster's icon. Ky opened her channel and the stationmaster's face came up onscreen, looking graver than its wont.

"I'm here," Ky said.

"I'm sorry to say I have had a disturbing message from the Vatta Transport ship en route to the station. Her captain—"

"Captain Furman," Ky said.

"Er . . . yes. Captain Furman insists that you must be an imposter, that the real Kylara Vatta is dead."

"What?" The other bridge crew in hearing turned to look at her, their visible shock paralleling what she felt.

"He says the Vatta family were attacked—which you told us—but insists that the person whose name and identification you gave must be dead, and that you are not she."

"I certainly am," Ky said firmly. "Did you transmit a visual image of me?"

"Not yet," the stationmaster said. "Do you expect he will recognize it?"

"He certainly should," Ky said. "I did my apprentice voyage on his ship, and then we . . . ran into each other last year in the Sabine System, when someone attacked their ansible platforms. I have no idea why he would think I'd died." Should she mention that it was more confrontation than meeting? Probably not.

"Because he was part of the plot?" murmured Rafe, just out of range of the pickup.

Ky didn't want to think about that. Furman was a stiff-necked prig, true, but that didn't make him a traitor.

"So he should be familiar with you; he has seen you recently enough—"

"I would think so," Ky said. "I was only thirteen on my apprentice voyage, but I'm assuming he had his screen on when we spoke at Sabine. We didn't meet face-to-face; we weren't docked at the same time." Again, the complexities of that whole situation—why she was docked and he wasn't, why she had not met him face-to-face—were more than she wanted to explain at the moment.

"He says the ship you're in was stolen by a renegade Vatta—which you also told us—and he says he thinks you must be Osman Vatta's daughter or granddaughter, pretending to be Kylara, the daughter of Gerard Vatta. That Kylara Vatta, if alive, would be on a ship named *Gary Tobai*, but he's sure you're—she's—dead."

"My cousin Stella's on the *Gary*; she should be here any day. Send Furman my picture and see what he says," Ky said. "If he still insists it's not me, he's lying and my cousin will vouch for me when she gets here."

"Captain, not to impugn your honesty in any way . . . will your cousin have any better identification than you? And will Captain Furman know her?" A moment's pause, then, "I must remind you, Captain, that even in moments of emotional intensity, using such epithets as *lying* is against our regulations, as provided in the hardcopy you were given. I am willing to overlook it this once, but such an infringement if repeated must be reported and will reflect on any judgment in this case."

"My apologies," Ky said, choking back what she really wanted to say. "I appreciate your leniency to a visitor and regret that my home world's standards of courtesy were so lax." It would not help her case, she suspected, to tell the stationmaster that Furman had called *her* a liar and that's why her father had sent him out here. The last thing she wanted was a forced implant readout, not with that *thing* Rafe's implant had inserted into her head.

"It is understandable, Captain Vatta," the stationmaster said, in the genial tone he had used with her before. "But you understand that we must strictly enforce our regulations or risk chaos, with so much outlander traffic in the system. Now I will transmit your image to Captain Furman and see what he says."

"Please do keep me informed," Ky said, trying to keep the edge out of her voice.

"Certainly," the stationmaster said.

"He's out to get you," Lee said, as soon as she'd cut the connection. "I remember—"

"So do I." Ky ruffled her hair with both hands. "Mad as a kicked wasps' nest, he was when he first contacted me, and madder when I didn't do what he told me. But I didn't think of him as particularly vindictive, just bossy and stubborn."

"That was before your father kicked him out of his cushy and very lucrative circuit and sent him out here," Lee said.

"I suppose. I still can't believe he'd lie about me. Do you suppose he really thinks I'm dead and Osman had a daughter . . . granddaughter . . . whatever? For that matter, *did* Osman have children?"

"Considering what Quincy told us about his sexual proclivities, he may've had dozens," Rafe said. "Whether he recognized any of them is another question, but Furman may know something we don't. And it would be interesting to know how he knows, if he does."

"Nothing in his records," Ky mused. "At least, I didn't see anything . . ."

"Nor I," Rafe and Martin said together. "But that doesn't mean much," Rafe went on. "I doubt he was the type to take care of his offspring, if he even knew they existed."

"If they exist, I wonder if they know about him," Ky said. "If they know they're related to Vatta. To me."

Rafe raised his brows. "You aren't thinking of looking for them, are you? Your original plan to rescue Vattas meant legitimate Vattas, didn't it? Not some renegade's by-blows."

"It's not their fault they're Osman's children," Ky said, feeling a sudden surge of protectiveness. "Probably raped their mothers and left them stranded somewhere . . . it's not fair."

Rafe rolled his eyes and Martin sighed; Lee merely looked amused.

"Stella said you had a rescue complex," Rafe said. "Now I see it. Odd, really, that combination of killer and rescuer."

"I'm not—" Ky stopped abruptly, a swirl of emotion almost blanking out her ability to speak for a moment. Another signal from her father's implant, as something she'd said triggered the opening of a secured file she hadn't noticed yet. Her father had also suspected that Osman would father children on helpless women; her father had worried about that, he and Stavros both. They had tried to trace Osman's movements for the first few years, looking in orphanages, paying for genetic screenings of possibles out of their own money. They'd found four, managed to have them adopted into more respectable Vatta families; they'd been sure there were more. She probed further, but her father had erased the names.

For a moment, Ky felt a stab of cold terror. Was she herself one of Osman's by-blows? Was that what made killing such an intense pleasure, and was that what had led her toward Spaceforce? She could well imagine her father, with his sense of duty and honor, choosing to adopt one of the children himself. And she looked nothing like her mother . . .

"Captain—what's wrong?"

She pulled her mind back to the present. "Implant alarm," she said, keeping her voice level. "Talking about Osman's possible children triggered a locked file. My father thought there were some."

"And?" prompted Rafe.

"And he thought he found some, had them adopted into good families. I don't know who. He erased the names." She was not ever going to tell Rafe—anyone— about that fear. She was not like Osman. She was not a vicious pirate; she was not a sexual predator; she was not an outlaw. Even if she was his child—and she could not believe that—she was not like him. She was her father's child, and her father was—had been—Gerard Avondetta Vatta, the respectable, honorable financial wizard at Vatta Transport's head.

Martin whistled. "I hope whatever made Osman Osman wasn't genetic," he said.

"I'm sure it was looked for," Ky said. "Early therapy might've changed Osman; if the children showed any behavioral problems, it would've been treated."

"But back to my point," Rafe said. "You can't think of going out to find and rescue Osman's children, when you have more important priorities. You need to find other family members, other ships."

"Like Furman's," Ky said. "He's got to realize that I am who I am, and that I'm now in charge."

"He's not going to like that," Lee said. "He's a senior captain; you were just upgraded from provisional."

"I'm a Vatta," Ky said.

"If he can cast doubt on that, I bet he will," Lee said. "You and Stella are both decades younger than he is."

"Crown & Spears has Jo's—Stella's sister's—genetic scan on file; they used it to compare with mine and confirm my family identity." She had forgotten that until now; a wave of warm relief came over her. Surely the comparison of her DNA and Jo's proved that she was Jo's first cousin, not Osman's daughter. Osman hadn't been her father's and uncle's brother, after all. "Besides, while Stella doesn't look much like a Vatta—she takes after her mother's family—I fit right in."

"For that matter, so did Osman," Lee said. "Like your father and Stavros, anyway. I wonder if his children look more like a Vatta, or their mothers."

"It doesn't matter what they look like," Rafe said, clearly impatient with this. Ky was grateful; it covered her reaction. "They could look like anyone, and the point is you have more important things to worry about right now."

"Like Furman," Ky said. "I wish Stella had arrived. She'd be much smoother talking to him than I will."

The stationmaster's next call confirmed her worries. "Captain Furman says that the image we sent superficially resembles Kylara Vatta, but he is sure she is dead, and thus you must be an imposter."

"He is . . . mistaken," Ky said, trapping *lying scumbucket* behind her teeth. "Crown & Spears has a sample of my genetic material and has already compared it to a known sample from my cousin Jo, my father's brother's daughter. Did he say where he got this certain knowledge that I was dead?"

"I'm so sorry," the stationmaster said. "A commercial concern such as Crown & Spears maintains private records to which we are not granted access. I'm afraid that their confirmation of your identity is not valid for official records. While I have no reason to disbelieve their results personally, our regulations are very clear: we need to establish genetic relationships based on samples obtained and maintained by official means before such can be used to establish identity. Would you be willing to give another sample?"

"Yes, of course," Ky said. "Anytime. But do you have existing records from my family to which to compare it?"

"I do not yet know," the stationmaster said. "This is an unusual situation, in unusual times. I will have that answer for you in a few hours. Meanwhile—and I regret very much placing such strictures on someone whose dealings with us have so far been amiable and honest— I must request that you personally stay aboard your ship until Furman arrives and a court date can be set for formal procedures, and that you allow one of our monitors to come aboard to ensure that you do not attempt to flee."

"May I ask why?"

"We take identity fraud very seriously, Captain Vatta. Captain Furman suggested that you had altered biometrics to assume the identity you claim. Altering biometrics is not illegal here, and we have clinics that perform humodification at various levels from superficial surgery to gene altering. But when identity fraud is suspected, we do not allow the person so charged access to these clinics until a full identity scan has been run."

"That's—" *Ridiculous* was hardly tactful and courteous. "—reasonable," Ky managed. "But couldn't you use some form of tracking device on my person instead? I'm a trader; I have business to conduct. I know back home that they use such to restrict the movements of criminals."

"The larger problem is your ship, Captain. We were prepared to accept your account of how you obtained it, but it is a ship with a bad history. We don't want to be held responsible for setting a criminal loose. I could petition to allow you to be fitted with a tracking device—we have that technology, of course—but we must disable your ship's ability to depart without warning."

"I understand that," Ky said. "As long as your means of doing so cause no permanent damage and we do not incur additional charges, I have no objection."

"Then I will speak to a judicar about an alternative way of controlling your movements. And your crewmembers, of course, are under no restriction at this time, other than the requirement to obey our rules."

"Thank you," Ky said.

"Do you by any chance have another member of the Vatta family aboard? Someone else whose DNA we could compare to yours?"

"Yes, but not a close relative," Ky said. "A young man whose ship was blown up at Allray; my cousin Stella brought him with her to Lastway."

"Do you know the exact relationship?"

"No, but I can find out. When will your monitor arrive?"

"She is at dockside now. If you would be so good as to grant her entrance—"

"Right away, Stationmaster." Ky cut the connection, shaking her head at the expressions of her bridge crew.

"Stop that. We have to comply with the law, for now. Not as if we weren't already, or I'd have said what I really think of Furman."

"With her aboard, you can't," Martin pointed out. "None of us will be able to . . ."

"If they agree to my being given a tracking device, she may not be here that long. Let me check. Martin, you go let her in." Ky called the stationmaster. "If I'm reading your regulations correctly, our ship is still considered the territory of its origin, is it not?"

"Yes, Captain. What is it?"

"My crew are concerned that their habitual behavior to one another, their freedom of expression, is not within the bounds of your regulations, and that they may be charged with an offense for something they say here, which they considered private space not subject to your rules."

"Oh—nothing to worry about there, Captain. We are quite aware that ship crews have their own way of speaking and behaving aboard their own ships, and that is not our concern. It is our concern only when they are dealing with our citizens on our territory. Our monitors are carefully trained, and will ignore everything other than their assignment. In this case, the monitor's assignment is simply to prevent your ship's departure from the station without my permission, and to prevent you personally from exiting until a determination is made of your identity or your request for an alternative method is granted. Does that fill your needs?"

"Yes, thank you," Ky said.

"In fact, if you personally should make statements that would be considered an offense outside the ship or if you were speaking with one of our official personnel, the monitor is instructed to ignore these unless they are directed at herself. Naturally, no discourtesy can be offered to her, as she is indeed one of our citizens."

"That is quite clear, Stationmaster," Ky said. "Thank you again."

"You are most welcome, Captain Vatta," the stationmaster said.

The woman who appeared on the bridge a few moments later, with Martin a careful two steps behind her, looked nothing like Ky had expected. *What is such a beauty doing in police work,* was her first thought. She was a match for Stella, only dark instead of blond.

"Captain Vatta? I'm Robinette Leary, monitor first class. I'm sure it's a bit upsetting, having a stranger forced onto your ship."

"Er . . . not at all," Ky said, floundering for the moment. The woman carried a bulky case.

"Don't worry; I'm not eager to take offense," Leary went on. "I'm not here to make trouble, just prevent it. So far we have no local complaints against you at all, but because of the way in which you obtained this ship, we are required to take all precautions to be sure of your identity."

"I understand," Ky said.

"I'm glad," Leary said, smiling. Her smile involved dimples in her perfect cheeks. She glanced around at the bridge crew. Ky could see for herself that her looks had affected the men—except Rafe, whose expression of advanced disdain might be a cover for the same reaction. "Let me reassure you all," Leary said. "I will take no notice of what you say among yourselves; our rules on courtesy do not apply here unless you deliberately insult me."

"So . . . I can call him a terminally stupid idiot"—Rafe nodded at Lee—"and you won't object?"

"Not at all," Leary said. "Does he?"

Lee grinned. "From Rafe, that's a compliment," he said. "I don't mind."

"I will consider it an education, but will refrain from

participation," Leary said. "Captain, as my primary duty is to see that neither you nor the ship departs, I will begin by sealing the bridge controls related to departure. If you would point out the relevant boards, please."

"Here." Lee moved aside, pointing to the controls that retracted umbilicals, sealed ports and hatches, and brought the insystem drive to readiness.

From her case, Leary took raised plastic covers that she fitted over those controls, being careful to cover only those Lee pointed out, and sealed the edges with bright orange tape. "This tape will turn green if it is lifted," she said. "It will not reseal. Tampering with official seals is an offense under our regulations, and will result in severe penalties. If for any reason you feel it necessary to gain access to these controls, you must have authorization from me or the stationmaster. A directional electromagnetic pulse device has been attached to your ship; removing more than four centimeters of tape will cause it to activate, and permanent damage to your control circuits may result. It may also cause temporary damage to persons on the bridge at that time. Do you understand?"

"Yes," Lee said. The monitor glanced around, waiting until everyone, including Ky, had agreed that they understood.

"If you have other crew who come onto the bridge, you must instruct them."

Ky nodded her understanding. The station com circuit bleeped again; she turned to the screen.

"Captain Vatta, the judicar has authorized use of a tracking device in your case. May I speak to Monitor Leary?"

"Of course," Ky said. Leary came forward.

"Monitor Leary, when you have secured the ship, you will please accompany Captain Vatta to a security station where she will be fitted with a tracking device."

"Bridge controls have been sealed, Stationmaster. Will it be necessary to place a guard on dockside?"

"I think not, Monitor. When Captain Vatta has been fitted with the device, be sure she understands all the restrictions, and then you need not accompany her further."

"Thank you, sir."

"Captain Vatta, the judicar granted this alteration of the original order only because of the time involved until Furman arrives and your need to conduct legitimate business. I trust you will appreciate the courtesy and not abuse it."

"By no means, Stationmaster," Ky said. "I am grateful for the consideration shown, and intend to be offship only in the necessary course of business."

FIFTEEN

Having the tracking device fitted took only a few minutes, and the technician treated Ky with perfect courtesy. Ky restrained herself from any of the witty remarks that occurred to her; she suspected that Cascadian bureaucracy would not take kindly to that kind of wit. Afterward, Monitor Leary handed her a hardcopy list of the establishments she was forbidden to enter.

"And now you are free to go, and I will not trouble you further," Leary said, smiling.

"Thank you," Ky said, adhering to the cultural demand for perfect courtesy.

A few hours later, she was back on the ship when she got the call informing her that there was no official source of Vatta genetic material on the station or in the system. The Cascadian Bureau of Investigation agent explained that no Vatta family member had ever been required to give one; no question of identity had arisen before.

"It's most inconvenient," the agent said. "We do have basic bioscan data, fingerprints and retinal scans and so on, but that's only good for determining if someone matches a single known individual identity. That's collected from captains on arrival, as you know, and we have data from Josephine Vatta, as well as several others. Ergash

Vatta, Melisande Vatta, Bromlan, Asil. But you aren't claiming to be any of those, and we had no reason to request a sample for genetic identity."

"So . . . what do you plan to do?"

"First we will inquire more of Captain Furman, who is already known to us as a legitimate Vatta employee. Do you deny this?"

"No, of course not. Assuming he's not an imposter, this is the man under whom I trained. He should know me, and identify me, correctly."

"We do have bioscan data on him, so when he arrives we can determine instantly if he is the same individual with whom we have been dealing. Do you have any identifying data?"

Ky queried her implant. In his personnel file she had both his bioscan and genetic pattern, as well as visual images; she offered to transmit those.

"Nothing external?"

"No. But since we hold opposing opinions, is there any reason for you to doubt the validity of my implant data if it confirms his identity?"

"Well . . . no. All right. Please transmit visual image first—full-face and profile if you have it—and then the bioscan data. We may not need the genetic data."

"Just a moment." Ky had not called on the skullphone, which she still found awkward to use, and now moved the files she wanted to send, plugged in, and sent them via ship com.

"Thank you," the agent said. "The visual matches but I'll send the bioscan to our records department."

"Once he's docked," Ky said, "you might ask him whether he has any bioscan data on me. He might have, since my father asked Furman to go to Sabine on my behalf."

The agent's brows rose. "You don't seem at all concerned that such data might implicate you."

"Implicate me how?" Ky asked. "I am Kylara Vatta, and I know that, and any real identity check will prove it. If the ansibles weren't down, you could contact Slotter Key for all the details."

"But they aren't working," the agent said. "According to Captain Furman, the real Kylara Vatta was on a very different ship, the . . . er . . . *Gary Tobai* . . ."

"Yes, I explained that," Ky said. "Are you sure that ship hasn't shown up in this system yet? I was expecting Stella to follow on directly, and she should be here by now."

"I'm quite sure," the agent said. "I will inform you if—when—such an event occurs."

"Thank you," Ky said, warned by his tone. "I didn't mean to impugn your watchfulness, it's just that I'm worried about her. I thought she'd be here by day before yesterday."

Stella stayed two extra days in Sallyon, doing her best to soothe the ruffled feelings of its administrators. "We are traders," she kept saying to one after another unhappy official. "Yes, Ky is a bit impetuous, but Vatta Transport is what it has always been, commercial and not military."

"In these dangerous times, we simply cannot have private individuals raising a military force . . ." This was the fourth official to call her in for a lecture. Stella held on to her temper with an effort.

"I quite understand. As you may have noticed, I'm not doing any such thing. I have traded ordinary cargoes—" The designer toilets had brought an excellent price here, as had the custom fabrics.

"But you are going to follow her, are you not? Your

listed next destination is Cascadia; that's where she went. That suggests to us that you are in league."

She was getting very tired of this suspicion. *I'm not like Ky at all,* she wanted to scream at them. In truth, she did not want to follow Ky. If Ky had gone rogue, as she suspected, she could not help Vatta by playing along. Besides, she could pick up little here that anyone in the Moscoe Confederation would want. Still, more than she wanted away from Ky, she wanted to get Ky into a small room and shake some sense into her.

"I have only this one small ship," she said. "And as you pointed out, these are dangerous times. I hope to persuade my cousin that her duty is to protect me, and other Vatta ships, perhaps by escorting us in convoy."

"We still find it suspicious—"

"You would find anything I did suspicious," Stella said, her temper finally fraying. "I have met all your restrictions; I have conducted only normal trade activities. You simply want to believe I am part of some vast conspiracy. Let me turn that around. How am I supposed to know that your hostility to an interstellar space force is not part of collusion with these pirates who have taken over Bissonet?"

The man turned pale. "How dare you—?" he began.

Stella stood up. "I could ask the same question. Perhaps you cannot grasp that family members may disagree, even vehemently. Ky and I are cousins, not even sisters, and certainly not twins. We have been at each other's throats more often than not since childhood. We are working together now only because of the peril that stalks our family. You met her; you have now met me. Can you really say we are alike?"

"My apologies, Captain Vatta," the man said. "To look at, to talk to, you have been nothing like your cousin. You are beautiful; she is—"

"Plain as a post," Stella said, in the tone of a beauty who has scant patience with the plain. She did not sit down again, but she stood less braced. "Always has been. Let's be honest here, gentlesir. Children in a family aren't all alike. I was the pretty one of the family—no credit to me; I was born this way. My sister Jo was the smart one; my brothers were the strong ones. Ky's mother kept talking to my mother about how to dress her up, make more of her, but no matter what, she was not going to look like me. And she minded, of course. Anyone would. She liked to think I was nothing but a pretty face."

"So she always hated you?" the man asked. Stella felt a stab of guilt at this—she had described a stereotypical jealous woman, and as far as she knew Ky had never cared enough to envy her—but she ignored it and went on.

"I wouldn't say hate," Stella said. "But we were rivals, of a sort, until she abandoned the competition." Again, that tickle of guilt. "She made herself different from me—rough where I am smooth, so to say. It comes naturally to me to look for a way to avoid problems, to cooperate; it comes naturally to her to attack problems head-on, to argue. This doesn't mean she's always wrong. But if it's possible to put someone's back up, Ky will do it."

"I see." He cocked his head. "So . . . you don't agree with her about this Bissonet business?"

"I don't know exactly what she thinks," Stella said, "because I haven't had a chance to talk to her. The invasion scares me; I saw what happened to my family back home. If this is the same enemy who attacked Vatta, they must be stopped or we're all in peril. But Ky as commander of a vast interstellar military force . . . that's ridiculous."

He relaxed visibly. "And you would tell her so?"

"I would," Stella said. "If I ever catch up I intend to

talk some sense into her. As her closest living relative, an older cousin, I think she'll listen to me, even given our past friction." She hoped she was right. She had the uneasy feeling that Ky was past listening to sense from anyone; that she was living out some adolescent fantasy of power and vengeance, perhaps intoxicated by something on Osman's ship or simply the possession of a ship configured for war. "Vatta needs her," Stella went on. "We need all our family members, and we need them all working for the family, to rebuild our business."

After that, the station authorities gave her no more difficulties; she sold off the rest of their cargo, and refilled the ship with goods Orem thought might sell on Cascadia. "Nothing likely to make the profit we did in Rosvirein and here," he said. "But we should cover expenses nicely." When the cargo had been loaded, Stella didn't push for a priority departure. She was already well behind Ky, and it would do Ky no harm to worry some. Maybe, if she worried, she would start to realize her responsibility to the family instead of daydreaming about a space navy.

The days in FTL flight passed uneventfully. Between sessions in which she moved from division to division to learn more about ship operations, Stella planned one speech after another, finding flaws in each that Ky would surely exploit. It was infuriating. Anyone with a gram of sense could see that trying to raise an interstellar force was a job for governments or powerful, experienced, military leaders, not a young woman who hadn't even finished her education. But the more she thought about Ky's objections and how to counter them, the more she saw that the basic idea—having a real interstellar force that could control if not eliminate piracy and prevent attacks on systems—was a good one.

Both Quincy and Orem agreed when she brought them into the discussion.

"The only choices I see—other than just letting the pirates take over, which we all agree isn't good—is that merchants form an armed league to fight them off or governments cooperate to create exactly that kind of inter-stellar force," Orem said. "The system governments never wanted merchanters to create a force like that; they were afraid that we'd become a menace—controlling supply, able to attack from space. They weren't any too happy about ISC having its own armed force."

"That may be," Stella said, "but that doesn't mean Ky's the one to do it. She's younger than I am; she didn't even finish at the Academy."

"Ky's smart," Quincy said. "No, she didn't graduate, but she had only a few months to go—she'd learned most of what they had to teach. And I've seen her in action."

"So have I," Stella said. "But even so, she's a Vatta. We need to rebuild Vatta; that's what she said she was going to do. We need every ship and every family member to stay focused on that as the top priority. It's one thing to say that this kind of force is needed, and even to suggest what components might be in it. But to take a Vatta ship and try to do it herself is . . . is irresponsible at best."

"Maybe," Orem said. "I haven't met her, of course; what I know I've learned from you, from Quincy and other members of the crew who were aboard with her. But rebuilding Vatta will take more than having ships to haul goods. It will take securing the spaceways, making them safe for trade again. If she can do that—if she can influence others to do that—that's an important contribution to Vatta's recovery."

"I agree," Quincy said. "And I don't see it as disloyalty to Vatta; I think she cares as much about Vatta as you do.

She sees beyond Vatta, though, to the society in which Vatta must function."

"I suppose," Stella said. "I still think she's not the right person to organize such a force."

"You're still annoyed with her for leaving you behind," Quincy said, with a knowing expression.

"I'm still angry about that," Stella said. "All right, I understand her reasoning at Garth-Lindheimer. What if they didn't adjudicate the ship to Vatta? We needed another ship. But Rosvirein I simply do not understand. You know the mess we jumped into there—if it hadn't been for Balthazar's expertise, we might all have been killed. And she left the moment trouble started, just bolted away; others stayed behind, and she could have. What kind of military commander is that? What kind of care for us?"

"Stella, I've told you—" Quincy began.

"I know what you've told me. I still think she could have stayed in dock, or found a way to meet us somehow. You just don't want to see her as anything but your marvelous Ky." Instantly she was ashamed of herself; she sounded like the jealous one now.

Quincy shrugged. "Either you'll understand someday, or you won't. I have work to do. Excuse me, Captain." And with a nod to Orem, she withdrew.

Stella sighed. "I'm sorry," she said. "I hate to upset Quincy. I do take your points, Balthazar, but I'm not going to agree that Ky is the right one for that job . . . not yet, anyway."

"I'm certainly not going to interfere in a dispute between my employer and her relatives," he said with a wry grin. "I hope when we get to Cascadia that she is still there and you can reach an agreement."

Gary Tobai dropped back into normal space right on target;

Stella had gained confidence in her experienced crew, but
this was always a tense moment for her. She didn't really
like space travel; she'd be glad when she could settle down
again on Slotter Key and stay there. That thought reminded
her of Aunt Grace. She'd better have a good report for
Aunt Grace if she hoped to live happily ever after.

As soon as scans cleared, Captain Orem called her forward. "Ma'am, there are two Vatta registry ships in system.
Fair Kaleen, which we expected, and *Katrine Lamont.* Do
you know anything about that one?"

Stella queried her implant. *Katrine Lamont,* transferred
to this route after the Sabine affair—*why?* she wondered—
captained by Josiah Furman. Excellent record until the
Sabine affair . . . what had he done? Had he been involved
with Ky in some way? Crossed her? Was she going strange
even back then?

"It's one of our larger ships," she told Orem. "Captain
Furman should be listed—"

"J. Furman, yes, ma'am."

"He's listed on this route, so that's fine. I'm glad to
see another Vatta ship whole and on its proper route; it
gives us something to work with." And it gave her someone
certainly sane to talk with, as well. Furman, she now
remembered, had been the captain on Ky's apprentice
voyage. Ky had thought he was difficult, but she herself
had been difficult at thirteen; her animosity to Furman
was surely no more than adolescent pique. Such an exemplary captain was surely levelheaded enough to be fair
with his employer's daughter. If Ky had complained about
him again at Sabine, that said more about her than about
him. Perhaps he would be an ally, someone to add weight
to her own words. Ky wouldn't like it, but she'd have to
listen.

Moscoe Confederation's system ansibles were working,

so she debated whether to call Ky or Furman first. Family won out. Before she sicced Furman on Ky, she should at least find out if Ky had come to her senses. Besides, the ship wasn't synchronized to local time yet. According to the information transmitted by the local system, they were more than a shift off.

Ky's skullphone pinged an alarm, then transmitted the automatic message: *Gary Tobai*'s beacon had been recognized. She let out a sigh of relief and sent a quick thanks for notification. Stella had hired experienced crew, yes, but too many things could go wrong and she had dreaded losing her nearest relative. She wanted to place an immediate call, but Stella would have things to do. She'd be talking to Traffic Control, to the various official entities. Later would be soon enough, though she wished *Gary Tobai* had a faster insystem drive.

Another call waited when she got back to the ship. "It would help in the adjudication if Monitor Leary observed your initial contact with your cousin," the agent said.

"Why?" Ky asked.

"For evidence," he said. "If your cousin recognizes you as her cousin. That is not sufficient, but it is suggestive."

"She might call anytime," Ky said. "Did you want Monitor Leary to come back aboard?"

"With your kind permission," he said.

Ky agreed, feigning a good grace she did not feel, and managed to smile politely at Leary when she came aboard. Shifts passed. Finally a call came in.

"I'm glad to hear from you," Ky said. "I was beginning to worry." No need to say she'd been worrying for days.

"We're all fine," Stella said. "And you?"

"There's a problem," Ky said. "The other Vatta ship in system, *Katrine Lamont*—"

"Yes, with Captain Furman. You don't like him, do you?"

"That's not the problem, Stella," Ky said. "He's claiming I'm an imposter."

"What?" It was clear from Stella's expression that this was not what she had expected to hear.

"You heard me. He thinks I'm—you will not believe this—Osman's daughter pretending to be Kylara Vatta."

"That's—that's ridiculous." Stella's eyes narrowed. "Whatever gave him that idea?"

"He thinks Kylara's dead, he says, killed in the attacks on Vatta. He thinks Osman's up to something and has put in a ringer. That's what he's telling the stationmaster, anyway. And with the Slotter Key ansible and those in between still down, I can't prove differently."

"Has he seen you? Surely he knows you."

"He does, which is why I don't understand it. He hasn't seen me face-to-face, but he's seen current visuals and he still insists I'm a look-alike imposter. It's strange . . . no matter what he thinks of me personally, surely he knows who I am."

"He should," Stella said. She sounded tentative, as if she were really thinking about something else.

"Crown & Spears has a genetic sample from Jo; they compared it to mine before giving me access to the corporate accounts—"

Stella's voice sharpened. "What have you done with the corporate accounts?"

"Nothing, really. I needed to pay docking fees on arrival is all. I've put it back, from a delivery payment. We had a load of medical stuff."

"You were carrying real cargo?"

"Of course I am, Stella. What did you think?"

Stella didn't quite meet her eyes. "I . . . was beginning to wonder."

"Wonder? About what?"

"The people at Sallyon were really upset, Ky, about your plan to form some kind of space navy—"

"The people at Sallyon are idiots," Ky said. "They're more worried about upsetting the pirates than protecting themselves and their trade." Surely Stella understood that. It was obvious enough. "Either system governments are going to have to get together and fund a real interstellar force, or we merchanters are, or we just give up and let the pirates take over system after system and run the universe. I'm not happy with that thought. They killed our parents."

"It's a job for governments," Stella said. "Not us. We have enough to do just putting Vatta back together, if we can."

This was not an argument Ky wanted to have at a distance; she needed to see Stella face-to-face. "I'm glad you're here, Stella. How long before you reach the station?"

"Sixteen days, Balthazar says."

"Balthazar?"

"Balthazar Orem, the shipmaster I hired back at Garth-Lindheimer. You may remember you left me stranded there, just like you did at Rosvirein and Sallyon . . ." Stella's beautiful face hardened; Ky realized that Stella was still angry. She had always been able to hold a grudge until it died of old age.

"Not because I wished to," she said. "I'm glad you found a reliable capt—shipmaster."

"I was very lucky on that account," Stella said. "And he agrees with me that merchants have no business trying to set up a military force—" That wasn't exactly what Orem had said, but never mind.

"You talked to him about my plans?" Ky said, with the

slightest emphasis on *my*. "When you knew them only by hearsay?"

"Considering the reputation you were leaving behind yourself, it seemed entirely prudent," Stella said. "I had no idea what I'd find when—if—we finally caught up with you."

Ky choked back the first three things she wanted to say. So Stella was back to confiding in a man, and willing to confide in the handiest, even if he was a new hire. How handsome was this shipmaster, anyway? She'd assumed that Stella was over all that headlong romantic stuff, but now she saw the ill-fated first love, the spendthrift careless husband, Rafe, and this shipmaster as points on a very straight line indicating that Stella hadn't changed at all.

"I look forward to your arrival," she said instead. "Then maybe we can clear up this identity problem and have a nice long chat about Vatta business." Without, she was determined, the intrusion of Stella's new love interest. "If you'll excuse me—"

"I'll call again tomorrow," Stella said. "I'm not going to wait sixteen days to talk to you. Who know what you'll get up to in sixteen days? You might run off again."

"I'm not going anywhere," Ky said. "The ship's locked down until the identity issue's settled."

"Good," Stella said. "Then I see no reason to hurry to solve it. If you are stuck there, you'll have to listen to reason."

The contact blanked. Ky stared at the screen, puzzled and annoyed both. Stella was angry with her; that much was clear. She understood a little of that; she had left Stella to trail behind through several systems. If she'd been in Stella's place, she'd have been annoyed, too. But surely Stella could understand that it had not been intentional.

Stella was acting as if she, Ky, had turned into some kind of monster, even an enemy of Vatta, when all she'd done was try to make things safer.

Sighing, she swung her command chair around and met the monitor's gaze. Leary's neutral expression could not conceal the interest in her eyes.

"She recognized you," Leary said.

"Yes," Ky said. "That was Stella, as I'm sure you noticed."

"Your cousin, I believe?" the monitor said.

"Yes. My father's brother's youngest daughter. Only living daughter now. It's her older sister's genetic material that Crown & Spears has on file."

"She doesn't look anything like you," the monitor said.

"No," Ky agreed. "She's the beauty of our generation; she takes after her mother's family more, and even there she's remarkable. The Stamarkos family have more blondes, but her mother is dark—darker than Stella, anyway. One of her brothers had light hair. Some of her Stamarkos cousins are blond. I used to wish I could look like her; my mother was always telling me to watch how Stella dressed, how Stella stood and sat."

The monitor cocked her head. "You really do seem to know her."

"I should. We spent a lot of time together as children. She's a few years older, but not that much."

"You were in school together?"

"No. My uncle's main residence was on the mainland, near the Stamarkos family's; my father preferred to live on Corleigh—an island."

"Then—"

"We were together on family vacations and outings," Ky said. "Alternately on the mainland and on the island. She knew our house as well as I did; I knew their house.

I even knew the gardener who—" She stopped abruptly. It wasn't this woman's business that Stella had become "idiot Stella" with that gardener. She became aware that Rafe and Hugh, as well as other bridge crew, were listening.

"The gardener who—" the monitor prompted.

Ky shrugged. "Old family stuff. The point is, we were in and out of each other's homes as children and young people. Stella and I were sometimes rivals—she always won—and sometimes allies, especially when we'd have mock wars in the orchards between her father's house and the Stamarkos house." The memory made her grin; this story couldn't hurt Stella's reputation. "Stella was always so perfect and her mother was a stickler for neatness. One time the Stamarkos boys challenged us and we spent three days building a fort on our side of the orchard while they did the same on theirs. Then we had to capture their flag, and they had to capture ours."

"How old were you?" Leary asked.

Ky thought back. "I must've been ten or so. Stella would've been twelve, thirteen, something like that. Usually she took along a change of clothes and washed her face in the canal before going home, but this time—" She broke off, chuckling.

"You can't stop there," Rafe said. "Are you telling me the immaculate Stella got mussed?"

Ky glared at him for interrupting. "She always got mussed; she just cleaned up before showing up in front of her mother. This time we carried the fight into the part of the orchard that hadn't been picked—which was forbidden. We just forgot; we were all throwing clods and overripe fruit off the ground, a running battle. Well, suddenly we were in among the pickers, and one of her brothers bumped into a ladder and a picker almost fell.

The orchard foreman was furious and chased us out, all the way back to the house. There was Stella, her hair in strings and full of dirt and fruit pulp, her clothes spattered with purple, red, yellow. Just like the rest of us, but it was Stella, after all. I thought Aunt Helen was going to explode. Uncle Stav just laughed, but then he made us all apologize to the foreman. The Stamarkos cousins were sent home and I heard later they were put on house arrest for two days. We were, too, and put to work as well. Within ten days, they had a new fence around the orchards and we had to walk a half mile to get to the Stamarkos cousins and play in open fields."

"If indeed you are the Kylara Vatta of her childhood, and she the Stella Vatta of yours, she should remember that story, don't you think?" Leary asked.

"Yes," Ky said. She knew Stella remembered it, but there were differences. Stella had blamed her, Ky, for urging her to play in the orchard even though she was really too old for such games. Ky had known better; even then, at twelve or thirteen, Stella liked to sneak off and try to meet one of the pickers she had a crush on. Ky had been torn between a desire to defend herself from Stella's accusation by telling all she knew, and the promise she'd given Stella to keep her secrets. She had resented Stella's unfair accusation then, flinging back at her the little bracelet Stella had given her at the start of vacation and storming off to an attic to sulk. It had worried her later: if she had told Aunt Helen then about Stella's flirtations, would that have prevented the far more serious affair with the gardener?

"I will suggest to the stationmaster that he ask her," the monitor said.

Ky wondered, for the first time in years, what had happened to the bracelet.

*　　*　　*

Stella bit her lip as she stared at the blank screen. Ky could be just as irritating as ever. Once she made up her mind she was impossible to reason with. She glanced over at Orem.

"What do you think?"

"She's very . . . determined, your cousin," he said.

"You don't think she's right, do you?"

"Ma'am, it's not for me to say. We've discussed this before. If this Gammis Turek fellow has indeed taken over a whole system at Bissonet, that argues for a lot of resources. It will take a lot of resources to fight him off. It wasn't very tactful of her to talk to other captains back at Sallyon without talking to their government first, though."

Stella seized on that word. "She's not tactful," she said. "Ky never has been. She got angry with me one time when she was nine or ten, something like that. I'd blamed her for getting me in trouble—and probably not entirely fairly— but she threw back at me a gift I'd given her, called me a liar, and wouldn't talk to me for the rest of the summer, which luckily was almost over. I tried to apologize but she stayed in a huff." She had also, Stella thought with a guilty twinge, kept Stella's secrets faithfully, angry as she was.

"Hot-tempered, then?"

"Yes. Impatient, impetuous, and very sure she's right."

"What are you going to do now?" he asked. His calm tone soothed her taut nerves; clearly he thought she knew or would think of something to control her wild cousin.

"I'm going to call Captain Furman," she said. She was sure Ky would consider that disloyal, but as long as Ky wasn't putting Vatta first, she was the disloyal one and Stella alone was faithful to the family. Recalling Ky to her family duty was *her* family duty, and it didn't matter that she'd be talking to someone Ky loathed.

Stella had never actually met Captain Furman; her implant had a summary of his personnel file and his image. His narrow face stared out at her coldly, thin lips folded tight. No one, she reminded herself, looked their best in an official identification portrait, but he didn't meet her standards of handsome.

When she placed the call, his communications tech, a round-faced woman about Stella's age, answered. "Captain Vatta? Which Captain Vatta?"

"I'm Stella Vatta," she said. "Stavros Vatta's daughter. I need to speak to Captain Furman."

"I'm afraid that's not possible," the comtech said. "He's eating now."

Stella felt a trickle of anger. That was not the way to speak to the daughter of Vatta's former CEO, even if the CEO was dead. "And I'm acting CEO of Vatta Transport," she said. The woman's eyes widened. "I'm certain that Captain Furman will want to speak to me. Now."

"Oh . . . oh . . . yes. Mmm . . . I'll send someone." She turned away from the screen and muttered something Stella couldn't quite hear.

"And while you're at it," Stella said, "do you have any Vatta family members aboard?"

"Ummm . . . I don't think so . . ." The woman was obviously upset, but surely she'd know the names of crewmembers. The *Katrine* was big, but most of that size was cargo capacity; her crew numbers shouldn't be over forty, and probably less than that.

Stella queried her implant quickly. Yes, the usual crew for this size ship was thirty-four to thirty-eight. "Would you check, please," she said, making it more order than request.

"Yes . . . er . . . Captain Vatta." She saw the woman look down as if scanning a reader. "Er . . . no, Captain

Vatta, we have no Vatta family members aboard at this time."

That was unfortunate. She had hoped for additional allies to put pressure on Ky. It was a little odd, too, since most Vatta ships did have Vatta family members. Not all were captains; they might be found in almost any of the ship departments, though perhaps with a preponderance in Cargo. She queried her implant again. While she did not have the full command set that Ky had received from her father, she had loaded the most current list of family members and their ship assignments. Odd indeed. Maynard Vatta and Baslin Vatta should have been on this ship.

She opened her mouth to ask the communications tech when the tech's face was abruptly replaced by that of Captain Furman. A very angry Captain Furman.

"Whatever you're playing at, it won't work, young woman!" he said, looking down at something below screen level. "And trying to intimidate my crew won't work, either. As soon as I dock, your entire fabrication will come apart!" He looked up, then, and the angry flush blanched to a sickly pale. "You're not—they said Captain Vatta—"

"I'm Stella Vatta," Stella said. "I did tell your comtech that. Who did you think it was?"

He took a long breath; normal color seeped back into his face. "Stella . . . not Chairman Vatta's daughter? I didn't know you were ship-qualified."

He had not answered her question, but she would pursue that later. "Yes, Captain Furman, I'm Stavros Vatta's daughter, and presently acting CEO of Vatta Transport." She watched that sink in; his expression hardened, sour as a plateful of pickles. "Now, whom were you ranting at?"

He took a visible deep breath. "There's a renegade

SIXTEEN

An icy chill ran down Stella's back; she struggled not to show her sudden unease. "What makes you sure she died? That this person is an imposter?" Her voice had gone up a tone; she took a long breath.

"She made herself a target," he said. "I suspect the attacks on Vatta were revenge for what she did at Sabine— did you know she actually killed two men? Herself? And got a valuable Vatta employee killed in the process? And she was in an old, slow, unarmed ship, and now this person claiming to be Kylara Vatta shows up in a fast armed merchanter that I know belonged to a renegade, Osman. How likely is that? There's a superficial resemblance, I'll admit—they're both young women, dark-haired, rather dusky—" He hitched his chin up and down, as if to show off his own pink complexion and pale eyes. "—but there's no way Kylara Vatta could have defeated Osman and captured his ship. She was only a—a—provisional captain, after all."

Warning bells clamored in Stella's mind. If only she weren't in Ky's old ship, something Furman hadn't seemed to notice yet, but he would. She wanted to let him think she believed him, that Ky was dead, that the person now aboard Osman's ship wasn't Ky, because every instinct told her Furman knew more than he should—no successful trader could be as stupid as he sounded. But before he figured it out, before he became suspicious of her, she had to tell him.

"Captain Furman," she said, putting all her charm into her voice, "I appreciate your concern, but I must tell you that I'm convinced my cousin is alive . . . I don't believe you can have noticed the ship I'm in—"

"Er . . . what?"

"It was Ky's ship, the one she renamed for Gary Tobai. She asked me to take it over for her when she transferred to Osman's ship."

He did pale a shade. "What! Impossible."

"True, though. Look at the Traffic Control ID codes if you don't believe me."

He glanced down, then stared at her a moment, jaw hanging, before he spoke. "But where did you—are you in league with her? Are you another of Osman's bastards?"

Stella snorted. "Hardly, Captain Furman. You should know better than that. Surely you've seen pictures of me. This is not a face easy to fake."

Now he flushed. "Er . . . no. I don't suppose it is, but . . . but I don't understand."

Was he entirely witless? Stella felt a flush of sympathy for Ky, and then stuffed it away. "Ky is not dead, Captain Furman. We met on Lastway Station, where she had taken this ship, and traveled together. We . . . er . . . ran into Osman . . ."

"Where?" Now his brows contracted, his gaze intent.

"I have no idea," Stella said. "I suppose it's in the log somewhere, but I haven't looked it up." She did not want to tell him the whole story, especially not here and now. "Ky did end up with his ship, and that is Ky docked at Cascadia Station."

"Are you sure?" he asked.

"You think I wouldn't know my own cousin?"

"You hadn't seen her in some time, had you? Small changes—I mean—how do you know the person you met at Lastway really was your cousin?"

"It seemed the reasonable explanation," Stella said. "She was in the right ship . . ."

"Yes, but—" He scowled, then brightened. "Suppose she had been killed wherever she was going when she left Sabine, and someone had taken the ship, someone who looked like her at least a little, and then that someone fooled you, and the meeting with Osman's ship was planned. I'll wager you never saw Osman, now, did you?"

A man welded to a pet theory, Stella thought, could bend the raw iron of facts into very fantastical shapes. "Well, no," Stella said. Not alive and in person, anyway. "I suppose," she said, to see how much rope he would take, "it could have happened that way. But it certainly seems like Ky."

"I mean, you have little ship experience, isn't that true?"

It had been true, but she had now amassed almost a half year of ship time and she'd paid attention. Still, let him think what he would. "Yes," she said. "This is my first experience of real ship duty."

"I can help you," he said. His voice acquired a fruity false sweetness. "I can protect you from this imposter. I'm willing to do that, but I'm not willing to pretend that this person is really a legitimate heir to Vatta."

"I see," Stella said. She did not think it would be wise to ask him where the two Vatta family members were who should have been on his ship. Family instincts were ringing alarm bells.

"As far as I know," he went on, "I'm the only surviving

senior captain, and if you're trying to reconstitute Vatta Transport, you need me."

"It's my belief that we need all our ships, Captain Furman," Stella said.

"Yes, but they're mostly destroyed, aren't they? Now, if I can get that imposter out of Osman's ship, and take it over in your name, that should be worth something, shouldn't it?"

"I'm not sure that will be necessary," Stella said, glad for the years of practice that kept her voice smooth when a flare of white rage almost blanked her vision. The nerve of the man. He thought he could take over Vatta, did he? He had probably intended to wait out the statutory limit of his contract and then declare himself the new head of Vatta, at least in this area. Now he thought he could evict Ky from her ship on specious grounds, present it to Stella as a gift, and . . . what? Insist on a partnership, at the least. The way he had looked at her, he might want more than that.

"Well, no, the *Katrine* should be sufficient for a welcome," he said. His smile made Stella want to smack his face. Sixteen days before she'd be close enough . . . she wanted to smack his face now. "But Osman's ship would be a great addition to our fleet."

"It's encouraging to see you identifying so closely with Vatta Transport," Stella said.

"I have given my whole life to Vatta Transport," Furman said. He seemed to literally swell with pride. "We—you and I—could bring it back from this disaster."

"I certainly couldn't do it alone," Stella murmured. She looked at him under her eyelashes, gauging his response. Yes. He was just as susceptible as most men.

"So . . . you'll work with me?"

"I do have the advantage of the Vatta name," Stella said.

"Yes, of course. I understand. And I expect you have useful knowledge I don't have . . . corporate accounts and things like that."

As if she'd give him that information. Stella forced a smile. "I have quite a bit of data, yes. I don't want to share it over a public link, however. Why don't you just go on and dock, and we'll talk it over when I arrive?"

"Not try to seize Osman's ship?"

"No, I don't think so. I think it's a situation where the Vatta name may be more useful with the authorities. More persuasive."

"Well . . ." He was clearly reluctant, but finally nodded. "Well, then, I'll just keep you informed, shall I? At least the authorities aren't going to let that imposter depart."

"If it is an imposter," Stella said. "I'm still not entirely convinced."

"I'm sure of it," he said, as if that should convince her. "There's absolutely no doubt in my mind."

Only, thought Stella, because his very small mind was full of his own conceit. "Then we'll talk tomorrow," she said. "Same time." And cut the connection.

"That guy's a crook!" her pilot said. "You don't believe a word he said, do you?"

Stella looked at her. "What makes you think that?"

"His eyes, the way he changed color like a mating stripe-tail, the tone of voice—couldn't you tell?"

"I am not," Stella said, "disposed to believe everything dear Captain Furman says. On the other hand, it suits my purposes for dear Captain Furman to think I believe him. You will kindly not trouble the poor man's mind with any confusion on that issue."

"Don't blow your cover, you mean?" The pilot's brows went up.

"Something like that," Stella said.

It was most annoying. She'd had such hopes of Furman, had seen him as an ally to force Ky to see reason and give up the nonsense about a space navy. She'd assumed that Furman, like her own shipmaster, would be at worst stolid but still a faithful Vatta employee, reliably hers to command. Now she had another person she couldn't trust in a position where she couldn't afford error. A greedy, ambitious, self-serving man, and someone who might be connected to both Osman and the conspiracy.

Not for the first time, Stella wished that Rafe had been on her ship instead of with Ky. He could have sorted out Furman, finding out more about the man than the man knew about himself. He was even closer: once Furman docked, Rafe should be able to deploy his considerable resources. But she would have to go through Ky to contact Rafe. Would Ky cooperate? She wasn't at all sure.

Over the hours between that call and the next, waking and sleeping, Stella puzzled over Furman. Why had he been so sure Ky was dead? Wishful thinking, perhaps? They'd never gotten along. Or had he known she was a target for assassination? Had someone told him she was dead, and if so, who? Why was he so sure Osman had children? Had he known Osman?

Could it possibly be true . . . could this Ky possibly be a substitution for the real Ky—and if so, to what purpose? More ruin of Vatta? Something else? She was sure she knew her cousin . . . and yet, Ky had done things, things that bothered her, that did not fit the Ky she'd grown up with.

When she woke and could not go back to sleep, she checked the crew schedule and found that Quincy was on duty. Quincy had been with Ky from the time she came aboard; she would know.

"Of course it's Ky," Quincy said. "Furman's an idiot; that's the stupidest theory I ever heard."

"There's no time a substitution could have been made?"

"How?" Quincy asked. "Spaceforce Academy would have checked her identity when she went in. She came aboard from a Vatta shuttle, straight from her father's house. I'll admit she walked some little distance through the station, but never out of sight of monitors."

"All the same," Stella said. "It's not that I trust Furman—I don't—but a fool may still know water flows downhill. What if he's right about this one thing?"

"Ask her about something only the two of you know," Quincy said. "A substitute can only know things that others know as well."

Stella wasn't so sure. What could she and Ky alone know? Perhaps there had been some secret in their childhood, but she couldn't think of anything that other relatives hadn't also known, could have talked about casually sometime in the years in between. The gaggle of cousins vacationing together had always been in one another's pockets. "What we need is a good genetic scan," Stella said. "That would establish her identity for certain, but we need reference scans that are back on Slotter Key."

"It's Furman's identity I'd be more worried about," Quincy said. "How do we even know he's who he says he is?"

That hadn't occurred to her. Furman as an idiot or a traitor, yes, but a Furman who wasn't Furman? "Ky is sure he's Furman," she said, realizing as she said it how foolish that was.

Quincy pointed out the obvious. "If you're not sure she's Ky, why would you take her word on Furman's identity?"

Stella scrubbed at her face with her hands. "At least they're not in this together . . . I hate this. Why can't Ky be reasonable?"

*   *   *

Ky wondered if Stella would contact Furman behind her back. Stella had been trained to be sneaky; of course she would. The one thing she could count on, though, was that Stella knew she, Ky, was not an imposter. She might be angry, she might think Ky was an idiot, but she would never think Ky wasn't Ky. Maybe she could get that through Furman's head.

With Furman only a day from docking, Ky wondered how she could penetrate his security. He thought she— the real Ky Vatta—was dead. Why did he think that? Had he known about the attacks on Vatta? Was he part of the attacks on Vatta? She wanted to believe that, but she knew her long-held dislike of him might be clouding her judgment. Or perhaps he wanted to discredit her simply to strengthen his own claim, as a senior Vatta captain, to speak for Vatta, to gain unquestioned access to Vatta accounts. Perhaps in the apparent collapse of Vatta's trade empire, he'd hoped to start his own, using the ship he had and any accounts he could plunder.

Or he could be honest and mistaken, her conscience reminded her. "I don't think so," Ky said aloud, without thinking.

"What?" Martin was staring at her, and she realized that she'd come out with that in the middle of a meal, with a forkful of something she hadn't really tasted halfway to her mouth.

"I was thinking about Furman," she said.

"Motives," Rafe said, with a sidelong glance at Martin. She wished he wouldn't do that. He could not resist being, or seeming to be, that fraction ahead of Martin. This time he was right, but she wasn't going to tell him so.

"Rafe," she said. He looked at her. "On the off chance that Furman thinks I'm dead because someone in the conspiracy told him so, I want you to penetrate his security once he docks, and look for anything interesting in his internal files."

"Scut work," Rafe said, his lip curling. She stared him down; finally he shrugged. "All right. But it'll take time I could be spending doing something more interesting—"

"You'll manage," Ky said. She turned to Martin. "Martin, do you consider our current security adequate to frustrate anything Furman comes up with?"

"If his background is what it should be, tradeship, then yes, ma'am. If he's a clandestine agent for Turek, then I'd put the ship on high alert."

"Do it," Ky said. "I used to think he was just an arrogant prig, but claiming I'm someone else . . . that's scary."

She turned to Hugh. "I'm concerned that he may withdraw substantial funds from Vatta accounts," Ky said. "While I'm here, and Stella's in the system, he should apply through one of us, as senior family members. But he's denying that I am a senior family member. What if he does the same with Stella? He could then claim to be the only person authorized to have access to those accounts."

"He is authorized now?" Hugh asked.

"Yes. Senior captains must have access to Vatta corporate accounts, both for deposit and withdrawal. In ordinary times, they report via financial ansible to the accounting department at corporate headquarters on Slotter Key."

"If he thought that Vatta was destroyed," Hugh said, "he might have thought he could withdraw Vatta funds without a challenge, and perhaps set up his own business."

"I can see him doing that," Ky said. "And in that case discrediting the legitimate heirs who showed up so inconveniently would be a necessary step."

"You're going to bar him from Vatta corporate accounts?"

"Perhaps. At the very least, I want his transactions monitored and withdrawals limited to those strictly necessary, such as docking fees." She placed the call at once.

Crown & Spears, now familiar with Ky and her dilemma, put her through to her personal representative at once.

"Is Furman making sense yet?" the woman asked.

"No," Ky said. "And it finally occurred to me that we may have a problem with the accounts."

"*We* know who you are," the woman said. "No matter what the government says, our tests show that you're a close relative of Josephine, and that's what matters to us."

"And I appreciate that," Ky said. "But if Furman had been hoping to get those accounts for himself . . ."

The woman smiled at Ky. "We're ahead of you there, Captain. This wouldn't be the first time someone tried to discredit a legitimate account owner. We have established procedures. Captain Furman will have very limited access to those accounts—none, if you'd prefer."

"I know he'll have the usual entry fees to pay," Ky said.

"We can accept a direct charge from the stationmaster's office," the woman said.

"Does Furman usually set up a separate ship account when he comes in?"

"He's only been here twice before," the woman said. "Let's see. No, he worked with the corporate accounts both time. He did deposit more than he withdrew. Would you like to see the details?"

"Yes, if that's legal."

"It's quite legal. You're the senior representative of the account owner, Vatta Transport, Ltd. You have a right to see anything pertaining to Vatta corporate accounts. Just a moment—" She looked down and away. "I've retrieved them . . . we do recommend, Captain Vatta, that in cases like this we courier the hardcopy to the account owner. Would that be acceptable?"

"Certainly," Ky said. She looked around. "Martin— would you come here a moment, please?" He came within pickup range of the comunit. "This is Gordon Martin, my security head; he will meet the courier dockside."

"Excellent," the woman said. "We'll send this over right away, within the hour. I see that Furman is scheduled to dock early first shift tomorrow. If you could let us know your wishes regarding his access to accounts by mid-third today—"

"I'll do that," Ky said. "I'd just like to look over those records first."

Within the hour, as promised, she had the records. The bank had thoughtfully highlighted Furman's transactions, making it easy to compare his expenditures with those of the other Vatta captains using the same accounts. At first look, nothing suspicious showed up. Entry fees, docking fees, supplies for the crew and ship, customs and excise, departure fees . . . all similar to those of the other captains. He had sold cargo and received delivery payment on both of his previous arrivals . . . amounts that fit fairly well with the usual income reported by the other captains.

Ky scowled at the report. She hated niggly work like this. She wished Stella were there to go over it instead of—or with—her. But secure link or no, there was always a risk in transmitting information that way. She would just have to wait . . . no. Martin's experience in inventory control might be useful.

"Of course," he said when she asked him. "I'll be glad to work on this. Nothing obvious, you say? All the better. That makes it interesting." Not the word Ky would have chosen, but she was glad Martin thought so. "What's the chance, do you think, that there is something to find?"

"I don't know," Ky said. "He may be totally honest and just holding a grudge against me because my father transferred him out here. Certainly he's not making the profit here he made on the route he used to have."

"He's not?" Martin grinned. "That's very interesting, Captain."

"Well, this one is new. He may not have the contacts yet—"

"Contacts, yes. I'll get right on this, Captain. I may come up with some things Rafe should look for when he goes prying, and I should certainly have some information for you in a few hours."

"Good," Ky said. She felt twitchy still. Crown & Spears would protect Vatta accounts. Leary had transmitted her suspicions to the stationmaster, so Furman might not have as much influence there. Stella . . . Stella was an unknown quantity at the moment, but surely she'd come around and see sense. So why, as the day wore on, was she still so tense?

She'd missed something. She'd missed something important. What was it?

Grace sat by the window of the upstairs sitting room as curtains of rain blew across the slope to the river. Already, summer was past its peak, here in the hills, and the late-summer rains made it seem more autumnal than it was. Her arm-bud itched abominably. She couldn't scratch it, in its sterile hood that made such an awkward lump around the end of her stump. She could see it, what there was of it—a tiny red nub like a blood blister within the inner sleeve that provided its protective cushioning and kept its surface moist. It would not develop skin, useful skin, until later.

MacRobert had gone. He was, she presumed, back at Spaceforce Academy, making the lives of cadets miserable. The President was dead, as she had wanted; she had not told MacRobert how much she had wanted to kill the man herself, to savor again that moment of supreme power. She liked MacRobert; she knew he liked her; there were some secrets not meant to be shared even though she never expected to see him again.

The Assembly and Council, after several shaky days and what was to others a surprising number of resignations, had settled into a more normal—she hoped healthy—pattern of behavior. No more attacks had come. She had been assured no more would, and that the government—the present government—once more considered the Vatta family worthy of protection. Various ministers had expressed themselves in the strongest terms: they were appalled, they were horrified, it should not have happened, it would never happen again. They hoped . . . each one said this, as part of farewell . . . that she could find peace, and forgive those who had removed themselves from any possibility of actual punishment.

As she watched the rain, though, she seemed to see the faces of the dead wavering there, as if printed on thin gray silk . . . those she knew well, Gerry and Stavros and their children, those she hardly knew, the men and women who had worked at headquarters, those on the ships, those in the factories and fields. So many dead. Even that pony face into which she herself had fired the mercy shot. All out there in the rain, all unsatisfied with her . . . because it wasn't over. Her duty wasn't over.

She turned away, pinching her lips as the protective bulb on her arm bumped the chair and demonstrated that the stump could still hurt worse than the arm-bud could itch.

"Grace—are you all right?" Helen, come to check on her.

"I'm fine," she said, knowing it was a lie.

"You're green around the mouth again," Helen said. Helen looked better, Grace noticed. Helen found it easy to believe the successors to a traitor President; she had slept easy, and she was eating well. The children were completely recovered, full of energy; she could hear them now, clattering up the stairs and yelling for "Gramma."

"Just tired," Grace said. "I think I'll skip dinner, go to bed early." She pushed herself up with her good arm and walked off toward her room, aware of Helen's concern like a hand on her back. The wrong hand.

Her room was dimmer yet and smelled of wet leaves and sodden grass. Grace shivered. They'd told her that her body might have unpredictable reactions to the arm-bud and its supporting interventions. They'd told her she might feel cold or hot, more tired or hyperactive, as the biochemical cocktails that sustained and accelerated the bud's development coursed through her body. She slid under the covers, still dressed, and hoped that tomorrow's unpredictable reaction would be on the other end of the scale.

She woke in the dark, as heavier rain pounded the roof above. Nothing hurt: no ache, no burn, no itch. Around the bed, just visible, were the faces again, all gazing at her.

"I'm sorry," she whispered, though she heard no sound.

Then she heard the sound. The faces faded back into darkness, as the footsteps came nearer, nearer. Not Helen's. Not one of the children. She reached out to her bedside table, feeling for the weapon the police had finally returned—with many warnings about its illegality and how lucky she was no charges had been filed. She couldn't find it; she scrabbled a wider arc and one of her rings clinked against the water glass. The footsteps stopped; she held her breath.

She knew the door opened by the change in air; she knew it closed by a faint thud.

They had lied or they had been mistaken; it didn't matter, really. Here was another attack, and she was not ready and could not even find her weapon. She lay rigid, determined not to make a sound, not to shiver.

Then the bedside light came on just as a drop of cold water landed on her arm. MacRobert, his rain hood dripping, with her weapon in his hand.

"You!"

"Shhh. You're whiter than the sheets and shivering. Let me get out of this."

To her utter astonishment, after putting her weapon well out of her reach he stripped off his wet clothes, revealing just the sort of body she would have expected.

"What do you think you're doing?" It was hard to express the outrage she felt in a whisper, but she did her best.

"Getting into bed with you," MacRobert said. "Move over." His hand slid under her back, warm and strong, and eased her to the other side of the bed as he slid under the covers.

"How did you—"

"Helen. She thought you needed me. She doesn't know I'm here yet, of course."

It was like having a fire in bed with her; she wasn't cold anymore. Her feet weren't cold. The light went out; he lay back with a contented sigh. "I hope you don't snore," she said, trying to muster the indignation she thought she should feel.

"I wouldn't know. There's been no one to tell me for years. By all means, should I snore, prod me in the ribs and wake me up." She felt the dip in the mattress as he turned toward her. "Grace . . . I know what your problem is."

They always had the same answer; she was disappointed in him. "It's not lack of sex," she said.

"Good heavens no! I wasn't going to say that."

"What, then?"

"You wanted to see him die. You wanted to kill him yourself. Am I right?"

Surprise held her rigid for a moment. "Yes," she said. "I did. I wanted him to know who did it."

He did not recoil, as she had half expected. "I thought so," he said. "You have the look."

"The look?"

"You enjoy killing. You're a decent person, so you don't indulge yourself in that pleasure, but when the occasion arises, you enjoy it." His voice was calm, as if he were describing the parts of a weapon.

"It doesn't shock you?" Grace said.

"No. And you might like to know that when the Commandant laid out for the President the net that had closed around him, the President's spontaneous response was 'How did she do this?' So he knew, though your name was never mentioned."

She was warm. She was safe. She fell asleep lighter of heart than she had been since before the troubles started, and when she woke the rain had stopped and the early sun through her window lit MacRobert's brown eyes.

"Did I snore?" he asked.

SEVENTEEN

"*Katrine Lamont* is approaching dock," the stationmaster said. "We've assigned docking nearby, but not on the same branch."

"Thank you," Ky said.

"Captain Furman remains convinced that you are not Kylara Vatta, daughter of Gerard Vatta, legitimate employee of Vatta Transport. We understand that he has been in communication with Stella Vatta, who now styles herself acting CEO of Vatta Transport. Do you dispute that?"

What was Stella playing at? They had not discussed how to organize the company in the future, and with only the one ship it seemed unnecessary to formalize anything. She'd suggested that Stella act as her financial officer, but CEO? "Dispute that she has been in communication with Captain Furman? No, why would I? I suggested it."

"That she is acting CEO of Vatta," the stationmaster said.

"We haven't discussed what our positions may be," Ky said. "Her father was CEO and mine was CFO. I'd have thought her expertise ran more to financial affairs, but we'll thrash that out later. Why?"

"For our purposes, we must know which of you is senior to the other. Organizationally, I mean; we already know she's older than your stated age. Which of you is in charge?"

The first half dozen answers that raced through Ky's mind were all unsuitable. She hoped her face hadn't revealed them. "I believe that's something Stella and I should settle between ourselves," she said. "I'll contact her now, if you'll excuse me. Thank you." Before he could answer, she closed the connection.

Gary Tobai was now within ten light-minutes, but Ky wasn't going to wait for the signal lag of lightspeed communication; she used the system ansible instead.

Stella answered the hail; she had evidently been expecting a call from someone else, because her expression changed when she saw Ky. Beside her was a man in a captain's uniform; this must be the "Balthazar" she'd spoken of.

"I was going to call you," Stella began.

"I just heard from the stationmaster that you're the acting CEO of Vatta Transport," Ky said. She could not keep the edge out of her voice; she knew she sounded angry. She was angry.

Stella waved her hand. "I had to say something," she said. "I thought it sounded impressive. And after all—"

"I thought we agreed, back on Lastway, to reverse our fathers' roles," Ky said. "I've been telling people you're my chief financial officer—"

"And you've been claiming the CEO title?" Stella had flushed a little; her eyes sparkled. "Don't you think that's a little presumptuous, with senior Vatta family members alive on Slotter Key?"

"You just did it," Ky said. "I don't see that's any less presumptuous."

"I'm older," Stella said. "And my father was CEO—"

"Not to intrude or anything," Rafe said. Ky turned to

look at him; he had positioned himself so the communications monitor would include him. "But the two of you can argue about this later, surely. The more delay, the more the stationmaster will suspect something's wrong with both your identities."

Stella opened her mouth but Ky was faster. "Joint," she said quickly. "We're joint acting CEOs, a necessity in this present emergency. It's so if either ship is destroyed, the company has a clear chain of command."

"That might work," Stella said.

"We'll both call the stationmaster," Ky said. "Hold this link. I'll call him and make it a circuit call." Stella didn't look enthusiastic, but Ky didn't care. She was not going to put herself under Stella's command. She keyed in the stationmaster's code, identified herself to his assistant, and he came on.

"I thought you'd like to hear this from both of us," Ky said. "You must understand that the situation is complicated by the fact that we're both ship-based right now, since Vatta headquarters was destroyed, and the ansibles are down most places."

"The thing is," Stella put in, "we're both acting as CEO for the time being. It's a safety issue; should one of our ships be lost, the other has a clear line of succession. We've had to operate in different systems, out of contact with each other since the ansibles were down."

"Co-CEOs?" the stationmaster said. "I don't think I've heard of that."

"It won't last," Ky said. "It's an emergency measure."

"But—who's really in charge? If you're both in the same system, as now, who is senior? I presume you don't always agree—"

Stella chuckled. "No, indeed. But if we need to, we go into closed session and argue it out. Ky's better at some things—she has more ship and actual trade experience—and I'm better at others—I have more experience at headquarters. We are, after all, on the same side."

"I see," the stationmaster said. "But Captain Vatta—Kylara Vatta—when I first told you that Stella Vatta was saying she was acting CEO, you seemed surprised and upset."

"Frankly, I'd assumed that if we were both in the same system, the first to arrive would use the title and the second wouldn't—just to avoid the kind of confusion we have here. But we hadn't discussed it, so we didn't have policy set up." Ky put on her blandest expression.

"It just didn't occur to me," Stella said, with equal blandness. "I'd gotten used to using it because we were separated."

"I see," the stationmaster said again. Ky was not at all sure he believed them. "So . . . in this instance, with you, Captain Vatta, being the first to reach the system, would you say that you are in charge?"

"Yes," Ky said, before Stella could answer. "Though I do consider Stella my partner, not my subordinate."

"And that's agreeable to you?" the stationmaster asked Stella.

Stella nodded. "Quite agreeable," she said. Ky detected, in that, the exact opposite meaning and hoped the stationmaster didn't.

"Very well, then," the stationmaster said. "I must remind both of you that there is a question of identity relating to Kylara Vatta, as Captain Furman has charged that she is not really Kylara Vatta, but an imposter."

"I don't agree," Stella said. "Obviously, I think he's wrong. But I would prefer to leave him in doubt of my opinion, since I want to know why he's so sure, and what his motives are."

"Ah. You haven't told him you're sure he's wrong?"

"I've listened to him," Stella said.

"Do you think he has committed some offense?"

"I don't know," Stella said. "I will say I found his attempt to discredit my cousin surprising in someone whose record as a loyal employee is exemplary."

"So you have no complaints against him at this time?"

"Other than his error, no," Stella said.

"Do you have any proof, other than your word, that this is in fact your cousin? Any genetic material we could compare, for instance?"

"No. Other than my own, of course. Though I do have, on my ship, an elderly crew member who knows her very well. Would her testimony be pertinent?"

"Yes, but probably not conclusive." The stationmaster sighed. "Your genetic material will probably serve, since Captain Furman has yet to question your identity. You are now what . . . fourteen days from docking, I believe?"

"Yes," Stella said.

"I had hoped for a quicker resolution," the stationmaster said. "I'm sorry," he said to Ky, "that you must be under surveillance for so long."

Ky shrugged. "It's not your fault, and this ship isn't as cramped as Stella's."

"I'm glad you see it that way," the stationmaster said. "Excuse me, please: I have other messages coming in."

"Of course," Ky said. His link closed; she looked at Stella in the monitor. "Well?"

"He's still suspicious," Stella said. She sighed. "Ky, I wish you could stay out of trouble in one system, at least."

"It's not my fault," Ky said. "It's that idiot Furman."

"It wasn't Furman at Sallyon. Or Rosvirein or Garth-Lindheimer."

"You're not blaming me for Garth-Lindheimer, surely!

I didn't do anything there but refuse to waste time and money dragging through their court system."

"You left me to clean up your mess," Stella said. "Short-crewed and with no clear directions."

"I didn't think you needed directions—if you recall you told me you didn't. If you're co-acting-CEO—"

Stella glared out of the screen. "I handled it, yes. That doesn't mean I liked being left behind like that. And then I get to Rosvirein and you're already gone and there's a missing person bulletin. Are you going to tell me you had nothing to do with that?"

Crossing mental fingers, Ky said, "Why would you think a missing person was my fault?"

"Why? Because who else would abduct someone like that—the bulletin said he was casual laborer suspected of working with local criminal elements and even pirates. You're the pirate hunter: isn't that just what you'd do?"

It's what she'd done, but telling Stella that she'd let Rafe and Martin question the man and he'd died and she'd spaced his body once she was far enough from the station would only escalate the fight that now seemed inevitable.

"I'm sorry you think that," Ky said, struggling to sound calm yet serious.

Stella pursed her lips, then her mouth tightened. "You've changed, Ky. You're not being straight with me, I can tell that much. We're going to have a serious talk when I get to the station. I want to know where your priorities are."

"Where they've always been," Ky said. She felt tired, as if she were suddenly in a higher gravity field. It was unfair for Stella to distrust her this way, to question her motives and priorities. "I want Vatta to survive and our enemies to fall."

"I wonder," Stella said, and cut the connection.

Ky slumped into her seat. She'd thought Stella was over whatever had her upset when she first came into the system. She had backed Ky with the stationmaster. Yet clearly she wasn't satisfied.

"Problem?" Hugh asked.

"Stella," Ky said. "I suppose it's old family rivalry or something."

"It would've made sense for her to say she was acting CEO—"

"Yes," Ky said. "I can understand that. I just wish she'd told me. If we'd had our stories straight . . . and then she's got this thing about my priorities. You'd think I'd gone off on a vacation or something . . ."

"Families." Rafe shook his head. "You can't live—"

"If you say *Can't live with them, can't live without them,* I will—" Ky noticed the bridge crew watching this interaction. "—be extremely displeased," she finished.

"I wasn't going to," Rafe said, with a blatantly false expression of innocence. "I was merely going to say that . . . that—"

"Yes?"

"You can't live with their expectations. Not forever." He smirked. "Stella's certainly sitting close to that new guy, isn't she?"

"Her shipmaster, she calls him. She's still calling herself captain."

"Well, she is. Technically."

"I suppose." Ky sat up straighter. "Fourteen days until she docks. I think I'll go work out. I don't want to get soft."

Stella managed to keep her face bland until she was in her cabin. She turned up the soundscreens to full strength and let loose with every blistering oath she could think of. Thanks to Rafe, she could go on for quite a stretch without repeating herself, and she did, ending with ". . . stupid little *prig*!" Even alone in her cabin, that seemed too tame an ending for what she felt. "Blast you!" she said to the walls. "As if I weren't older than you. More experienced than you. I'm not the one who alienated an entire system . . . and you have the nerve to humiliate me in front of the stationmaster. And Rafe was there listening, I'm sure, soaking it up, never happier than seeing families quarrel." She threw the pillow off her bed at the wall. It did no good, but it did no harm. "Maybe in fourteen days I won't want to kill you on sight," she said, more quietly.

Then her lip curled involuntarily and a ripple of laughter shook her. No. It wasn't funny, or if it was funny, she wasn't ready to see it yet.

She had as much information about Furman as Ky did, barring Ky's two encounters with the man. If she figured out what his game was before Ky did, that would restore her credit—in her own mind at least. Although she did not have the information in her own father's implant, she did have the updates Grace had given her, including financial and personnel data current as of the destruction of headquarters. She pored over it.

Furman had been with the company twenty-nine years. He had been hired away from an insystem carrier in another system, when a Vatta captain died, along with many others, in an epidemic. It had been quicker to hire him and get the ship moving again than to send someone out to take over. He had satisfactory reports, and steady promotions, until he reached senior captain. Stella paused. His personnel record had a mark she didn't recognize, a typographical squiggle with no explanation, one year after his promotion to senior captain. She shrugged and went on reading.

Furman continued to accumulate good reports and promotions to increasingly lucrative routes. His on-time and early-delivery record was the best in the company; he had received commendations and bonuses. Then, less than a standard year ago, he had been sent to Sabine to find and assist Ky. Immediately after that, he had been transferred to this route, on the far side of Vatta's operating territory.

Stella paused again. Something was wrong. Why would such a good employee, so diligent, so valuable to the company, so well compensated, be transferred here? He wouldn't ask for such a transfer; it was against the pattern she saw in his record, the pattern of cautious but determined ambition. He must have done something, and logically that something involved Ky. He'd known her before; she hadn't liked him. Perhaps the dislike was mutual? But surely he wouldn't have said anything about it, even if it was. He was mature, experienced, socially adept as any trader must be; such a man would not risk his career to complain about his employer's daughter. What could have happened? Had Ky complained about him to her father?

Nothing showed up in the files that her implant carried. She racked her own memory of that period. She'd been away on company business; she hadn't even known Ky was in the Sabine system until after the ansibles were back up, and Ky was on her way somewhere else. Her father had given no details, beyond the fact that Ky had been there, had been injured but was now fine, and the crisis was over. Nothing about Furman, nothing at all.

That in itself was strange. Usually he told her family news right away. She'd known the same day when Ky left the Academy; he'd told her everything he knew, or found out, in the days after Ky left on her voyage. That's why she'd written the note, in a flush of sympathy, imagining how the perfect daughter, the one always in control, must feel such a disgrace. Why hadn't her father told her about Furman being sent to help Ky, and what went wrong, and that Furman had been transferred to another route?

Had it been to protect Ky? Had Ky complained for no reason, slandered Furman? Furman could indeed be irritating; she'd seen that for herself, but she could not imagine anything he could have done to deserve being yanked off one of the best routes in the Vatta system and sent to another, as far from headquarters as possible.

She wondered if Ky would tell her the truth about it, if asked. Then she remembered that Quincy had been aboard at the time.

"Furman was furious," Quincy said when asked what had happened. "He was angry about being pulled off his route to come to Sabine, that I could understand. But he started scolding the captain as if she were a naughty child, instead of a grown woman who had done very well in a difficult and dangerous situation."

"Scolded her . . . you're sure he did, and that wasn't just her interpretation?"

"I'm sure," Quincy said. "I wasn't on the bridge to hear it, but Lee was, and the Mackensee communications tech they had aboard. Furman laid into her in a white fury, told her she had ruined the company's reputation and cost it millions, and so forth and so on. He wanted her to let him sell off the ship for scrap—"

"This ship?"

"This ship, yes. We needed repairs, true enough, but it wasn't beyond repair, as you can see. Ky had cargo to take to Belinta, and cargo at Belinta bound for the next stops, but Furman wanted her to come aboard with the crew, and he'd pick up and deliver the Belinta cargo."

"Is that what she was supposed to do?"

"No. Not according to the sealed message her father sent with Furman. Furman was just there to render aid. It was his idea to take over and treat her like an idiot. Ky wouldn't put up with it, naturally. She told us all what he wanted and what she was going to do instead, and offered to let any of the crew who wanted leave with Furman."

"So . . . did she complain to her father about Furman? Is that why he's out here, and not on the Beulah Road route?"

Quincy shook her head. "She couldn't have complained if she'd wanted to; remember, the Sabine ansible platforms had been blown up. ISC brought in repair crews, but no private ansible communications were permitted; we left before the repairs were done."

"It just doesn't sound like Furman, from his record," Stella said. "I don't understand—"

"He's got something of a reputation," Quincy said. "He's a good captain, right enough: a stickler for safety, for efficiency. Excellent on-time delivery stats. But he can be a petty tyrant with his crew, especially the lower grades. Mostly he's just kind of prissy, but every once in a while he blows up. You know he courted a Vatta girl once, years back . . ."

"What?" That was the last thing she'd expected to hear.

"Oh, yes. Up-and-coming young captain, rapid promotions for efficiency. Met—what was her name? I can't quite remember. Harmon's oldest daughter—"

"Mellicent," Stella said. "What year was it?"

"Let me think. It's twenty years ago, about, but I'm not sure. Anyway, he asked permission to court her—he didn't grow up on Slotter Key, you can tell—and her father said yes, but he thought she might already have formed an attachment. As polite a warning as he could give, but Furman didn't understand it. Mellicent was a typical Vatta, headstrong and impatient. She had that intense, energetic kind of dark beauty, nothing at all like you, but attractive to a lot of men. Furman sent her a careful progression of gifts: the birthday card, then the flowers, then the box of candy, and so forth. Everything perfectly conventional and respectful. Then he began to ask her out. She went with him to a provincial fair, but he got sick on one of the carnival rides. After that, she always had an excuse, but he still didn't take the hint."

"I never imagined Furman as a suitor," Stella said. "Ambitious, wasn't he?"

"I don't know," Quincy said. "Vatta girls have to marry outside the family, after all, and a loyal, efficient, up-and-coming captain isn't that bad a choice. Other captains had taken her out. Of course, they took her dancing and sky-sailing and reef-diving, not to a poky agricultural fair."

"So she didn't encourage him."

"No. In fact, he came back from a voyage to find she'd married in the meantime, not a word to him about it."

Stella checked the date of Mellicent's marriage in her files. About a year after that mysterious symbol in Furman's personnel record. Did it mark the start of his unsuccessful courtship? "How did you know all this?" she asked.

Quincy gave a small snort. "That kind of thing travels faster than light. Employees marrying into the family was nothing new, but it was always good for gossip. Besides, while Furman was a good captain, he wasn't that popular."

"A reason for him to be bitter . . . I wonder why he stayed with the company. A man of his qualifications could find a place somewhere else."

"Yes, but we do—did—have one of the most generous compensation packages in the industry. You know Vatta's never had a problem hiring away from other firms; people want to work for Vatta. Wanted to."

"I suppose. I wonder if he took against Ky because of that. Mellicent was dark; Ky is dark."

"Maybe. I think he's just one of those sour people who would rather complain than change things."

"But then, if Ky didn't complain to her father, why was Furman transferred?"

"My guess is that he said something to her father, something her father took amiss. I don't know, though. It's all guesswork, and we'll never know unless Furman tells us."

"Which is about as likely as time running backward," Stella said. It sounded as if Furman was an unlikely ally, though. If he blamed Ky for his transfer, then maybe that's why he was trying to discredit her, claim she was an imposter. "Did Osman have any children that you know of?" she asked Quincy.

"Children? Not that I ever heard of. Why?"

"This claim Furman's making that Ky isn't our Ky, that she's one of Osman's children and her appearance with his ship is part of some plot of Osman's—it doesn't sound like the sort of thing he'd have the wits to invent, if it was known Osman had none. You never heard any rumors of anything like that?"

"Nothing," Quincy said. "Osman was a sexual predator; everyone who came near him knew that much. But that doesn't mean he had children, or children he'd acknowledge."

Stella didn't mention the information in the family files. "If you didn't know, I wonder how Furman heard about them."

Quincy looked thoughtful. "That's . . . an interesting

question. Assuming there are any such children. And even if they're not, why would he pick on that explanation for Ky faking an identity?"

"It makes me wonder if Furman had any dealings with Osman," Stella said. "The Beulah Road route . . . I think I'd better look that up."

"You don't think there's any truth in it . . ."

"Of course not," Stella said. "Ky is entirely too irritating to be anyone but herself."

The Beulah Road route as outlined in the Vatta Transport Manual was a five-stop circuit, named for the first system after its intersection with the Congrove. Beulah Road, Planters Rest, Arlene, Hope Landing, New Jamaica. One intermediate jump point between Beulah Road and Planters Rest, two between Planters Rest and Arlene, two again between Arlene and Hope Landing, three between New Jamaica and Beulah Road. The standard time en route, per section, compared with Furman's reported times was . . . very interesting.

Furman made up one day on the Beulah Road–Planters Rest leg; he had been in a day early 95 percent of the time for the past ten standard years. Well-organized ships could do that, with fine-tuning of the drives and a little higher fuel consumption to allow a faster run-in and thus require more deceleration near their goal. He spent that extra day in port, keeping precisely to Vatta's timetable so that shippers could rely on him. His times on the second and third legs were very good indeed, indicative of an efficiently run ship; he rarely made up a complete day unless he had an early-delivery bonus pending. Then he might show up two or even three days early. But on the fourth leg, with three intermediate jump points to traverse, each requiring a slowdown to drop in and out, he seemed to go faster instead. He arrived at New Jamaica an average of four days early.

Stella stared at the navigation manual until she was cross-eyed, then called in her pilot.

"I'm trying to figure out how a ship goes faster than the listed travel times on green-keyed mapped routes. Much faster."

"That's easy." The pilot gave her a challenging look. "They're not using the green routes."

"Excuse me?"

"They're using the yellows," the pilot said.

"But that's illegal," Stella said, and got another look much like the first.

"Yeah, and it's dangerous, which bothers most people more," the pilot said. "I won't do it, even for a bonus. What routes are we talking about?"

Stella pushed over the reader. "How could I figure out what routes he was using instead of the ones he should've been using?"

"One of your other ships, eh? Let's see. That hull . . . that drive . . . no way he could be making up time like that on green routes."

"Why would he do it?"

"Speed pays. Faster delivery, early-delivery bonuses, no overtime charges. Stupid, because eventually you'll run into something . . . not all the yellows are yellow for the same reason, you know."

Stella didn't know. "Explain, please," she said.

The pilot was still looking at the reader, her fingers flickering over the controls. "Some of the jump points are yellow because they're unstable—they wobble around, they change focus, that kind of thing. Some are too close to a large mass. You may get by with a yacht or something, but not with a big freighter. Some systems are inherently dangerous, lots of rocks loose in the system. Some, there's concern about the stability of a star; wouldn't want to be translating through there just as it went blooey. And some, it's unfriendly natives. The people don't like travelers, or they like them in the wrong way."

"Pirates?"

"Could be. Nearby systems report problems to the Pilots' Guild, and they classify them as green or yellow. We pilots prefer to err on the side of caution, so probably some yellows aren't that unsafe, but I'm not trying them." She nodded at the reader screen. "Aha. Look at this."

The figures meant nothing to Stella until the pilot explained. "My guess is he's running yellow routes the whole way."

"But he's not coming in that early on the second and third legs."

"That's because he's spending time off the clock," the pilot said. "Somewhere on those legs, my guess is, he's meeting someone at one of these four jump points. Probably BV-328, RV-43, or GV-16, since they're all in un-inhabited systems. BV-24's inhabited; if they hung around there longer than necessary, someone might notice."

"Meeting someone."

"Yes. I don't know who this is you're checking up on, but if it's an employee I'd say check the balance sheets. They're jumping slow, hanging around, meeting someone, maybe exchanging cargo, maybe just information."

"Is this something a ship captain could do without the crew's knowledge? Without at least the pilot knowing?"

"Not unless the pilot was knocked out and locked in a closet. The rest of the crew . . . I don't know. If they think it's supposed to take six days of FTL flight with a jump-point transition in the middle and it takes six days of FTL flight with a jump-point transition in the middle, they might not."

Furman's counterpart, running the same route backward, had never matched Furman's times. Why hadn't someone at headquarters noticed? Missing cargo would've been noticed; shippers had never complained of shortages in consigned cargo. Private cargo, then? Crew allotments? That would require crew complicity. Stella called up the records. He'd had the same senior crew for years, and the number of Vatta family members in the crew had dropped steadily.

Captains were allowed to pick their own crews, certainly, but Vatta crew usually had priority for openings. Furman had no openings. According to the records, the only people who ever asked for transfers out, who ever got sick, who ever retired, were Vattas.

"I need to get back to the bridge," the pilot said. "If you'll excuse me—"

"Yes, go ahead," Stella said. "Thank you for your help." That was automatic; she barely noticed the door closing. When had Furman started this—whatever *this* really was? Was it related to his unsuccessful attempt to marry into the family? Had he been crooked before he ever joined Vatta? Or was it something else, simple greed perhaps?

It made a horrible kind of sense. Furman, angry and hurt at what he may have felt was an insult, but unable or unwilling to confront his employer, had not seen the cream-puff Beulah Road route as sufficient compensation. Had he even known what Osman Vatta was, when he met him—Stella wondered where, and how—and began clandestine meetings where they exchanged . . . what? Nothing too large, nothing bulky. Something quick and easy to move from ship to ship, in the emptiness of a system with only a jump point and perhaps an automated ansible.

Something Furman could sell, in those extra days on New Jamaica.

Had Ky been aboard, an unwanted apprentice too quick-witted for her own good, on one of those voyages?

For one mind-boggling moment, Stella wondered if a substitution could have taken place then, Osman's daughter for Gerard's—the real Ky killed and her body spaced—but it was too absurd. The Ky who came back from that voyage was the same difficult, sulky teenager who had left on it. No substitute could have gone un-detected.

The critical thing was Furman, Furman's treachery, Furman's equally treacherous crew, the danger they posed to Vatta now, and her own inability to do anything until she got to Cascadia Station. She was stuck out here, days away, while Ky was right there cheek-by-jowl with Furman.

Furman couldn't do anything more without the help of the Cascadian government, she told herself. Surely he would not attack Ky's ship, or Ky herself, directly. He would have to wait until she herself docked, until the station-master had obtained the genetic samples he wanted and had them compared. She could call Ky and warn her, but Ky was already suspicious of Furman; surely she would be careful. Besides, if Furman was as bad as that, why risk a call that might be intercepted?

EIGHTEEN

As soon as Ky knew where the stationmaster was assigning Furman dockspace, she sent Rafe and Martin out into the station.

"You know what we need," she told them. "Furman doesn't know either of you—he can't—so he and his crew shouldn't be that wary of you."

"Unless the stationmaster rats us out," Rafe said.

"Why would he?" Ky asked. "He wants to know the truth as much as anyone."

Rafe rolled his eyes. Martin said, "Thing is, Captain, if Furman's been paying off this stationmaster . . ."

"I know," Ky said, "but Furman hasn't been on this route that long. Only two previous visits. If the stationmaster were already in his pocket, he'd have me in custody somewhere else."

"Maybe," Rafe said.

Ky settled back to wait. Martin returned about the time Furman docked, to report that he had placed unobtrusive sensor devices to keep track of activity near Furman's ship.

"Where's Rafe?"

"I don't know, Captain. He came and went several times, carrying boxes, and he had gone again when I was through. He said he'd be in touch."

"I hope he finds something useful," Ky said. "I don't have the kind of evidence they're asking to prove my identity. If they don't take Stella's word for it—and mine for hers—we could be in serious trouble. I just don't understand why Furman is insisting that I'm not who I obviously am. He knows me. And how did he come by the information that Osman had children my age?"

"He wants this ship, or he wants you immobilized, or both," Martin said.

Ky thought a moment. "If he wants this ship, I'll bet it's not to return it to Vatta . . . maybe he wants to form his own fleet?"

"Assuming he's bent," Martin said, "*Katrine Lamont* and *Fair Kaleen* would give him two tradeships, one of them armed, in which he could set up even in today's dangerous climate. If he knew what he was doing, he could even offer convoy escort service. He wouldn't even have to be very bent to think that with Vatta headquarters gone, and a lot of the family dead, his duty to Vatta no longer mattered."

"If that's what he thought, I must've come as a nasty surprise," Ky said. "A Vatta related to a corporate executive, right out here. And me in particular."

"You probably did," Martin said. "His first instinct would be to deny it—it is improbable on the face of it. From what he knew about you, as an apprentice on his ship, it could be hard to imagine you, at your age, defeating Osman. He would have known Osman was a renegade; that would have been shared with senior captains, surely."

"Yes," Ky said. "It's in the sociopolitical hazards section of the standard senior captain's briefing. It wasn't in my original implant because I was just a provisional, and they had no record of Osman operating on the Belinta-to-Lastway route."

"So," Martin went on, "he might be guessing about Osman having children; he may've assumed anyone that age would. It would make things easier for him if you were Osman's daughter and not your father's."

Again that tickle of fear. Could she be Osman's daughter, adopted into the family, raised as Gerard's?

"I can't believe that a child of Osman's would look exactly like me," Ky said. "And he saw me—onscreen, at least—back at Sabine."

"That's the other possibility, certainly," Martin said. "He knows perfectly well who you are, but he's trying to pull a bluff, hoping that you have no way to prove absolutely that he's lying. Stella showing up must be another complication for him."

"She's turned out to be a complication for me," Ky said. She would like to have vented her frustrations to Martin, but Stella was, after all, a family member, quite possibly the closest relative she had left.

Her next call came not from Stella but from planetside, from the canid reproductive specialists.

"This is Mellowyn Davin of the Eglin Veterinary Clinic . . . We hadn't heard back from you about your dog. Are you still interested in a semen harvest?" It was not the same voice she'd heard before, and the woman's appearance—she had paid for a full video link—was that of a middle-aged professional.

"Are you interested in purchasing semen?" Ky asked, struggling to pull her mind back from Furman's accusations to this trade and profit possibility. "I understood from the person I spoke with before that you have concerns about whether our dog is a descendant of dogs stolen from your planet."

"I'm so sorry," Davin said. "That was our front-office

assistant, and she should not have hinted at any such thing. Some people do believe spacers stole our dogs long ago, but I assure you the government is now well aware that it's not true. I apologize for her rudeness; she should have transferred your call to one of the partners right away."

"I see," Ky said. "Suppose you tell me what would be involved in the process."

"I imagine you would not want to transport the animal to the surface," Davin said. "We would send a team up to Cascadia Station—by the way, do you know if this animal has ever bred successfully?"

"No," Ky said. "He was still quite young—estimated by the vet on Lastway to be no more than a hundred twenty days old, a third of a standard year. He would be close to three-quarters of a standard year by now."

"We would need to test the dog for known communicable diseases, run a genetic scan for genetic problems, do a semen test for sperm quality, and then, if the dog checked out, collect semen. The tests would take some hours—aside from the blood test, nothing painful to the dog. I'm presuming he's had standard immunizations?"

"Yes, on Lastway. I do have that paperwork."

"And the breed?"

"That I don't know. The dog had been dumped in a waste container, from which my crewmen rescued it."

"Dumped! For disposal?"

"Yes. In fact, we were encouraged to allow the vet to euthanize the dog—"

"Barbaric!"

"—and instead chose to adopt it, at some considerable cost to ourselves."

"That was a good deed, Captain," Davin said. "So you do not know what kind of dog?"

"The vet at Lastway told us it was a small terrier breed, possibly something called a Jack Russell, but whether it was pure in breed or not, he was unable to determine."

"Ah. Small breeds do mature faster than large breeds . . . tell me, has the dog exhibited any sexual behaviors? You don't have a female dog as well, do you?"

"No, we don't have a female . . . does grabbing people's legs with his forepaws count as sexual behavior?"

"Indeed it does. Your dog may well be mature enough for sperm collection, and since all our terrier lines are very inbred and require constant genetic tinkering, we can hope this one's different enough for a good outcross line." Davin cleared her throat. "About cost . . . as we do not know yet if the dog is healthy, with good genetic material and viable sperm, we would expect to be reimbursed for our costs in bringing a team to the station. Counting all costs— transportation for the team of three, materials for the tests and lab time, all that—it's in the range of twelve to four- teen thousand. I can assure you that if the dog is suit- able, that this cost would be quickly recovered from sales of his sperm, but that's a chance you would have to take. Alternatively, with a young dog that has never been exposed to breeding, we would be prepared to assume those costs ourselves for an equal share in the profits. You would risk nothing, but your profit would be lower."

"I understand," Ky said. "Are you prepared to suggest what the sperm might be worth?"

"I prefer not to," Davin said, almost primly. "However, there are entries in the database that you can look up. May we expect to hear from you soon?"

"Yes," Ky said. "If you'd transmit the site locations you mentioned."

"Certainly." Across the bottom of the screen flowed a list of search terms and sites both.

"Thank you," Ky said.

"Thank you for saving the dog," Davin said.

Ky set Toby the task of looking up the going rate for canine sperm, per insemination. "Rascal's your dog," she said. "You should do the research."

"I don't want him hurt," Toby said. "Will they have to hurt him?"

"They want a blood sample," Ky said. "Check for parasites, disease, that kind of thing. But it's just a needle-stick, and he's had those."

Toby nodded. He worked his way down the list; Ky left him to it and called up the remote visuals Martin had planted. Furman had docked; Furman's crew had begun offloading cargo. The cargo she could see all looked ordinary: standard bins with standard markings on the side, consignors' labels neatly placed. She hadn't seen Furman yet; she wondered if he would call or attempt to contact her directly.

"I don't believe it!" Toby said, breaking her concentration.

"What?"

"Five thousand credits for a single insemination? Rascal's a little gold mine." He grinned at her; Rascal, in his lap, seemed to be grinning as well.

"It would take three to cover the cost of bringing the team up here," Ky said. "After that, it's gravy. But how many can a dog that age do?"

"I don't know yet," Toby said. "I'll keep looking."

Ky turned back to her screen. She wasn't worried that Furman's crew would notice the visual pickups; all docks were monitored and ship crews expected that. Cascadia had lax regulations for such things; if people wanted to add their own surveillance gadgets in public places, they were free to do so, as long as they obtained a permit and certified that the gadgets didn't interfere with the official ones, and the owners granted Cascadia the right to the recordings if a criminal act occurred. She had sent Martin to the permits office the day before, hardly believing that he would actually get a permit to bug dockside space, but the permits had been granted without question.

Unloading looked more complicated than she'd expected, but *Katrine Lamont* was a larger ship and carried more cargo than she'd ever dealt with.

On the stationside of the dock area, consignors' representatives were already lined up, ready to check bills of lading and certify delivery. Furman's cargomaster, a tall bald man with the Vatta logo on the back of his shipsuit, directed the placement of bins as they came off the ship. Finally he halted the offloading and walked over to the gate where the consignors' reps waited.

"Messinam Imports?" The audio pickup, perfectly placed, relayed his voice to Ky's ear.

"Here."

"Come on, then." The cargomaster led the rep over to the bins; the rep checked bin ID, labels, routing numbers, then nodded, thumb-marked the cargomaster's hardcopy, and went back to the gate. The cargomaster peeled off a layer of hardcopy for the Cascadia Customs officer, and a Cascadia Station work crew loaded the bins onto a moving belt that took them through an opening in the bulkhead. From there, Ky knew, they would move to the Customs inspection bay, where both the consignors' representatives and Cascadia Customs would open and inspect the containers.

When the first lot of bins was off the dockside, the cargomaster told his crew to bring out the next.

"Isn't that the captain?" Martin asked. Ky zoomed back

out—she'd been trying to read the consignor's name off one bin—and caught a glimpse of someone in a captain's uniform and cape angling across the dockside to a different exit. Martin already had him centered on that screen; Ky moved to look over his shoulder.

"Yes, that's Furman," she said.

"Looks in a temper," Martin said.

"He usually does," Ky said. "But where's he going?"

"I put a pickup in the next compartment," Martin said. "We'll see him choose a direction, at least."

Furman had gone through the opening labeled CREW EXIT ONLY. On the far side, a Customs and Immigration desk blocked his progress; they watched as he handed over an ID kit and submitted to a thumbprint and retinal scan. Martin used that brief time to imprint Furman's image and ID data into his own security AI; the system would now recognize Furman wherever Martin had pickups.

Furman left the Customs desk with a final nod to the clerk, then paused to pick up a leader-tag. They could not tell what destination he'd asked for.

"Bank or here, on a bet," Ky said.

"Bank," Rafe said from behind her. She jumped; she hadn't heard him come in, and no one had said anything.

"And you were where?" Ky said, trying for icy composure.

"Here and there. It's interesting: the man has lockouts very similar to those Osman had on this ship."

"Learn anything yet?"

Rafe grinned. "I have a nice full data cube ready to untangle . . . haven't done that yet." He opened his hand in front of her; the glossy cube lay there, full of mystery and promise.

"Don't let me stop you," Ky said.

"Want to know if he's really going to the bank?" Rafe asked, tossing the cube from hand to hand.

"What did you do, bug the entire station?" Martin asked.

"No. I did, however, bug him as he strolled along following the tagger's directions. He ran right into me; he wasn't looking."

Martin's mouth quirked upward. "I think there's a story in that, right?"

"A story?" Rafe cocked his head. "Well, I suppose. Someone happened to be carrying a large container of liquid in the passage, from a pub interior to one of the tables overlooking the walkway. None too steadily; I suspect the fellow was a new hire. Our good captain didn't want to be splashed; between watching the man with the pitcher of ale and five glasses on a tray, and trying to keep up with his tagger's direction, he didn't notice the person squatting down to look at a walkside display of plaster figurines—"

"You," said Ky.

"No," Rafe said, with a lift of his eyebrows. "I was the person just inside the door who rushed out and helped him up. Suspicious brute, our captain. He was sure someone had stolen something from him, but no one had. We're all honest here in Cascadia. He had to pat all his pockets and pouches, though, to be sure. If I had wanted any of his valuables, it would have been easy—" He shot a look suddenly at Ky. "You do realize I haven't done anything illegal."

"Yet," Martin said, echoing Ky's thought.

"It did happen that in the course of brushing the dust off his cape—and for a man of such long experience, Captain, he certainly does have a fine, unmarked cape. Yours, I've noticed, is already showing some wear—in the

course of brushing off his cape for him, I did just happen
to lose a burtag."

"You *lost* it," Ky said, struggling not to laugh.

"Lost it. It stuck to his clothes, I imagine. At least, when
I queried it, it was moving along at about his speed.
According to my implant, he's now on the same corridor
as the bank. Yes . . . yes. He's heading for the bank."

"I'm surprised you didn't plant an audio tag on him as
well," Ky said. She couldn't keep the amusement out of
her voice.

"That *would* be illegal," Rafe said. "I prefer not to break
the laws, wherever I am."

"Really." Martin looked him up and down; Rafe didn't
respond, except to raise an eyebrow.

"It's not illegal to tag someone to follow their movements," Rafe said. "I checked. Audio is illegal, but visual
isn't."

"You have a permit?" Martin asked.

"I obtained my own permits," Rafe said. "That way
there's no confusion about who had permits for what."

"I see," Martin said.

"As Captain Furman is not a citizen of the Moscoe
Confederation, local law says that I am under no obligation to notify him with due courtesy of my intent to track
his movements . . ."

"Technically, that is correct. However, arranging for him
to fall down is a direct injury, and in public. For that you
should have notified him," Martin said. "I hope no one
on the scene figured it out."

"Why would you think I arranged for him to fall down?"
Rafe asked.

"Because you said—"

"I described a series of events," Rafe said with perfect
calm. "That does not mean I caused those events."

"No, but—"

Ky intervened. "Stop it, both of you," she said. His bow to her was a model of grace.

"Captain—" That was Toby. "I have a cost analysis ready."

Ky dragged her attention away from Rafe and Martin, and said, "Yes, Toby?"

"It all hinges on how many collections they can do while we're here: I don't know how long we're staying, or how often Rascal can be collected. I did research the market, and we could easily sell enough for one hundred inseminations. The crossover point is eight collections: below that, the sharing with the vet clinic would be more profitable, but if we can do more than eight, we'll be better off paying them and taking the whole profit. Of course, that assumes we can do the collection, or we can make the customer pay for the collection. Some might."

"So—what do you think is best, Toby, from a trading standpoint?"

He scowled in thought. "I was wondering. If we just hire them to do the test, they don't have much incentive to support Rascal's suitability. If we go in with them, it's in their best interest to make sure he works out."

"There's the public relations side, too," Ky said. "If it turns out that we want to trade here again, and perhaps ask Rascal for another contribution, we will need a good relationship with a vet clinic. Our profit's lower, but I'm inclined to work with the clinic on this. How about you?"

"Me?"

"He's your dog, Toby. I don't think the company has any precedent for this particular situation, so I'm going to assess ten percent of the profit to the ship, but the rest of it's your money. You're going to want to finish your education, and we don't know how things are back home for you."

Toby's eyes were wide. "But Captain—that's too much. Twenty-two hundred per collection?"

"You can always invest it in company stock when we have some again," Ky said. "But for now, that's what I'm suggesting."

"Yes . . . yes, ma'am."

"I'll call the clinic back, then," Ky said. This time she was put through immediately.

"Captain Vatta—you have made your decision?"

"Yes, thank you. We want to take you up on your offer of cooperation, splitting the profits of sale of the dog's semen. Do you have a standard contract for that?"

"Thank you! That's wonderful. Yes, we do have a standard contract, which I'll forward to you at once. Er . . . what is the animal's name?"

"Rascal," Ky said, very glad now that Toby had insisted on changing it from Puddles.

"Rascal? Is that all? I mean . . . most animals used for stud service have . . . er . . ."

"Fancy names?" Ky said.

"Yes. Perhaps we could use a breeding name, something more . . . er . . . impressive?"

Ky turned away. "Toby, your pup needs a fancier name. Make something up."

"Vatta's Ridiculous Rescue," Rafe suggested with a sardonic grin.

"Vatta's Nipping Nuisance," Lee said.

"Star Rover's Rascal," Toby said, glaring at the older men.

Ky turned back to the screen. "How about Star Rover's Rascal?"

"That's better. We'll put the name in the contract. I'll

assemble a team and we'll be on our way . . . probably tomorrow."

"Excellent," Ky said and closed that connection. She glanced at Rafe, who was staring at scrolling figures on a cube reader screen. "What's that?"

"That, my dear Captain, is the contents of Captain Furman's secure files." His tone denied the reality of *secure*. "Very interesting man, our captain. He's been double-dealing Vatta for years."

"Furman? He's so upright you could use him for a flag-pole."

"Hardly." Rafe squinted at the dataflow, entered a command, and the screen froze, full of figures Ky didn't recognize. Rafe apparently did. "This is the sum of his various accounts, the ones he holds as sole owner, both in his own and other names."

"Other names?"

"Yes. He has a half dozen aliases. And one in particular will interest you. Olene Vatta."

"There isn't any such person," Ky said after a moment's query of her implant.

"You may not think so, but there's a bank account on New Jamaica in the name of Olene Vatta, and the money sloshing about in it came from two sources: Furman and another Vatta with the initial O."

"Osman?" Ky's voice almost squeaked. She took a deep breath and consciously steadied her tone. "Are you suggesting that Furman was actually dealing with Osman?"

"I'm not 'suggesting' it. I'm saying it's true: Furman was working some kind of scam with Osman. From what I've found so far, money flowed both ways, but most of it flowed from Furman to Osman Vatta. At first I thought Osman was blackmailing Furman, but now I think Furman was fronting for him, selling something Osman sent him, and sending money back."

"What?"

"Think about what's on this ship. Those salvaged implants. Those data cubes of readouts from implants. Valuable information."

That part of Osman's cargo had given Ky the creeps. Putting together salvaged implants and their files with what she'd found in Osman's cabin, she could imagine all too easily how his prisoners had "disappeared."

"What I don't know," Rafe continued, "is where the transfer was made. Furman traveled a well-known route through reasonably respectable systems. Osman's presence there would've been noted. And you said Furman had a reputation for early and on-time deliveries, so I don't see how he'd have had time to meet Osman between systems."

"Maybe those files will tell us," Ky said.

"Maybe. But I'll probably need navigational help if they do. I'm not a pilot or navigator."

"Just keep after it," Ky said. "I would love to put Furman in the villain's seat." Another idea hit her. "If Furman's involved, he'd have access to current Vatta schedules . . . maybe it was Furman who gave the attackers the locations of Vatta ships and crews."

"I thought you'd decided it was Osman," Rafe said.

"But if they were working together—wait—wait—" The horrific vision propagated in her mind. "Furman knew," she said. "Furman has been working with Osman. So Furman tells Osman, gives him all the schedule data, all the call signs, all the passwords. And Osman tells his allies, those pirates. Only Furman's been transferred to this new route . . . and what do you want to bet he was supposed to meet Osman here, or in another port of this route, but here is logical . . . it's so close to Nexus."

"Furman was spying on ISC's defenses," Rafe said. "Has to be. Hated being sent out here but then found a way to profit even more."

"You're not setting foot off this ship until we know who he's been working with," Martin said.

"Agreed," Ky said. "But when this identity thing is settled—"

"It's not going to be settled," Martin said. "You're too dangerous to him. You've got Osman's ship; Furman doesn't have to know Rafe to know that something incriminating him might be on *this* ship."

"It might be still," Rafe said. "I haven't had time to go through half the files; I prioritized on things that might kill us quickly—"

"I'm not blaming you," Martin said. "Just pointing out that Furman must worry that there's data somewhere on this ship that could point to him . . . and you, Captain, of all the Vattas, are the one most likely to give him trouble."

"But why did he turn on us?" Ky wondered aloud. "We have excellent compensation; people want to work for us. He came here of his own accord—"

"Some people are never satisfied," Rafe said. "Or maybe Osman got to him somehow, twisted him around—"

Ky delved into the personnel section of her implant and was startled to find gaps, obvious erasures, in Furman's record. They could only come from her father—it was his very personal implant—unless Grace had been able to make changes after Gerard died. She glanced at Rafe; he might well know how to interfere with implants or even recover data that had been erased. But no: he was not Vatta, or sworn to Vatta. It was too dangerous to risk. She would figure Furman out on her own.

* * *

As the days passed, Stella's worry grew, and she finally decided that she could not wait to call Ky about Furman. The man was too dangerous. This business with Furman might even focus Ky's mind back on the Vatta family and business, make her realize that she needed to concentrate on saving the family first.

To her surprise and annoyance, Rafe answered the comunit instead of Ky. "Stella! What a delightful surprise. You're as lovely as ever—"

"Haven't gotten into her bed yet, have you?" Stella asked tartly.

"Stella, dear Stella, don't tell me you're jealous because I'm here and you're there. Ky tells me you have a handsome new shipmaster—isn't that enough to play with?"

She should have known better than to tackle Rafe; he always had a comeback that stung worse than her attacks. "I need to talk to Ky," she said.

"Our esteemed captain is busy at the moment, improving her physical skills with Gordon Martin. Her combat skills, I hasten to add; I'm sure she and Martin have nothing on otherwise. Are you sure I can't help?"

"Quite sure," Stella said. "*Katrine Lamont* has docked, hasn't it?"

"Yes, why?"

She was not going to tell him and let him relay what he chose of it to Ky; she was not going to miss the triumph of having figured out so much, either. "Just call her, please. I do think it's urgent."

"Very well. Excuse me a moment." He vanished from the visual pickup; apparently he was going to go after Ky in person. Stella spotted Toby across the bridge, with Rascal by his side as usual.

"Toby!"

He turned, spotted her image on the screen and came

over. He had grown even more since she'd seen him last. "Stella! I'm glad to see you. Have you heard about Rascal?"

"Rascal? No, tell me."

"They don't have many dogs here," Toby said. "And they're really valuable. We've had offers for him up to thirty thousand credits—"

"You're going to sell him?"

"No! No, I'd never sell Rascal. But Captain Ky thought of using him to breed, for artificial insemination, and she found this vet clinic that'll do the collection. And she's giving me ninety percent of the profit, for my education if . . . if something's happened to my parents back home."

"That's—very generous, Toby."

"I thought so. I told her it was too much, but she said Toby was my dog, and I should profit from it. They said it won't hurt Rascal at all, just one needle-stick for the blood test."

"That's wonderful," Stella said. So Ky was thinking about family after all, at least about Toby.

"I was so worried at first; I thought she might make me sell him because the price was so high, but she didn't." Toby's voice broke suddenly, shifting registers; he flushed and shook his head.

"Never mind, Toby," Stella said. "Happens to all boys."

"I know," he said in a croak an octave lower than before. "Rafe told me. Gordon told me. Everyone's told me. I hate it."

"Excuse me, Toby," Ky said, coming up behind him. He flashed her a grin and moved away. "Hello, Stella. Things have been happening here—"

"Toby told me," Stella said. "But I have news for you. I started looking into the doings of your Captain Furman, and you'll never guess what he's been up to. He's been—"

"Illicitly trading with Osman Vatta," Ky said, finishing her sentence.

Stella felt a stab of resentment. "How did you figure it out?"

"I didn't, exactly. Rafe got into his files aboard *Katrine Lamont*. How did you figure it out?"

"Personnel records," Stella said. "And I talked to Quincy. And then I worked through the Beulah Road route, checking the timings, and talked to our pilot. I think the trouble probably started with Mellicent."

The look on Ky's face was gratifying: clearly she had not figured out that part of the story. "Mellicent," she said finally. "Harmon's daughter? What does she have to do with it?"

"Furman courted Mellicent years ago."

Ky's brows rose. "Ambitious, wasn't he?"

"That's what I said. Quincy said it wasn't that unusual for daughters to marry successful captains, and he'd already made a name for himself. Anyway, he wasn't successful; she married someone else without telling him. I think that may've set him off, convinced him that he wouldn't rise to his potential with Vatta."

"I haven't figured out how he had time to deal with Osman," Ky said. "He was always coming in early or on time at least—"

"My pilot figured that out. He was using nonstandard routes to save time, building a reputation for efficiency."

"He took *our* ships on yellow routes?" Ky looked as if someone had hit her over the head. Stella had not expected that level of shock.

"Yes. That's what my pilot says, that there's no way he could have been that short on those routes on the—the green routes. She thinks he rendezvoused with Osman in one of the uninhabited systems, a transfer jump point, I think she called it."

Ky nodded. "That makes sense. I hadn't checked his routes yet. We do know he was meeting Osman regularly and money flowed between them. And he had accounts under other names."

"Do you have any idea what he was trading?" Stella asked. "I haven't been able to think of anything."

"Data, mostly," Ky said. "We didn't have a chance to talk about that, but there are indications on this ship that Osman took prisoners and acquired their . . . um . . . knowledge, the kind of thing that's readily salable. Rafe's still stripping the files, looking for details. I haven't reported any of this to law enforcement here, because we don't have it all collated yet, but I think Captain Furman may also be responsible for telling Osman just how to set up the simultaneous attacks on Vatta."

Stella felt her stomach turning to ice. "He killed my father? Your parents?"

"Not himself, but he made it possible. I'd bet on it." Ky's face was as grim as Stella herself felt. "And now he wants this ship, and probably your ship, and thinks he can set himself up as his own trading company."

"That's in his files?"

"That's obvious, from everything he's been doing. Why else try to discredit me?" Ky shook her head. "He's not going to get away with it. With what you've got, and Rafe's getting from his own files, we should be able to take care of Captain Furman, permanently."

NINETEEN

Ky half expected Furman to come to her ship in the tedious days before Stella brought in *Gary Tobai*, but he didn't. He made no protest to the limits she'd put on his use of the Vatta corporate account. He did not even call. Instead, he filed formal charges against her with the local government, charges relayed by the authorities along with the date she must appear before a judicar in formal proceedings. Martin continued to monitor the activity on dockside, but everything looked normal. Shippers' agents came, inspected cargo shipping labels, and the cargo bins moved into Cascadia's automated cargo-handling facility to be loaded onto short-haul carriers.

Rafe continued to analyze the data he obtained from Furman's ship files. Much of it was encrypted; though Vatta had its own encryption formats, Furman had used something else. Ky, prompted by Stella's discoveries about Furman's Beulah Road route, looked for anything resembling a jump-point designation, but so far they hadn't found it. What they had found were yet more indicators of financial irregularity. Furman had never diverted Vatta funds directly; he had not embezzled, in the usual sense. He had, however, maintained noncorporate accounts at every port, often under an alias.

"I suppose other banks aren't as good about checking identity as Crown & Spears," Ky said. She'd used Crown & Spears because her family did; she knew little about why it had been chosen. Furman had accounts with First Travelers, Allsystems Bancorp, Geneva Bank & Trust. Only one account was in his own name.

"He may have provided his real identity and asked to open the account in another name," Rafe said. "That's legal in some jurisdictions. All three of those banks do it where they can. Allsystems Bancorp, in fact, is a fairly shady enterprise."

"But don't they have to be licensed? Why would a system government license them if they're dishonest?"

"I didn't say they were dishonest, exactly. As to why— banking can be a very profitable business for the government, too. A little tax on transfers can help pay for a lot of infrastructure."

When Ky compared the data from her ship's autolog with the information Stella had provided, she found that Osman's ship had indeed been at all three of the jump points she mentioned in the past twelve years, apparently alternating them. This still did not prove that anything had passed between them.

"We need the autolog of Furman's ship," Rafe said. "But I can't get into it. Not yet, anyway."

Stella arrived before Rafe could break the access codes. She came at once to meet with Ky, bringing along a legal professional recommended by Crown & Spears. Ky had hoped for a private chat, a chance to mend familial fences, but Stella's perfect jaw was set in a way that offered no hope of that, at least not until the legal matter of Ky's identity was settled.

"We don't have time," Stella said. "You have to appear

tomorrow, first shift." Ky went back over what she'd already told the authorities, reassured that at least Stella didn't think she was a changeling. The judicar had submitted questions for her to answer on official record.

Ky had never been to court on Slotter Key, or for that matter anywhere else. Her legal representative, here called a barrister, gave her another list: Rules of Conduct in Court. Some of it made obvious sense: speaking in turn, not interrupting, avoiding the use of inflammatory language. The rule requiring barristers and judicars to wear a wreath of fresh green—pine for barristers, fir for judicars—seemed as bizarre as the shape of the space station itself. Pledents—"those who plead," her barrister explained—must wear green as well: a stole over the right shoulder if the accuser, and over the left shoulder if the defender. If the defender made a counteraccusation, the defender then wore green stoles crossed on the chest, secured by a plain green belt.

"Appropriate court stoles may be rented or purchased," her barrister said. "As you are not a citizen, yours must have a single stripe of orange one centimeter wide, which must be centered in the stole when it's worn. It is extremely rude to appear with an uncentered stripe."

The courtroom itself was a room narrow for its height, slightly wedge-shaped, with a plain dark wood bench on a raised platform along either side and across the narrow end. At equal intervals on both sides were half columns that appeared to be replicas of tree trunks with coarsely textured bark; the entire narrow end looked like one massive trunk, and Ky realized, glancing up, that the ceiling was higher there. The floor was covered in a resilient, dark, textured material that dampened sound. Between the "trees," the walls were dark green, subtly patterned with darker tones as if by layers of leaves in a shady forest.

Overhead seemed to be a mix of lighter greens and golds, again patterned subtly. Brilliant spotlights stabbed down here and there, and the effect was much like walking through such a forest, especially because of the pine smell from her barrister's wreath.

As defender and counteraccuser, Ky was assigned the bench on the left as they entered, and Furman was assigned the right. Guided by her barrister, she and Stella filed in between their bench and the narrow, slant-topped table in front of it. As they sat down, the tabletop lit and displayed the case number, her name, her barrister's name, and asked for her thumbprint to verify that she was in fact the person seated there. Ky complied.

Down the room, the door opened again and Furman came in, scowling. He wore only the one stole, its orange stripe correctly centered, and his barrister, like her own, wore a wreath of pine. They worked their way into their own space across from her. Ky watched as Furman pressed his thumb to his own tabletop, presumably for the same reason she had.

A dark opening appeared in the narrow end of the room, and a light shone on it. Ky's barrister nudged her and she nudged Stella; they all stood. The judicar seemed to climb up from below the opening; they saw his fir wreath first, like a bushy green bird's nest, then his face, and finally his body. Ky felt an almost uncontrollable urge to giggle, which she knew was merely anxiety, and tightened her lips. Laughing in court was a grave offense.

"As trees contend with trees for light, so do persons contend with persons for the truth, which is the mind's light," the judicar said solemnly. His face, under the fir wreath, was broad, sun-marked, with laugh wrinkles at the corners of the gray eyes. In his gray-streaked beard, he had tied the lengths of green silk with which he would bind his verdict.

"Barristers!" That came out in a rough bark that made Ky jump. Her barrister and Furman's bowed. "Can you not bring your clients to agreement without troubling the Tree?"

"No, Forest Lord," they said in unison.

"Pledents!" Ky understood that he was now speaking directly to her and to Furman. "Can you not share the light as trees do, without contention?"

"No, Forest Lord," Ky said; Furman echoed a moment after her.

"Very well. Be seated."

The bench was hard. Her barrister had explained that the Cascadians did not approve of lengthy legal wrangles, so the benches had no cushions, backs, or armrests. No one was allowed to lean against the wall, either . . . the walls were wired, and leaners got a sharp shock. Her back twinged already.

"The pledent Furman has alleged that the defendant Vatta is not in fact the individual Kylara Vatta as identified on entry to the Moscoe Confederation," the judicar said. "The pledent Furman has alleged that this individual is instead another member of the Vatta family. This court finds no reason why that should matter to the Moscoe Confederation."

"That's ridiculous!" Furman said, standing up. His face had gone red. His barrister grabbed his arm and pulled him back

"The pledent will be seated," the judicar said. "The pledent will recall the rules of this court and this Confederation, in which rudeness is not tolerated, and refrain from gratuitous insults to the bench." He cleared his throat. "The pledent's barrister will remind his client that pledents are not to speak without direct address from the court. The pledent's barrister may now explain why this court should care which member of a foreign family is here."

"My client begs the court's pardon," Furman's barrister began. "As do I, for failing to instruct him adequately in the procedures and rules of this jurisdiction—"

"The court hears your apology," the judicar said. "Go on."

"Captain Furman states that the ship known as *Fair Kaleen* was operated by one Osman Vatta, a man related to the Vatta family of Vatta Transport, Ltd., but exiled from that family for a number of crimes—"

"Crimes never brought to court?"

"It is my understanding, Forest Lord, that the family wished to avoid public shame. At any rate, this Osman Vatta stole a Vatta ship and operated as nothing more than a common pirate. *Fair Kaleen* is well known in other jurisdictions as his ship, and was interdicted in those systems because of his piracy."

"Yet never brought to court?"

"It is an armed ship, Forest Lord, and the said Osman was, apparently, expert in evading pursuit." The barrister paused, as if for another question, then went on. "Captain Furman furnished me with replicas of legal notices from other systems substantiating his claim that *Fair Kaleen* was known to law enforcement as a pirate ship."

"I see. Is Captain Furman claiming that this woman"— the judicar gestured at Ky—"is Osman Vatta?"

"No, Forest Lord. Osman Vatta would be a much older man; Captain Furman believes that this is Osman Vatta's daughter."

"And how would Captain Furman know so much about an outlaw?" the judicar asked.

"The information was supplied by Vatta Transport, Ltd., as part of security briefings to all its captains," the barrister said.

"Including information about this woman?"

"Not specifically, no. But that Osman Vatta had children, yes. This woman, pretending to be Kylara Vatta, daughter of Gerard Vatta, until the late disasters the chief financial officer of Vatta Enterprises—which includes Vatta Transport, Ltd.—cannot be that individual because Captain Furman has personal knowledge of Kylara Vatta. She served on his ship as an apprentice."

"I see. I will now hear counterargument from the defendant's barrister."

Ky's barrister laid out her claim of identity, including an explanation for her possession of Osman's ship. Furman's barrister countered with his version of events.

"Captain Furman contends that the genuine Kylara Vatta, who apprenticed on his ship, was incapable of capturing Osman Vatta's ship with the old, slow, unarmed vessel to which she had been assigned. She lacked both the armament and the expertise—"

"Captain Vatta reminds the court that she had almost completed the Slotter Key Spaceforce Academy prior to resigning to enter the family business, and that she had purchased defensive armament that was used in the conflict—"

Back and forth the barristers went. Ky's back ached.

Finally the judicar held up his hand. "I will hear from the pledents and defendent directly. You will answer my questions briefly and to the point. Captain Furman. You have heard the evidence that this woman is in fact Kylara Vatta. On what do you base your claim that she is not?"

"I know her," Furman said. "This is a stranger."

"You last saw her in person how long ago?"

"It would now be . . . perhaps ten years standard."

"She was a young girl then, and now she is a woman; many people change in that period of time."

Furman flushed again. "It is not Ky. It cannot be Ky. The Ky I knew was an impulsive, argumentative, difficult adolescent, always getting into trouble. While it never surprised me that she was expelled from the Academy, there is no way she could have defeated Osman."

"What do you believe happened?"

"I believe Osman killed the real Kylara, and substituted one of his own children, who had the family resemblance, coaching her in her story."

"And this would fool her crew?"

Furman shrugged. "It worked. But notice that she left her most experienced crew—the ones who knew the real Kylara best—on the ship Kylara had captained."

"You have entered in confidence five incidents from Kylara Vatta's experience aboard your ship that you believe the real Kylara would recall. Do you attest that these are true representations of those events?"

"I do," Furman said.

"Captain Vatta," the judicar said. Furman opened his mouth as if to say more; his barrister pulled him back. "Were you in fact an apprentice on Captain Furman's ship?"

"Yes," Ky said.

"You were asked to submit five incidents from your time serving under Captain Furman that you believed he should recall. Do you attest that these events occurred as you represent them?"

"I do," Ky said.

"That is very interesting," the judicar said, "because I find no point of correspondence between these accounts. More than that, the two of you picked no incident in common. It is possible that in the course of a year's journey, many more than five memorable incidents occurred, and that what a captain finds worthy of memory is not what a young girl finds worthy . . . but it is a discrepancy I cannot ignore. Captain Vatta, Captain Furman was asked to supply the names of crewmembers on his ship during your apprenticeship. I want you to name as many crewmembers and their positions as you remember." Ky's barrister stirred; the judicar went on. "I am well aware that Captain Vatta may not remember them all, or that Captain Furman may have provided inaccurate information: we shall see. Go ahead, Captain Vatta."

Armed with her father's command implant, Ky didn't need to remember all the names, but some she would not forget anyway. "Toron Barclay was the chief engineer," she said. "A big, husky man with thinning red hair. Everyone teased him about it. Elly Prost was his number two, tall, skinny. Jan Arbeit was the number three; he was much younger." She had been accused of flirting with Jan because they'd played simulation games with each other so often, but she'd had no interest in him that way. "Apprentices rotate through the different areas, but I spent the most time in Engineering. In Cargo . . . let me think. Ganli Zludist was cargomaster, and his number two was Serge Paolin. I don't remember the number three . . ." She had been barred from the bridge except for a few brief visits; she didn't remember the pilot, the navigator, the communications tech, except as vague faces, and said so, though the implant furnished her with the names.

The tedious questions went on and on.

"This is your cousin, you say?"

"Yes. Her father and my father were brothers."

"She looks nothing like you."

"Yes. My mother was dark; her mother's family had many blondes."

"Stella Vatta. Is this your cousin Kylara?"

"Yes," Stella said. "It is."

"It is not something about which you could be mistaken?"

"No; I have known her from childhood."

"The testimony is confusing," the judicar said. "I understand that Crown & Spears has genetic evidence that Captain Kylara Vatta is indeed a Vatta and closely related to a family member about whom there is no previous question, Josephine Vatta. This person would be your sister, Stella Vatta?"

"Yes, my older sister," Stella said.

"Then I would expect a genetic scan to show that you and Kylara Vatta are as closely related. Though we cannot admit in this court the evidence from Crown & Spears, having no proof that their sample of Josephine Vatta's genetic material is in fact hers, establishing a first-cousin relationship should be simple. Do you consent to having this test performed?"

"Yes," Ky and Stella said together.

"Good. We shall invite the technicians to enter."

The technicians inserted the samples into the machine, and in a few minutes obtained a readout.

"These individuals are indeed related," one of them told the judicar. "But not closely. There is very little chance that they are in fact first cousins."

"What?" Stella blurted. "Of course we are."

"I'm afraid not," the technician said. "Here are the scans."

"I told you so!" Furman said. Again, his barrister restrained him.

"This is a surprise to you?" the judicar said to Stella.

"It certainly is. I've known Ky all my life, and she's known me. We're cousins. There must be some mistake."

"You have no other sources of Vatta genetic material?" Stella held up her hand. "Yes, Stella Vatta; you may speak."

"Er . . . there is genetic evidence from Osman Vatta," Stella said.

"What?" Ky clapped a hand over her own mouth and glanced apologetically at the judicar.

"You've forgotten, Ky. You had me retain a tissue sample from Osman's body in the freezer, remember?"

"I thought you'd give it to Mackensee," Ky said. "They took the body, didn't they?"

"Yes, but I thought you wanted a sample for us—to prove that it was Osman you'd killed, that it really was his ship. Anyway, it's still there."

"If they'll accept it—with no proper chain of custody— it should help a lot," Ky said. She looked up at the judicar. "We also have a distant relative, a boy, with us."

"Are you *in loco parentis* for this boy?"

"Yes."

"And will you and he consent to his contributing a sample?"

"Yes, of course."

"Court will recess briefly to allow one of our monitors to retrieve the sample; Stella Vatta may guide them; Captain Vatta will remain here, as will Captain Furman."

At least, Ky thought, they could stand up and move around instead of sitting on those hard benches. She and Furman made no attempt to approach each other.

Again the technicians inserted samples into the machine, this time all three available Vattas, plus Osman's sample. Again, the brief wait. Ky's stomach churned.

"We have the results," the senior technician told the

judicar. "There is a strong likelihood that all four individuals are related, though not in equal degree. Samples one, three, and four are distantly related—farther apart than second cousins, in all likelihood. Sample two is distantly related to samples one and three. Between two and four, however, there is a much closer relationship: first degree, in fact. In my professional opinion, two and four are parent and child."

"And the names? Which are parent and child?"

"Osman Vatta and Stella Vatta."

Ky stared at Stella. Even though it had occurred to her before, it seemed far more likely that she herself might be Osman's daughter. Stella? The beauty of the family a daughter of that ugly and violent man? It could not be possible—yet something told her it was.

"No!" Stella said, her voice rising; her face had gone chalk white.

"Silence," the judicar said. "This is indeed a surprise; I thought the accusation was that *Kylara* Vatta was Osman's daughter—"

"Maybe they both are," Furman's barrister said.

"They cannot be," the technician said. "Kylara Vatta and Stella Vatta are only distantly related. If they were half sisters, that would be obvious."

"You were unaware of this?" the judicar said, looking at Stella.

"Yes—it can't be right," Stella said, still pale. "I—I was born on Slotter Key. I remember—our house, growing up, my parents—"

"Perhaps you were adopted very young," the judicar said. "Perhaps you were not told—"

"But that's—" Stella turned to Ky. "*You* know, Ky. I've always been there—always."

"You are the elder," the judicar said. "She could not

know for certain that you were born to your legal parents. If indeed you were adopted . . ."

"Ky, please!" Stella reached out, then withdrew her hand.

Ky reached out, grasped Stella's hand, and squeezed it. "You're my cousin, always, whatever the test says," she said softly. "Don't worry, Stella. We'll figure this out."

"Silence," the judicar said, but without heat. "I understand this is a shock to both of you, but we must go on with this hearing, and appropriate decorum must be maintained.

"Stella Vatta, although your unbidden words are against the regulations of this court, I judge them forgivable due to the element of surprise. However, you must be silent unless directly addressed." He waited until she nodded.

"The test makes it clear that Kylara Vatta is not the child of Osman Vatta, and thus the first pledent's accusation is proved false. Given that she is not the child of Osman Vatta, there is no reason to think she has falsified her identity, and I find that the person representing herself as Kylara Vatta is in fact Kylara Vatta, and until further evidence is submitted suggesting otherwise, I rule that her account of events leading to her capture of the ship *Fair Kaleen* be accepted."

"No!" Furman was on his feet, his barrister clinging to his arm. "You can't—she's lying!"

"Captain Furman, you are in contempt!" The judicar's voice matched his scowl. "You have repeatedly broken the rules of this court, and have exhausted my patience. You have illegally insulted Captain Kylara Vatta—"

"They're in it together. They must be. Osman's daughter corrupted Ky, and they're working together—if you can't see that, you're stupid—!"

"Bailiffs." At the judicar's word, they came forward to

surround Furman. "Your barrister will instruct you as to the penalties attendant on insulting the court, Captain Furman. Your trial will be scheduled promptly."

Ky watched in stunned disbelief as the bailiffs bound and gagged Furman, and dragged him from the courtroom. Though her barrister laid a cautionary hand on her arm, she wasn't tempted to move or speak. When the courtroom doors closed behind Furman and the bailiffs, the judicar turned to her.

"Under our law, the misbehavior of one pledent does not prove that the pledent's case is false. But clearly you are not the child of Osman Vatta, which was Captain Furman's accusation. That being so, I have no reason to disbelieve that you are the person you say you are, in legal possession of Slotter Key's letter of marque and a ship captured from the pirate Osman Vatta, and to order that officers of the court immediately remove the tracking device you were made to wear. I offer this court's sincere apologies for any inconvenience or embarrassment you suffered as a result of that requirement." One of the bailiffs came to Ky and touched the anklet with a control wand; it fell open, and the bailiff picked it up with an apologetic nod. The judicar went on.

"As for Stella Vatta, your testimony and hers suggests that she was adopted very young, and thus her legal identity is, in fact, consistent with her claimed identity. Even if that were not the case, no charges were laid against her, and if you—as a Vatta whose identity is not in doubt—accept her as your cousin, then her identity is of no further interest to this court."

He paused and took a sip of water. "Now, I understand that you had laid countercharges against Captain Furman, and this court was prepared to hear them. However, you might wish to confer with your barrister about those charges, and whether they might not be better brought at Furman's trial for gross discourtesy." He paused, nodded toward their barrister and said, "You have permission to confer."

Ky's barrister leaned over to her. "We can pursue your original case if you wish, but since Furman will be executed for the undeniable behavior here—"

"Executed?" Ky struggled to keep her voice low.

"Gross discourtesy in a court of law? Absolutely. He offered you and the judicar both mortal insults. He persisted in discourteous behavior despite warnings from the judicar and his barrister."

"But—but I'm sure he didn't understand the penalties—I'm sure he meant no mortal insult—"

"Captain Vatta, you have been here only a short time; Captain Furman has visited the Moscoe Confederation before. He has had more time to absorb the requirements of our legal system; he is also older than you, and thus held to a higher standard of behavior. We do not tolerate discourtesy from anyone, but those senior in age or rank are held to a stricter standard, and punished more severely should they offend. Is it not so on your home planet?"

"Er . . . no," Ky said. "That is, it is for some things, but not others, and our standards for courteous behavior are quite different."

"Yet you have not offended, nor has your cousin. Despite your youth and your relative inexperience, neither of you has lost control and offered insult. At any rate: with Furman out of the picture, his ship clearly belongs to Vatta Transport, of which you are both part, and would require no re-registration to operate under your command. You would but have to apply to the appropriate office to specify which of you—or whom else—would become captain of that ship."

"I . . . see," Ky said. "So you're advising me not to enter the plea that Furman was working with Osman Vatta and bilking the company?"

"The judicar also sits on a hard bench," the barrister said. "I believe he would appreciate the end of this particular exhausting session. I also believe your evidence is not needed to condemn Captain Furman, but you could bring it to the attention of the judicar in written form, where it might influence his trial. Though once a man is dead, you cannot kill him twice."

"Isn't there anything but the death penalty?" Ky asked. She was not sure why she wanted to plead for Furman's life—particularly if he had been involved in the attacks on her family—but she felt a strong impulse to intervene.

"There is another measure, but it is rarely employed as it is considered inhumane—"

"More inhumane than killing?" Stella asked.

"Oh, yes. If you simply kill someone, they are merely dead. For those who believe in an afterlife—and I am one of those—the person is still who he or she was in life, and if too harshly judged in life receives recompense, or if too lightly judged in life, receives punishment. The only other procedure restructures the personality, making the individual incapable of the crime for which he or she was punished . . . but that person then accrues the rest of a lifetime as another person. The afterlife is clouded; there are arguments about what happens."

Ky wanted to pursue that, but a soft throat-clearing by the judicar suggested that this was not the time. "I agree at least not to pursue my complaint against Furman at this time."

"Good," her barrister said, and rose. "Forest Lord," he said. "My client abides by your judgment but may wish to offer information later. Is that satisfactory?"

"Quite," said the judicar. "I shall await any useful information later." He rose; they all rose; he turned and descended back into the great tree trunk.

Ky's barrister ushered her, Stella, and Toby out, leaving the technicians fussing with their machine on the courtroom floor.

"That was . . . very strange," Ky said, when they were in the passage outside. "I'm still somewhat confused. Would you come aboard my ship and explain further?"

"Certainly," the barrister said. "But you must understand, at my fixed hourly rate. Now if we were merely to have a meal together—and it is now time for lunch, I believe—then we might have a friendly conversation that would cost you for the meal but nothing else."

"I—I want to go back to the ship," Stella said. Tears glittered in her eyes; her hand in Ky's was cold.

"What's wrong, Stella?" Ky asked. She knew the moment it came out of her mouth that it was the wrong thing to say, but she couldn't unsay it.

Stella paled. "Don't be stupid!" she said. "I find out that I'm not who I thought I was, that my father was a renegade, a thief, and . . . and worse . . . and you want to know what's wrong?"

"I'm sorry," Ky said. "I thought . . . I meant . . ."

"I'm going back to the ship," Stella said, yanking her hand out of Ky's grasp. "I'm going to pack. You can have it all . . . all the ships, all the company. It's yours. You know what you're doing; you're always so sure of yourself." She whirled and strode off. Toby looked as shocked as Ky felt.

"Excuse me," Ky said to the barrister. "Family crisis. Come on, Toby." She hurried after Stella, Toby at her side. "Stella!" she called. "Stella, wait—don't go—" People in the passage turned to look at them, and politely turned away.

Stella slowed, but did not turn. When Ky caught up with her, Stella's face was streaked with tears, her mouth set in a stubborn line.

"Stella, please," Ky said. "In law you're my cousin, whether it's birth or adoption. It doesn't matter . . ."

"It matters to me," Stella said. "To be that man's daughter—no wonder I messed up my life. My father—my *adoptive* father—should have kicked me out then and there. No surprise they didn't think I'd amount to anything." She walked faster again; Ky stretched to keep up. "And then . . . and then to lie there, blinded and tied up and waiting for . . . for a monster to come kill me, I thought, and for it to be my own . . . my own father. My real father—"

Ky could think of nothing soothing to say. "He's dead now," she said, hoping that would help.

"Killed by you," Stella said. "That makes me feel *so* much better." She took a shaky breath. "I should be grateful, I'm sure. I should be grateful for being rescued from whatever life Osman would have given me—"

That was so true that Ky dared not say anything. Stella in a rage, Stella having a tantrum—she knew that Stella of old.

"And I am grateful," Stella went on, more calmly. "I had a good childhood. My . . . the parents I thought I had . . . were good to me." Her voice rose again. "But still . . . they should've told me something. I should have had some warning that I wasn't really Jo's sister, that the differences I felt weren't my fault. That there were things I should be watching out for."

"You were a child," Ky said.

"Not for the past ten years," Stella said. "Were they ever going to tell me? Or was I supposed to go through life not knowing there was an explosive secret hanging over my head?"

In the ordinary life they'd known, not knowing wouldn't have caused her any problems, Ky thought, but Stella was clearly in no mood to hear that now.

"You are a Vatta, though," Ky said. "And you've been working for Vatta, since—"

"Since Aunt Grace took me on," Stella said. "And I wonder if she knows, the old harridan. Damn her, for not telling me. She of all people should have known better."

"But it hasn't stopped you doing your job," Ky said. "You aren't a thief. You aren't a murderer. You are a competent woman with many talents—"

"Including some I inherited from my father Osman," Stella said. "No, Ky, I'm not the person I thought I was. I'm not reliable. I proved that once, and it's there in my genome, as well. You don't need me."

"I do," Ky said. "I do need you."

"Right. That's why you kept zipping from system to system, not waiting for me . . . all you need me for is a place marker. To lie there with a bag over my head pretending to be you, to follow you around in an old tub until you deign to slow down and tell me what to do—"

The abrupt switch caught Ky off guard. "What's that about?" she asked. "I thought this was about Osman being your biological father."

"It is . . . it was." Stella strode past a group of people waiting outside a pastry shop so fast that they all turned and stared.

"Slow down," Ky said. "Station rules . . ."

Stella stopped, and Ky almost bumped into her. "Ky, will you please just go . . . somewhere . . . and let me get back to my—to the ship? I do not need to be nursemaided."

Ky was aware of the onlookers and made an effort to keep her voice very low. "Stella, you should have an escort when you're not aboard ship, just as I should. We don't know if Furman had someone watching us, if we're still being hunted. If I send Toby with you, will you promise not to go anywhere alone, or—or do anything, and we can talk later?"

"All right," Stella said, more softly. "But who's going to guard your back?" She grimaced. "I may be Osman's by-blow, but I don't want you dead."

"That's good," Ky said. "I think—I know—we can work this out if we just sit down and talk, but if you want some thinking time—"

"Yes," Stella said, between her teeth.

"All right. Toby, please make sure that Stella gets back to her dockside safely."

"Yes, Captain," Toby said. "I won't let anything happen to her."

Ky watched as they moved off down the passage, then turned to look at the crowd near the pastry shop. As one, they all turned away.

TWENTY

Ky used the skullphone in her implant to call back to *Fair Kaleen*.

"Furman blew his own case," she told Hugh, who answered. "And there's a complication."

"Isn't there always? What this time?"

She hesitated a moment, then decided that they would all have to know soon enough. "They did genetic tests on Stella, Toby, me, and Osman's tissue," she said. "Stella is Osman's natural daughter . . . found in an orphanage, apparently, and adopted in infancy by my uncle Stavros."

"She's . . . oh, my."

"Yes. Don't tell the others yet, but she's having a rough time right now. I let her go back to her ship with Toby, for the present."

"You need an escort?"

"I probably should." Ky didn't want to wait around, but it was just possible that Furman or Osman or someone else had agents on the station.

"You definitely should. Stay where you are—where is that? I'll send a pair. Gannetts, will that do?"

"Fine. I'll be eating lunch at a café right here—the Rainbow Arch, it's called. Smells good."

"Find a table with—"

"My back to a wall and an exit nearby. I know." Hugh was as bad—or good—as Martin when it came to security matters.

Her next call was to Quincy, on *Gary Tobai*. Stella hadn't reached the ship yet, so she briefed Quincy on the discovery.

"Well, that explains things," Quincy said.

"No, it doesn't," Ky said. "She hasn't changed into a monster just because Osman was."

"I didn't mean that," Quincy said. "I meant it explains why she never got ship duty like nearly all you Vatta youngsters. She didn't go offplanet until she was over twenty, did she?"

"Not that I know of," Ky said. "The thing is, she's very upset—"

"Naturally—"

"And she said she's going to leave Vatta, go off somewhere."

"Ridiculous. She mustn't. You want me to talk to her?"

"Let her tell you," Ky said. "But try to keep her from walking out on us."

"I'll keep her busy," Quincy said. "I'm not going to tell the crew, though. Not yet, anyway."

"Right."

Ky found a seat both Hugh and Martin would approve, and ordered lunch. Maybe this would give her time to think over what to do about the day's revelations. Two of the Gannetts, Arnie and Gus, arrived before she'd finished eating. She nodded and they sat down on either side, refusing food.

"We'd just eaten, ma'am," Arnie said. "Don't you rush."

"I won't," Ky said. But she also couldn't think in the café's bustle.

Back aboard ship, she went into her cabin and resorted

to old-fashioned marker and paper to organize her thoughts. With Furman arrested and sentenced to death— she should do something about that, but what?—and her identity as Vatta's heir now accepted, she had three ships at her disposal. Three ships, but did she have three crews? Furman had quietly eliminated Vatta family members from his ship; did that mean the crew were all disloyal? Surely not all of them . . . but whom could she trust?

The dots and circles and boxes she doodled didn't really help. If she didn't trust Furman's crew, then . . . she called Quincy.

"If you were a captain up to no good in a Vatta ship, which crewmembers would have to be in on it?"

"What?"

Ky explained.

"Well . . . your pilot and navigator, if it involved route changes or unscheduled stops. If cargo's unloaded or taken on, at least the cargomaster. Engineering wouldn't have to know, necessarily, or Environmental. They might but they wouldn't have to. My guess is that Furman first eliminated family members who might be nosy, then anyone else with too much initiative."

"So . . . what chance is there that those in on it will try to run with the ship?"

"Minimal, I'd think," Quincy said. "Though you will have informed the stationmaster not to give it clearance— you did, didn't you?"

She hadn't yet. "Not yet, but I will. Thanks, Quincy." The stationmaster agreed to put a lock on *Katrine Lamont* and also halt cargo clearance.

"You'll want to change the captain of record, I'm thinking," the stationmaster said.

"Yes, but I haven't hired a new one yet," Ky said. "I'll have to check at the Captains' Guild."

The next step, clearly, was to go over and take formal possession of that ship, ideally before the crew realized Furman was under arrest. This might require assistance from the station's law enforcement. She asked about that.

"I can detail a couple of patrol personnel to go with you, if you expect trouble," the stationmaster said.

"Furman will have told the crew I'm an imposter," Ky said. "They may not believe me when I say my identity was proved in court and he's in custody."

"Ah. I see. Well, when do you think you'll go?"

"Immediately," Ky said. "At least, I'll start immediately. You have my com code."

"Yes. I'll alert the station nearest that ship's docking slot."

Ky called Martin and Rafe in. "Rafe, I want you monitoring all your surveillance gear near or in *Katrine Lamont*. I'm sure some of that crew are in on whatever graft Furman was pulling, and it would help to know for sure which ones. Replacing an entire crew here is going to be difficult, if it's possible at all. Martin, I want enough of our weapons-capable crew as necessary to set up a round-the-clock watch on the *Kat*; I'm going to remove the entire crew, and then send them back in small groups."

"They're not going to like that," Rafe commented.

"They don't have to like it, but I am not about to leave that ship in the hands of Furman's accomplices. I want a guard on the engines and environmental systems; Quincy thinks these sections are least likely to be in on it, but that's where sabotage could do us the most harm. Martin, gather your team while I go talk to our own bridge crew."

At *Katrine Lamont*'s dockside, a crewman in Vatta ship-suit stood watch, as was proper. His eyes widened as he spotted Ky and her entourage, and she saw his hands move on the dockside comunit.

"I'm Captain Kylara Vatta," she said, though he must have known that. "Captain Furman will not be returning to this ship; it will be reassigned by Vatta headquarters."

"It—you—he said you were a fake," the man blurted.

"As these gentlemen will explain," Ky said, gesturing to the two local patrolmen with her, "my identity was proven in court. I am Kylara Vatta, daughter of Gerard Avondetta Vatta, and in this jurisdiction acting head of Vatta Transport, Ltd."

"So you—you're going to take over the ship?"

"I'm going to reassign it, not take it over personally, but there will be an immediate inventory of assets," Ky said. She nodded to Martin and the squad he had chosen. "The crew will be escorted offship while the inventory proceeds, and then decisions will be made about changes in assignment."

"But you can't—I mean—"

"Your name and specialty?" Martin stepped forward; the man paled and licked his lips.

"Uh . . . Demi Pelagros. Cargo handler, class three."

"Very well. Step over here, please."

As Martin had recommended on the way over, Ky then called the ship's general intercom. "All personnel aboard *Katrine Lamont,* report to dockside immediately."

First to appear, as expected, were cargo handlers wearing their reflective mesh vests with the Vatta logo on the front and the ship's name on the back. None was the bald man with the cargomaster's patch, however. They looked uncertainly at Ky, but lined up next to Pelagros as instructed. Then a mix—Engineering and Environmental techs. Again, the heads of these departments didn't appear with their people.

The dockside unit buzzed; Ky picked up the headset. "What's going on?" someone asked. "Is there a problem?"

They would have their own surveillance, Ky knew. This was delaying, nothing more or less. "All personnel report to dockside," she said. "You will be informed when you arrive."

"Who are you? I'm Acting Captain Bender, while Captain Furman is ashore. Where is he?"

Ky said nothing. Seconds ticked away; then a group of five appeared in the hatch. Two women, three men, all in Vatta blue with the armbands of senior crew; one was the tall bald man she'd noticed on scan before. Ky kept her expression bland as they stared across the dockside space at her.

"What's going on here?" a hard-faced woman asked. "I'm Bender—who are you people and what are you doing on our dockside?" Her gaze raked the *Katrine Lamont* crew. "What are you doing with our people?"

"You're the senior engineer?" Ky asked.

"Yes, of course," Bender said. "And you?"

"Kylara Vatta," Ky said. "Is this all the crew?" She knew it wasn't.

"I suppose," Bender said, but her gaze wavered. Ky reached over and put her command wand into the dockside unit. Instantly information poured into her implant: three crew were still inside the ship.

"Go on in, Martin," she said. "There are three—one on the bridge, one in crew quarters."

"Captain, I have two on surveillance," Rafe said in her ear; Martin glanced at her; she knew he'd also received Rafe's information. "The other one's disabled the pickups in his area. I can map the pickup failure."

"Good job, Rafe," Ky said. She waited where she was. She had wanted to board first, but Martin argued that she must stay outside, under the protection of the police, until he had secured the ship.

It took almost thirty minutes to find and escort out the last crewperson, who had been found hiding in a concealed space similar to that Ky had found in Osman's ship. Martin's team went through the ship carefully, compartment by compartment, searching with every tool they had for anyone else, while Ky addressed the crew.

"Captain Furman claimed that I was not Kylara Vatta— a lie, as he knew me personally. Moreover, I was able to prove my identity to the satisfaction of local authorities. He was found in contempt of court and will be sentenced in the next day or so. He is, of course, no longer a Vatta Transport employee."

She paused. Most of the crew simply looked stunned, but the senior section heads glowered. "Those of you who did not obey the order to leave the ship have forfeited your employment. Personal items will be retrieved for you from your quarters; evidence of criminal activity will be turned over to local authorities."

"You can't do that—" This was a man wearing the green armband of Environmental. "We got rights—"

Ky stared him down. "I am Vatta, on this station. This is my ship."

"It is not—it's the captain's ship—you can't just come in here and—" He lunged toward her, reaching for his hip. Her own shot caught him in the chest, Martin's in the head. He fell; the other senior crew did not move, and the local police merely watched.

"As I was saying," Ky said, "evidence of criminal activity will be reported to local authorities. Those of you who obeyed may be rehired, if you pass all security investigations. You will need to present applications. When my people are sure the ship is secure, you will be allowed to retrieve personal items, under supervision, one at a time. Is that clear?"

A mutter that might have been a chorus of *yes, ma'ams*.

Ky tipped her head to one side. "Is that clear?" she asked again.

This time the answers were louder, except from the senior crew.

"Then you'd best be off. Give your names to these gentlemen—" Ky gestured to the local police. "Find yourself a place to stay. None of you will be staying on the ship for at least three days."

Slowly, with many backward glances, they moved out the dock entrance, one by one showing their identification to the police.

"If I were you," the senior police officer said, "I wouldn't hire any of 'em back. But you will have to give them their personal effects."

"As soon as the ship's secure," Ky said. "We'll clear out the crew compartments and put their gear in a safe location they can access. I'll probably rent one of the cargo inspection compartments for a day; that will be convenient to the ship, if anyone claims something was left behind, but maintain ship security."

He nodded. "That makes sense and is legal within our system."

Four hours later, Ky was back aboard her own ship. Rafe had already reported, via skullphone, on the most important of his discoveries during that period of surveillance, and all three ships were now secure. Martin's crew had begun removing the former crew's personal effects to the cargo inspection area she'd rented. Ky looked forward to a relaxing cup of chocolate in her cabin before tackling the other problems, but even as she walked in, she got a call from her barrister.

"Were you serious about wanting to try to ameliorate Furman's sentence?"

"I don't want to be impolite," Ky said. "But a death sentence for being rude to the judge does seem harsh by our standards."

"I suppose it does to outsiders," the barrister said. "But there is evidence that Furman knew our laws; he had been here before and both times he certified his understanding and acceptance, as you did this time. In our experience, adults who cannot control their behavior any better than that will cause others damage. However, if you want to attempt intervention, the available alternative punishment is personality restructuring, with the individual then put in custody of a guarantor. If you petition for this, you will have to stand as guarantor; Furman will become, essentially, your ward."

"Personality restructuring . . ."

"We actually consider that harsher than death, since it makes the individual into someone else, someone who is not legally competent. The judicar did say that this was a most unusual case, and you had behaved very well; thus he is willing to consider that option if you request it, but you must take responsibility for Furman if that is the case."

"He would be . . . changed completely, you're saying."

"I'll send you a file. It explains the process. Furman exhibited verbal and potentially physical violence toward others; he had also demonstrated dishonesty. The potential for these would be eliminated from his behavior . . ."

"I see," Ky said, though she was not sure she understood how this would work. Slotter Key's constitution did not allow for meddling in the personality of any competent adult.

"I'll send the file on over," the barrister said.

Ky leaned back in her chair and started to put her feet up, but the comunit buzzed again. Muttering a curse, she answered.

"Stella needs you," Quincy said. "Now."

"On my way," Ky said. She explained briefly to her bridge crew on the way out.

"Want me to come?" Rafe asked.

Ky shrugged. "If you think you can help. But first I have to talk to her. She may not want you to know."

Stella's captain had cleared out of his cabin so she and Ky could talk, a courtesy Ky appreciated. The once familiar cabin now seemed cramped and very clearly belonged to someone else. Someone—Stella, she assumed—had had the stained carpet removed and replaced with a nubbly gray tweed, the cabinets and desk refinished. Orem's captain's cape hung from a hook; his books and not hers were on the shelf above the desk. He had chosen a plain dark blue bed covering, and his master's certificate had a two-color mat in tan and green instead of her plain black frame. Stella stood stiffly on the far side of the cabin, her beauty marred by tears and obvious misery.

"Stella," Ky said.

"I know what you're going to say," Stella said. "You're going to say it's all right and it doesn't make any difference, but it does."

"Something like that, yes," Ky said. "Though of course it makes a difference to you."

"Why didn't they ever tell me?" Stella said. "If I'd known—it's even in pop psychology articles. Everyone knows adopted children should be told . . ."

"Yes. And they keep writing those things because not all parents tell their adopted children." Ky sat in the desk chair. "Sit down, Stella."

"On my captain's bed—that's a great image, Ky."

Ky stood up. "Fine. I'll sit on his bed. I can put my feet up that way. I've had these formal shoes on too long."

"And I really appreciate your subtle way of reminding me that you've been working all afternoon while I had hysterics," Stella said, throwing herself into the chair.

Ky felt decades older than Stella. "That sounds like someone who is about ready to quit having hysterics," she said.

"I don't want to be ready," Stella said. "It's been the worst day of my life, and that includes the day I found out I was pregnant with that scum's baby and he'd used the family codes to run off with a chestful of Grandmother's silver. I suppose I can still call her Grandmother—"

"Yes," Ky said. "And I'd think that would be worse, because you knew it was your fault. This—you're not responsible for Osman's sperm or your parents' decision not to tell you."

"But I'm—" Stella shuddered. "I'm contaminated. Then it was just on the outside—well, not in my genes anyway—but this—I'm part of him in every cell, whether I want it or not."

"And part your mother, who must've been a beauty," Ky said.

"Ky, I'm really not in the mood for you to be nice to me. When everyone else finds out I'm Osman's daughter . . . I'll be no use to Vatta at all. No one will trust me."

"Want to bet Aunt Grace doesn't know?" Ky said. "And she trusts you."

Stella started to speak and then looked thoughtful. Ky pressed on.

"She knew people could make mistakes and get over it. She didn't look at you as just the beauty of the family, and clearly she thought you were trustworthy. And so do I. In the first place, we don't have to tell the whole universe you're Osman's biological daughter: you're the legal daughter of your legal parents, Stavros and Helen. In the second place, even if people find out, or you choose to tell them, that's just a tiny part—the smallest part—of who you are."

Stella looked at the deck. "And you keep doing everything—you saved our lives when Osman attacked, you have Rafe—"

Ky stared at her. "Rafe? I don't have Rafe. Not in any sense you mean. Yes, he's been traveling with me, and yes, his expertise with electronics has been useful, but we aren't . . . anything."

"He likes you," Stella said.

Ky snorted. "Stella, he may be beginning to respect me, and he hasn't tried to trick me lately, but I don't think he's capable of liking me or anyone else."

"Maybe." Stella swiped a hand across her face. "I must look awful. Excuse me." She went into the attached 'fresher; Ky listened to the water running and wished her feet didn't hurt as much as they did. Stella might be calming down for now, but would she be able to adjust to this new identity?

The Stella who emerged from the 'fresher seemed calm and capable.

"So what do you want me to do, Ky?"

Ky looked at her a moment, then said, "What do you want? And what do you think you can contribute?"

"Aside from my ability to strike men dumb? I'm a good data collector and analyst. But even though I've studied, I'll never make a good ship captain."

"No reason you should be," Ky said. "We need someone on the trading side, someone who's an insider in our business. You have more of that background than I do."

"Are you serious about starting an interstellar space force?"

Ky shrugged. "Someone has to. This pirate group has enough ships to attack whole systems—no one system can stand against it. Either we combine against them, or we might as well lie back and give them whatever they want."

"Which seems to be rape and pillage."

"Right. Some of the other privateers, including one from Slotter Key, seemed to agree with me, but the Sallyon government was afraid. They forbade anyone to talk about it, especially me."

"I know you think this is important, Ky—and I can see that it is—but what I don't see is how it advances Vatta's interests, except indirectly. We have only two ships—"

"Three, with Furman's."

"Right. Three, then. And one of them a top-line ship. That's much better than when you just had this one—but it's not much to start a shipping line with."

"Vatta Trading started with one," Ky said.

"Yes, but its captain wasn't trying to fight a war. I don't see how you can do both."

"I can't," Ky said. "That's why you need to become our business leader, our CEO. It was stupid of me to make a fuss when you used the title. We can hire captains and crews, but we must have someone in the family heading the whole enterprise . . . and that's you."

"I'm not really senior," Stella said. "Aunt Grace . . ."

"If she'd wanted it, she'd have had it years ago. Do you really think either of our fathers could have held it against her? No. And yes, there are older Vattas, but most of them haven't been as active in the business as you, and a lot of them are dead. Besides, they're out of contact, stuck in a system without a functioning ansible. You can't run a business without communications. You have already demonstrated your ability to talk to banks, contractors,

shippers—look at your record in just this short time—
and that's on top of your insider knowledge."

"I suppose . . . ," Stella said.

"Here's what I think," Ky said, kicking her shoes off
and rubbing one sore foot. "You should set up a satellite
corporate headquarters—temporary, I'm sure, because the
ansible service will come back—and start being the face
of Vatta Transport. Let good crews run this ship and *Katrine
Lamont* on whatever routes you find. Handle the finances;
if you find other Vatta ships, bring them in and get them
back to work, too. There should be two more on this
route."

"You trust me . . ."

"Of course I trust you!" Ky let some of her frustration
seep into her voice. "Stella, I've known you since I can
remember. You are not Osman. You are not like Osman.
I mean, how much am I like my mother?"

"Point taken," Stella said. She looked, Ky thought, much
more focused and almost like the practical Stella of old
. . . Stella had never been *all* pretty fluffhead except for a
few adolescent years. "And then when ansible service is
restored . . ."

"If it's safe, you get yourself back to Slotter Key. Talk
to the seniors and explain that you're taking over because
you're best suited—and I said so. Most of 'em don't know
you have any relation to Osman at all, though I'll bet
Grace does. And I'll bet she'll back you, and . . . there
you are. Corner office, with windows."

"If we ever have an office building again," Stella said.

"We will," Ky said, forcing confidence into her voice
that she did not entirely feel. "You'll make it happen."
Stella nodded, this time with conviction, and Ky went on.
"Meanwhile, I'll try to see that what happened this time
can't happen again—because those responsible will be as

dead as Osman. If I don't have to worry about running a trading business at the same time as fighting a war, I'll do my end better. And Grace did say I was to fight the war, right?"

"Yes, she did." Stella rubbed her temples. "All right. So do you know where I should set up a headquarters? Nothing looks safe to me right now."

"Nothing is," Ky said. "But I think the enemy's busy consolidating its hold on Bissonet right now. Look for a system that has ansible service now, and connects to as many others as possible. Go there, and take Toby—he needs more school, so that's another consideration. Hire some good people—"

"I don't know if Aunt Grace's diamonds will stretch that far," Stella said.

Ky waved her hand. "We have accounts here—we have accounts a lot of places. Furman just delivered cargo and got paid; I'm sure the obvious part of that is in the Vatta accounts at Crown & Spears. Once Vatta's seen to be an active concern again, we'll have access to those other accounts."

"I could just stay here."

"You could, if you decide it's the best place. I leave that up to you. How about it?"

"All right. Yes. Though I wish you were with me—"

"Stella, I still know too little about trade and profit, and you can't possibly do what I was trained for. Now, do you want Rafe to work with you on security issues setting up?"

"You'd give him up?"

"He's not mine," Ky said. "I brought him along in case you needed him, but it's up to you. Either of us could find a use for him, or he may run back to the ISC. As he keeps reminding me, that's his primary loyalty."

Stella looked thoughtful. "I don't think I need him. Maybe it's time for him to go back to ISC and figure out what's wrong there . . . though I'd think he'd be useful to you if you get this space navy thing going."

"We don't need someone with divided loyalties," Ky said. "And I think it would come to that. Logically, ISC's monopoly was broken when the first shipboard ansible was out of their control, but I doubt they're ready to admit that yet. That means my use of the ansibles—let alone my providing them to others—will be difficult for him to accept. At some point the strain may be too much."

By the time Ky got back to her own ship, Stella had come up with a rough business plan. She would keep *Katrine Lamont* on the same trade route, since they had ongoing contracts; she would send *Gary Tobai* out on speculative trips to reestablish contacts. She would try to contact the ships Ky had found, the ones that had not believed her identity, and reconnect these scattered remnants of Vatta's fleet. She had laid out the crew she'd need to hire and the probable profit and loss for the next half year, appending an assessment of the markets through which she'd passed while following Ky to Cascadia. The *Gary,* she was sure, could make a profit just from connecting the Cascadia route to Rosvirein.

"Brilliant," Ky said when she contacted Stella again.

"What I need now is your authorization to Crown & Spears," Stella said, with no hint of the emotional storm she'd been through a few hours earlier. "I've also contacted local educational authorities; they want us both to apply for guardianship—he's still underaged here—but the facilities are excellent, both here and down-planet."

"Stella, you're working miracles," Ky said. "I'll contact

Crown & Spears right away." She glanced at the chronometer; they still had an hour for that.

Stella shrugged. "I'm doing my job," she said. "Now for the budget. This part you may not like. How much do you want for operating *Fair Kaleen* as a warship? I assume you'll need weapons and things from time to time, and you have your payroll. How are you going to finance that? There's no way you can pay your own way if you're fighting and not trading."

"You're right," Ky said. "And I have no idea what I'll need, or how much you can let me have. I'll get back to you. Now, what about hiring crew for the *Kat*?"

"That's my job," Stella said. "Don't worry about it."

"The crew Furman had—"

"Won't be reliable. I understand that. Believe me, references will be checked." She smiled for the first time. "Ky, I appreciate what you've done, but now it's time to let go. You'll have enough to command, once you get out there among the enemy."

Ky blinked. Stella had the right of it, but that didn't make it palatable. Could she really trust Stella to be stable, to stay this sensible, businesslike person and not dissolve into the hysterical Stella of a few hours ago? She had to: there were no alternatives.

"Sorry," she said. "This is all new to me, too."

"I know," Stella said. Her smile widened to a grin. "And it's funny, but I was scared before and now I'm thinking how much fun it's going to be. A lot of work but also . . . fun."

"I'll call Crown & Spears," Ky said. She didn't want to pursue what was fun and what wasn't.

Crown & Spears, smugly gratified to find that their assessment of Ky's identity was accurate and they had backed the right horse, expressed complete willingness to do whatever Captain Vatta wished in the matter of corporate and ship accounts. Stella Vatta would have to come in for a complete identity record, of course, but certainly the daughter of the former CEO was eligible to take over . . .

"Stella was adopted at birth," Ky said, to forestall any comparison of Stella's DNA sample with Jo's. "But I've known her all my life and can vouch for her."

"That's fine, Captain Vatta. We just need hers on file so that no one can assume her identity. Is she on file at other Crown & Spears branches, do you know?"

"I'm sure she is on Slotter Key," Ky said. "We all were typed, as children, with the local bank there; I don't know about other branches, but I'm sure she'll tell you. She has more experience in the administrative end than I do, and less in ship handling, so she is the logical choice to set up a temporary headquarters."

"Of course." The woman on the screen smiled. "So she will be staying here, then?"

"I'm not entirely sure," Ky said. "She will be making an appointment with you, I expect. I'm not staying; I have a ship to run."

"Cascadia is an excellent choice for start-ups," the woman said. "We will be glad to assist her in locating office space and ancillary services."

"I'm sure she will find you most helpful," Ky said. "But the decision is hers. We agreed that my talents are best used on shipboard."

"Ah. Then I wish you well, Captain."

Ky called her barrister next, to report that the family crisis appeared to be over, but Stella was henceforth the acting head of Vatta Transport.

The barrister stared out of the screen with professional lack of expression. "If you're quite sure—"

"I am."

"Have you made a decision about Captain Furman?"

She hadn't thought about Captain Furman for hours.

"I can assure you that the products of personality restructuring are harmless and obedient," the barrister went on. "You need have no fear that he would be obstreperous, though he's likely to be less intelligent than he was, and he will have little initiative."

For a moment, the image of Furman as her servant—submissive, permanently under her control—roused a flash of satisfaction. She could pay him back well and truly for the misery he had caused her. Then that same image revolted her; he would be a permanent temptation to a part of herself she despised. And yet the alternative was death.

"Could Stella be his guardian?" Stella would not have the same temptation.

"No," the barrister said, shaking her head. "This offer was made only to you, personally. And I remind you that it is considered the crueler punishment here."

"I don't want to be cruel," Ky said. "I just—condemning someone to death—"

"It's not your judgment," the barrister said. "That judgment is our responsibility."

It was their legal system, not hers, that would impose the punishments. Death, or destruction of him as a person, and reconstruction into what—to her imagination—seemed little more than a disabled slave. Did they suffer, the ones who underwent that procedure? What was the least evil here? Once again, when she tried to access the color bands of Saphiric Cyclan meditation, nothing happened.

"When do we have to say?" she asked.

"By tomorrow, second shift." The barrister frowned. "I

can see this bothers you, Captain Vatta; clearly you are an ethical person, and you see this as a choice of evils. We see it differently, and this is our jurisdiction. Perhaps I could recommend a religious counselor who could explain our point of view better?"

"No, thank you," Ky said. Hard as the decision was, it would not come clearer by waiting; she knew that. She knew which she would prefer, if she were in Furman's place. Was that what he would prefer? He had forfeited his right to her consideration of his preference, but she would take that last step. "I want to ask Captain Furman his preference. Is that possible?"

The barrister frowned again. "He is under close guard. I suppose I can ask the impoundment officials. This is highly irregular."

"If I can't speak to him, I will let your judgment stand," Ky said. "Since life as someone else would be more abhorrent to me than death. But if I can ascertain his preference, then I feel bound to abide by it."

"I will ask."

TWENTY-ONE

Captain Furman's answer, relayed from the impoundment, was, in the words of the impoundment officer, too profane to repeat precisely. "Basically, he said he'd rather be dead than under your guardianship," the officer said. "He claims your family has done nothing but cheat and rob him since he first started working for it, but given his behavior since we took him into custody, I am not believing anything he says."

"He wanted to marry into the family," Ky said. "The girl married someone else while he was off on a voyage."

"Ah. That sort. Well, it's none of my business, Captain Vatta, but if I were you, I'd rather have a rotting fruit salad in my locker than have this one around, personality restructuring or no."

"Thank you," Ky said. "I will communicate with my barrister."

The barrister nodded approval when Ky gave her decision. "Very wise, Captain. You have the prisoner's own preference, and you have our tradition that death is a kinder punishment. You need not worry that he will suffer, except in a few days' anticipation, which we can alleviate pharmacologically. Our method of execution is completely humane."

Ky wondered if any death could be considered completely humane, but this was not the time to bring that up. "Thank you for your help," she said. "My cousin Stella will be taking over as corporate manager, and I'm hoping you can suggest someone for corporate assistance if she chooses to stay on Cascadia."

"Quite so," the barrister said. "I will be delighted to be of service."

Two down, more to go. Ky looked at her message stack. The canine reproductive services report informed her that Rascal was not only healthy but very fertile indeed, and the first straws of his sperm were already being traded for an astonishing price, higher than that originally mentioned. Toby's education should be assured, at any school Stella found for him. She called Toby up from the engine room; Rascal, as usual, trotted along behind, tail wagging briskly.

"Things are going to change," Ky said, after he sat down across from her. "Stella's taking over as head of Vatta; she knows more about the business end than I do. You will stay with her—"

"I like ships!" Toby said. "And I'm not useless; I've been working hard—"

"I know. But you need to finish your education. You've had your apprentice voyage; now it's time to go back to school. Stella can arrange that for you."

"What about Rascal?" Toby reached down to scratch behind the dog's ears.

"You'll keep him, of course. He's your dog now. Here on Cascadia, if Stella sets up here, he's very valuable, and he's already brought in enough to pay for most schools. With his potential in this system, you'll have a nice nest egg when you come back to the fleet."

"Will there be a fleet?" Toby asked. He looked very

grown-up, except that his feet and his body still weren't quite in proportion.

"Yes," Ky said firmly. "Stella's going to rebuild Vatta Transport, and I'm going to do what I can to make space safe for all traders again."

Toby scowled a moment; Rascal jumped into his lap and licked his face. Toby laughed, then, and grinned at Ky. "I guess it won't be too bad. School, I mean. Other kids again. More space . . ."

"Stella's deciding where to set up," Ky said. "When she finds a place, you need to be ready to go."

"I might even get home again someday," Toby said. "If my parents—" His voice trailed off.

"If your parents are alive—and they could be—they'll be very proud of you," Ky said. She would miss Toby's bright-eyed presence, and even the *clickety-click* of Rascal's nails on the deck. But not the responsibility of having a youngster aboard in dangerous times. "How long will it take you to pack?"

"Not long," Toby said. "I'll be ready."

Next in the queue were memos on the cargo that she had carried, that the *Kat* had carried—queries from buyers, requests from shippers for space on the next departure. She shunted those to Stella's account. A relief not to have to deal with that anymore. Then the application for a new registration for her own ship. With her identity officially confirmed, so also was her right to possess the ship. Re-registration would be approved on payment of the fee, and what name would she like to use?

She had thought of many names, names as old as fighting ships from the wet navies of Earth's ancient past: *Vengeance, Victory, Vanguard, Invincible, Defiant, Dreadnought, Enterprise.* If she wanted the vessel to pass as a tradeship with a privateer's authorization, she should use a more peaceful name, but if she committed to a purely military mission . . . a fighting ship should have a fighting name.

Could she use one of the old names without disrespect? She shrugged. Probably every space militia and every wet navy had reused the best of them; originality mattered less than the effect of a name on the crew and the enemy. Osman's ship deserved a good name, a strong name. *Victory* was too pretentious; it would be foolish to claim victory before winning it. *Vanguard*, though: that would work. A pioneer, a leader, that's what she meant to be. Where she meant to be.

No ship in the current Cascadia registry used that name. She entered it; the ship chip would be programmed and delivered within twenty-four hours after payment of the very large fee. She entered the fee transfer.

Next morning, the systemwide ship status board listed *Sharra's Gift* insystem, headed for Cascadia on a fast transit, with docking expected in three days. Ky suspected Argelos had come looking for her, and went on with preparations for departure. By the start of second shift, Stella called to report that she'd found living and office space.

"You want me to send Toby over?"

"If he's ready. You'd better send an escort, in case someone throws a fit over that dog."

"We can put Rascal in a carrier."

"Good idea. I found a garden apartment up on West-five, would you believe? These people are crazy about trees."

"I'd noticed," Ky said.

"Thanks for setting things up with Crown & Spears. They've informed their branches within ansible range, so we can transfer funds among them as needed. I wish we could get at Furman's accounts."

"It'll cost us in legal fees," Ky said. "Even if other jurisdictions honor Cascadia's judgments. But it's up to you."

"I've already got the core crew for the *Kat*," Stella went on. "She'll be ready to go only a day or so late. And we have cargo."

"Excellent," Ky said. "I'd like to put a shipboard ansible in *Gary Tobai* and also leave one for you here. That way we can stay in contact. Maybe you can find someone to manufacture them here, get them aboard all Vatta ships." Though that would be perilous, if ISC found out.

"That's a good idea," Stella said. "It gives Vatta a definite trade advantage, too. Send them right over; I'll tell the captains to expect them. Are you sending an installation crew?"

"Yes," Ky said. "And something else—there's a Slotter Key ship insystem—"

"I saw that," Stella said. "Friend of yours?"

"I think so. I've got to talk to my crew—do you think I should talk to the Cascadia government about my plans?"

Stella considered a moment. "I'd ask Rafe, actually. My sense is that they're either easygoing or very rigid, from issue to issue; he's been here before so he might know which."

"I need to talk to him anyway," Ky said.

Rafe listened to her plans.

"I think it's time for me to leave you," he said when she had finished.

Though she had half expected this response, Ky felt a pang. She had grown used to his quick wit, his astonishing technical expertise, even his ability to throw her off balance. She waited to see if he would say more.

"Starting an interstellar space force is your thing, not mine," he went on. "And I need to get back in touch with

ISC. I haven't gone to the local office; my instincts tell me something's wrong at headquarters, and I don't want to advertise myself right now."

"I thought you weren't supposed to go home," Ky said.

"This is an emergency situation," Rafe said. "Something's wrong—beyond the pirates, I think—or a lot more of the ansibles would be back up. My father may not want me to stay, but he's not likely to have me intercepted on arrival, and I've got important information that I don't want to transmit by any other means. Those shipboard ansibles you won't promise not to use, for instance."

Ky nodded.

"And some of your crew will be glad to see me go," Rafe said. "Martin still doesn't trust me, even though he likes my skills. I'm going to go tell Stella where I'm going; I'll be back to say a more formal good-bye."

On that, he turned away, and Ky went back to her planning. How was she going to finance a fleet? Outfitting one ship had been expensive enough, but outfitting more . . . she had to get the cooperation of allies, governments or . . . or someone. Stella called to say that she was ready for Toby and gave the address of her apartment. Ky saw him off; the ship seemed too quiet when he'd left, even though he hadn't been a noisy boy. It was the dog, she told herself. She was glad to be rid of it. It smelled; ships had enough off odors without dog.

The next morning, she was finishing the order to the chandler for rations when Rafe appeared at her office door, dressed in a stylish business suit instead of the casual shipsuit he'd worn for weeks.

"You scare Stella," he said, lounging against the bulkhead.

"I doubt it," Ky said, marking the order COMPLETE and

sending it on. She turned to the wish list the Gannetts had given her for additional munitions.

"Seriously," Rafe said. "And she's not easily scared. She's quite brave, Stella, in her own way."

Ky could not think of anything to say to that—she hadn't ever said Stella wasn't brave—so she went on scrolling down the list of munitions. Cascadia didn't have anything as big as MilMart Express, back on Lastway, but they had two dealers who carried most of what the Gannetts wanted. Question was, could she afford it?

"I wonder if you even know what you are," Rafe went on, in the half-teasing tone that heated the back of Ky's neck.

"I think so," Ky said, without looking up. "Human, youngish, female . . . which to you means natural prey, I suppose." She glanced at him.

For an instant before his mask slid back in place, Rafe looked both startled and horrified. "You wrong me, Captain. My natural prey is smug fools. Young women . . . well, those who aren't smug fools anyway . . . find in me the older brother they wish they'd had."

Ky let out a snort of laughter. "You? A protective big brother?"

Rafe scowled at her. "I see you don't believe me, and that's within your rights. Think anything you like of me. But, Captain—I was serious about you scaring Stella, and about you yourself. You know what you have inside, and I'm not talking about the cranial ansible."

Ky felt a cold chill.

"You're a killer, Captain. I'll wager anything you like that you didn't know it until it happened. That you thought you were the way Stella described you to me years ago— a nice girl, a conscientious, earnest, dull, hardworking, respectable member of your family." He cocked his head.

"I'm right, and you know it. Good Ky, the straight-arrow counter to foolish Stella." He paused; Ky said nothing. She could feel her heart pounding in her chest. "And then you killed for the first time. And deep down, somewhere inside, you felt something you had never felt before. You liked it."

"I—" Ky clamped her jaw shut again. He was right; he had seen it. Did everyone see it?

"I saw you, you know, when you came from killing Osman. Up to then, all that glee, all that determination to mix it up yourself with the invaders—that could've been the military training you had, or the bravado of ignorance. I wasn't sure. But after that—I knew. You didn't just kill him; you enjoyed killing him."

The images flooded her mind: the whirling chaos of that fight . . . the final moments, when she had, indeed, taken great pleasure. Shame flooded her; she felt her face going hot with it even as Rafe's voice went on.

"The thing is, Captain, when a good person like you discovers a bad pleasure—a guilty pleasure—there's things you must do to survive. You're not an Osman; you don't want to be like him—"

"Maybe—" Ky choked, but forced the words out. "Maybe I am like him; maybe this is how he started."

"No." Rafe's voice held no doubt. "No, you're not. You're a good person—a decent person—who happens to take pleasure in killing bad people."

"No good person—"

"Listen to me. I know what you're dealing with." Rafe reached out—rather gingerly, Ky noticed even in that moment—and touched her shoulders. "You are not the first person to have this experience. Most people, you're right, don't enjoy killing. They throw up, they cry—"

"I threw up. The first time."

"Yes. Normal physiological response. I'm sure they told you that in the Academy."

"Yes, they did." Ky tried to steady her breathing.

"Most people take no pleasure in killing; that's probably biologically important, or we'd have wiped out the human race before now. But a small percentage do, and it's like being able to taste certain flavors or smell certain smells—it's innate, not something you choose. Do you understand that?"

"I . . . don't see how it can be. Not on worlds like Slotter Key anyway. We have genetic screening; parents can choose gene-mod packets . . ."

"But the gene components of pleasure in killing aren't defined," Rafe said. "At least not on my world, which is at least as advanced as yours."

"How do you know that?"

"How do you think?" He grimaced. "Captain, what I recognize in you is what I carry in myself." He stopped, and stared into nothing; Ky did not move or speak. Finally he went on. "When I was quite young, ten or eleven, someone subverted the security at our summer cottage. They got in sometime during the afternoon, we think. Hid until after we children were in bed. My parents were out for the evening; the nanny was downstairs chatting with the cook." He paused, shook his head. "I woke up—I still don't know why. A noise, a movement of air. Whatever, I woke up all at once, and turned on the light." Another pause, this one longer. Ky recognized his inward expression.

"He was in a programmable skinsuit," Rafe said. "Black when I turned the light on, but shifting in a few seconds to a mobile camouflage—you had those in the military, I'm sure." Ky nodded, but said nothing. "Hard to follow the movements, with the colors flaring and fading across the suit. I was off the bed in a flash, you can believe, and tried to get to the door past him; he grabbed me and I started fighting. I'd been taking martial arts classes since I was seven, but I was only a child, and he was an adult. I used everything I had, but he would've taken me . . . except that I'd bought a display sword, one of those Old Earth replicas, and my instructor had had me practice a few strokes. I managed to grab it off its display hanger and hit his wrist hard enough to make him let go. The thing was blunt, of course, and probably wouldn't have gone through the skinsuit even if it'd been sharp, but edge-on the blade had enough force to crush his windpipe with the backswing from that first blow. I didn't even realize what I'd done—he let go, and I went for the house alarm."

"Mmm . . . ," Ky said, just to keep him talking.

"It wasn't working, of course. I had only a child-level implant, but everyone in our family had a skullphone link; I activated the emergency alarm. I remember, at that point, seeing him lying on the floor of my room, and feeling . . . triumphant. I didn't know yet he was dead or dying. I just knew I'd taken down an adult. I wasn't scared. Didn't have enough sense to be scared. I thought I was being very clear and logical, thinking through what had happened. I needed to protect my sister, and there might be more bad men. I would need a better weapon. My father's hunting weapons were locked up, and I didn't have the combination, but about then the man's skinsuit shut down its camo program, and I could see his weapons. I took his sidearm—I remember being very careful with it, finding the safety and flipping that off—and then went out into the hall." He sighed. "I shot the first moving thing I saw, which was good, and the second, which wasn't . . . it was our terrified pet gammish, perfectly harmless. The third bad guy fled. When my parents and the emergency crews arrived—within seconds of each other—I was positioned correctly to cover the front door, had given my sister the second dead intruder's sidearm and told her how to cover the back door. She was hysterical, because she'd had to go through the kitchen, where the cook and the nanny were both dead."

Ky could think of nothing to say; she looked at Rafe's somber face, imagining the eleven-year-old. How he must have felt, and looked.

"I was taken to therapy, to deal with the post-traumatic stress I was expected to have," Rafe went on. "And, being eleven and an honest child up till then, I told the therapist exactly how I felt. Which was not, I learned quickly, how I was supposed to feel."

"It must have been very difficult," Ky said, and his mouth quirked.

"Yes, it was, a bit. The therapist warned my parents that I was at risk of becoming a criminal, said that I needed intensive therapy for a long period, and would probably do best in a closed environment." He swallowed. "My sister was afraid of me, they all said. She had seen me kill the second intruder; he had her bound, gagged, and slung over his shoulder when I shot him. She saw me shoot our pet. And I admit, I slapped her to make her quit screaming when I wanted her to guard the back door. Everybody decided I had never been the good boy they'd thought I was up till then; that I'd been hiding a monster inside."

"But you saved her, and yourself."

"Yes, but eleven-year-olds aren't supposed to be able to do that," Rafe said. "And they certainly aren't supposed to argue with the therapist and insist that they're proud of killing two grown men, professionals. That they liked the feeling." He shook his head with a rueful grin. "That came from being a spoiled son of privilege. I'd heard my father tell people off—and my mother, too, for that matter. It never occurred to me to lie, or that I could get in trouble for telling the truth."

"That's awful!" Ky felt a surge of indignation. "They should've seen that you were a hero."

He shrugged. "You know better. What would your family have thought about the way you killed Osman? Don't you have some nonviolence in that religion Stella was telling me about? How are you getting along with that, by the way?"

"Not," Ky admitted. "I can't seem to make it make sense anymore."

"Yeah. Same here. I can remember picking flowers to put on the altar at home, but after all that . . . I can't remember why. Anyway, after six months or so, the family sent me off to a boarding school for troubled boys; the therapist told them it was the only chance for me to become a responsible citizen. It was educational in a way they didn't anticipate. I came in naïve, the obvious victim and fall guy, so of course I was in trouble for things I never did. Decided it was more fun to be in trouble for things I'd actually done, and then that it was even more fun not being caught. All this merely confirmed the therapist's warning, of course. I actually believed it myself for a long time. Anyone who enjoyed violence or killing was doomed to be bad to the bone. Might as well be bad and enjoy it."

"Is that why your family sent you away?"

"Part of it. I came out of that school still interested in learning—I had managed to make good grades in academic subjects even while in trouble all that time—but university was just too . . . tempting. After the third pregnancy, when the girl was a Council member's daughter, my father had had enough."

"So . . . do you still think that way? Once bad, always bad?"

"No. But it's taken me years, and I don't want you to make my mistakes. Ky—Captain—you're the same person you were, with a big lump of self-knowledge you didn't have before. I've watched you since I came aboard; I've seen you doing a lot of things, including dumping me on my back. You're smart, you're honest—more honest than Stella or me, when it comes to that. You're fundamentally decent. The little thrill you get when you kill someone doesn't change any of that."

"It's not—it's not right!"

"Killing the *wrong* people isn't right. Feeling what you feel is just . . . feeling it. What you have to do—what I had to do—was figure out how to control it, not let it ride me either way. It's easier if you don't spend the next ten to fifteen years identified as a potential sadistic serial killer . . . that's what I'd like to save you."

"You didn't want to kill that man—that agent back on Lastway," Ky said, putting together some history.

"No. I could see that his death might be necessary, and that ISC might have terminated him, but I didn't want to be the agent of his killing. It's . . . too easy to go that way, become an assassin, paid or inspired by my own ideals. I won't let that happen again."

Which meant it had happened. Ky suppressed a shiver. "I worried—"

"Of course you did. That's why you don't need to worry."

"I even thought, when I knew my father had died, at least he wouldn't have to know about me—"

"Mmm. Not much on afterlife, are you?"

"Saphiric Cyclans believe in return without awareness," Ky said a little stiffly. "But I'm not sure I'm a Saphiric

Cyclan anymore. And I'm clearly not a Modulan."

Rafe waved his hand. "Theology aside, do you understand what I'm saying? You're not sadistic; I've never seen you do one cruel thing. You're not eager to kill; I watched you with that spy who died unexpectedly. So far you have killed only at need, to save your ship and crew. You will not slide into the other kind of killing unless you let yourself, and it's my opinion that you are not likely to slide that way—unless you think it's inevitable."

"So—you're telling me not to worry about that jolt of pleasure?"

"Not exactly. Humans are humans; we seek pleasure. You might be tempted more than most, in circumstances where it's a close call whether it's necessary or not. You need to admit it, at least to yourself, that you might be tempted, and watch for it, and control it. But you are planning to fight a war. You will kill again—that's what a war is. And you will enjoy it again, because that's how you're constituted. If you let fear of that pleasure keep you from fighting as you should, you'll get other people killed. And knowing you, that'll drive you into a whirlpool of guilt." For a moment his face expressed sadness and exhaustion; then he forced a crooked grin. "If you're trying to think how to say that you don't want to be like me, don't bother. I know that, and I know you won't be. Does that help?"

"Yes." Ky felt as wrung out as he had looked, and dredged up the outrage at his parents and therapist. "I still can't imagine telling you—a child—that you were doomed to be evil when you'd just saved yourself and your sister. They should have been proud of you." Even as she said it, she wondered if her father would have been proud of her.

"I killed two grown men," Rafe said, shrugging. "I didn't express remorse. Looking at it from their point of view, I can understand, though I still don't agree. And part of it was the very expensive and exclusive therapist they brought in, recommended by my family's religious adviser. Later on, I learned that he followed a form of psychological theory not much respected in the rest of the universe. But my father asked for the best, and got the most expensive."

"Does your father still think you're that bad?"

"I'm not sure. We haven't met face-to-face for years, but the work I've done for the company has seemed to soften his attitude. The last time we spoke by ansible, he said he was willing to see me again. It wasn't quite an invitation to a banquet of fatted calf, but it was at least not hostile."

"So . . . is that where you're going?"

"Yes." Rafe looked away, as if embarrassed. "I'm concerned that in this crisis, they haven't pinged my cranial ansible. Yes, it takes an external power source to use for two-way communications, but I'd know if they sent an alarm. Cascadia's close enough to home—and the ansibles are up here and there—so I should have heard something."

"Wait—you said the shipboard ansibles can't link into the regular net—"

"Cranials can," Rafe said. His eyebrows rose. "In fact, Captain, if you want to cheat ISC of ansible charges, it's quite possible. I can teach you—"

"Never mind," Ky said. "I don't expect to be using this thing."

"A good commander ignores no advantages," Rafe said, more seriously. "But back to my proposed itinerary. I could call home via a commercial service, but if there's trouble on the ground, that would alert the bad guys. Considering my father was a good guy, in spite of everything, if I just go there, I'll be among the hyenas before they know what's hit them." His grin was feral.

"When—" the rest of *will I see you again* stuck in her throat. From his expression, he heard it anyway.

"I don't know," he said. "Someday, maybe, when you least expect it, you'll smell limes and think of me, and there I'll be, peeling one. With, I assure you, no intent other than flavoring a drink."

Ky laughed in spite of herself. "Rafe, you always have an intent. When are you leaving?"

"Today. There's a tradeship—not Vatta, alas—and I have a ticket. Under one of my traveling names, of course. Just time to teach you the tricks of our shared ability, if you're willing."

Ky nodded. It would be stupid to ignore an advantage. She could imagine what her crew would think of the two of them spending time in her locked cabin, but this was not something she could explain. She was no more eager than Rafe to reveal the existence of technology that would make her more of a target. Two hours later, Rafe concluded the session by pointing out that she lacked the boosted external power jack he'd been given.

"You can use the one you've got," Rafe said, "but it's not designed for the load the ansible needs. You're going to be limited to reception and very short transmissions. I don't recommend you use it except in emergencies."

"I don't intend to," Ky said, wrinkling her nose. Her first experience of the weird sensations and unpleasant odors generated by its use had been a strong deterrent to experimentation.

"And don't do direct implant-to-implant downloads, as we did, or you'll pass this on to someone else."

"I don't intend to do that, either."

"Did it load the connection codes into your implant? That would be in a subfolder under ISC . . ."

"Yes," Ky said.

"You're the honest sort who wouldn't use them to make free calls, but again, if you're ever stuck . . . those codes will work via any ansible interface." He stretched. "Well, I'll be on my way. I don't suppose you'd let me demonstrate my respect and affection—"

"No," Ky said. "But thank you for asking."

"You are a cruel and heartless woman," Rafe said. "But someday . . ." And with that he was gone.

TWENTY-TWO

Two days later, *Sharra's Gift* docked at Cascadia Station and Captain Argelos called Ky. "We need to talk; where can we meet?"

"My ship's secure," Ky said. "You'll have noticed it has a new name . . . *Vanguard*."

"Good. I'll be there in less than an hour."

Ky ordered in refreshments and told her security crew what she wanted. When Argelos arrived, she let Martin meet him at dockside and escort him to her office.

"Things went very sour at Sallyon after your cousin left," Argelos said, even before sitting down. "Quite a few Bissonet ships have shown up there since you left. Merchanters, private yachts, one Bissonet Space Agency ship, a couple of privateers, each with worse news than the last." Argelos drained his mug. "Idiots at Sallyon still don't want trouble, they say, but unarmed traders started pulling out right after you left, and that's continued. Does the Moscoe Confederation know about your ideas?"

"No," Ky said. "I've had other problems here. A former Vatta employee turns out to have been one of Osman's spies and he tried to compromise my identity."

"Ah. But you've got that straightened out, I see."

"Yes." She wasn't going to explain further. She still had complications from that to clear up. "I plan to tell them about my plans, though, so I don't get in the kind of trouble Sallyon gave me."

"Good. Thing is, I think you're right. We've got to have some kind of interstellar force. It's clear from Dan's report—sorry, Dan Pettygrew, captain of one of the Bissonet privateers that made it out in one piece; I've known Dan for years—that the pirates have at least sixty, maybe more, ships. That civilian ship's scans didn't show all of them, by any means. They simply swamped Bissonet's defenses, which assumed attacking forces of no more than four or five ships at once. Like most systems."

"If that was a Bissonet privateer, why didn't he fight?" Ky asked.

"Against a force of sixty ships, when Bissonet had only ten ships in the system? It would've been suicide. Anyway, Dan agrees that we need to combine as many of the privateers as we can, and any other force that wants to join. I told him about you, and that makes three of us . . ."

"I see. Are there any others?"

"Dan says there was another Bissonet privateer, someone I've never met, who was close to jumping out as the raiders came in. That's the other one who showed up, a woman named Andreson who's been a privateer for years and started trying to gather a force to liberate Bissonet. The Sallyon Port Authority threw her out, just like they did you."

"Is she coming here?"

"No. She's taken two other Bissonet ships to a system a jump away from Sallyon. I have the coordinates. Says she's interested in talking to you and joining forces with anyone who'll fight the invaders. She thinks Slotter Key privateers would make good allies, and your name impressed her. She knows Bissonet can't do it alone, not now." He poured himself another glass and took a drink. "But the thing is, she's going to expect to be running things. I know you've got a military background. As far as I know, Bissonet didn't give its privateers any special training so we don't know what she really knows about space warfare, in terms of handling formations. She says she does."

"Anyone else?" Ky asked.

"There's a Captain Zavala, from over in the Loma Linda Cluster, registered out of Ciudad," Argelos said. "He knows that fellow I told you about before, Ortiz. And there's a ship from Urgayin, but I'm not sure about that one. Urgayin has a bad reputation . . . of course, so do we. But still—"

Ky queried her implant. Vatta did not have a direct trade route with Urgayin; the implant notation was Dangerous: pirates masquerading as privateers. "Did they go with Andreson to the rendezvous?"

"As far as I know, yes. Andreson said to meet there; everyone was leaving Sallyon at random intervals to avoid port authority suspicion. I left first, to come find you and see if you were interested."

"Are you?"

He drained half his glass before answering. "Yes . . . and no. I mean, you made sense, and you're from Slotter Key. And you're a Vatta. All that means something to me. Obviously, though, we need more ships and people involved, and we can't gather Slotter Key privateers with the ansibles down. I'm just not sure about Andreson. She's likely to give you trouble, for one thing."

"Why?"

"Like I said, she expects to command, and she's going to think you're a rival."

"If she's more experienced—"

"She's older than you, more years as a captain and a

privateer. But when I asked her if she'd ever commanded in a multiship engagement, she got huffy. Said she knew more about space combat than any half-baked youngster."

Anger washed over her; Ky barely managed a level tone. "I'm not exactly half-baked—"

"I know that. But her age, her experience . . . and she claims she and her companion ship took out two pirates on the way out of Bissonet." He tilted his head. "Going to fight her for it?"

"Not now," Ky said. "It's more important to get an inter-system alliance than who commands it. I'll at least talk to her." She had to start somewhere, and five more ships plus a prickly commander was better than just Argelos.

"I'll stick with you, then," Argelos said. "The odds are better with more of us than with me going out alone. I don't want to be solo against a fleet of pirates." He took another sip. "You seemed to think you had some sort of plan, back on Sallyon. Was that all youthful enthusiasm?"

"Plans depend on resources," Ky said. "I have to have numbers to put in the boxes. A plan for eight ships isn't like a plan for eighty."

"I can see that. But still—some kind of overall organization?"

"Definitely," Ky said. "What I know is Slotter Key's Spaceforce model; I've tried expanding it for multisystem use, but I'm sure there'll have to be adjustments. Still, we need a command structure, a support structure, all that kind of thing. And we must have someone in command who has experience in multiship engagements."

He grinned. "I was hoping you'd say that. It's not that I think this is just a Slotter Key problem that has to have a Slotter Key solution, but I don't want to find myself on the tag end of a gaggle of privateers commanded by someone who has no qualifications other than the number of ships he brought to the party. After all, my authorization is from Slotter Key."

"How many privateers have fought in groups?" Ky asked.

"Not many," Argelos said. "I've worked with another Slotter Key privateer a few times—we'd set up a trap—but nothing more than that. Sergei Morales, out of the Loma Linda group, he was telling me once about putting all the Loma Linda privateers together for a few operations. But he told me that in a bar on Placitas when he was more than a little drunk."

"Ideally, we need a commander who's done multiship combat before," Ky said. "A merc, in fact. They're the ones with the experience."

"Mercs don't work with privateers," Argelos reminded her. "At least, the good ones don't."

"True," Ky said. "At least, not often. But they fight each other, and they know what we don't about full-scale warfare. I had the theory in the Academy, but I haven't actually done it."

"Wait—you had mercs with you when you took this ship, didn't you?"

"Not to take this ship," Ky said. "They cleaned up Osman's allies, two other ships."

"They didn't capture this ship for you?"

"No. I . . . er . . . did that myself."

He looked at her with a new expression. "Really. So that talk about you killing Osman wasn't just random rockfall? You actually fought him off and killed him? Yourself?"

"Yes," Ky said. Tension skewed her voice; she fought it down. "It was . . . very personal. He wanted this ship; he wanted me dead. I didn't have experienced soldiers . . . I had to do it myself. As I did at Sabine. If you heard about that."

"Only rumors," Argelos said. "You will forgive me, I

hope, if I discounted them as mere rumors. A young woman your age—and you don't look—"

"Spaceforce-trained," Ky said.

"Yes, but . . . forgive me again, but didn't it bother you?"

"Of course it bothered me!" Ky looked him in the eye. "I threw up; I cried. But it had to be done."

Argelos shifted in his seat. "Yes. Well. You look so . . . so young, and Vatta doesn't have the reputation of breeding soldiers. I should have known, I suppose. When you talked about privateers combining, I assumed . . . but never mind. You're tougher than you look, clearly. So what kind of organization did you envision?"

"Like this," Ky said. She called up the files she'd been working on. "Initially, I don't expect to get much if any support from system governments. I'd hoped we would— but Sallyon showed that most will be slow to respond. So we have to arrange our own supply and support bases. That's when I started thinking of ways to incorporate experienced mercs."

He looked at the charts, then at her. "You've really thought this through. My Spaceforce adviser should see this. Would you let him?"

"Only if he agrees to secrecy," Ky said. "I'm still wondering if he's the one who tipped off the Sallyon administration that we were discussing joint operations."

"It's possible, I suppose," Argelos said. He looked at the charts again. "I notice you don't have numbers in some of these boxes."

"I don't know the armaments the pirates carry. Do you?"

"Some of them, certainly."

"Good; you can help me fill in the blanks." Ky looked up to find Argelos looking alarmed. "You said you'd be with me," she said. "What's the problem?"

"It's my adviser. He thinks we should just head back to Slotter Key—"

"If your adviser is against this, what will you do?"

"I . . . don't know. He's young, as I said. I wouldn't have gone against Berman's advice—the adviser I had before—but I'm not sure of this one. If he comes up with what I consider valid objections, then—" He shrugged and spread his hands.

"I can't tell you more of what I know if you're not with me—with us," Ky said.

He looked at her in silence for a long moment, then nodded. "I'm with you. At least as far as contacting other privateers and trying to form a joint force of some kind. I do think you should consider working with the Bissonet privateers. Dan's solid—like I said, I've known him for years. If we decide it's not a good deal, we can always leave."

"So where is the meeting place?"

"Corson's Roads; it's a smallish place, mostly a repair facility set up a long time ago when FTL engines needed tuning more frequently. We've both been there before. He'll bring the other Bissonets, if they show up at Sallyon."

"How far?"

"One jump from here, too. It's relatively convenient to Sallyon, Cascadia, Bissonet, and Bernhardt."

"The pirates wouldn't have it staked out?"

"They might, but it's a dwindling economy since the long haulers took over. Not much to rob."

Ky considered. Bissonet's privateers would have a personal and urgent interest in defeating the pirates, which meant they'd probably welcome any assistance, but for the same reasons might want to run the show for Bissonet's purposes, not the benefit of all.

"I'll go there," she said. "Tell me more about the people you think we'll be meeting."

On the voyage to Corson's Roads, she scheduled more weapons drills. Ky didn't take the time to drop out of FTL and blow up a few rocks, as they had on previous runs, but she and her new weapons officer made up scenarios that gave the batteries practice in loading various munitions and responding to emergency situations. Jessy turned out to be wickedly inventive with such scenarios. On one of Ky's tours through the ship, she overheard the battery crews commenting on this in one of the servicing compartments.

"Just one drill after another." Graydon, number three battery, sounded annoyed.

"Better this than no drills." That was Jon Gannett.

"Not saying it isn't. But I'll bet we're fitter than any of those other crews."

"Fitter than the pirates, is what we need to be," Pod Gannett said. "I had a word with that Argelos' number one gunner, back on Cascadia. They don't drill but once in ten days, and they know when."

"Captain's smarter'n that," Graydon said. "Can't say I like having my rest shift busted up, but at least it feels like a real fightin' ship. She may be young, but she knows what she's doin', I'm thinkin'."

Ky backed up twenty steps and made an intentional noise. When she walked into the compartment, five of them were bent over a missile, apparently calibrating the targeting computer. "Good work on that last drill," she said. They had, in fact, exceeded the parameters she'd set by 10 percent.

"Thanks, Captain," Jon Gannett said.

A few days later, they down transitioned into Corson's

Roads System. Corson's Roads ansibles were nonfunctional; its Traffic Control beacons operated only on request from incoming ships. Only eight ships lay docked there, three with Bissonet registry, one from Ciudad, one from Urgayin, as well as the two Slotter Key ships and a small, slow insystem freight hauler. The station had the bleak, worn look of any depressed business district. The repair docks with their huge derricks and machinery lay empty, unlighted, visible only to scan. Small as the station itself was, its commercial concourse had too many closed-up spaces, too few pedestrians, and most of those had a hard-edged disgruntled expression. The Captains' Guild had no facility here; Crown & Spears had no branch office, though Ky noticed a blank spot on one storefront that might have held their logo in more prosperous days. The whole place gave Ky an uneasy feeling. Their scans had found no mysterious ships in the system, but what kept the economy going at all, if not some clandestine trade?

Argelos had arranged, through his acquaintance, a meeting in what was supposed to be the best of the local restaurants. Ky left her escort at the restaurant entrance; she could see that the place was empty except for those she came to meet, and she was more worried about the criminal element outside.

The three Bissonet captains sat along one side of a table like a row of officers at a court-martial, a formation clearly chosen to intimidate. They stood when Ky approached. All wore gray tunics over blue trousers tucked into low boots. All had long hair worn Bissonet-fashion, the woman's coiled high on her head, the men's draped over one shoulder and tied with Bissonet blue and gray.

The hawk-faced woman Argelos had described, Petrea Andreson, stood between the two men; her hair was so pale that Ky couldn't tell if it was beginning to gray or not. Her hard-boned face was puckered on one side by a scar that she hadn't bothered to have removed. Ky wondered why. She recognized Dan Pettygrew's plain, ordinary face from his broadcast interview back on Sallyon; the other man, Simon Battersea, captain of the smallest Bissonet ship, was vid-show handsome with a thick mane of red-gold hair in a loose braid, and intense dark eyes.

"You're Captain Kylara Vatta?" Andreson said, raising one pale eyebrow.

"Ky Vatta, yes," Ky said. Surely they would recognize her from the picture she'd sent.

"Let us sit down," Andreson said. She and her companions sat; Ky slid into a seat across from them.

"I'm sorry for your loss," Andreson said. "We heard about your family."

"Thanks," Ky said, surprised at the offer of sympathy.

"I understand you want an alliance with us," Andreson said.

"More than that," Ky said. The familiar argument she'd made so often scrolled through her mind. "I think we—privateers loyal to our own governments—need to form an interstellar force to defeat this new threat—"

"Yes, yes," Andreson said, waving a hand to stop her. "I understand all that. But right now we don't have an interstellar force, and you need allies to start one, right?"

"Right." Argelos had said the woman was blunt and pushy; she was living up to her reputation.

"What makes you think you're the one to do this?" Andreson asked. "Rather than, for instance, someone with actual experience in space warfare?"

"I thought it up," Ky said. "And as for experience, I've been in a few fights—"

"A few fights." Andreson's tone was as dismissive as

her earlier hand wave. "That's better than nothing, but not good enough for us, Captain Vatta. I know you were at the Slotter Key Space Academy, but I don't know how good they are—if their training is comparable to Bissonet's—and besides, you didn't graduate. I can't say that gives me much confidence, and I doubt it will encourage many others to join you."

"Your point?" Ky said, folding her hands and hoping her eyes didn't reveal her anger.

"We are more than willing to attack the enemies who attacked Bissonet. I agree that they are not going to stop there; I agree we need to join forces to go after them—though I think all surviving Bissonet and Slotter Key privateers together would not be enough. But you, Captain Vatta, are too young and too inexperienced to hold such an alliance together. It will take someone with maturity, someone with years of deep-space command, to do the job. I hope you can see that."

Andreson had the votes, if it came to voting. She could always take her ships and go somewhere else. Ky tried for a tone that combined reasonableness with firmness. "My goal is to defeat the enemy and make the spaceways safe for trade again," she said. "I would hope that is the goal of everyone involved in this."

Andreson relaxed slightly. "That is my goal as well, though I would include freeing Bissonet from its invaders. But you are from a trading family: what does Vatta expect to get out of this? I'm not going to put my ships at risk to build your family's wealth." Her gaze flicked for a moment to Simon Battersea.

"I hope Vatta will prosper again in a safe trading environment, just like any other trading company," Ky said. "Right now all trade—and all legitimate governments—are at risk."

"Here is my proposal," Andreson said. "Your idea certainly has merit, though you aren't the first to come up with it. But I am not putting myself under your command, nor are any of my captains. We are already used to working together—" Pettygrew stirred, but said nothing. "I have almost thirty years of deep-space command, and while we had no fleet-sized actions in that time, I have commanded in smaller multiship engagements. If you want to come in with us, I'll be glad to accept your help, but I will expect the same kind of discipline that you would have given to your planetary militia."

Even though she had already decided to yield command, Ky still felt a pang at this. She liked Andreson's bluntness; it felt like honesty. The woman probably was a competent commander; just surviving that long as a privateer meant something. But still . . . she did not look forward to taking orders from someone she hardly knew.

"I'm assuming Argelos will do whatever you decide," Andreson went on. "If you have any ability to command, he will follow your decisions. And we have two others who might be willing to join us, a fellow from Ciudad and Ernst Muirtagh from Urgayin. That would give us seven ships. Enough to practice maneuvers with, and then we'd have something to show, to encourage more to join us."

"Have you considered talking to any of the good mercenary companies?" Ky asked. "They have resources the seven of us don't have."

"Mercs!" Andreson snorted. "If there are any good mercs, they'd certainly be out of our price range. Unless you're paying."

"I'm not going to let some merc tell me what to do," Simon Battersea put in, with a quick toss of his head. "I'm a patriot, not a gun for hire."

"Enough, Simon," Andreson said. Again a quick sideways glance. "I'm sure Captain Vatta was thinking of their resource base. But I for one don't think they're needed, and I would regard them as a security risk. Those who will fight for anyone might easily be bribed."

Ky could not imagine the Mackensee commanders being bribed . . . certainly not easily . . . but realized she wouldn't convince Andreson.

"How many ships do you think we'll need, ultimately?" she asked instead.

"Unless they're attacking planetary systems, I don't expect they'll show up in more than small groups," Andreson said. "Three, four, maybe five. They can't be everywhere in force, and as long as the ansibles are down, they can't communicate among their scattered forces."

"You are aware they have shipboard ansibles?"

"There is no such thing," Andreson said.

"There are," Ky said. "I found them on Osman's ship. It's how they've been coordinating their attacks."

"But—ISC always said it was impossible—" That was Battersea again. Ky wondered about his relationship to Andreson.

"ISC said it was impossible to knock out ansibles systemwide, too. I'm telling you . . . when I got Osman's ship, I found these things, and the installation and user instructions."

"And you have them . . . how many?" Simon Battersea leaned forward.

"Enough to equip this many ships, at least. And they don't know we have them."

"Do you have their codes?" Andreson asked.

"No. The electromagnetic pulse that knocked out Osman's ship systems—it's complicated; I'll have to tell you about that battle sometime—also knocked out the code records in the one he had installed. The uninstalled ones seem never to have had the codes loaded. If I understand the instructions, they're initialized with the ship chip; they transmit using ship chips as initiator codes. They don't interface with system ansibles—"

"How do you know that?"

"Says so in the instructions," Ky said. "I don't begin to understand it—maybe because ISC didn't authorize them or something." She wasn't going to tell these people about Rafe.

"So . . . you're saying you can offer us instantaneous ship-to-ship communication even if the system ansibles are down?" Andreson looked doubtful.

"Yes. And in systems where there are no ansible stations."

"And what do you want in return? You aren't demanding command as the price of that?"

Ky shook her head. "I care more about getting it done than who's commanding. This should give us equality in communications."

Battersea snorted, but Andreson nodded. "I appreciate that, Captain Vatta. I misunderstood you, I think. I will try to deserve your trust."

"I'm concerned that this is not a secure location," Ky said.

"Quite right. I will hold a captains' meeting aboard my ship for any serious planning. You will meet the other captains there as well." She glanced quickly at her companions. "We should eat, I think; it would be the normal thing to do. We have eaten here before, Captain Vatta. I can recommend the baked fish. Or, if you do not eat fish, the curried lamb."

Ky punched in her order, and the Bissonetans punched

in theirs. While they waited for the food, she said, "It struck me that you wanted to discuss business before eating; on my world, we do not usually talk business until after the meal."

"Ah . . ." Captain Andreson smiled a little. "On Bissonet, we do not want to share a meal with those whom we do not trust, so we make the deal first. It would be almost impossible to refuse a suggestion, after eating together. Does not the sharing of food create an obligation among your people?"

"Not to agree to a business deal, no," Ky said. She had never imagined that result of a business lunch. "It does put people in a better mood, usually, but that's all." Precepts from Saphiric Cyclan doctrine swam up through her memory . . . the obligation of host to guest, for instance. Did that apply? Had her father thought it applied? She felt vaguely guilty for not having paid much attention. "I think," she said, "it's perceived as a courtesy not to disturb each other's digestion."

The other three looked at her with an expression that made her uneasy. "Your people worry about digestion over business ethics?" Battersea said finally.

"Not instead of, but in addition to," Ky said. She could tell they were not convinced.

"Simon," Andreson said, this time without looking at him. He shrugged. Ky realized that he reminded her somewhat of Rafe, but without Rafe's hard edge of experience.

A constrained silence lasted until their food orders arrived.

"What did you think?" Martin asked when Ky got back to the ship.

"I don't know," Ky said. She had tried to sort out her thoughts, but they were still jumbled. "They've worked together before—that's a plus. They have more experience than I have, that's certain."

"Is it the right kind of experience?"

"I don't know." Ky ran her hands through her hair. "I certainly hope so, because there's no chance the Bissonet contingent will accept anyone else as commander. The problem is, we don't have anyone else who even claims to have experience in multiship engagements. My instructors said the difference between one-on-one and small-group engagements was greater than that between small groups and large groups until you got up to dozens. I don't see how I can put my theoretical knowledge up against her practical experience, at least not until I see how she organizes training. You might prefer it, but the other Bissonet captains won't, and I haven't met the others." That was another concern: she wished she had a way of meeting the other captains before the joint conference, but Andreson would resent that, she was sure. "I'll be meeting with Andreson—that's their senior captain—on her ship tomorrow morning. I'll find out more there, meet the other captains. When I get back, I'll meet with our senior staff."

"What are your criteria, Captain?"

That was the problem. She didn't know how to assess the competence of someone that much older, someone who claimed experience she didn't have. "It has to make sense," she said finally. "If she wants to rush into a fight without training us as a unit—that's not going to work. I want to see a plan, first for training and then for engagement."

Andreson had a plan, and laid it out for them. They would leave Corson's Roads and make two jumps to an uninhabited system—she had the coordinates—where they

would train in maneuvers and gunnery until she was satisfied that they could fight an engagement together.

"How long do you think that will take?" Isak Zavala of
Ciudad, captain of *Dona Florenzia,* asked. His wavy red
hair was tied back with a black ribbon; his uniform had
a high collar, and he sat very stiffly upright. Ky had noticed
his formality of speech, and his distinct accent.

"I can't tell until I've assessed your ship handling and
your weapons crews' efficiency," Andreson said. "We can't
rush into combat untrained." This made sense, but something in her tone suggested that she resented Zavala's question.

Zavala's lips tightened, but he said no more. Ernst
Muirtagh, captain of *Belcanto* from Urgayin, held up his
hand, and Andreson nodded at him.

"What I want to know is how we're financin' this," he
said. "Who's payin' for the munitions, the fuel, the rest
of the supplies? If we're supposed to support ourselves,
we'll need to spend time tradin' . . . or gettin' some juicy
prizes." He said that last with a knowing leer at the others.

"It is not about profit," Zavala said. "It is altogether—"

Muirtagh interrupted. "Everything's about profit, one
way or t'other. And I sure don't have the resources to fight
a war without I get some support."

"Gentlemen," Andreson said, in a tone that made
them both stop short. "It is a reasonable question. We
hope in time that planetary governments that feel themselves under threat will contribute to our support, but
it's true that at present this is a drain on us personally.
If we can free Bissonet, I know our government will
reward us—"

" 'Snot gonna happen with just us seven, now is it?"
Muirtagh said. He lounged back in his chair. "I can't afford
to run my ship on fine words, not for very long. I imagine

that's what Zavala was thinkin', too, when he asked how long the trainin' would take."

"It was not," Zavala said hotly. "I was merely—"

Muirtagh waved his hand. "Doesn't matter. The point is, unless one of us is independently wealthy on the grand scale"—he glanced around at their faces—"we have to have some way to support ourselves. So say we defeat some little group of pirates—how do we divide the prize money?"

"There are more important considerations—" Andreson began, but Muirtagh interrupted.

"I don't think so," he said. "Not if we want to keep ourselves afloat. I don't see it does any harm to talk about it, and I propose we divide anything we get into nine shares. One for each of us, an extra for our leader here, and one to be given to the ship that's done the most in that engagement, by majority vote."

Andreson had flushed, but as he gave his proposal, she calmed again. "That seems reasonable to me," she said.

"I thought it would, bein' as you'll be our leader," Muirtagh said with a grin.

"I shall reserve my extra share for unexpected expenses affecting the entire group," Andreson said. "I am not in this for profit any more than Captain Zavala is. My homeland is captive."

Muirtagh nodded. "That's fine with me. Whatever. Now . . . where are we going to do this training?"

"Here." Andreson passed around a navigation chip. "The coordinates are on it. It's a system I happen to know about—uninhabited, no ansibles, nothing to draw attention to it. Two jumps away. We'll rendezvous by the largest planet—the data are on your chip."

"So—when do we start?"

"We'll start training as soon as we're all there,"

Andreson said. "We leave here when Captain Vatta has installed our new communications system."

Everyone turned to look at Ky.

"What communications system?" asked Zavala.

Ky wished Andreson had waited to tell them—waited even until they were at the training site to tell them. But it made more sense here, where it would be much easier to move the ansibles from her ship to theirs. "Shipboard ansibles," she said. "The pirates have them; Osman Vatta had them. I offered to give you each one."

"How much will it cost us?" Muirtagh asked.

"Nothing," Ky said.

"I did not know such things existed," Zavala said.

"They're about the size of a small scan console," Ky said. "You'll need to make room for them—I suggest on or near the bridge—and you'll need a power source. My Engineering crew has the exact dimensions and will install them for you."

TWENTY-THREE

"This is a rotating cluster," Martin said, watching the scan. Ky had positioned her ship exactly where instructed, but *Dona Florenzia,* instead of being directly aft of her at twenty-thousand kilometers, had lined up behind *Cornet,* on the right. *Sharra's Gift* was on the correct side of the formation, but a sloppy three thousand kilometers behind her assigned spot.

"We're on target, though," Ky said. "Good job, Lee."

"What is the purpose of this formation?" Lee asked, not taking his eyes off his board. "It looks admirably suited for getting us all blown away at once. That is, if everyone gets to the assigned place . . ."

"It lets us all shoot someone in front of us without worrying about hitting each other," Ky said. "Except for the *Lady,* which is guarding our rear."

"With one little beam weapon?"

"And her missiles," Ky said. "And she can lay a mine-field back there to screen us, too."

"So you think it's good?"

Ky shrugged. "Not exactly what I'd have chosen, but it's also good for practicing getting into, and maneuvering in, formations. You don't want to start with some of the trickier formations when people can't keep station in this one. We're all pointed the same way, at least."

"Oh, good grief," Lee muttered. *Dona Florenzia,* apparently noticing that she was behind the wrong ship, had tried a quick correction rather than the right one, and was now gaining on the front of the formation, angling toward *Vanguard.* "I'm going to have to shift, Captain."

"I'll tell Capt—Admiral Andreson." Ky activated the shipborne ansible. She wasn't looking forward to this. So far Andreson had taken her election to admiral as proof of godlike powers.

"*Flower* communications," someone answered.

"Captain Vatta, *Vanguard,*" Ky said. "*Dona Florenzia* is out of position and closing on us; I will be moving *Vanguard.*"

"Hold your position," Andreson said. "I've ordered the *Lady* back to her assigned position; she's just maneuvering."

"Our scans show possible intersection."

"Nonsense. There's plenty of room. If you were more experienced—"

"Lee, give us a kick. Just what we need."

"Yes, Captain."

"*Vanguard* under acceleration," Ky said.

"I told you to hold position!" Andreson said. "That is gross disobedience."

"Better than a collision," Ky said. "Plot it on scan. I did."

"You—oh." The scans now showed that *Dona Florenzia* would plow right through the position Ky would have been in. "Even so, you should have waited for me—"

"Admiral, you have many responsibilities; I would suggest that captains need to be aware of their surroundings and make minor adjustments as needed. As soon as we can, we will resume our assigned station." She could

imagine Andreson's eyes narrowing, the suspicious tight-
ening of her mouth.

"You take a lot on yourself, Captain Vatta," Andreson
said finally. "But I am not one to deny merit where it
exists, even if it is expressed so . . . inappropriately. We
are, after all, from different cultures. Perhaps in yours jun-
iors contradict seniors so blatantly."

We elected you, you arrogant twit. For your three ships,
not *your brains.* Ky knew she couldn't say that. "I'm sorry
if I've offended you, Admiral," she said. "It's certainly
true that Slotter Key has its own way of doing things."
And if Bissonet was defended by people like Andreson,
no wonder the pirates had chosen it for their first system
takeover.

It was the fifth day since they'd begun training, with
just the six ships. Muirtagh had never arrived; Andreson
was convinced he had just made a course error, but Ky
worried that he wasn't coming, and might have been a
pirate plant. In that case, the pirates would know that
they weren't the only ones with shipboard ansibles.
Andreson had shrugged off that threat.

"Even if he doesn't come, he may just have decided
that it wasn't profitable for him," she'd said. "No need to
think he's selling us out."

No need, but also no need to think he hadn't. Argelos
had told her that his adviser was also concerned, but not
enough to argue with Andreson.

Maneuvers continued rough the rest of that day. Just
getting the ships into the simple formation took hours,
and trying to maneuver the formation as a whole led to
more of what Martin called rotating clusters. At the end
of the day's work, when Andreson called all the captains
into the communications net, they all looked and sounded
two stages beyond grumpy. Andreson's scathing analysis,

accurate though it was, didn't help. An extended and exhausting wrangle followed.

It turned out that Zavala, whose errors caused the first blowup, had only an incomplete command of what Ky had assumed was the common trade tongue familiar to spacers everywhere, and most of his crew knew only a few basic commands. He had honestly mistaken which ship he was supposed to follow, and claimed that the admiral's command to correct his position had forced him to accelerate faster than he chose.

"That's ridiculous," Simon Battersea said. His *Cornet* had turned in the third best performance, according to Andreson. She had scored herself first and Ky second. "The orders were perfectly clear: line up behind Vatta's ship—"

"No word of Vatta was spoken," Zavala said. His ice-blue eyes, striking under dark brows and that red hair, flashed angrily. "I have the order here. It says, 'In direct line from the flagship, form line behind intervening ship and hold position at three thousand kilometers.' From my initial position, your ship was directly in line with the flag-ship."

"It didn't mean initial position," Simon said. "That was obvious to everyone else—"

"Simon," Andreson said. He sat back, lips pressed together. She seemed to speak to Zavala, though with the vidscreen showing a window for each, Ky couldn't tell where she was looking. "I'm sorry, Captain Zavala, that my orders were unclear. I meant, of course, a line parallel to our course, from my ship back through the formation. But I understand I will have to be very clear." Though the words were courteous, the tone was similar to Simon's and implied that Zavala had to be really stupid to mistake the intent. Zavala's pale face flushed.

"Your correction, I understand, was also an attempt to

follow my orders, but it did require Captain Vatta to accelerate and lose her perfect position. I shall be very careful in the future to give precise orders," Andreson said.

"That would be wise," Zavala said. He had lost the flush, but Ky noted a telltale paleness around his mouth. He was still very angry.

"Tomorrow, we will learn this formation," Andreson said. The graphic came up on the central window. "Perhaps being in closer order will prevent confusion."

Ky opened her mouth then shut it. Close-order drills with ships were, in Spaceforce, not recommended until units could keep position in the more open—and safer— formations.

"You were going to say something, Captain Vatta?" Andreson said.

"My crew could use more practice in the open formation, Admiral," Ky said.

"Your crew did exceptionally well," Andreson said. "You don't need the practice, and frankly, I don't think more practice will help the others. Close formation will force precise response to precise orders. We will do this one, and we will do it at one-kilometer intervals."

Which meant ships that erred were likely to collide and damage or destroy one another.

"That's too close," Argelos said. "By your own plots, we were all out of position more than a kilometer sometime today."

Andreson's mouth widened in a feral smile. "So I expect you all to be more careful. We cannot defeat Gammis Turek's pirates, who are experienced in ship maneuvers, by being sloppy."

"But, Admiral—" That was Pettygrew, the other Bissonet captain. "We don't have the experience yet—"

"And we won't get it if we don't practice," Andreson

said. "You're from Bissonet, Captain Pettygrew; you know what the stakes are here. We have no room for careless, sloppy, incompetent ship handling."

"Are you saying I'm incompetent?" Zavala asked.

"I'm saying we must all improve," Andreson said.

"You said Captain Vatta didn't need to improve—"

"No, I said Captain Vatta didn't need to practice that particular formation any longer."

Ky looked at Zavala's face; he was clearly not convinced. "I do not think it is safe," he said. "It will do us no good if we collide."

"Then don't collide," Andreson said. "If you are careful, nothing will go wrong."

The next day's maneuvers began badly again. Zavala refused to close within five kilometers; Ky, all too aware of *Cornet* on one flank and *Bassoon* on the other, sympathized with him, but had no attention to spare for the argument that raged on the com. When Andreson called for the formation to rotate about its long axis, a tricky evolution, *Cornet* wobbled, coming within seven hundred meters of Ky before opening the distance again. By the time they broke for lunch, tempers had frayed all around. Zavala had retreated to a thousand kilometers; the others pulled back at the announcement of a meal break despite Andreson's orders to hold formation.

"My pilot needs a break," Argelos said. "And before you say it, I know if we were in a battle he wouldn't get one. Still . . ."

"Mine, too," Pettygrew said. Ky said nothing to Andreson, but nodded when Lee asked permission to open a distance from the two nearest ships.

"She's nuts," Lee said when he had pulled them back to a thousand kilometers from the nearest ship. "If we're that tight, we're going to worry more about hitting each other than where the enemy is, and it gives them a target barely five kilometers across."

"She's scared," Martin said. "I've seen that before. That kind of anger is fear, really. She wanted the job, but she's beginning to realize what it takes and she thinks she doesn't have it."

"Hugh, is that your reading?"

"Oh, definitely." Her second in command had remained cool all through that difficult day, but she could tell he was worried. "She thinks the only way to hide it is to act scary herself. Thing is, she's going to drive Zavala away."

"You think so?" Ky said. "He seemed so enthusiastic when we met—"

"Ciudad's part of the Loma Linda group," he said. "We had some recruits from there, and one or two officers. Culturally quite different from Slotter Key. Take you, for instance: you're used to giving orders to men and having them obeyed, and it doesn't bother Lee or Martin or anyone else—male or female—that you're a female captain. Ciudad's different: they aren't into gender equality much at all. It's hard enough for Zavala to obey a woman in command, and she's not doing anything to make it easier for him. If he's here another three days I'd be surprised."

"Should I talk to him?" Ky said.

Hugh shook his head. "You're a woman, too. He may think you're not as bad, but still you're female. And you're not the problem. She is."

"Captain, you've got a call . . . from Zavala."

"Right," Ky said. She opened her screen.

"Captain Vatta," Zavala said. His expression was calm, but she noticed the tension around his eyes.

"Captain Zavala," she said. "How may I help you?"

"I do not think you can," he said. "It is that woman—she is impossible!"

Fragments of lectures on military etiquette raced through her mind. Junior officers criticizing seniors behind their backs—disloyalty . . . but this was not Slotter Key Spaceforce Academy. This was . . . nothing yet. Nothing if it fell apart.

"We're all new at this, Captain," she said.

"I am making allowances," Zavala said. "I am telling myself that she has never had such command before, that she may be under great stress. But to speak to me that way, to call me a coward, in front of all of you—that is not something a man of my people can accept without disgrace. It must be answered with honor."

Ky had the feeling that she was missing something important. "You will forgive me," she said, feeling her way. "I was having such trouble in the close formation that I was not listening to everything she said."

"Ah." A world of meaning in that tone, if only she knew what it was. "So you did not agree with her?"

"No, Captain Zavala. I was distracted; I'm sorry. For what it's worth"—not much, she was sure—"I thought your distance was prudent, much safer than the close-order drill."

His gaze sharpened. "Prudent. You are thinking I thought only of safety?"

She had said something wrong; she tried to think why. "Captain Zavala, I was thinking only of safety. You did say, didn't you, that it made us more vulnerable to attack, all bunched up like that?"

"It is stupid," Zavala said. "But she called me a coward, an old lady—"

"That was rude," Ky said.

"It was worse than rude," Zavala said. "It is a mortal insult, and I must answer it with honor."

Again Ky could not quite understand; she was afraid that any question would make Zavala angrier. "When you say *answer it with honor* . . . ," she said.

"I mean a duel, of course. A duel of honor. Do you not have such?"

"Not on Slotter Key," Ky said. "A duel of honor is a trial of some sort? A test?" Running, she thought, or climbing, or even a fistfight, primitive as that sounded.

His eyes widened. "A duel of honor is fought with the blade and the heart, until they are one." He thrust his right forefinger into his chest. Then he shook his head, speaking very distinctly as if to a small child. "It is a fight with the sword, Captain Vatta, that ends in the death of one, either challenger or defender."

"You're going to challenge Petrea Andreson to a duel?" Despite herself, that ended in a near-squeak. She bit back *That's absurd,* which gave her time to think of all the ways this was a very bad precedent to set.

"I must," Zavala said. "And I would like you to be my second. She will have a male second, of course, and then we men will fight because no woman can duel."

A prickle of irritation. "Why not?"

"Dueling is between men. Women fighting is just—" His hand waved dismissively. "There is no honor in it. No insult to you, Captain Vatta, for your defense of your ship, which we have heard about. That is different. For a woman to fight in defense of her family or home—or their extension in planet or system—is normal. But the duel of honor belongs to the realm of men."

"And you expect us to stand by and watch you fight?"

"It is how it is done," he said, with the dignity of someone who knows all the rules and intends to follow them.

"What if Captain Andreson refuses your challenge?"

"If her second will not fight me, then I leave. I will not stay here to see my honor dragged in the dirt." He paused, then went on. "You do not have duels or affairs of honor on Slotter Key?"

"We don't have duels," Ky said. "We do have honor."

"How can you have honor if there is no blood price?" Zavala asked.

A vision from the implant of her home in flames, her dead mother's face, blocked out the screen for a moment. "There is a blood price," she said, her voice thick.

"You killed your kinsman Osman, I was told," he said. "For killing your parents, is that not so?"

"It was not a duel," Ky said. "It was vengeance." Very satisfying vengeance, though she knew she shouldn't feel that way.

"I think we are not that different," Zavala said. "So will you be my second? You are the only one I can ask."

Ky hesitated. "What would my responsibilities be?"

"You don't—oh. Of course. After I challenge her, you and her second will make the arrangements for the duel. It is different because in my civilization we do not challenge women, but you will explain it. I will meet her second in an honorable duel. As we are shipboard, the weapons choices available will naturally be limited to those that will cause no harm to the ships. That is why I said sword." His voice was completely calm now, as he pointed out the practical aspects of dueling to the death on shipboard, and told her that Andreson, as challenged, would have the choice of weapons: one of three styles of sword. "And I have a handbook that you can read, for the correct wording at the time . . ."

This was surreal. This made no sense. They had real enemies in the universe, and he was about to kill someone, or be killed, just because he felt he'd been insulted? Perhaps she could persuade him. "Captain Zavala, while I agree that what she said was wrong, and an insult, still . . . this is a perilous situation we're all in. Turek and his pirates are out there trying to capture more systems and dominate everyone . . . isn't that more important?"

His face hardened. "Nothing is more important than honor. Without honor, how can I fight Turek? I must have the confidence of my crew. How can my men respect me if I accept insult without defending myself?" Then he gave her a tight smile. "But, Captain Vatta, it is the duty of one's chosen second to test one's resolve, as you have just done. As I said, you are more like me than I would have thought possible."

"I see." She didn't see, not completely, but she did recognize intransigence. He was going to duel or he was going to leave. At least arranging the duel would take some time and maybe he would cool off, or maybe Andreson would apologize. Neither was likely, but that was all the hope she could find. "Then I accept—I agree to be your second in this matter, though I wish it could be deferred."

"You should have been the commander," Zavala said. "You would not have let this happen."

That was true in one way, but she suspected that Zavala's cultural heritage provided him with unseen trigger points that would give any female commander problems.

"You do understand," he went on, "that if she refuses my challenge, I will be forced to withdraw from this alliance."

"Yes," Ky said.

"I recommend that you also withdraw, not because you are my second, but because that woman will get us all killed, if she goes on like this, and then where is your idea?"

"It's because it's my idea that I can't withdraw," Ky

said. Though Andreson might very well send her away just for cooperating with Zavala. "I must share the risk."

"As you wish. I will send my challenge to Andreson before the meal break is over."

Ky had no appetite after that, but forced herself to eat something. She would need it if this went as badly as she feared.

She did not expect what Zavala did next: he hailed all the ships, bringing everyone online to hear his challenge. She had assumed he'd make the challenge in private, and she would have a chance to ask Andreson to apologize. Instead, in formal phrases, stilted in their translation from his native language, he called upon Andreson to give him satisfaction of "mortal blood on the field of honor."

"What are you talking about?" Andreson asked, looking more annoyed than anything else.

"A duel, madam, for the insults you have laid upon me, to prove in blood whether such be deserved."

"Duel? Nobody does duels anymore."

"On the contrary, madam—"

"That's *Admiral*—"

"No, madam, it is not. When an affair of honor is involved, formal ranks are discarded. You will wish to name a second—a male second, I must insist—"

"Excuse me!" Andreson had flushed. "I haven't said— I'm not about to—"

"You refuse my challenge? Then, madam, it is you who are a coward!"

"Wait a minute!" That was Pettygrew of *Bassoon*. "This is—this is ridiculous. We have a real enemy—"

"A point made by Captain Vatta," Zavala said.

"You talked to her first?" Andreson pounced on this distraction. "You and she have been talking about me behind my back? That's outrageous!"

"I asked her to act as my second," Zavala said. "She attempted to dissuade me from pursuing the duel, as is the duty of a second to the challenger, but she has agreed."

"You traitor!" Andreson glared from the screen at Ky. "How dare you conspire behind my back—"

"I wasn't conspiring," Ky said.

"You agreed to be his second. I call that conspiring."

"I don't," Pettygrew said. "If he called her and asked her to be his second—that's what happened, isn't it?"

"Yes," Ky and Zavala said together.

"But she agreed," Andreson said.

"I don't see anything wrong in that," Pettygrew said.

"Nor I," Argelos said. "I have known Captain Vatta longer than you and I do not think it is any more than a courtesy to someone not from our culture."

"Well, I'm not going to get into a physical fight like some backwoods barbarian," Andreson said, her upper lip curled. "It's disgusting."

"I'll be your champion." Battersea had drawn himself up stiffly. "It would be unseemly for you to fight, Admiral, but if that's what it takes to convince this . . . this person . . . then I'm willing."

"Simon, there's no need," she began, but Ky interrupted her.

"If he is your second, then Captain Zavala will meet him."

"It's absurd—"

"Let me, please," Battersea said, leaning forward.

"Have you ever dueled?" Ky asked.

"What does that matter?"

"Only that what Captain Zavala intends is a fight to the death. One of you will die. One of your ships will no longer have a captain, and may be lost to our cause."

"Oh, he won't kill me." Battersea looked faintly amused.

"I am an expert with a variety of weapons, and I have the choice, don't I?"

"Yes: a choice of which kind of sword."

"Simon, I don't like this," Andreson said. "It's not civilized—"

"And now you insult my whole people!" Zavala said. "We are an ancient and honorable civilization where it is not the practice to insult others. That is civilized."

"Don't be silly, Captain Zavala," Andreson said. "I'm not insulting your people. Every culture has fossils in its cultural closet; we still have people who use drugs that rot their brains, despite everything our government can do. Your people may be civilized in every other way, but settling problems by brawling—"

"A duel is not a brawl," Zavala said. "But whatever you think of it, I must have an answer. Will you accept the challenge of mortal blood and send your second to duel, or will you not?"

"And if I don't you'll run away?"

"And if you do not accept my challenge, I will proclaim your cowardice and remove myself from your command."

"You can't call me a coward just because I won't risk a . . . a friend at a time like this."

"You called me a coward for less."

"I just meant—"

"Your answer, madam!"

"You can go if you want. I'm not going to sanction dueling."

"Very well. Then I withdraw from this alliance. I do not place my crew under the command of a coward and fool. However, my regard for the rest of the officers involved is such that I give my word I will not reveal the location or plans to anyone else at any time."

"You—!" Andreson spluttered a moment, incoherent,

then recovered herself. "Good riddance," she said to the whole group. "We're well shut of such an unstable person. And you've had more than enough time for lunch . . . back to your positions. We need work, not silliness."

Zavala's ship had withdrawn another ten thousand kilometers when the shipboard ansible bleeped. Ky turned it on.

"Captain Vatta, my apologies for involving you in what was not, after all, an affair of honor."

"You didn't intend it to go this way."

"No. But I should have anticipated it. I wanted to ask you about the communications device you installed on my ship. If I am not in your alliance, you will not want me to have it, I think. Should I put it in storage for you at my next port after informing you where it is?"

The image of a shipboard ansible languishing in some commercial storage facility startled Ky into speech. "No! I mean, I am concerned that it might fall into the wrong hands. Keep it. We might cross paths again." Perhaps, if Andreson imploded, he would come back to the alliance. An idea occurred to her. "Or perhaps you could communicate the idea of the alliance to your government, let me know what they think."

"I know what they will think. They will think they want nothing to do with anything run by that woman. Any woman, I would say, but as you have said, the threat is very real. If a successful force were commanded by an honorable woman—" The stress on *honorable* was remarkable, considering that he wasn't shouting. "—then they might consider it. But that woman—never." He shrugged. "Still, if you permit, Captain Vatta, I will retain the communications device and perhaps contact you from time to time with information I consider useful."

TWENTY-FOUR

Ky stared at the scans, littered with the course traces from the day's maneuvers. Andreson's analysis had been scathing, as usual, and this time Ky's crew had not escaped criticism. Yet even now, more than twenty days into training, Andreson seemed to have no understanding that one maneuver was more difficult than another, especially in closer formations. Ky, Argelos, and even Dan Pettygrew had tried to talk to her, but each passing day seemed to make things worse. No, she would not vary from her training schedule. No, they would not practice gunnery at all until they had satisfied her in all formations and maneuvers. No, she would not set out a detection beacon in the outer system, or entertain the suggestion that Muirtagh's nonappearance was ominous and a security breach. Ky had hoped that Zavalos' departure would get her to ease up, but if anything she had become more rigid, more autocratic.

Ky was aware that her crew didn't like Andreson's manner any more than she did. The enthusiasm they'd shown originally for this training had gradually ebbed into a sort of wary obedience that Ky had never encountered and wasn't sure how to handle. Nobody refused orders; nobody questioned her, but the ship felt different, colder in some way.

She herself had lost confidence in Andreson's ability to handle multiple ships at all, let alone in combat, but what other choices did she have? She could pull out, but where would she find other allies, especially after abandoning her first? She could try to convince Argelos to come with her, and then go searching for other Slotter Key privateers, but she had no guarantee that they would listen to her. If Pettygrew would come over to her, they could vote Andreson out, but all her training opposed any attempt to unseat a commanding officer. She had agreed to accept a subordinate position; it was her job to make it work, to be supportive.

She felt frustrated and exhausted both. All her instincts, which had served her well before, insisted that Andreson was wrong, that Muirtagh had betrayed them, that the pirates might show up any moment, in force. And yet she felt she had to set an example of correct behavior. She had made a mistake before, when she'd insisted on tackling Osman in spite of the warnings of more experienced military commanders, and it might easily have cost the lives of her entire crew; she would not make that mistake again. Andreson wasn't all bad, after all; clearly the woman had courage and wanted to close with the enemy.

When the ansible light came on, Ky groaned inwardly. This would be Andreson again, with another set of stupid complaints. Andreson insisted on keeping them in close formation, where ansible communication wasn't necessary and lightspeed worked just as well, and then used the ansible for almost every briefing. She touched the controls to open her end of the connection.

"Captain Vatta!" For a moment she didn't recognize the voice or face. Then the com board displayed the name: Zavala's *Dona Florenzia*.

"Captain Zavala? What is it? Where are you calling from?"

"I'm here in the system, four light-minutes from your position. Eight enemy ships are here, too. Arm yourself."

"What? Who? Why are you back here?" Even as she asked, Ky tapped the controls to bring weapons systems up live. She saw heads turn to her, eyes wide; she nodded.

"Captain, Muirtagh did betray us—you. I intercepted a message that they knew where you were, knew you had shipboard ansibles, and planned to attack. There are eight, in two groups of four. I expect them to jump to intercept me. I am about to engage them."

"Alone? You can't possibly—"

"Please, Captain. There is no time. Honor required that I tell you, and that I come to your aid; you might not have believed me if I had contacted you from a distance. They entered the system hours ago, but several New Standard AU from the primary. They have been using calibrated microjumps to close in: they will be visible on your scans soon, but by then much closer, and attacking. You must persuade *that woman*"—even in an emergency, his voice was edged with scorn—"to take up a defensive formation or withdraw. They are heavily armed; I recommend withdrawal."

"I can't make her do that," Ky said. "She won't listen to me."

"Then you should withdraw."

"I can't leave the rest of them—"

"I knew you were a person of honor, Captain Vatta. I was right to return." His head turned away from the screen; she heard noises in the background. "It will not show on your scan for four minutes," Zavala said. "But we're now engaged. I will transmit to you the information my tactical computer gets—it may help you."

Ky's blood ran cold. He had no chance. Up on her screen came a string of numbers; she shunted them to Jessy's board, then opened the intercom.

"Enemy's insystem; prepare for battle. This is not a drill. Repeat, this is not a drill." The bridge crew stared at her, eyes wide, then turned to their own boards.

"Battery one, ready," came Jon Gannett's voice. "No target data."

"Estimate four minutes—no, three and a half," Ky said. Zavala had left his voice channel open; she could hear his crisp, calm orders to his crew in their own language. Though she could not understand the words, she could imagine what they would be. Their voices, in the background, were barely audible, but none sounded panicky. She didn't try to speak to him. Zavala spoke to her directly only once more.

"Captain Vatta, you also need to know what I was told at my last port. They have taken another system. They know about you—they know you have Osman's ship. You must not let yourself be destroyed, Captain Vatta."

"I don't intend to be destroyed," Ky said. "I will do my best for the others."

"We have serious damage," Zavala said. "Our shields are down. We have perhaps one more shot—." Then a burst of white noise, and the connection ceased.

Ky turned to her shocked bridge crew. "We have to tell the others," she said as she tried to open a channel to Andreson. Andreson had the unit off; it should be beeping at her com officer, but he might be on break or something.

Finally he answered. "*Flower* com; what's the problem?"

"Raiders insystem," Ky said, and started to transmit the coordinates she had, but he interrupted her.

"Raiders? What d'you mean?"

"Get the admiral: we have raiders insystem, estimate

two to four light-minutes or less." She overheard a murmur of voices from the other ship.

"There's nothing on scan," the com officer said.

"There will be. They're close, they'll show up anytime now."

"She won't like it," he said. "She doesn't want to be disturbed for the next two hours, she said."

"I don't like it," Ky said, putting an edge on her voice. "Get her."

Andreson looked rumpled as well as annoyed when she appeared onscreen a few seconds later, her pale hair standing out in damp spikes. Had she been in the shower? "What is it, Captain Vatta? Do you think you have better scans than we do?"

Ky suspected that she might, but didn't say so. "No, Admiral. I had had an ansible message from Captain Zavala just now. He is—was—in this system and reported eight enemy ships—"

"He led them here!" Andreson said.

"No," Ky said; she knew she sounded angry. "He did not. He found out in his next port that they knew about our training location and were planning to attack us; he was afraid we might not receive, or pay attention to, an ansible message. He chose to come back here, knowing the danger, to give us a chance to survive."

"Well, where is he then? I see nothing on scan!"

"Scan lag," Ky said. She could not believe that Andreson didn't figure that out for herself. "They're close enough that they blew Zavala's ship, and he was four and a half light-minutes away from me. I have Zavala's data from the battle; he sent it to me from his tac computer . . ."

"What battle?"

"The one in which he was killed," Ky said, anger getting the better of judgment. Her chronometer ticked down the seconds. She should see something anytime now . . .

"Oh." Andreson sounded abashed, for once. "I'm—that's too bad. But I don't see—"

On Osman's enhanced scan, a fuzzy speck appeared, then two more, then three, then two . . . emerging from jump in a classic attack formation. Two groups of four, properly spaced to avoid damage from the destruction of a nearby ship, and converging on the tight formation Andreson had demanded.

"They're on my scan now." Ky sent the position data to Andreson's ship. "Eight of them. There's Zavala, jumping into the middle of that mess—" A ninth speck had appeared.

"Why did he do that?" Andreson asked.

Wrong question, wrong time, but maybe the answer would shake Andreson out of her immobility. "To help us. What are your orders?"

"I don't—I can't—this isn't how we planned it."

War didn't care about plans; Ky remembered one of her instructors saying that; surely anyone engaged in warfare knew that. Ky tried analysis. "They're in the system; we're maneuvering close to serious mass, so we can't just jump out of here."

"Is that what you want to do?" Andreson asked. "Run away?" She sounded scornful.

"No, but we are outnumbered. Maybe Zavala did them some damage and maybe not. We won't know until we can see the battle on scan, and by then they'll be much closer. They could pop out of FTL flight in the middle of our formation, if we got really unlucky."

"We need to boost out, then, get away from here—"

"Not necessarily. We can use the mass to shield us, if they're in close . . ." She wanted to explain to Andreson the sequence she and Hugh had come up with in case of attack, but she wasn't sure how much Andreson could absorb. Meanwhile, her crew used Osman's enhanced scan to detect the enemy weapons and shunt those data to her board. Missile batteries . . . she had to assume well stocked with missiles. Beam weapons—she couldn't yet tell how they were mounted, but twice as many as their own force mustered. They'd better run; they weren't going to defeat this force.

Once she'd marked them as enemies, the tactical scan back-computed their courses, finding images no one had noticed with all the junk in this part of the system. The current scan suggested that they were within four light-minutes, their position four minutes ago. Time had passed—how close were they now? For an instant, she wondered why instantaneous communications had not led to FTL scan that would give the real-time position of ships in space. But she had no leisure to think about that.

"Arm weapons," Andreson said. "Maintain course and formation. Uh . . . general call, all ships—" That was to her crew, no doubt. It was stupid to continue on their present course, to make such easy targets of themselves.

On her own scan, Zavala's ship still moved, as did the enemy's. Serene little blips—one green, the rest red, jewels on velvet sliding on glittering wires of their calculated course, the fine lines of missiles in flight, the slightly thicker ones of beam weapons reaching out, all as elegant as an etched circuit. It was hopeless; Zavala and his crew were already dead, but Ky could not help watching as the deadly lacework closed about *Dona Florenzia* and then she flared to debris as her shields failed.

Though they outnumbered him, the enemy had had to maneuver a little to attack him. Zavala's sacrifice had bought them another minute or two, and disarranged the neat pincer attack: now the group on the other arm of the

X would reach them first. One of them lagged; Ky could not tell if it was damage or intention, but again, it might help. It was a tiny advantage, but in this desperate situation every advantage counted.

"We have to open out," Ky said, watching for any sign of comprehension in Andreson's frozen expression. "We're bunched; we're easy meat here—"

"We can protect each other," Andreson said.

They could have if they'd ever practiced it. If they had defensive assignments. If they could manage evasive maneuvers in close formation. If, if, and if.

"We can't," Captain Argelos said. "We need to get spaced out, Ky's right."

"This is no time to argue," Andreson said.

"Right," Argelos said. "I'm not arguing; I'm moving out."

"You can't—!" Her face contorted into a mask of fear or rage; Ky was not sure which.

"Captain Vatta, what's your analysis?" Argelos said.

Ky stared at the screen, momentarily taken aback. Then she glanced at her tac analysis. "We can improve the odds by dropping toward the planet, work with that gravitation to build velocity and get some of that mass between us and at least one of the groups. Spread out enough to make targeting harder for them and give us room to shoot without hitting each other. Have to watch out for the smaller satellites and the rings . . ."

"Shoot me your figures," Argelos said.

"You're a coward!" Andreson said.

"You're an idiot," Argelos said, his voice cold as frozen air. "I should never have agreed to your command." On the screen, his ship's icon grew an orange triangle of delta vee, lengthening as he pushed his insystem drive to its capacity and it drew away from the formation.

"Captain?" Lee said, hands poised above his board.

"Go!" she said; Lee's hand moved and their ship surged ahead; in that instant she saw a line of incandescence streak the atmosphere below them—a ranging shot with a beam weapon as the enemy ships appeared out of a microjump, now only light-seconds distant. A moment later a white flare grew around *Cornet* as one of the enemy's beams hit its shields squarely. Their own shields flared slightly with backblow; then they were beyond that range. *Flower*'s batteries launched at the attackers.

"No damage," Hugh said. "Our shields are still one hundred percent."

"Target acquisition, battery one," Jon Gannett said in her earbug. "Permission to engage?"

"Engage," Ky said. The ship shivered as their number one battery launched.

"Target acquisition, battery two!"

"Easy beam distance, Captain."

"Engage battery two. Go ahead, beam, one discharge." Again a slight shiver, but no dimming of lights or any sign that the massive power discharge had caused them any difficulty. On scan, *Flower*'s missiles were almost to the enemy group; she watched them sparkle against powerful screens, not penetrating, or miss entirely.

"Lousy gunnery," Jessy said. "Wrong fusing options, among other things. They'd better get out of there."

But even as he spoke, multiple missiles hit *Cornet*'s weakened shields, and its ansible link went dead. *Flower* killed acceleration, its lengthening wedge dropping to nothing, and swapped ends, bringing its forward-mounted beam weapon into play, stabbing out at the nearest enemy ship. That was a solid hit, but the enemy shields held. *Flower* had only one beam weapon, with a slow recharge rate; more flights of missiles left its batteries, but they were no more accurate than the first. *Cornet* continued to be pounded by missiles and then another beam; it burst open and most of its arms blew up with the ship. Now the enemy beam concentrated on *Flower*.

Ky had no time to worry about *Cornet* as a pod of missiles probed their screens; none penetrated, but the telltales showed that it had been a near thing.

"One of ours got in," Jessy said. "Second ship in the formation."

"Damage estimate?"

"Impossible to say. Scan's getting messy." It was, indeed; the overlaid symbols for courses of ships and courses of missiles, color-coded for relative velocity, crisscrossed the screen.

"How low d'you want to go?" Lee asked suddenly.

"As low as we can," Ky said. "Just like we plotted before." Those few hours, when she and Lee and Hugh and her weapons teams had discussed what could be done if someone attacked while they were pinned against a mass that prohibited an FTL jump. They hadn't expected to have to use those figures, not without going over them again. "Our best bet is to make them swing around with us, force them all into a stern chase; the more velocity we pick up, the faster we'll reach a jump radius on the other side, and that's really our only option." If the enemy captains were smart enough, they'd hold back one group, but maybe they'd believe they had easy prey.

"*Bassoon*'s with us," he said. "And it looks like *Flower*'s boosting at last."

Another salvo flared against their shields without penetrating. "They want us to run," Ky said. "They think they can pick us off singly." She called to *Bassoon* and *Flower*. "Keep up with us," she said. "Maintain ten-klick spacing."

"I can't," Andreson said. "We've got damage. We don't

have full power on insystem, and we can't jump." Her face was as cold and closed as ever. "Get them out, Vatta, if you can. Go find better partners. I did my best, and I'll get one of them before they get us, if it's the last thing I do."

It would be the last thing she did, if she could do it. Andreson had never lacked courage, just skill and that indefinable instinct that made a good combat commander. "I know you did your best," Ky said. "I'll do mine, Admiral." That title was the only comfort she could give, as *Bassoon* edged nearer and *Flower* fell behind, with three ships now concentrating on her.

Where were the others, the ones that had engaged Zavala? Would they reconstruct the pincer formation on different axes? She would have, but she had no idea how pirates thought about space war.

Their velocity increased steadily as they dove into the planet's gravity well, using it for additional acceleration. Now the enemy missiles burned out their engines before reaching them, and the enemy's beam weapons concentrated on *Flower.*

Flower blew just as they were about to pass out of line-of-sight around the planet's curve.

"They'll be on us in a bit," Ky said. "Launch mines."

"How many?"

"Half of what we have. We'll hold the other half for the ones on the other side."

"That's . . . several hundred . . ."

"Better too many than too few," Ky said. "If we get through this, we can buy more mines; if we get killed being cheap . . ." She spoke to Pettygrew on *Bassoon.* "Don't fall behind. There are some hazards back there now."

"Doing our best," Pettygrew said.

"Vatta, do you have a plan?" asked Argelos. *Sharra's*

Gift showed weapons hot on scan, but she was still accelerating faster than *Vanguard*.

"Are you with us?" Ky asked. "Or have you decided to go solo?"

"Solo against eight? No. My adviser's telling me the only chance is to link up with you, if you have a plan in mind." A pause, then, "He doesn't."

"I have an idea," Ky said. "Drop back a little, and hold at about ten klicks off me, if you can. If they're smart, we'll meet four of them as we come out the back side of this maneuver. And if we're lucky, it'll be only four against three at that point. Damage?"

"None," Argelos replied, and then Pettygrew.

"Fine, then. Ready for attack; fire the moment you have a firing solution, pour it on. They have calibrated microjumps, but they should be crossing our course on insystem drive; we may get some of them. Then we try to break through and get to jump radius. Be ready to jump the instant you can; don't wait for anyone else. We won't be at the mapped jump point, so just get out of range—"

"I can't calibrate short jumps," Pettygrew said.

"Doesn't matter. If you get a few light-hours out, you'll be able to detect the jump point before they can find you again. Or do an uncalibrated jump out one light-year. There's not another star that close, and unlikely to be a large mass. Rendezvous—" Where should they go? Where would they not be expected to go . . . ? "Ciudad," she said. "We can tell them about Zavala's heroism."

"We'll have to be lucky as well as good," Argelos said, after a minute or two. "But my adviser said it's possible."

His adviser, who hadn't come up with a plan of his own. Ky wondered again just who the adviser really was.

"We won't have much maneuvering ability on insystem

at those velocities," she reminded them. "But anything might help us avoid a beam, so we'll spiral around each other in an open formation, ten thousand klicks. Pettygrew, can your tactical computers handle that and the firing solutions?"

"Yes, ma'am," Pettygrew said. He sounded steadier, almost confident.

"I can, too," Argelos said.

"Then we should start now." Moment by moment she talked them into the starting positions she wanted, and specified the diameter of the spirals.

"There goes one," Jessy said suddenly as they completed their second circuit of the spiral. The first group of the enemy, three ships spaced evenly and one lagging, had appeared around the planet's limb on scan; one had encountered a mine, its shields flaring in response. "And another—" A second flare on scan. As the flares died, the ship icons reappeared, but now decelerating, opening a distance. "Aha. If they slow to worry about mines, they'll have to power up to get out of the well, where they are. Very good thinking, Captain."

"I want them dead," Ky said. Surely they'd hit some of the other mines; surely some of them had done damage . . .

"One down!" said Hugh. A flare surrounded the icon of the last ship in pursuit and did not die. Two of the pursuing ships had fallen farther behind.

"Lowest point," Lee said. "We start coming up now . . ."

Ky watched the plot for a moment. They had gone very low indeed, inside the rings, much closer to the second smallest satellite than she liked, and Pettygrew would be closer still. But *Bassoon* would miss it, and now they were on their way out. Her stomach tightened. They should find the second group soon.

Behind, flare after flare showed where the pursuers kept running into mines. None was quite powerful enough to cause damage, but each hit on the shields cost them power, and they could not afford even an instant with the shields down, an instant in which to fire their own beam weapons. They fell farther behind, not yet negligible, but not an immediate threat. The immediate threat was ahead of them, four ships armed and dangerous and eager to kill.

Ky felt in herself the same eagerness. She had told her companions to make a run for it; she intended to make a run for it herself, but . . . she wanted a solid kill, something more satisfying than having the damaged pirate run into a mine.

When the first enemy ship appeared on scan, she grinned. Scan lag was negligible, less than a half second; Jessy had target acquisition instantly, and as quickly he attacked. The beam lanced out, visible only on scan until it touched the enemy's shield, which flared. "Keep it on," she said.

"Got it," Jessy said. "We're bleeding charge, though."

Every fraction of a second the beam held, that ship could not lower shields to use its own beam, and she was closing to missile range. Recharge would take time. She had three other ships to worry about. What was the right balance? "Recharge at thirty." Ten seconds, fifteen, twenty, each as long as a lifetime. The flare brightened as the enemy's shields resisted the beam, then disappeared from scan, to be replaced an instant later by the larger flare of a ship's disintegration. Ky grinned at Jessy. "Good hunting."

"Shields up," Jessy said.

A second ship appeared, and a moment later a third. These had been following the same course as the first, higher in the well, and they launched barrages at her, as she did at them. *Bassoon* and *Sharra's Gift* also launched as Ky had instructed, widening the bracket she had established. On acutely opposing courses, they passed each other without incident, missiles on their way and not yet arrived, shields tight, beams—if they had beams—inactive. Ky kept an eye on her own ship's recharge. She had to save some capacity for the other ships, the fourth of this group and the survivors of the other, which if they reached jump radius could come after her charges in calibrated microjumps.

The fourth enemy ship appeared, lagging with intent, farther out from the planet, very close to jump radius. Missiles launched now would have a stern chase, and almost certainly fall short. *Vanguard*'s beam charge was only up to 68 percent. Converted to seconds of full power, that wasn't enough to blow the enemy ship or delay its attack as her group passed. If she pulled shield charge . . . dangerous as that was . . . yes. But it could be fatal. Her skin felt hot; she felt no fear, but keen awareness of the others on the ship, the people her mistakes could kill. "Random pulses," she said. "Worry them, see if that's enough."

Suddenly *Bassoon*'s shields flared; the enemy had struck at the smallest ship, though it was more heavily armed than *Sharra's Gift*. They'd done that before, attacking *Cornet* first. The same ship? Or the same tactics, dictated by the same mind?

"Full on," Ky said. He raised a warning eyebrow; she shook her head. "We have to get his attention off *Bassoon*. Make him close up."

"We may run out of power . . ." Already their beam had touched the enemy, whose shields flared, then steadied, though the power of its beam dropped by a third.

"We'll use shield charge," Ky said. "Drop the shields." He gave her a startled look. "They can't get us with missiles now," she said. "And he'll have to button up if we go to full power and hold it."

He nodded, lips compressed. Their own beam strengthened to maximum power as the shields went down, no longer fragmented by the need to pulse in time with shield vibrations; the enemy's shields expanded on the scan. Five seconds . . . ten. *Bassoon*'s icon now showed no attack stressing its shields. No responsive beam stabbed out at them, but Ky knew this would last only as long as their full power held full on the enemy. If they lost lock, or their beam failed, they would be unprotected.

"What d'you think you're doing?" Argelos, calling from *Sharra's Gift,* sounded anything but calm. "Did you take damage?"

"No," Ky said. "I'm inflicting it. Keep going."

"But if you—"

"I'm aware of the risks," Ky said. "Both ways. Be sure your spiral doesn't cross the beam path." It shouldn't, unless he changed course.

"I—oh. Yes."

On scan, the enemy's shields showed the first warning flutter. Suddenly their icon showed the brilliant turquoise vee of maximum deceleration; before Ky could open her mouth to warn Jessy, he had compensated. Their beam maintained its target lock.

"Gives us longer in effective range," he said. "But we're down to fifteen percent of the beam charge."

"We'll hope the other group didn't leave someone behind to catch us on the way out," Ky said.

"Trouble behind," Lee said suddenly. One of the pursuing ships had gone to maximum acceleration, disregarding the danger of mines, and its beam stabbed at their unprotected stern.

Before it had a good lock on them, *Bassoon* decelerated

and rotated into their rear; its shields were up, full strength, and the searching beam flared on them.

"Got your back," Pettygrew said.

"Thanks," Ky said. "Do you have anything to throw at them?" She certainly could not launch the remainder of her mines while he was back there.

"We're dumping what we have . . . if we're lucky . . ."

Ky looked again at the scan. Her sustained beam attack was burning its way through that enemy's shields; they showed flutter on the scan, but the ship was moving out of her most effective range now, and reserve charge was down to 40 percent. A brighter flare of shields, then the intense blossom of explosion. Almost immediately the ship behind them slowed, its icon also showing rapid deceleration and *Bassoon*'s shields no longer flaring with attack.

"It's not the whole ship," Jessy reported. "Just the insystem drive unit blew, I think. I don't think we can blow the whole ship on this course with the power we have left."

"Cut it, then," Ky said.

Ky felt her muscles loosening slightly, and in the same moment realized she was drenched with sweat. The worst threats were gone, she hoped, though the enemy's ability to perform calibrated microjumps meant that one of them could still attack her group, if they could get back outside the jump radius before she did.

She gave orders for her weapons crews to rotate, catch a quick meal, and insisted that the bridge crew eat as well. She contacted the other two ships, making sure they understood what to do next. Then, leaving her bridge crew to watch the scans, she herself settled in with the scan data to analyze what had happened from start to finish.

It took longer than she expected to locate the brief disturbances in the flux that revealed the enemy's arrival and those first few hours of cautious approach. The precision of their movements suggested considerable practice in multiship maneuvers and warfare as well as excellent communications; Ky chewed on her lower lip, comparing what she saw with what she remembered from her classes at the Academy. Basic tactics for space warfare had been much the same for decades, based on the limited utility of ship-to-ship communications unless a handy ansible was available or the ships were within a light-second or so of each other. Shipboard ansibles changed that. If Zavalos had not been able to contact her synchronously, she would have been at a worse disadvantage.

Four hours later, they reached the minimum jump radius. The enemy had not pursued with insystem drive, somewhat to her surprise. Though they had destroyed two ships and seriously damaged a third, they were still outnumbered and considerably outgunned. Ky did not relax until all three of "her" ships went into jump, emerging six to ten light hours farther from the primary. With the shipboard ansibles, it was easy to locate each other.

"We're not going to the mapped jump point," Ky said. "They know where it is; they could expect us to rendezvous there, and ambush us. We're going here—" She transmitted the coordinates. "A messy jump shouldn't matter that much; jump duration is only forty-three hours. Be sure to come in at low relative velocity."

"And then what?" Argelos asked.

"Then we head for Ciudad. I'll give you the routing in the next downjump period. Jump on my mark—" She counted down, and *Vanguard* moved into jump as smoothly as ever.

TWENTY-FIVE

"Secure the ship for FTL transit," Ky said to Hugh. "Set regular watch schedules; be sure offwatch gets some sleep. You, too. I'll want a tally of expended munitions, any wear or damage reports from the batteries, as well as a supply list for our next port."

"Yes, Captain," he said. He looked rested and almost relaxed; she supposed he had been able to sleep a little, as she'd told him to on the run out to this jump.

"You have the bridge," she said, and stood. Her vision wavered, and she was instantly furious with herself. It was her own fault she hadn't slept . . . she realized suddenly that Hugh's prosthetic arm had steadied her. "Thanks," she muttered.

"Get a good rest," he said softly. "We're safe now."

That echoed in her head all the way to her cabin, where she made herself undress and shower before falling across the bed. Safe *now*. Safe now, when she'd finally made a sensible decision, but not safe at all before, when she had trusted the wrong person yet again. Though this time not for the reasons she'd mistaken before, not because she felt the least sympathy for Andreson.

She wanted to roll over, bury her head in the pillows, and not come out until . . . until what? Until things were all fixed again, until the past returned? That was ridiculous. The past wasn't coming back. Nothing she could do would bring her parents to life again, or any of the others who had died. Nothing she could do would restore the family homes, offices, ships. Nothing she didn't do would accomplish that, either. It was impossible. What she did and did not do could not matter to them. Despair weighed her down, smothering darkness. Why even try? No one understood, really. Stella thought she was crazy to attempt to form an interstellar force. Probably the rest of the family would agree, if any more of them had survived.

She had thought she was making progress. Those first months, just staying alive had been a triumph. The plan she'd made at Lastway had seemed huge but still possible. The letter of marque had given her the right to arm a ship . . . and then she'd imagined an alliance of privateers forming a real interstellar navy. Could it have worked? Maybe—but the first attempt had been a disaster; nobody would listen to her ideas now. Now her enemy knew she existed, knew she was dangerous, knew she knew who he was. She had brought more trouble on Vatta instead of protecting the family interests.

Just like her childhood. Just like all the times she'd tried to do something useful or helpful and instead it had all blown up in her face. Only now it wasn't scoldings and sighs and rolled eyes: now it was human lives. She hadn't been able to convince them the threat was imminent; she had made things worse.

"How many ways are there to screw up?" she asked the overhead. No reply, and then, from a mix of memories, she seemed to hear Rafe's mocking voice, telling her she hadn't begun to plumb the depths of error yet. That was a daunting thought. She wondered idly what Rafe would do in her situation, and then where he was and what mis-

chief he was up to. At least she had not trusted *him*—
much, anyway—though she fell asleep remembering their
last conversation, and dreamed of storming in to scold his
parents for treating him so badly.

Slotter Key

Grace Lane Vatta stood in the row of Vatta family members huddled inside a portable all-weather shelter to one
side of the gaping hole where Vatta headquarters had once
been. The tangled debris had long been hauled away, the
basements cleaned out, the cracked foundations excavated
and replaced. Today, an entirely unauspicious day of cold
slashing rain, was the formal ceremony of beginning anew,
laying the cornerstone of the new building. It could not
be put off for better weather, since too many dignitaries
had the date on their crowded calendars. A second shelter
held the press corps, ready to swarm out when the ceremony began.

Now workmen in dripping rain gear eased the huge
block of Modessar granite into place, aligning the holes
drilled in its base with the reinforcing stubs in the foun-
dation, the whining of the crane's winches hardly muted
by the steady drumming of rain on the plastic roof. The
stone, shiny with rain, looked thunder-dark this stormy
morning, but the names of those who had died in the
attack glittered on the two sides that would be exposed,
incised deeply and then imprinted with gold leaf. It had
cost an enormous amount, and some had complained, but
Grace had been adamant, harder than the granite. "The
dead paid more," she'd said, and the others had given
way.

Behind the family were the dignitaries: the new
President, the new provincial governor, the new mayor, the

new Commandant of Spaceforce, the same Commandant of Spaceforce Academy, the CEOs of major banks . . . Grace felt itchy, but decided it was just her arm-bud. MacRobert was back there, along with the rest of the security detail, and she knew where all her weapons were.

When the stone had finally settled, and the masons had checked the alignment in all dimensions, the workmen detached the cables and drew back. The family members stepped forward, into the rain. Reporters poured out of their shelter, but the security detail held them back. Lights flared, and the mutter of voices stilled as Jo's children walked up to the cornerstone with the bottle of wine.

Helen stood on one side, Grace on the other, as the children recited the lines they'd been taught and smacked the bottle against the hard granite. Glass shattered; wine red as blood mingled with the rainwater and Grace felt for a moment the same black rage that had taken her when the attacks were new. The moment passed; people started talking, scurrying back to shelter as the rain came down harder. The crane moved off with a dismal clanking of treads; official staff with official umbrellas helped dignitaries back to official cars.

After the ceremony, back at the Stamarkos town house where a lavish buffet ran the length of the formal parlor, Grace stared at the well-fed, gossiping crowd with disgust. How could they eat now, of all times? She backed into the quietest corner of the room.

"It was supposed to be a happy occasion," MacRobert said in her ear. He offered her a glass of something colorless; she shook her head. "Proof of Vatta's resilience."

"Proof of the guilt some people feel," Grace said. "They fawn on us now—"

"Inactivity drives you crazy," he said. "But you will survive this convalescence."

She turned to look at him. "You know too much about me."

"So I should. Shall we go somewhere?"

"I want to know where Stella is and what she's doing. And Ky."

"Ky," said MacRobert, "is no doubt being every bit as difficult as you are. By the way, did you know that our new President is planning to offer you a high-level position in Defense?"

Grace blinked. "He is?"

"Yes." MacRobert said nothing more, just looked at her.

"It's a control issue," Grace said.

"Well, yes," MacRobert said, tugging at his ear. "He's not crazy; he wants you where he can watch you. Still . . ."

"How high-level?" Grace asked.

"My, is that ambition I hear in your voice? I can't discuss it here; the place isn't secure enough, and no one else—well, almost no one—has the clearance. I don't know about you, but nothing on that table appeals to me. Tea in a quiet place, however . . ."

"Sounds like an excellent idea," Grace said. Her dark mood had disappeared.

"That's what I told him," MacRobert said. She almost stumbled at that, but MacRobert had her gently by her good arm.

"You mean—? Damn it, Mac, you are a very canny fisherman."

"It's all in the lure," MacRobert said, easing her past two gesturing politicians without putting her arm-bud in danger.

Ky woke sixteen hours after she went to sleep, feeling dull and miserable, and knowing she needed to conceal that from her crew.

"I slept too long," she said in response to Hugh's greeting. "But I'm fine."

"I have those reports," he said. "In brief, we sustained no damage or major wear to any battery, and no injuries. Quite remarkable, under the circumstances." His expression was, she realized with a shock, admiring.

"It was a mess," Ky said. "We were lucky to get out alive, and I was an idiot ever to sign up with that woman."

He shrugged. "What's done is done, and she's dead, and you got the rest of us out alive. And some of them are dead."

"We ran like rabbits," Ky said, eyeing him. Was it really approval?

He grinned. "Like fanged rabbits, Captain. And it was the only thing to do." He leaned closer. "Cheer up. I know what you're feeling—you wanted to do better. But you're alive and you'll have another chance."

His mood was infectious; Ky felt a tentative surge of confidence returning. "I certainly hope so," she said.

"That's the spirit." As if he were her father or uncle or something.

"Um . . . did I remember to tell everyone how well they did?"

"Yes, Captain, you did. Right after that first jump, and again later—but you were dead on your feet by then."

"Good." She'd managed some duties well, then.

"You commended Captain Argelos and Captain Pettygrew, too, in case you're wondering."

"Better."

"I'd suggest something to eat—"

Appetite returned in a bound. When had she eaten last? Long before she'd fallen into bed. "Yes," she said. "What meal is next?"

"Pirate stew," Lee said over his shoulder. Someone else

snorted; Ky looked around and realized they were all unreasonably gleeful. Well, they were alive, and no enemy could reach them in FTL flight.

"Fried pirate," Ky said; there was a general chuckle. "Make that two," she added.

By the end of that shift, she had visited every compartment on the ship, spoken to everyone, conveying the message that the captain was awake, alert, sane, and confident. Everyone seemed to believe that, even though she herself wasn't as sure. Was it sane to think she could still pull long-term victory out of what now seemed a trail of bad decisions and defeat?

The alternative looked worse . . . if she backed off now, the pirates would have no effective opposition. No, crazy as it looked, she had to keep trying, until she succeeded or they killed her. With that decision made, she settled in to use the days in FTL flight to best advantage.

They needed an organization. They needed strategy and tactics and operational doctrine and logistics and all those military things that had seemed simple and clear-cut at the Academy, laid out in the texts with neat diagrams and clear explanations. She called in everyone in the crew who had served in a military unit of any kind.

"Tell me everything you can about your organization," she said. "Not the secret stuff, of course, but the plain vanilla of it: how was it organized? Who made what decisions? Who could countermand that decision? We're trying to combine people who have different organizations. Yet functionally, they do much the same thing—fight ships in space from ships in space. So if I can figure out how it overlaps, make it easier for people from other organizations to combine and work together—"

The first startled resistance melted away as she

explained, showing them the skeleton table of organization she had drawn up, based on Slotter Key's Spaceforce. "You mean we call the officer who buys supplies the procurement officer and you call him the supply officer?" asked Jon Gannett.

"Exactly," Ky said.

Hugh leaned over to look. "Well, if you take away the labels in the boxes, it looks pretty much like ours."

Jon Gannett nodded. "Like ours, too."

"So creating a combined table of organization won't be as bad as I thought," Ky said. She glanced around the table; they were all looking at the diagram, and after a moment looked up to meet her gaze. "Next," she said, "we have to come up with tactics that work."

"We could just do something stupid again, wait for them to pounce, and then surprise them by suddenly becoming brilliant," Martin said. That got a chuckle.

"I'd rather we were brilliant from the start," Ky said. "And we have a few weeks to get that way before we get to Ciudad."

"You're not giving up." Jon Gannett made it a statement, not a question.

"I don't give up," Ky said. There was a moment's startled silence, then she went on. "And since going at it the wrong way nearly got us all killed—"

"Not your fault," Martin said.

"Joining up with Andreson when she made it clear she would insist on command was my decision," Ky said. "But I can't undo it; what I can do is not make that mistake again. So—let's use the time we have to figure out how our three surviving ships can convince potential allies that they should join us. I think having a good organizational plan in place and some tactical analysis should help with that."

"Yes, ma'am, that should help a lot." Hera Gannett, normally quieter than Jon, beat him to it this time. The others nodded.

"And then," Ky said, "when we have the allies and the plan, we will hunt those scumsuckers down and blow them all away." She grinned at them, one after another, and, one after another, they grinned back.